Praise for *Dawnflight*:

"An appealing story about Arthur and Guinevere, [*Dawnflight*] depicts fifth-century Scotland as one of warring tribes and marriages that unite enemies. Female warrior Gyanhumara is set to marry Urien when she first meets Arthur. Once met, never to forget... A compelling tale of war and allegiances." ~Camilla Cowan, *The Dallas Morning News*

Kim Iverson Headlee constructs "... a credible Dark Age Britain where Gyanhumara (Guinevere) and Arthur meet [and] fall passionately in love... The day-to-day historical context is vividly depicted... Gyanhumara is a fascinating combination of contradictory qualities." ~Raymond H. Thompson, Acadia University, Canada, *Arthuriana*, Quarterly Journal of the North American Branch of the International Arthurian Society

Dawnflight "... is such an accomplished piece of storytelling magic and lovely characterisation... a story both delicately and powerfully told. The atmosphere of the novel is rich in allusion and yet it is very much an original creation. A wonderful feast for the reader!" ~Carole Nielsen, editor, *Arthurian Association of Australia Newsletter*

"Intense."
~Jessie Potts, *USA Today*

Morning's Journey

*7/31/21
Enjoy the journey,
Chris!*

*Kim Iverson Headlee
Stories make us greater.*

KIM IVERSON
HEADLEE

Pendragon Cove Press

Published by
Pendragon Cove Press

Morning's Journey
Copyright ©2013 by Kim Headlee
All rights reserved

http://kimheadlee.com
https://twitter.com/KimHeadlee
http://www.facebook.com/KimIversonHeadlee

All rights reserved, including the right to reproduce this book or portions thereof in any form, with the exception of brief excerpts for the purpose of review.

This book is a work of fiction. Names, characters, places, and incidents are products of the author's imagination or are used fictitiously. Any resemblance to actual events or locales or persons, living or dead, is entirely coincidental.

2nd Printing, Pendragon Cove Press, December 2014
ISBN-13: 978-0-9905055-3-2
ISBN-10: 0-990-50553-7

1st Printing, Lucky Bat Books, June 2013
ISBN 1-939-05128-2

"The Caledonian Warrior's Lament" lyrics ©2013 by Kim Headlee
Interior art ©2013 by Kim Headlee
Cover design ©2014 by Natasha Brown
Cover photos:
Handsome man ©by Ollyy, Shutterstock ID 127374206
Fashion girl portrait ©by Yuriyzhuravov, Dreamstime ID 26373605
Decorative font: Neverwinter, public domain

Gràdhaich domhain air son an neart-tiodhlac.

Bí thu ghràdhaich domhain air son a'mìsneach-tíodhleach.

Caledonian Proverb

"Love deeply for the gift of strength.

Be loved deeply for the gift of courage."

Contents

Chapter 1   9

Author's Notes   378

People   379

Glossary   389

Acknowledgments   416

Interior art   417

About the Author   420

Chapter 1

THE CLASH OF *arms resounds in the torchlit corridor. Blood oozes where leather has yielded to the bite of steel, yet both sweating, panting warriors refuse to relent.*

Her heart thundering, Gyan grips her sword's hilt, desperate to help the man she loves. Caledonach law forbids it.

Urien makes a low lunge. As Arthur tries to whirl clear, the blade tears a gash in his shield-side thigh. The injured leg collapses, and Arthur drops to one knee. Crowing triumphantly, Urien raises his sword for the deathblow.

Devil take the law!

Gyan springs to block the stroke. Its force jars her arms and twists the hilt in her grasp. She barely holds on through the searing pain.

Urien slips past her guard to slice at her brooch. The gold dragon clatters to the floor. Her cloak slithers to her ankles, fouling her stance. As she tries to kick free, Urien grabs her braid, jerks up her head, and kisses her, hard. Shock loosens her grip. Her sword falls. She thrashes *and writhes, but he holds her fast, smirking lewdly.*

"You are mine, Pictish whore."

Urien's breath reeks of ale and evil promises. She spits in his face. He slaps her. She reels backward, her cheek burning. He grabs her forearms and yanks her close.

"Artyr, help me!"

No response.

Her spirits plummet. Weaponless, she can do nothing—wait. A glint catches her eye.

When Urien kisses her again, she surrenders. He grunts his pleasure, redoubling the force of the kiss. Slowly, she works her hands over his chest until her left hand touches cold bronze on his shoulder. She snatches the brooch and rips it free, hoping to stab him with the pin.

Her elation vanishes with her balance as her tangled cloak thwarts her plans. Face contorted with rage, Urien lunges and catches her wrist. She grits her teeth as his fingers dig in to make her drop the brooch. Pain shoots up her arm. She pushes away. Together, they fall—

GYAN GASPED and sat bolt upright, pulse hammering. Sweat plastered her hair to her head, which felt like the ball in an all-night game of buill-coise. Bed linens ensnared her legs.

Fingers grazed her shoulder. She recoiled and cocked a fist. Her consort ducked behind his hand. "Easy, Gyan!" She relaxed, and he wrapped his arm about her. "What's wrong?"

She pressed the heels of her hands to her eyes. "A dream," she replied, hoping that for once he'd be satisfied with a vague answer.

"Some dream."

She sighed. "It was the fight—and yet not the fight." Gently, she traced the thin red line at the base of his neck where she'd scratched him with Caleberyllus to seal his Oath of Fealty to her and to her clan. But dreams cared naught for oaths. "This time, Urien won."

Arthur grimaced. "That's no dream." He hugged her, and she burrowed into his embrace. "I'd call it a nightmare."

"Ha." She bent forward to disengage the linens from her feet. The unyielding fabric ignited her ire. She pounded the straw-stuffed mattress, furious at Urien and even more furious at herself for allowing him to creep into her wedding chamber, if only in spirit. "Why must that cù-puc keep coming between us?" She gazed at the table where Braonshaffir, named for the egg-size sapphire that crowned its hilt, lay sheathed inside its etched bronze scabbard beside Caleberyllus. Indulging in the fantasy of her new sword shearing through Urien's neck, she bared her teeth in a fierce grin. "Just let him cross me openly, and by the One God, I'll settle this matter!"

Arthur's warm sigh ruffled her hair. Together they righted the linens, but when she would have risen, he clasped her hands and regarded her earnestly. "I can't afford to lose either of you."

She looked at those hands, young and yet already scarred and callused by years of war: hands that cradled the future of Breatein. "I know." Briefly, she squeezed his hands, hoping to convey her desire to help him forge unity among his people, the Breatanaich, as well as with Caledonaich, her countrymen.

One legion soldier in five called the northwestern Breatanach territory of Dailriata home, and one in three of those men hailed from Urien's own Clan Móran. In a duel between Gyan and Urien, Arthur's Dailriatanach alliance would die regardless of the victor.

If politics ever failed to constrain the Urien of the waking world, however, she couldn't guarantee that diplomacy would govern her response.

She averted her gaze again to the table where their arms and adornments lay. Their dragon cloak-pins sparked a memory. Something else had been odd about that dream, but its details had receded like the morning tide. She couldn't decide whether to be troubled or relieved.

Closing her eyes, she inhaled deeply, trying to purge Urien map Dumarec from her mind. Moist pressure against her lips announced her consort's plans. She welcomed his kiss and deepened it. He ran his fingers through her unbraided hair, following the tresses down her neck and over her breasts. Her nipples firmed under his touch. She arched back, and he kissed his way down to one breast, then the other, drawing the nipples forth even farther and awakening the exquisite ache in her banasròn.

The swelling shaft of sunlight heralded a reminder of their duties.

"The cavalry games will be starting soon, mo laochan." No other man had earned the Caledonaiche endearment from her, and none ever would. Her "little champion" bore her down onto the pillows, and his lips interrupted any other comment she might have made. As they explored the curve of her throat, she whispered, "We must make an appearance."

"We will, Gyan." His fingertips teased her banasròn, discovering its damp readiness. "Eventually."

She stilled his hand. He looked at her, puzzled.

Being àrd-banoigin obligated her to ensure her clan's future by bearing heirs, but was she ready to abandon the warrior's path and devote her life to a bairn? She gave a mental shrug. A swift calculation assured her that her courses would return soon, leaving the question to be faced another day. Smiling, she began caressing one of the reasons he'd earned "laochan" as an endearment.

He cupped her face and kissed her, urgency for both of them soaring on the wings of desire. His thigh rubbed hers with slow, firm strokes. Gyanhumara nic Hymar, Chieftainess of Clan Argyll of Caledon, yielded to her consort's unspoken command. She opened to him, and he plunged her into their sacred realm of mind-blanking bliss.

Whenever Arthur map Uther, Pendragon of Breatein, issued an order, on the battlefield or off, only a fool disobeyed.

TRENCHER LADEN with goat's cheese and steaming black bread, and the kitchen's clamor and aromas and warmth at his back, Angusel mac Alayna stood in the feast hall's doorway. Most joining-ceremony guests—clan rulers and their escorts, religious leaders, craftmasters, and merchants prominent enough to have been extended an invitation—hadn't stirred from their quarters. Some sprawled where sleep had overtaken them, snoring fitfully through ale-soaked dreams.

"Over here, lad!"

Though he couldn't see the voice's owner, he knew only one Caledonach who could sound like a thunderclap without trying. He headed toward the shout.

He found Gyan's father at a table below the dais, methodically destroying a loaf of bread and a mound of bilberries and slices of early apples, pausing at intervals to bury his face in his tankard. After wiping the creamy flecks from his graying sable mustache and beard with the back of a hand, he resumed the attack on his trencher. Peredur and Rhys, Gyan's half brother and clansman, flanked him.

All three had dressed for battle in traditional Caledonach bronze helmets and forearm guards, boiled-leather tunics, thick leggings, and knee-high boots, nary a detail missing except their weapons.

"Sit, sit," urged the Chieftain of Clan Argyll between mouthfuls with an impatient gesture toward the bench. "Hurry. After you finish eating, you must change."

Angusel glanced at his sky-blue linen tunic and back at Chieftain Ogryvan. "My lord?"

"The games, Angusel. The games!" As Angusel obeyed and dug in, with Rhys pouring him a tankard, the chieftain explained, "The drink has left Conall in no shape to ride. We need a fourth."

Surprise made him gag on a hunk of cheese. He swallowed hard. "Me, sir?" He took a swig of ale without tasting it. He could think of a hundred reasons why this was a bad idea, starting with his age and lack of experience.

"Of course, you." The chieftain grinned. "Do you see anyone else?"

Angusel looked about. Another man sat crumpled over the far end of the table. With his cloak balled into a pillow, his clan affiliation couldn't be discerned, but the loudness of his snores proclaimed him to be in no condition to ride, either.

He cleared his throat. "But, my lord, I am not of Argyll."

"Not by blood, Exalted Heir of Clan Alban," Chieftain Ogryvan allowed, "but your heart is Argyll."

Angusel's hand went to the scar at the base of his neck, symbol of his oath to the woman whose father regarded him so intently.

That oath made his spirits sink. These three men were the best horsemen of Clan Argyll and stood among the best in all Caledon. How could he agree to ride with them when his skills seemed so pathetic in comparison?

Rather than admit that, however, he tried a more practical argument: "I am deeply honored to be asked, my lord, but I have not done the trial of blood. You don't want an untried boy on your team."

"We know the role you played in the Scáthinach invasion. Your choices and courage saved countless lives, Gyan's included." Peredur snaked his arm through the clutter of half-consumed food and drink to grip Angusel's forearm. "I gave up leading my ala's team for this chance to honor Argyll and my sister." His smile made him look so much like Gyan that Angusel sucked in a swift breath. "If you join us, she'll be doubly pleased."

"Aye!" Chieftain Ogryvan thumped the tabletop. The pewter tankards and plates and utensils clattered. The snoring feaster woke with a startled grunt, glanced blearily about, and grimaced. Head in hands, he slid back into his dreams. The Argyll warriors chuckled, not loudly. Gyan's father continued, "Young you may be, but calling yourself untried is too harsh, Angusel."

"My lord, I—" Angusel looked at his trencher, but for once, eating couldn't have been farther from his mind. "I can't."

"Why not?" asked Rhys, grinning at a passing serving lass and elbowing Angusel in the ribs. "Fancy another type of sport, then?"

Angusel shook his head. "I don't want to make Argyll lose." He met Rhys's inquisitive gaze. "My oath forbids it."

"Nonsense, lad." The quietness of the chieftain's tone commanded Angusel's attention. "Gyan told me what you two were doing in your spare time before the invasion."

She had been helping him hone his horsemanship skills, but he remained laughably far from claiming mastery. "Then you should know, my lord, that I am the last person to ask."

"My daughter spoke of your progress with highest praise. She doesn't utter empty words."

True, he thought. But Argyll's competition included not just other Caledonaich, but the best horsemen of the legion and the northern Breatanach clans. If he could have made water at that moment, it surely would have come out cold.

"If we cannot find a fourth," said the chieftain, "we must forfeit."

"Think how disappointed Gyan will be, knowing you could have—"

Chieftain Ogryvan's upraised hand cut Peredur off. "Will you join Argyll, Angusel of Alban?"

Forfeit. Disappointment.

His gut twisted. A fortnight ago, he had sworn to serve Gyan for the rest of his days, a task he desired with his entire being, even if it meant sacrificing his life. Although he could refuse her father's request, his heart told him it would shake her confidence in him, a thought too painful to bear.

"Aye, my lord. I will ride with Argyll." Silently, Angusel prayed to all the gods that he wouldn't fail her.

Uren map Dumarec of Clan Moray of Dalriada watched the departure of the Argyll cavalry team through narrowed eyes. Overbearing Ogryvan and his pet, Peredur. Rhys the Rat. And youngest and smallest in stature but the biggest troublemaker of the lot, Angusel.

To think he might have become kin-by-marriage to those Picti vermin. Well, Arthur could have the whole bloody lot.

He rubbed the woad Picti betrothal tattoo encircling his left wrist, one bitter reminder of the woman who had broken that betrothal so she could marry Arthur. The other reminder he didn't have to see. He felt its shameful sting whenever he wrinkled his brow.

Reliving the fight soured his mood. He'd lost more than Gyanhumara at the point of Arthur's sword. Arthur had removed him from command of the Manx Cohort—a thousand foot and horse—and recalled him here, to Caer Lugubalion, to lead the only all-horse cohort. This amounted to about the same number of soldiers, but the Manx unit because of its diversity had been a more challenging command and a logical stepping-stone to greater power. Now, Urien commanded a unit composed almost entirely of accursed Picts; of the eight alae, only First Ala's roster contained Brytons.

It wouldn't surprise him to learn that Gyanhumara was agitating for Arthur to put one of her clansmen in command of the Horse Cohort. The bastard probably was itching for such an excuse to discharge Urien altogether. He considered resigning his commission; if he left the army, it damned well would be on his terms, not anyone else's.

Army politics aside, losing Gyanhumara meant losing her lands, which would have doubled Clan Moray's wealth, and it had destroyed his opportunity to make a bid for the Pendragonship.

No one stole that much from him with impunity.

But the thrust of his revenge would have to wait until after his father's death. The choice to remain under Arthur's thumb at headquarters carried a hefty price: the curtailment of freedom. Being chieftain would eliminate the problem. Certain elements of the plan could be accomplished now, however.

He thumbed a rivet on the silvered bronze of his games helm, which his family had owned for five generations. More than a helmet, the exquisitely sculpted Roman cavalry centurion's mask covered the entire face, with slits for eyes, nose, and mouth.

Too bloody hot to wear in combat, the helm's purpose lay not in the deflection of enemy blows, but ornamentation.

When Urien had learned that Arthur would be staging cavalry games as part of the entertainment for the wedding guests, he'd quickly selected his team and commissioned identical helms for them. Not precisely the same, for the bronze of the new helms had tin overlay, unlike Urien's silvered helm. Even a chieftain's son had limits.

Silver or tin, the sun's glare would render them identical.

He grinned at his distorted reflection.

Chapter 2

ARTHUR AND GYAN mounted the stairs of the canopied viewing platform to the throng's thunderous cheers. There to greet them, garbed in his garrison commander's ceremonial uniform, stood the man who had performed their Christian joining ceremony the day before, called Bishop Dubricius in his temple and everywhere else Merlin.

"High time you two arrived." The dark sparkle in Merlin's eyes revealed the jest. "I was beginning to wonder how much longer I could keep them amused."

The warrior-priest gestured at the people packed onto the tiered wooden seating behind the fence surrounding the parade ground. More had climbed onto the barracks, smothering the red tile roofs. Gyan noticed that several enterprising souls had perched on ladders or each other's shoulders, scrambled onto crates and casks, piled into unhitched wagons, shinned trees—anything for an unobstructed view.

On the field, Arthur's foster brother, Caius, commander of the garrison at nearby Camboglanna, was leading the infantry cohorts through a series of complex formations. Three thousand armored men marching and turning with split-second precision presented quite an impressive sight.

Yet the escalating chants revealed the crowd's craving for the promised excitement of the cavalry games.

"You ought to get married yourself, Merlin," Arthur shot back. "Then we shall see how prompt you can be the morning after your wedding night." Impudence invaded his grin.

"Ah, youth." Sighing, the warrior-priest surveyed the cloudless heavens. "They never appreciate their elders." He winked at Gyan. "I am depending upon you to keep him in line, Chieftainess, since he no longer heeds me."

Arthur chuckled. "No worries there. I have two counselors now."

With the corners of her mouth quirking downward, she wondered when she'd begin fulfilling that role, since in a sennight she would assume command of the Manx Cohort. She eagerly anticipated the challenge of leading a thousand foot and horse but not the prospect of again being separated from Arthur by a hundred miles of sea.

"Only two counselors?" A man stepped from behind Merlin, grinning to rival the sun. "Arthur, you wound me."

Returning the grin, Arthur planted hands on hips. "If I had wounded you, my friend, your blood would be telling the tale, not your tongue."

Gyan said, "Commander Bedwyr, it is a pleasure to renew our acquaintance under—shall we say—less awkward circumstances."

When she had met Bedwyr map Bann at the Dùn Ghlas shipyards, he'd been clad in a workman's plain tunic and breeches. Now, rather than a Ròmanach-style legion uniform, Bedwyr wore a finely tooled, dark blue leather jerkin and leggings to match. Stag-embossed silver discs adorned the jerkin's front. A silver torc gleamed at his neck. Its ends bore the same stag-head design that decorated the pommel of the silver-hilted dagger dangling from his belt. His cloak rippled the shade of new grass, woven with crossing strands of silver and black. The silver dragon badge, ringed with blue enamel, provided the only hint of his affiliation with Arthur's forces. Its eye was a yellow-green gemstone the Ròmanaich called heliodor and the Caledonaich called sunstone.

As she moved closer, extending her hand, she noticed his salty tang, blended with the scents of rope and leather, evoking the sea. She clasped Bedwyr's forearm in a warm gesture of greeting that he seemed glad to return.

Merlin regarded Bedwyr, knitting his eyebrows.

"At Caerglas last spring," Bedwyr explained, "this sly lady conversed with me through an interpreter without once letting on that she knew our tongue. I never suspected a thing." Hand to heart, he bowed deeply to Gyan. He straightened, but his smile didn't. "You have a rare jewel, Arthur."

Arthur chuckled. "Well, Bedwyr. When did you become the gallant?"

"Your lady wife brings forth the best in me," he admitted.

"That had best be all she brings forth in you." Arthur clapped his friend on the shoulder to the rhythm of both men's laughter.

Gyan cast a beaming glance at her consort. "Jealous already, my love?" She felt her grin turn wicked as she winked at his fleet commander. "Bedwyr, I insist you call me Gyan. All my friends do."

Arthur and Bedwyr shared a glance and a laugh.

"Bedwyr is right. You are a rare jewel, Gyan." In truth, her name meant "rarest song," but she wasn't about to correct her consort in front of his companion. He wrapped an arm around her waist and leaned close enough for his lips to brush her ear. "I will tolerate no one stealing you from me," he whispered.

"Ha. As if I'd let—" The warmth of his mouth upon hers abbreviated her remark.

Their kiss ended too soon for her taste. Arthur broke away and faced the steps. Two more people ascended to the viewing platform: Arthur's younger sister, Morghe, and their mother, Chieftainess Ygraine, whose name reminded Gyan of the Caledonaiche word for sun. Though of the same height, mother and daughter exhibited countenances as dissimilar as the sun and the moon.

The nature of this moon Gyan knew all too well from her association with Morghe on Maun. Like the heavenly orb, Morghe by turns could appear dark or light or something in between as her moods and purposes suited her. At present, she displayed radiant smiles for everyone. No telling how long that demeanor would last. For unlike the moon, Morghe could be as unpredictable as a blizzard.

Morghe lingered at the far end of the platform, facing the parade ground, as Ygraine advanced toward Bedwyr, Merlin, Arthur, and Gyan.

To the sun, Gyan's mother-by-law, Gyan directed her gaze.

Ygraine's ivory gown, edged in a pattern of crenellated crimson squares, fell in graceful folds to her feet, its colors straight off the Clan Càrnhuilean banner. The gown's sleeveless style, reminiscent of attire depicted on the praetorium's Ròmanach statues, honored her late husband, Arthur's father. Strings of seed pearls laced the curls piled atop her head in a manner Gyan suspected also was Ròmanach, since she hadn't observed it on most of the other Breatanach noblewomen. Ygraine's clan brooch, a silver unicorn rearing within a circle of reddish gold, adorned the mantle. A gold dragon dangled from a black cord at her neck, its design similar to the badges worn by Arthur's officers. Hinged at the neck and tail, her dragon writhed and flashed with her every movement.

Although Ygraine had to have at least twoscore and ten summers—her oldest grandson, Gawain, was Gyan's age—the years had spared her comeliness. Clearly, she'd bequeathed to Arthur her red-gold hair and arresting blue eyes. Decades of duty had engraved their mark on her brow but hadn't vanquished the boldness of her stride or the pride of her stance.

If Gyan could be as well-favored at that age, she would consider herself blessed.

"Chieftainess Ygraine." Merlin thumped fist to chest in salute. "It truly gladdens my heart to see you looking as lovely as ever."

"Ha, you old flatterer." Fists on hips, Ygraine grinned. "Your silver tongue could confound the devil himself."

"Would God that it could be so, my dear lady. The devil is a subtle and persistent adversary, indeed."

"Some things never change." Ygraine flicked a hand at Merlin's legion badge. "Including you. Still playing soldier, I see."

"Your son refuses to let me retire." Merlin glanced, smiling, at Arthur before returning his gaze to Ygraine. "He has his father's single-mindedness of purpose." The smile widened. "And his mother's powers of persuasion."

As Ygraine returned the smile, Gyan got the distinct impression that she and Merlin shared a private jest.

Arthur exchanged a look with Bedwyr that bordered on consternation. "If this is true," Arthur said, "then I must persuade you both to continue your reunion elsewhere so I can start the cavalry games." He motioned at the restive crowd. "Before we have a riot on our hands."

Ygraine laughed lightly. "A pleasure to see you too, Arthur."

"Forgive me, my lady mother. Of course I'm glad—and honored—to see you. It's only, well . . . forgive me."

Gyan arched an eyebrow. Though she found it highly amusing that the conqueror of thousands could be bested in a single verbal stroke by his mother, she decided she'd be a poor wife indeed if she failed to come to his defense. She clasped his hand.

"Chieftainess Ygraine, your son is a man of single purpose. He does whatever is best for his people. And now, my people as well." Gazing at Arthur, Gyan infused her expression with love. Her pulse quickened as he rewarded her in kind. "It is but one of the reasons I love him so." She reached behind his head and drew his face to hers. Closing her eyes, she blotted out all other sensations as her tongue probed and twined with his.

The crowd's impatient chants soon gave way to ribald shouts.

"Now who's inciting a riot?" Merlin asked with mock asperity.

Arthur gave Gyan a grateful smile as they parted. He turned and approached the rail, his gold-trimmed scarlet cloak unfurling in the morning breeze.

"Well spoken, my dear. Arthur is indeed evenly yoked." Ygraine's smile radiated approval. "Well come to the family, Gyanhumara."

Gyan nodded, smiling. "I bid you well come to mine too, Ygraine." As a peer, she had no qualms about using the woman's given name, but she hadn't contemplated the idea of calling her "mother."

Death had robbed her of the right to call any woman by that title.

With an incline of her head, Ygraine withdrew to join Morghe at the end of the platform, and Bedwyr returned to his place beside Merlin.

Down on the field, Caius glanced toward Arthur, nodded, and barked a set of commands. The men clotted into thirty rectangles to march past the platform. Under the Pendragon's gaze, the soldiers' movements adopted noticeable changes: lifted chins, puffed chests, livelier steps, and smart salutes.

Arthur beckoned to Gyan, and she took her place at his side. She'd spurned a gown in favor of her leather-and-bronze battle-gear. Gold dove-headed torcs flashed at her throat and upper arms. Braonshaf-fir hung at her left hip from the bronze dragon sword belt. Over it all draped the gold-edged, scarlet-and-saffron-banded blue mantle, symbolic of her status as Chieftainess of Clan Argyll. On its folds rode her consort's gift, the sapphire-eyed gold dragon.

After the last century had disappeared through the gap in the wildly applauding throng, a troop of mounted heralds galloped onto the parade ground sounding blasts on great curved brass horns. Men with sacks slung over their shoulders swarmed over the field, carefully spilling the sacks' contents into the dust. Four long, narrow white ovals marked their passage. Inside the far curve of each oval lay a set of three concentric circles.

Next entered two groups of men on foot. Wearing nothing more than sandals and white tunics girded with leather belts, the first crew lugged armloads of javelins. Gyan recognized the men to be the cavalry squads' drudges. Four of their number split away and took up positions in the near curve of each chalk track. The rest congregated nearby under the stern gaze of their overseer.

The other men had donned helmets and mail shirts. Weaponless, they hefted tall, curved shields, and each man carried a staff bearing a different cavalry standard or clan banner.

As four of these soldiers marched into the rings inside each track, Gyan cocked a questioning eyebrow at her consort.

"The targets," Arthur explained.

"I guessed as much. Why not use straw bales?"

"Straw is fine for practice, but the crowd"—he raised his voice over the swelling sea of voices—"craves blood. The javelins are blunted to reduce the risk, but to the crowd it looks no different." His expression took on a determined cast. "I will not fall prey to the ways of my forebears." She intended to ask him to explain when a smile broke across his face. He pointed. "Here come the contestants!"

Threescore and four horsemen spurred their mounts in a slow canter around the perimeter of the parade ground. A rainbow of banners, horsehair crests, cloaks, and saddle blankets wafted in the breeze. Helmets, body armor, shield bosses, and harness fittings gleamed. Many warriors waved at people beyond the fence, and the audience devoured every moment.

The eight alae of the Horse Cohort each had entered a team. Caledonaich rode in seven alae, the result of the Abar-Gleann treaty. These men wore their variously patterned clan cloaks over traditional Caledonach black leather battle-gear—another condition of the treaty, since Arthur couldn't afford to equip a thousand new conscripts with Ròmanach armor.

Selected from the only all-Breatanach ala, the eighth team wore scarlet officers' cloaks. Curiously, their identical helmets obscured their faces, rendering identification impossible. The frozen silvery stares gave Gyan a preternatural chill.

"Arthur, where did First Ala get such strange headgear?" Urien, as prefect of the Horse Cohort, might have put himself on the team, and no one would ever know. She squinted at them, looking for clues in their rank badges, bodies, horses, and riding styles to no avail. "Why would anyone want to fight half-blind like that?"

"Those helms are made only for cavalry games. And—" Arthur frowned as the teams lined up before the platform.

"And what?" Gyan asked.

His fingers closed over hers. "They don't reduce vision as much as you might think."

"You have worn one?"

"My father's." The frown gave way to a rueful smile. "With all the battles, I haven't had a chance to use it lately. Perhaps we"—his quiet emphasis on the last word sent a thrill up her spine—"can change that. Permanently."

She glimpsed that future pooled in the fiery depths of his eyes, a future holding no threat of enemy attacks, when warring peoples would become as brothers, when warriors could hang up their weapons and turn their hands and minds from destruction to creation. A future of happiness and prosperity, a future to believe in, a future well worth the cost in sweat and pain and blood to bring to life.

A mild cough disturbed her reverie, and Merlin approached the rail on the other side of Arthur, with Bedwyr a pace behind him. Gyan again studied the parade ground.

Eight independent teams rounded out the field. Clans Argyll and Alban represented the Caledonach Confederacy. The other six teams included Breatanach clans Cwrnwyll, called in Caledonaiche Càrnhuilean, the Rock-Elbows People; Moray, called Móran, the Many People; Lothian, called Lùthean, the People of Power; and three others whose banners Gyan didn't recognize.

"Bedwyr," she said, "is your clan down there?"

"Aye, Gyan! Clan Lammor's banner is the green stag's head on silver." He waved at his clansmen, a gesture they cheerfully returned.

"Ah, of course, Làmanmhor, the People of Great Hands—such as those who made your exquisite jerkin?" That won Bedwyr's nod and grin. Gyan surveyed the Làmanmhor team. By the expert way they controlled their mounts, they looked as likely a team as any to win the laurels. "Why aren't you riding with them?"

Arthur shot his friend a grin before looking at Gyan. "If you saw him ride, my love, you'd know why he serves in the fleet."

She would have explored his comment further, but her attention riveted to a nervous horse on the Clan Móran team. As the warrior quieted the animal, Gyan couldn't find Urien riding with his clan, which meant he'd probably chosen to lead the masked First Ala riders. She tried to curb her growing dread as she observed her clan's team. Her father, naturally, led them, joined by Per, Rhys, and . . . Angus? Surely she had to be mistaken. She looked again.

Angusel of Clan Alban regarded her proudly amid his Argyll teammates. She answered with the Caledonach warrior's salute: upraised sword hand clenched in a fist, splayed, and clenched again.

Arthur drew Caleberyllus and held it aloft, gazing at the crowd until every face turned toward him. "Let the games begin!"

ANGUSEL SWILLED dust from his mouth, spat, and splashed the rest of the water on his face. He wished he could douse his entire body but doubted whether anything could wash away the fatigue.

Argyll had outperformed its opponents in the earlier rounds. Not surprisingly, so had Alban. Two of the Pendragon's Horse Cohort alae also had survived the morning trials, the Sixth—Argyll's current opponent—and the oddly armored First. Soon, two more teams would go down in defeat.

In this game, accuracy counted as much as speed. Angusel had watched more teams be eliminated by failing to score direct hits on their targets than by being too slow to finish the relay, although the sacrifice of speed for accuracy didn't assure victory, either.

As Angusel glanced at the games marshals, who were busily recording details of each rider's performance on damp clay tablets while their assistants copied the completed notations to parchment leaves, he appreciated being a participant and not a judge.

One of the members of the Sixth Ala team cut the far corner too closely. Rider and mount went down amid a choking cloud of dust, and the crowd uttered a collective gasp. As the dust cleared, the horse rolled to its feet and cantered off the field, but the warrior writhed on the ground, clutching a leg and howling.

A pair of medics raced to his side carrying a leather sheet stretched between two stout poles, and they carefully loaded him onto the litter. Before they could bear him to safety, another shout went up. Angusel faced the adjacent track.

An important rule involved passing a bronze ring between team members. Possession of the ring by the fourth member at the end of his ride didn't garner extra points. A nuisance, to be sure, but to drop the ring meant elimination.

Amid cursing warriors and snorting horses, Clan Alban's ring gleamed serenely in the dust. In the space of a dozen breaths, the final two teams had been decided, and Angusel had never dreamed he'd be riding with one of them. The honor's magnitude drove all thought of fatigue from his mind.

The chief games marshal halted the competition to give the remaining teams a chance to refresh themselves, change horses, and inspect their gear.

"Fresh mount, lad?" Chieftain Ogryvan nodded toward the Argyll groomsmen, each holding the bridle of a rested horse, as Peredur and Rhys made their selections. "We have plenty."

"Thank you, my lord. But no, I—" Grinning, Angusel stroked Stonn's dappled gray flank. He'd seen to his stallion's needs after each round, walking him slowly to cool him down, checking for stones in his hooves, and taking care not to let him stay too long at the trough or hay crib. "*We* are just fine."

"Very well. Mount up!" This command, shouted to the entire Argyll team, barely carried over the bleating pipes that signaled preparation for the start of the final race.

A hush descended. The pipes skirled again, and the first two contestants spurred their horses ahead of the crowd's tumultuous roar.

As in the preliminary rounds, each rider had to complete three passes around the track. In theory, it wasn't difficult to collect a javelin from the drudge, fling it at the armored human target standing in the opposite curve, and swing around to begin again while the horse galloped as fast as the warrior's nerves allowed.

Theory had little to do with reality.

Peredur raced a flawless round, his best of the day. With each pass, he widened the gap between him and his opponent, who struggled with a skittish mare. By the time Angusel guided Stonn into position for transfer of the ring, Peredur had pulled half a lap ahead, scoring direct hits with all three throws.

Angusel set heels to Stonn's flanks and snatched the ring from Peredur's outstretched hand. After slipping it onto his left wrist, he poured his concentration into the ride.

Give Stonn his head on the straightaway . . . slow him just enough to grab the javelin . . . lean into the turn . . . judge the rate of closure on the target . . . take aim, throw!

He let his ears tell him how successful the throw had been. A metallic thump meant a direct hit. If the javelin missed, the crowd's cheers and jeers conveyed whether or not it had landed within one of the nested chalk circles.

His cast fell short but landed inside the innermost circle. After correcting for the distance on his second attempt, he heard the javelin bounce off the soldier's shield. As he began his third pass, his jubilation grew.

He had given no thought to his opponent. After making his final toss, he looked up to see the other warrior beginning his third pass. Fitting four ovals onto the parade ground hadn't left much room between the tracks. Still, if both horsemen rode carefully, they could pass each other without mishap.

Angusel tightened his grip with knees as well as hands.

The warriors had drawn abreast when the Bhreatan horse shied. Shouts rang out. Stonn reared and threw back his head, pawing and screaming. Angusel's head collided with Stonn's. His vision grew blacker by the heartbeat. He clung to consciousness as desperately as he clung to Stonn's neck. He had to complete his round! His honor, and the honor of Clan Argyll and its chieftainess, depended on it.

A shadow appeared before him. It might have been Rhys. Or another rider. Or a fence post or the gods alone knew what. Angusel squinted at the shape, fervently hoping for Rhys.

Gods, how his head throbbed!

Groaning, he braced against Stonn's neck, stretching out his leaden arm. He felt the ring slide off and heard shouts and receding hoofbeats. His fingers went numb, and he lost his grip.

He slammed to the ground. Darkness reigned.

Chapter 3

"ANGUSEL!" THE ANGUISHED cry tore from Gyan's throat. Several inquisitive faces turned her way.

She'd already thrown a leg over the rail before Arthur's hand gripped her arm. "Gyan, no!"

"Arthur, let me go." Not a plea, but a command.

The Pendragon did not obey. "It's too dangerous down there."

"Ha. I took my first steps around wilder horses than these."

"For me, then. Please." The last word barely reached her ears.

Most of the horsemen eliminated in the earlier rounds still roamed the field, either astride their mounts or attending their needs as the final race ended. Guards strained to hold back the crowd. Other folk scurried about on foot: women dispensing food and water, lads running errands for the games marshals, medics toting bandages and ointments, grooms lugging armloads of fodder and pails of oats, drudges collecting spent javelins from the tracks. Anyone with even the remotest excuse had contrived to be on the parade ground.

Reluctantly, she swung her leg back over the rail and called to a guard standing below her. "You, soldier! Order the medics to bring the injured Argyll horseman up here." She silently prayed that Angusel hadn't been badly hurt.

The guard glanced at Arthur, who nodded tightly, lips pursed. The soldier thumped his leather-clad chest and departed to do Gyan's bidding. She realized she'd trespassed upon her consort's authority and flashed him an apologetic smile.

After committing Angusel into the One God's hands, she turned to discover Caius on the platform. His legion ceremonial uniform had been styled much like Arthur's, in silver rather than gold, matching the silver dragon brooch pinned to his silver-bordered scarlet cloak.

Fair of face and hair, broad of shoulder, sturdy of limb—and legendary in the bedchamber—she understood how so many women could fall under Caius's spell.

"Well come." She offered her sword hand for the warriors' armgrip. "My brother."

Caius grunted.

She ignored his reluctance to clasp the blue woad Argyll Doves adorning her forearm. "Your men marched well, Caius."

"From what little you saw, Chieftainess"—the title came dangerously close to sounding like an insult—"how can you possibly make an assessment?"

"Some manners would become you, Cai." Bedwyr laid a hand on Caius's shoulder, his glare charged with warning. Caius shrugged it off like a grouchy hawk in molt.

For Arthur's sake, Gyan strove to keep her tone pleasant. "An oversight I do regret, General, I assure you. I never would have believed a large body of foot soldiers could execute such complicated moves had I not seen it for myself." Her smile rose on the wings of a pleasant memory. "This morning, my husband was most insistent."

If her use of Caius's rank pleased him, he didn't show it. "Aye," he allowed. "Arthur is nothing if not insistent."

"And I insist, Cai," said Arthur, quietly but firmly, "that you show more courtesy to my bride."

The two men locked gazes. Caius burst into laughter.

"You two, what a pair!" Still chortling, he slapped Arthur's shoulder. "Saints in heaven, preserve us all!"

She failed to see the reason for Caius's mirth, but Arthur shared the laugh as he reached for her hand.

"Time to reward the victors, Gyan." He signaled a boy holding four wreaths standing a respectful distance away. The lad marched forward to surrender them to Gyan and withdrew with a bow.

Amid the chorus of cheers, three of the four Argyll horsemen cantered to the platform.

Despite her anxiety for Argyll's absent teammate, she couldn't suppress the surge of pride for her clan's victory. The winners received more than the traditional laurel crowns. To the throng's obvious delight, she leaned over the rail to bestow upon the brow of each warrior a lavish kiss.

A hand pulled her back from the rail. "He's here," Arthur said.

She looked past him toward the far end of the platform, where two medics descended the steps and departed in opposite directions as fast as the crowd would allow. On the platform, crimson-and-green-banded sky-blue cloaks of Clan Alban swirled beside legion scarlet as several men stood in a semicircle. Ogryvan, Per, and Rhys dismounted and made their way toward the group, as did Ygraine and Morghe. From the back, Gyan recognized Merlin by his silver ceremonial uniform and balding, iron-gray head. The slender, white-robed figure at his side presented another welcome sight, although how Niniane, renowned physician and prioress of Rushen Priory, could have reached the platform so quickly from where she'd been standing with other members of the clergy was a miracle in itself.

A thicket of legs concealed the object of everyone's attention from Gyan's view. She sensed rather than saw her consort's presence as she neared and the group parted to admit them.

Blood and dust masked Angusel's face. More blood matted his curly black hair and spattered his battle-gear. If his chest moved beneath its leather shell, only a person with a falcon's eyes could see it.

"I've sent a medic to fetch my medicines, Your Grace, and another for water and bandages." Niniane regarded Merlin, clutching her crucifix. "With this crowd, it may be some time before they return."

"Then we must do what we can for the lad, Prioress," he said.

With the ease of a man half his age, the warrior-priest sank to his knees beside Angusel. Niniane joined him. They loosened the thongs holding Angusel's breastplate and pushed it aside. Angusel didn't respond. His limbs might have belonged to a child's rag doll.

Morghe stooped to pick up the breastplate, clutching it possessively. A mixture of sadness and fear pooled in her violet eyes, totally at odds with the Morghe Gyan knew. Then she recalled that Angusel and Morghe had been close companions before he'd chosen to devote himself to Gyan's service. Ygraine wrapped her arm around Morghe's shoulders.

A medic joined the group, water sloshing over the rim of his bucket and a bandage roll tucked under one arm. Prioress Niniane tore off a strip and dipped it in the water. While she swabbed the blood and grime from Angusel's too-pale face, Merlin laid an ear to the sweaty undertunic pasted to Angusel's chest.

When Merlin lifted his head, his look wasn't encouraging. "His heartbeat is weak and irregular." Gyan's hopes fell.

"What more can we do, Your Grace?" whispered Niniane as she gently wrapped Angusel's bloody head. "Without my herbs and salves—"

Merlin bowed his head and softly, in Ròmanaiche, began to pray. Niniane's hand rested lightly on Angusel's bandaged brow. She, too, bowed her head and added her treble voice to his chant.

Caledonaich and Breatanaich alike moved to adopt an attitude of supplication. Morghe tightened her grip on Angusel's breastplate and closed her eyes. Like Merlin and Niniane, most of the other Breatanaich—Arthur and Ygraine included—bowed heads and clasped hands together. Where room permitted, some knelt. The Caledonach way required eyes open, face turned skyward, arms outspread.

Gyan scanned the heavens, but the God she sought reigned above the Caledonach pantheon.

Earnestly, she begged the One God to heal her fallen comrade at whatever cost . . . even to the sacrifice of her life. She refused to contemplate how devastating his death would be to her.

She heard a ragged gasp and glanced down, dashing away tears. Angusel's chest rose and fell with a strong rhythm. His eyelids fluttered open. Slowly, he raised a hand to his temple and moaned.

An image flashed to mind of a day several months earlier, when she'd seen a slave injure his back so badly that everyone believed he'd never walk again. After the intense prayers of his fellow Breatanaich, Rudd had limped from the accident site.

Today's results startled her no less.

"It does work," she murmured, in Breatanaiche, to no one in particular.

"Indeed it does, Chieftainess." The warrior-priest pushed to his feet, captured her hand, and gave it a pat. "If you have faith the size of but a mustard seed."

Merlin and Niniane stepped back into the circle of onlookers as Gyan dropped to one knee beside Angusel.

"Did—did we win?" His Caledonaiche words sounded alarmingly weak.

"Yes, Angus," she answered in kind. Only then did she remember the fourth laurel crown, some of its leaves bruised by her fist. She pressed the fragrant wreath to his palm and closed his fingers around it. "You rode superbly. You have brought great honor to Argyll, to Alban, and to my consort and me."

He rewarded her praise with the crooked grin she'd come to love so well. Returning it, she silently thanked the One God for Angusel's healing and vowed to discover the identity of the horseman who'd brought harm upon her sword-brother, though her heart presented but one choice.

And the machaoduin would pay for his near-fatal mistake.

URIEN FINISHED fastening his new bronze cavalry prefect's brooch to his cloak and slipped its iron cousin into the pouch tied to Talarf's saddlebow. "If anyone asks, Lucius was the second rider." He kept his voice low, mindful that the games helm's mouth slit amplified sounds, and glared at his teammates. "I rode fourth."

His men nodded, one with more vigor than the other two. Although the helms robbed identity, Urien knew the confident one. His clansman and longtime friend, Accolon, had done a commendable job of feigning trouble with his horse to set the stage for the accident. Of Accolon's loyalty, Urien had no doubt.

For the benefit of Lucius and Cato, Urien said, "The man who fails to remember this won't live long enough to regret it."

With an angry jerk on the reins, the heir of Clan Moray wheeled his mount around and set heels to flanks. Talarf sprang toward the viewing platform, followed by the rest of the team.

There she stood, the woman who should have been his: tall, proud, and as stunningly beautiful as on the wet October day he'd met her, clasping hands with the man who'd stolen her. After being forced to attend their wedding and nuptial feast, Urien thought he'd been exposed to all the pain he was ever going to feel. Seeing her again, though, like this . . .

The heat under his helm wasn't the only thing to rise, damn her.

His gaze roved to the woman he would be marrying instead. In the last fortnight, Morghe had insinuated herself into Urien's affections so thoroughly that the sight of her violet gown coyly draping her figure's bewitching curves made him yearn for time to speed ahead to their own nuptials, and to the devil with Gyanhumara and Arthur and everyone else.

To the devil, in fact, was exactly where Urien itched to send the Caledonian whore. Morghe's proximity to Gyanhumara sparked an idea. He grinned behind the mask.

"First Ala team," said Arthur, "identify yourselves."

Urien's leisurely compliance didn't appear to irritate Arthur as much as he'd hoped it might.

Gyanhumara stared at Urien, her face stripped of emotion. She might as well have been wearing a games helm.

"First Ala team reporting as ordered," Urien said. "Sir."

Executing a salute with enough enthusiasm to keep it from being construed as an insult required more precision than a cavalry drill, but Urien's latest stint at headquarters had afforded many opportunities for practice.

"Your team rode well today, Prefect," Arthur began, cordially enough, though he chose not to employ the title "tribune," Urien's preferred manner of address. "However, I noticed the difficulty your second rider experienced in the final race." His face transformed into a mask as rigid as the one tucked under Urien's arm. "Who was he?"

"Lucius, my lord."

"Is this true, Decurion?" asked Arthur sternly.

"A-aye, sir. 'Twere an accident, Lord Pendragon. I swear!" Lucius twitched in his saddle under the Pendragon's fierce scrutiny.

"Your negligence could have cost your opponent his life. Decurion Lucius, you are banned from cavalry games for one year," Arthur said.

"Banned from—from games?" Lucius didn't disguise his astonishment. I can still fight with First Ala, my lord?"

"Of course. With no reduction of rank or pay." Arthur's countenance relaxed slightly. "You are far too valuable an asset to your unit. And to me."

Lucius responded with a salute and a look that, for all his attempted self-discipline, appeared decidedly grateful.

"What says Chieftainess Gyanhumara?" Urien ignored Lucius's gasp and stared at her. "Surely you would want something more done to the man who hurt your friend."

She exchanged a swift glance with Arthur, but whatever silent message passed between them, Urien couldn't decipher it.

"I support my consort's decision." Eclipsing her sword's pommel with her fist, she spat the words through clenched teeth. "Angusel has taken no permanent harm. Luckily for you, Urien map Dumarec. Being the leader makes you responsible for the actions of everyone under you," she snapped. "Good and bad alike."

Urien scarcely heard Arthur's agreement or curt dismissal. He glared at the woman who'd caused all his problems.

Somehow, he would break that iron pride of hers. Urien ran his tongue across his lips. Revenge would taste sweet, and like a prime vintage, he would savor each drop.

BY THE time Arthur escaped from the dining hall, the moon had sailed high overhead. Gyan had made a sensible retreat much earlier. Part of him didn't regret having spent time with his men, but the rest of him wished he'd chosen to accompany her.

The statue of the Roman goddess Diana in the praetorium's courtyard loomed before him. Moonlight transformed the water cascading from her jug into a silvery stream, and it glittered in the ripples around her feet. This chunk of marble had witnessed countless hours of Arthur's time as a student, sometimes with Merlin at his side to lecture and rebuke and praise, but more often not. Arthur map Uther preferred the luxury of solitude.

He wondered whether marriage would change that. Yet having Gyan for his partner made it a welcome prospect.

As a boy, he had viewed the stone goddess as the perfect embodiment of womanhood. Every detail shone flawlessly beautiful, down to the neatly sculpted fingernails. When the first stirrings of manhood had come upon him, he'd found fleshly women to be somewhat less than perfect. Some, a lot less. More than once, the doubt had nagged him that he'd ever find his own goddess on earth.

In Gyan, that doubt never would trouble him again.

"She is beautiful," murmured a female voice. Arthur turned to see Ygraine gliding toward him. He noted with a flash of irritation that the guards had withdrawn from their posts, except the pair flanking the door, and they stood too far away to overhear a conversation conducted in normal tones. The teeth bared by Ygraine's smile gleamed like moonlit pearls. "I haven't forgotten how much a little privacy costs."

He snorted as an image of her and his father came to mind. Shoving it aside, he squelched the urge to reprimand her for bribing his guards. The men would hear from him soon enough.

"Don't be too hard on them, Arthur," she said, as if hearing his thoughts. "They believe they're doing us a favor." As he glared at her under lowered eyebrows, her grin widened. "Your father used to get that same look whenever I did something like this."

He conceded with a sigh. Some battles weren't worth the effort.

Of the reasons Ygraine might seek private speech with him, he had a reasonable guess. Very little befell Clan Cwrnwyll without the consent of its chieftainess. After having grown to manhood in the fosterage of Cai's late parents, Ectorius and Calpurnia, he felt less like Ygraine's son than her liegeman.

"If you are displeased because I didn't consult you about my marriage—"

She waved dismissively and gathered her skirts to settle onto the pool's raised lip. "I gave you both my blessing yesterday, and I'm not of a mind to retract it now. Last night, Cai told me everything the bards couldn't: that certain events rather . . . outpaced everyone." She patted the lip beside her in an invitation. When Arthur shook his head, she chuckled softly. "Arthur map Uther, you are most definitely your father's son."

Unsure whether she meant that as a compliment, he let it pass. "Did he also tell you that by the laws of Gyan's people, we've been married for a fortnight already?"

"No." Her finger furrowed the water, and the carp swam over to investigate. Ygraine's features creased into a thoughtful expression. She flicked the drops away. "Quite convenient, I must say."

"Yes," Arthur said. If canonical law, to which the Brytoni clans adhered, had contained such a provision, there would have been no question about the legitimacy of Arthur's birth or his assumption of

Clan Cwrnwyll's chieftainship upon Ygraine's death. He didn't crave either status, but he despised his options being constrained by events beyond his control. "Quite."

Up jerked her head, and she shot to her feet. Arthur could feel her wrath ignite. Facing an enemy army alone and unarmed seemed much more appealing.

"I chose my destiny years ago, Arthur, and I'd do it all over again. Lord knows I paid for that choice by having you . . . and losing you..." She drew a breath, puffed it out, and drew another. "I've always regretted that things didn't work out differently for you. And for us. Your father included. If you think I don't care about what happens to you, then I strongly suggest you think again." When he didn't reply, she sighed, turning toward the pool. "You have a lovely, spirited bride. I see a lot of Uther and me in the two of you." Her short laugh sounded rueful. "Much more than I'd expected. I had hoped to use the occasion of these festivities to get better acquainted with her—and with you." Ygraine's shoulders shifted in another sigh, and she faced him. "Forgive an old woman for indulging in vain hopes."

He may have considered Ygraine to be many things, but never old. Yet as he studied her face, he noticed abundant evidence in the creased brow and the frown lines dragging at her mouth, lines etched by responsibility and, amazingly, regret. He began to understand how much he truly meant to her—to say nothing of her sacrifice to improve his chances of surviving the political chaos spawned by the death of her first husband, Gorlas, which had cleared the way for her union with Uther. Years' worth of animosity fueled by ignorance melted with the warmth of filial devotion.

"I—" His voice felt husky from the ambush of emotions. "I forgive you." He surprised himself by how deeply he meant it. Clearing his throat, he held out a hand. "Mother."

With a beatific smile, she clasped his hand. "We'll talk later, son." Letting go, she aimed a nod at the building's torchlit entrance. "You oughtn't keep your bride waiting."

Impish irreverence prompted his grin. "That's the best advice you've ever given me."

As he took his leave and strode off to heed that advice, Ygraine's answering chuckle floated after him. "So far."

HER BACK to the door, Gyan balanced atop a backless Ròmanach chair in the anteroom of the quarters she shared with her consort, feeling Cynda's comb's tug as she pondered the circumstances of Angusel's injury. The physician expected him to be fully recovered in a few days, but the news didn't prevent her from dwelling upon Urien's probable involvement in the "accident."

"You're terribly quiet, my dove." Gyan could hear Cynda's mirth as she eased the tangles from Gyan's hair. "Thinking about the pleasures your consort will be giving you, I don't doubt. So . . . how skillful is he? Is he ardent? Tender? Forceful?"

Gyan had to laugh. "As if I'd tell you!"

"Aye, well, when you get to be my age, lass, you'll ken that tales are the only things left to stir the blood."

Cynda sounded so wistful. Gyan shifted to look at her and wondered when Cynda's worry lines had gotten so deep. "You, old? Nonsense." She faced forward for Cynda to continue her work. "Now that I'm married, why don't you marry again, too?"

The pulling stilled. A virulent fever had taken Cynda's husband and wee bairn a few days before Gyan's birth, heartbreaking for Cynda but fortuitous for the motherless infant Gyan. No one else had claimed Cynda's affections.

"Cynda?" Gyan prompted.

"Nay, lass, I think not." Cynda chuckled as the pulling resumed, a fair bit rougher. "I couldn't hope to find a man half as handsome—or roguish—as yours."

A pair of lips brushed Gyan's cheek. Startled, she whipped around to find Arthur bent over beside her, comb in hand and looking as smug as a cat beside an overturned jug of cream.

"Beathach!" She swatted his shoulder and switched to Breatanaiche. "Beast! Must I guard my back in our own chambers?"

"Not an unwise idea, my love." As he surrendered the comb to Cynda, his expression turned pensive. "Best not to take chances."

"You're right." If Arthur could slip in without Gyan noticing, so could anyone else. She sighed. Would Urien forever wedge himself between her and Arthur, even during their most private moments?

In Caledonaiche, Gyan bade Cynda retire for the evening. While the older woman unfurled her pallet on the antechamber's tiles, Arthur bolted the door and escorted Gyan into their bedchamber. After securing the inner door, he pulled her into his arms, but the insistent probing of his tongue between her lips failed to lure her thoughts away from her enemy.

"Gyan?"

Dodging the question wasn't an option; she suspected Arthur would sense dissembling. "Urien was lying."

"I know." He gripped her hand and started for the bed. Although sex and sleep bottomed her present list of priorities, she didn't resist him. "But without proof, I couldn't take him to task for it." Frustration and regret sculpted his words.

She disengaged her hand to sit on the bed, contemplating the predicament into which Urien had thrust Arthur. A war-chieftain devoid of conscience would have chosen a permanent solution.

Such a man Gyan never would have married.

Chin on fist, she regarded Arthur as he peeled off the layers of his uniform. Soon, he stood before her wearing nothing save a narrow cloth band to guard his loins. The sight should have goaded her desire, but her mind's eye conjured the image of Angusel's bloody body surmounted by Urien's smirking face.

"What could he possibly hope to gain by hurting Angus?" she whispered, eyes downcast. "Unless . . . unless he thinks that by hurting those I care about, he is hurting me?" A gasping sob burst from her throat. "It does hurt!" She leveled her gaze at her consort. "Artyr, he must be stopped."

HER PAIN-WRACKED declaration, as her right hand groped reflexively for her absent sword hilt, wrenched Arthur's heart. The lapse didn't diminish the fierce determination painted across her brow. Yet something else dwelt there, too. A hint of—what? Regret?

Grasping her hands, he went to one knee at her feet. "I swear to you, Gyan, I will not let him harm you." He kissed her fingers.

"It's not me I'm worried about. If anything happened to me, you'd carve him into pieces too small for worms. And he knows it."

"Damned right." The praetorium's hypocaustum didn't run during high summer, but tonight the room felt unseasonably chilly.

He couldn't suppress the shiver.

Expression softening, she tugged on his hands. "Come on up here, you great idiot, before you catch your death."

Gratefully, Arthur joined her on the bed and crawled beneath the coverlet. With a hand on her arm, he tried to convince her to lie beside him, but she refused to budge. He sat up to begin massaging her shoulders. She sighed softly.

He leaned over to whisper, "Speak to me, my love." Her hair smelled faintly of rose petals, and he wanted nothing more than to forget their problems and pursue much more pleasurable activities. If she was concerned about a feud with Urien, however, the pleasures would have to wait.

For a long moment, she sat silently, head bowed.

"If only we could settle this matter between ourselves—just him and me, sword to sword. But he seems determined to involve my friends, probably my kin, too. I had so hoped to prevent a war with Dalriada." She slumped back against his chest. "Now, it's inevitable."

"Is it?"

"Of course!" She pushed away and twisted toward him, her eyes flashing scorn. "Where is that fabulous strategic sense of yours? Can you not see the pattern?" Though not especially loud, the words shot from her lips like arrows. "If I choose not to react to his attempt on Angus's life, he will only keep trying until I do. Maybe not Angus, next time, but someone else."

Mentally, he conceded the validity of her point. Still, perhaps other alternatives existed. He asked, "What if the collision truly was an accident?"

"Ha! To believe that you would have to presume Urien was telling the truth." She regarded him solemnly. "You'd best find someone else to lead the Manx Cohort, Artyr. I suspect I am going to be rather busy." With a sigh, she averted her gaze.

"This is exactly how he wants you to react." He slipped his fingers beneath her chin, forcing her to look up. "I need you on Maun. Not at Urien's throat. Let me deal with him."

"You think my being on Maun is going to solve anything?" She shook free of his touch and folded her arms.

"No," he admitted. "I'm hoping distance and time will help you see your course more clearly. I'll wager Urien believes he can defeat Argyll in a pitched battle."

"You don't think I could win?" Her plucky defiance coaxed a brief smile to his lips.

"I didn't say that."

Far from it. She had killed a Scotti general after suffering hours of exposure to wind and rain, deprived of food and drink. If Arthur hadn't witnessed the fight, he never would have believed the tale. Her right arm still bore the bandage from the deep cut Niall had inflicted during their duel.

"But if Urien believes he has the advantage," Arthur continued, "he will be difficult to defeat."

Especially if she committed Argyll to a war without thinking this through, but Arthur couldn't say that in so many words. Being her consort gave him access to her wealth but no voice in Clan Argyll's government. That duty she shared with her father, and by Caledonian law, Ogryvan would be chieftain for as long as he remained fit for the task. Arthur could advise Gyan—Ogryvan also, if the chieftain cared to listen. If the rulers of Argyll chose to ignore his advice, however, Arthur couldn't do a bloody thing about it.

"You wouldn't help me if I had to fight him?"

"Of course I would, Gyan." He inhaled another whiff of her rose-scented hair as he summoned the courage to tell her what she probably least wanted to hear. "But I do counsel restraint."

"Restraint? Ha! Then who will be his next victim? My father? My brother? One of my clansmen? You, Artyr?" She thumped the blanket with a fist. "I cannot let him hurt anyone else because of me!"

He gripped her shoulders. The eyes that met his gaze gleamed with feral intensity.

"That's exactly what would happen if you go to war." She started to protest, but he cut her off. "I can guard myself against treachery. I imagine your kin and clansmen can, too. If you attack Dunadd, it will appear to all Brydein as an unprovoked act of Caledonian aggression. Think what that would do to our treaty."

He didn't mention that the outrage of the Brytoni Council of Chieftains at Argyll's "unprovoked act of aggression" probably would prevent Arthur from sending his foot troops—provided by those same Brytoni chieftains—to help her. Never mind the inevitable political muddle if Arthur ordered his mostly Caledonian cavalry cohort to stay clear of an Argyll-Moray war.

Or, God forbid, the pressure the council might exert upon him to annul his marriage.

A legion of emotions paraded across Gyan's face: surprise, denial, anger, horror, and, finally, acceptance. Perhaps she'd discovered these other possibilities, too. Arthur hoped so. "Oh, God, no . . ." Her tortured whisper grieved him. "What am I to do?"

He hugged her. Her cheek felt like a firebrand against his chest.

"We will take the only sensible course: watch and wait." He brushed his fingertips across her cheekbones.

"I will go to Maun, then. For you." Her steady gaze heralded her resolve. "What of—him? Is it wise to let him command Caledonians?"

Arthur had wrestled with that issue often since recalling Urien to headquarters, liking the answer no more now than before.

"He is one of my best commanders. And he's no fool. Chieftain's son or not, he wouldn't dare provoke me openly." For Gyan's sake, he refrained from adding, "yet."

"If there's a way to defy you, Artyr, he will find it."

"I know." Urien had begun perfecting his almost-insubordinate attitude when he lost the Pendragonship appointment, long before either of them had met Gyan. Only the respect and alliance given Arthur by Urien's father, Chieftain Dumarec, restrained him from meting out the punishment Urien so richly deserved. "I can handle him, Gyan. Don't worry about me." He flashed his most convincing grin.

Her mouth twitched. "As you command, Lord Pendragon." The smile vanished, and she squeezed his hand. "I pray Urien won't destroy the Caledonian-Brytoni unity we're working so hard to achieve."

That prayer Arthur fervently shared.

Chapter 4

As the Wintaceaster palace guards departed to resume their posts, closing the ornately carved oaken doors behind them, Prince Ælferd Wlencingsson dropped to one knee. The room's lone occupant lounged in a purple-cushioned gilt chair near the hearth with a full view of the chamber's entryway, flanked by a brace of wolfhounds lying sprawled across the flagstones. They perked their ears to the soft ringing of Ælferd's bronze-linked hauberk but otherwise declined to move.

"Rise, nephew," intoned King Cissa. "Come and refresh yourself." Ælferd obeyed as the king's sharp claps pierced the air.

A trio of gold-collared Brædan thralls appeared through a curtained inner doorway. The male slave carried a tall-backed chair, which he placed near the king's. One woman brought silver goblets and a matching pitcher of wine; the other bore a platter of strawberries, cheese, and bread. The hounds scrambled to sit on lean haunches, eyeing the women.

The young woman with the wine was pretty, for a Bræde. Rich brown tresses spilled across milk-white breasts bulging above the gold-edged blue bodice. As she bent to set down her burden, the king's fingertips strayed to that flawless bosom. Cissa smiled slyly. The Brædan princess accepted her master's caress with the stoic remoteness of one resigned to fate.

Silver streaked the other woman's black hair, but her face was surprisingly handsome in spite of its frown lines. She carried herself with dignity and elegance, arranging the food on the table with practiced efficiency. Both women retreated behind the curtain.

Ælferd placed his griffin-crested helmet next to the platter, hitched the folds of his green-and-gold cloak around him, and sat while the Brædan prince poured the wine and sipped from both goblets. The king selected a hunk of cheese and passed it to his taster, bidding his nephew to do the same.

"One cannot be too careful these days," said the king. "Good health, nephew." Cissa lifted the goblet to his lips, swallowed, and rubbed the back of his hand across his mouth.

"Good health, my lord." Ælferd let the first mouthful sit on his tongue to savor the wine's mellow sweetness, calculating how much he'd have to bribe the steward for a cask. His men had earned it tenfold for their efforts in wrenching the Roman fort, Anderida—now known by its proper Saxon name, Anderceaster—from the fat hands of the southern Brædeas.

"Now, Ælferd. Tell us about Anderceaster." Settling back, feet propped and goblet in one hand, the king began to chew on his cheese, now and then tossing tidbits to his hounds, who gobbled them greedily.

"There's not much to tell, my lord. Those Brædeas possessed no champion like Arthur the Dragon King. My men fought like the true heroes they are, and the Brædeas"—Ælferd cast a grin at the thrall standing behind the king's chair—"fought like craven pig-dogs."

The Brædan prince didn't react to the insult, or to any other aspect of the report, including the fact that Ælferd's men had slaughtered the Brædan soldiers to the last man. The Bræde stood impassively, moving only to refill the goblets and taste the food at his master's command. Ælferd began to wonder whether the man was deaf or just stupid.

"Well done, nephew. Your father would have been proud."

Ælferd felt his chest swell. Years ago, disease had robbed him of the chance of ever proving his worth to Wlencing in this life. But since his father could well be watching him from Woden's Hall, it had never stopped Ælferd from trying.

Continued the king, "Let this represent a token of our pleasure."

Cissa gestured to the thrall, who bowed and disappeared into the side chamber. The Bræde returned with a small gilt box. Kneeling, he presented it to Ælferd.

Inside, nestled within the purple folds of a swath of fabric, gleamed a massive, garnet-studded gold buckle.

"Many thanks, Uncle Cissa," whispered Ælferd.

The king nodded. "Clearly, you are ready for a more difficult undertaking. Oversee the rebuilding and provisioning of Anderceaster, and begin staging the troops and ships I send you."

"My lord?" A sweaty itch tickled under the wide bronze band binding his hair, and he wished he'd shed his cloak, too. He couldn't imagine what sort of operation would require ships as well as soldiers. Crossing the Narrow Sea to invade Brædan-infested Armorica, perhaps?

King Cissa gently shook his goblet. The liquid swirled, casting the illusion that he held a whirlpool of blood. "A gem of an island gleams in the navel of the Ærish Sea." He downed the wine, looked up, and caught Ælferd's gaze. "I want it."

Ælferd raised his eyebrows. "Maun, sir? That's so far—"

His uncle glared at him. He swallowed his protest. The time and wealth required to provision such an expedition represented only part of the problem. Arthur's men garrisoned the Isle of Maun: men reputed to fight like demons, with a she-devil named Guenevara to lead them, and the most fearsome of the lot, if her battlefield beheading of the Ærish invasion commander wasn't some minstrel's ale-inspired fantasy.

Ælferd's throat went dry, and he clenched his fists to keep from touching his neck. He drained his goblet, but the wine had lost its allure.

"I am well aware of the distance, Ælferd, along with the cost in men, supplies, and time." That damned itch attacked Ælferd's forehead again, and he resisted the urge to claw the band from his head. Avarice flashed across Cissa's face as he explained, "This operation will give me a strategic base for launching attacks against the Brædeas of West Brædæn, the Ærish of Æren, and"—avarice transformed to malice—"against this upstart whore's bastard, Arthur, who has the gall to style himself Dragon King of Brædæn."

With the formidable Riothamus dead these past two decades, Armorica would make an easier and far more sensible objective, but Ælferd dared not voice his opinion.

What the King of the West Saxons craved, he always obtained. And the son of Wlencing vowed to do all within his power to satisfy that craving.

A FAMILIAR pealing echoed in Dafydd's ears, shattering his dreams and continuing long after he'd opened his eyes. Too long after. The matins bell rang only twelve times, and this had to be, what—eighteen, nineteen, twenty? He hadn't heard such a clamor since...

He jerked upright, perspiration beading his brow.

Lord God in heaven, not another invasion!

He threw on his outer robe, pulled up the hood, slipped into his sandals, and hurried outside as the other conical, mud-daubed wattle sleeping chambers disgorged their residents. The entire time, he strained to hear the ominous sounds he and the rest of the monks knew all too well, but he could discern nothing beyond that incessant ringing.

At last, mercifully, it stopped. As he wandered about with the others in sleep-hazed confusion, a pair of brethren appeared and directed the crowd toward the abbot's house.

The bell's summons made sudden, dreadful sense.

And Abbot Lir had yet to announce a successor for his duties as overseer of the monastery, the library, the brethren and students, and one of the holiest relics in Christendom.

Head bowed as he trudged in the silent file, he earnestly prayed for Father Lir and his successor.

Near the abbot's house, the line lost cohesion as brothers coalesced into quiet groups of three or four.

Dafydd, as the newest member of this community of faith, though not the newest in this type of service to the Lord, chose to stand apart. Grief for Father Lir's condition resurrected his grief for his children. Scotti invaders had killed his daughter, Mari, scant weeks ago. His infant son, Samsen, had succumbed to illness half a year before that. He pressed a hand to his moist eyes.

A soft, familiar hand slipped into his. He opened his eyes to see Katra standing beside him, concern and questions graven upon her face. Their only surviving child, twelve-year-old Dafydd the Younger, stood solemnly beside her. The elder Dafydd surmised they'd heard the bell from their quarters in the monastery's guesthouse. He circled his arms around his wife, and she laid her cheek against his chest.

"Father Lir?" she whispered. "Is—is he—"

Unable to trust his voice, he shrugged.

"Brother Dafydd?" Katra stepped back to make room for Brother Stefan, master of the library and students. Stefan pointed toward the door of the abbot's house with his cane. "He wants to see you." Beneath Stefan's customary gruffness ran a current of envy and disbelief.

Queasiness troubled Dafydd's stomach. Glancing at Katra and their son, then at Brother Stefan, he asked, "May they come, too?"

Stefan nodded, turned, and hobbled toward the house.

Dafydd followed, with Katra and young Dafydd a pace behind him.

Light escaped through cracks and knotholes in the cottage's shutters. Moonbeams gave its whitewashed stone walls a ghostly gleam. He shook his head to dispel the association. A quick squeeze of his wife's hand helped to reaffirm his grip on reality, and together they followed Brother Stefan inside.

The abbot's table, chairs, and sideboard appeared in good condition but of a modest design. A braided rug of undyed wool covered half the floor. A bank of candles illuminated the crucifix nailed to one wall.

Embroidered pillows piled on a bench beneath the window offered the only touch of luxury. Their sun-blanched colors made Dafydd wonder how long ago they'd been made, and by whom. The abbot's mother, a sister, or . . . wife? The Church of Brydein preferred her servants to remain free of worldly concerns but encouraged them to marry if the yearnings of the flesh burned too hotly.

He quelled his curiosity as he watched Stefan approach the bedchamber door to rap upon it with the tip of his cane.

The infirmarer opened the door. Dark shadows beneath his eyes betrayed his lack of sleep. The infirmarer shared a glance with Stefan, frowning, and gave a brief shake of his graying head. Stefan responded with a terse nod. Pulling the door open wider, the infirmarer beckoned everyone into the room.

The only light emanated from a pair of candles, each sitting atop a small table to either side of the bed. The abbot's sleeping chamber was furnished much like the other monks' quarters, only square rather than round, which provided more room between the bed and the walls. Into this space crowded the infirmarer, Katra, Dafydd, and their son. Stefan, grunting and leaning heavily on his cane, eased to his knees at Father Lir's side. Head bent, Stefan gently grasped the abbot's withered hand and pressed it to his forehead, his shoulders trembling.

Grateful that everyone else's attention centered upon the supine figure, Dafydd wasn't sure how much longer he could control his reaction to the sight of Father Lir's sallow, emaciated face and shrunken frame barely elevating the coverlet. Memories assailed him of the abbot's kindness since Dafydd's arrival on Maun, months before he'd renewed his vows.

His heart clenched.

"Stefan. Is he here?" The whisper crackled like a handful of dead leaves.

"Yes, Father, but I still think—"

"I know." The abbot's lips stretched into a thin smile. "I have ever valued your counsel, my son, and your faithful service." His voice sounded stronger. He disengaged his hand from Stefan's to beckon to Dafydd. "But this time, you do not know all the facts."

Dafydd's queasiness intensified. Facts? What facts? He, Dafydd, possessed no aptitude for administrative tasks. He could no sooner assume Father Lir's position than sprout wings and fly. He didn't even have command of his feet to obey the abbot's unspoken request.

Stefan said, "Forgive me, Father. I mean no disrespect. But I—that is, when Quintus died, I thought—"

"You thought you'd take his place as my successor. In truth, you would have." Father Lir's eyes fluttered closed. When he opened them, he looked squarely at Dafydd. "If not for our newest brother."

Surprise propelled him forward. He knelt on the opposite side of the bed. "Father Lir, I—" He shook his head in wonder. "I am honored, of course." Katra gave him an encouraging smile. To the abbot, he said, "But I'm too new to this community. I know too little about its workings. I—I can't—"

"Hush, my son." Father Lir laid an alarmingly cold hand on Dafydd's cheek. "God knows your weaknesses and delights in using them so that His power and glory may be manifest to all." The hand fell away. "He also knows your strengths. Including your shepherd's heart."

True, Dafydd thought with a brief smile. During his decade as a slave at Arbroch, it had been his pleasure to serve the Lord by tending to the spiritual needs of the other Brytoni slaves. It also had been a blessed joy to lead one of their Caledonian captors to a saving faith in Christ.

The rest of Caledonia might be ignorant of the Way, but he hoped Chieftainess Gyanhumara's conversion would prove to be a fruitful start.

One thing, however, he couldn't fathom. "I can see becoming abbot in perhaps ten years, but why now? The monastery, the school, the Chalice... Father, won't everyone think I'm too inexperienced?"

"Undoubtedly." The abbot locked gazes with Stefan, who frowned and looked down. Father Lir turned luminous eyes upon Dafydd. "Those who would disagree with my decision, even yourself"—Dafydd winced at the truth of the abbot's assessment—"have no choice but to accept it. Your appointment was foretold to me."

Stefan's head lifted. "Foretold?"

"Decades ago." Father Lir's gaze seemed miles away. "By Bishop Padraic of blessed memory." He focused upon Stefan, another ghostly grin bending his lips. "You do remember him, don't you, my son?"

Stefan snorted. "What did he tell you? This man's name? The date and manner of his arrival? The number of hairs on his head?"

Disapproval invaded Father Lir's expression. "Envy and pettiness have no place in the heart of any servant of our Lord, Stefan." Chastened, Stefan nodded. Father Lir said, "Padraic prophesied that I would know my successor by his mark of service." He gave a dry chuckle. "I confess to you all"—by the deliberate way his head turned, Dafydd realized Father Lir was including Dafydd's wife and son, as well as the infirmarer—"that I had no idea what he meant. Not until I saw..." He lifted a trembling hand to point at Dafydd, who understood and adjusted the neckline of his robe to bare his neck. "That." The hand dropped.

Stefan's eyes widened and narrowed as he studied the scar left by Dafydd's iron slave collar. "Father, you never told anyone of this prophecy. Again, I mean no disrespect, but how do we know—"

"That I'm not making it up? That I haven't taken leave of my senses? That this isn't some plot of the evil Adversary to bring ruin to the monastery and the Chalice?" The thin smile returned. "You don't. You must take it on faith." Pursing his lips, Father Lir bobbed his head slowly. "Just as I must take it on faith that my appointment of Brother Dafydd will cause no divisions after my passing."

The master of the library and students regarded Dafydd. Finally, Stefan shook his head and extended a hand across Father Lir's chest. "If this is your will, Father, I am not the man to oppose it."

Dafydd couldn't tell whether the remark had been directed at Father Lir or their heavenly Father. Either way, Stefan's statement heartened him, and he clasped the hand that had waged war in the earthly as well as the spiritual realms for more than half a century. Stefan had a firm, honest grip that Dafydd hoped would signify an equally firm and honest pledge of support.

The abbot laid both ancient, leathery hands on theirs. "Not my will, my sons, but the Lord's." His voice caught, and he gave a rattling cough. "May He guide your steps and guard your ways . . . Dafydd and Stefan and all who serve Him here . . ." Father Lir closed his eyes and sighed. Dafydd blinked away tears to look closely at the abbot. The aged eyes opened, but they seemed focused inward. "Listen . . . ah, listen to that glorious chorus . . ." A beatific smile spread across Father Lir's face. His eyes glazed.

Dafydd bowed his head to the coverlet. Katra laid a hand lightly upon his shoulder, but he didn't have the will to look up.

No prayers would come.

In his mind, he saw an image of a vigorous young man: Father Lir in his youth, Dafydd had no doubt. Brilliant light flared around him as he stood arm in arm with a lovely young woman, both being greeted by two beaming children, a girl and a boy.

A gasp of recognition lodged in Dafydd's throat.

The girl could be none other than his beloved Mari, which meant the boy—if this were a true vision and not some devilish trick—portrayed the glorified form of his baby son, Samsen.

Desperately, he tried to keep sight of his precious children and the man who'd become as dear to him as his earthly father.

The dimming vision wrung his heart.

The new abbot of St. Padraic's Monastery and Keeper of the Chalice heard no voices, no heavenly chorus... nothing but the sounds of his own grief. Yet for the brief, blessed vision he remained supremely thankful.

CHAPTER 5

SEATED BEHIND THE table in his private workroom, Arthur watched Gyan as she scanned the scouting report, her brow wrinkled and lips pursed. The report was written in Latin, and he wondered if she would request his help with the translation.

Clutching the dispatch, she strode to the wall covered by the tapestry-size map of Brydein. Burned onto deer hide, the map showed the isles of Hibernia, Mona, Maun, Vectis, and the land belonging to Dalriada and Caledonia, in addition to the larger island of Brydein. Brytons held Mona, Maun, and the western half of Brydein as far north as the Antonine Wall; Caledonians lived even farther north; Scots and Attacots divided control of Hibernia; Angles, Frisians, and Jutes occupied central and eastern Brydein; and, entrenched in the south, thanks to the long-dead Brytoni warlord Vortigern, Saxons.

Fists on hips, Gyan gazed at the map. Finally, she turned toward Arthur. "I don't understand."

"The Saxons have taken Anderida, and—"

"Translating the dispatch wasn't hard." The parchment rattled as she waved it impatiently. "You would not have held my ship unless you thought this news represented a threat." She laid the dispatch on a side table and folded her arms, smiling smugly.

"You're right." He found himself missing her keen insight already. With a sigh, he rose from behind the table to join her in front of the map. "The Saxons may launch an attack on Maun."

Her smile deepened. "You've gone mad." She jabbed a finger at the inkblot representing Dun Eidyn, in northern Angli territory, the closest enemy-held fortress to Arthur's eastern outposts. Less than three years before, it had belonged to the Brytons. At Dun Eidyn, Arthur had lost his father, gained command of the remnant of the legion, and inherited a powerful foe in a single spear-cast. "There lies your greatest threat."

He couldn't deny her assessment. The Angli occupation of Dun Eidyn and their role in Uther's death, coupled with the maddening fact that Arthur didn't yet possess the military might to address this problem on his own terms, pricked like a bur under the saddle. Beneath the desire to protect his fellow Brytons, swift and cold as a snow-swollen river, coursed thirst for vengeance upon that Angli bastard, King Colgrim.

Ruthlessly, he fought off that temptation. He'd be a fool to engage the Angli without assurance of victory.

Silently wishing circumstances could be otherwise, he said, "Colgrim has been quiet. No large troop movements, just a few border skirmishes and raids. Nothing Loth can't handle by himself." Not that he believed his proud brother-by-marriage would ever request his assistance, even if the Angli laid siege to Dunpeldyr itself, though for the sake of Annamar and their children, Arthur earnestly hoped Loth would exercise good judgment, should the worst come to pass.

"A Saxon invasion of Maun would require a tremendous undertaking." She traced a line from the port of Anderida into the Narrow Sea, around the tip of Dumnonia, past the Brytoni territories of Dyfed, Powys and Gwynedd, and across the Hibernian Sea to Maun. "All that distance by ship. The cost in provisions alone would be—"

"Well within Cissa's means," Arthur supplied. She opened her mouth, but he held up a hand. "The Saxons are fast outgrowing the lands Vortigern deeded to them. Plagues, crop failures, and Scotti raids have decimated the Brytoni population west of Deira. It's foolish to hope Cissa doesn't know this. If he has set his sights on this territory, then capturing Maun for a base would be a vital first step." Thankfully, she made no further attempt to argue. One lesson he'd learned in the week since the wedding was that having his wife as one of his military subordinates was going to be a bigger leadership challenge than any he'd yet faced. "I've ordered copies to be made of the most recent reports. Troop strengths of the Saxon kings, ship descriptions and numbers, and so on. Study those reports as your duties permit."

"An order, Lord Pendragon?"

He read the tease in the cant of her eyebrow, but apprehension prevented him from responding in kind. "A request."

"I will, then." Glancing at the map, she slowly shook her head. "I still think you're worrying for no good reason."

He hoped with all his heart that she was right. Abandoning the pretense of acting like her commander, he gripped her hands and all but lost himself in the fathomless depths of her sea-green eyes. "My love, I just want you to be prepared for the possibility."

"I know, Artyr, and I do appreciate it." Her throaty whisper ignited his passion.

He wrapped his arms around her and bent to kiss her, struggling to keep that passion in check. If he were to give it free rein, he would never be able to let her go. Judging by her response—warm, yet reserved—he presumed she felt much the same way.

The devil take it! God alone knew when he would see her again. He crushed her to him, redoubling the pressure on her lips, which tasted faintly of the honey she'd slathered on her bread. Seized by a hunger that outstripped physical need, he sought her tongue with his. His hands found the voluptuous curves of her leather-covered buttocks. With a husky sigh, she reached up to run her fingers through his hair, shifting beneath his kneading hands to nestle closer to him. The touch of her lips, her tongue, her hands, her body awakened his need for her like never before, yet it would have to go unslaked. With her ship's captain undoubtedly chafing to set sail, they'd already stolen too much time.

Reluctantly, he released her, though they did not step apart. She continued to hold his gaze, asking, "What of the replacement commander and cavalry troops for Tanroc? I expected them to sail with me."

"There have been some"—he curbed his grin lest it betray his surprise—"delays. I'll send them as soon as I can. The reports should be ready by then, too." This reminded him of a report Merlin had given him, though Arthur wasn't sure how she'd react to it. "There is something else you need to know, my love." He drew a breath and softened his tone. "The Abbot of St. Padraic's has died."

THE NEWS hit Gyan like a fist in the gut. "Father Lir? When?"

"Three days ago."

She buried her forehead against his neck. His arms tightened about her, but that only intensified her sorrow. The Scáthinach invasion had broken Father Lir's spirit and, ultimately, his heart. If anyone deserved to transcend the tears of this world, this gentle servant of the One God did. With a long blink and an even longer sigh, she gripped Arthur's tunic and battled to keep grief from crippling her.

"I suppose Brother Stefan has taken over?" she whispered, unwilling to dare a louder tone.

Arthur released her and strode to his worktable. After thumbing through a stack of parchment, he pulled out a sheet, returned to Gyan, and handed it to her.

As she read the message, written in precise Ròmanaiche with a neat, compact script, she guessed the author before reaching the signature.

Confirmation prompted her smile. "Abbot Dafydd, now, is it?" she murmured, half to herself. "Good for him!"

While this success never could erase the decade he and his family had spent in slavery to Clan Argyll, she hoped he was as happy with the appointment as she was for him.

Arthur placed his hands on her waist. "I thought you'd appreciate that."

"Very much. So Merlin and the other bishops have been invited to attend his investiture, but what about you? Will you join them?"

"This is an ecclesiastical matter."

"Ha. You think I won't attend the ceremony? They'd have to set an army around the church to keep me out! And it would do no good." She felt her smile fade. "You won't come even as an excuse to visit me?"

He uttered a bark of laughter. "As if I need one." His mouth descended upon hers, leaving no doubt as to the depth of his love. "Gyan, you know I cannot make promises that are too easy to break. But if I get the slightest opportunity to come to Maun, I will." Again he kissed her, hotter and more lingeringly than before. "Go, my love, before I change my mind and give someone else the Manx command."

"I wish you would." She laid a finger on his lips before he could speak. "I appreciate that you think highly of my leadership abilities, but . . ." Sighing, she dropped her gaze. His finger gently but firmly lifted her chin, and his earnest expression compelled her to continue. "Artyr, I am afraid."

"Of the Saxons?"

She gave a contemptuous snort. "Of disappointing you." Contempt gave way to concern. "And," she whispered, "of my own men."

He already had made it clear to the cohort what the cost of disobedience would be, but Maun's Clan Móran contingent couldn't possibly be pleased with having a new commander who was Caledonach, a woman, and their future chieftain's greatest enemy.

"Clan politics have no place in my legion," he growled. "All who fight under the Scarlet Dragon must answer to me." His gaze softened. "I don't like it, either, but I must watch Urien, and I want him as far away from you as possible."

"I wish we had another option."

"I could always send you back to Arbroch." The sapphire twinkle in his eyes betrayed the tease.

"Ha. And I could always take another swing at you."

Their laughter died, and she touched his cheek, imprinting its warm, smooth feel upon her palm. He pulled her hand away and kissed it. "I will support whatever course of action you take with the men. Be tough but fair, Gyan, and you'll do just fine."

"I HOPE you are right," Gyan murmured.

Arthur hoped so too.

After giving him one last kiss, she disengaged and left the chamber. Her departure ignited an acute burning in his chest, as if his heart had deserted him to accompany her.

The Manx Cohort's obedience came reluctantly, and as Gyan had feared, respect was all but nonexistent. The former she didn't hesitate to demand. The latter she'd have to earn, but with combat drills and the managing of the mundane activities around the fortress as her only tools, it promised to be an arduous journey.

At the worktable in the anteroom of her private quarters, with the never-dwindling stacks of supply requisitions and unit reports piled about her, she was pondering the cohort's morale problems when Cynda entered from the bedchamber. She approached Gyan, clutching a web-snarled broom in one fist and a small metal object in the other.

"What do you make of this? I found it in a corner."

Like petals of a rose, Cynda's fingers opened to reveal a bronze legion brooch encircled by a green-and-red enamel ring. Dried blood darkened the pin's tip. The damage to the dragon's jet eye gave it a half-lidded, dangerous expression.

Its features pointed to only one owner.

Into her mind's eye sprang the terrible dream images that had plagued most of her nights since the last turning of the moon.

"Gyan? You look as if a goose has trodden upon your grave."

She grimaced at Cynda's unwittingly accurate word choice. Given half a chance, Urien would tread—nay, dance upon her grave.

Setting her jaw, she pushed to her feet, glaring at the brooch. A warrior unable to face fear wasn't fit for the rank.

"Please pack it away." No telling when such a trinket might prove useful, but if she never saw the accursed thing again, she'd count herself that much happier. She flung her clan mantle about her shoulders with feigned indifference, glad to secure a gold dragon to its folds, not a bronze one.

"Where are you going?" Cynda trailed in Gyan's wake as she stepped briskly toward the door.

Gyan needed the larger working area and its unsurpassed harbor view, so moving to different chambers wasn't an option. At present, however, even the eternally fiery caverns of ifrinn seemed preferable to Urien's haunt.

For Cynda's sake, she stated, "Tanroc. To inspect the progress of the palisade's repairs. I should be back before the evening meal."

An hour later, confronted with the sight of the thorn-hedged fort and its inner palisade's charred remains, the Scáthinach invasion assaulted her in all its bloody detail. Standing clear of soldiers hauling wood and rubble, she closed her eyes. The clang of hammers and mallets evoked the clash of arms. Her memories intensified: the deaths of the monks, her capture, being forced to watch the slaughter of soldiers and common folk alike, the nauseating stench of burning flesh . . . and the seething frustration born of the powerlessness to prevent any of it.

She clenched her fists, the nails digging into her palms.

"Aunt Gyanhumara? Everything all right?" The male voice spoke in Breatanaiche.

Aunt? She opened her eyes with a start and relaxed her hands. One of the workmen stood before her, soot smeared across his face so badly that she scarcely recognized him. The bone dragon pinned to his undyed tunic marked him as one of the legion's foot soldiers.

"I am fine, Gawain." Odd to think of him as her sister-son-by-law, since they were of an age. The relation he shared with Arthur showed in his handsomely angled features. There the resemblance ended, for Gawain was shorter and stockier, his hair raven dark. "And it's Commander Gyan, soldier." She underscored her tease with a smile. "Back to work."

"Aye, Commander Gyan." His grin assured her that one Breatan on this isle didn't resent her authority, thanks be to the One God.

Gawain saluted smartly. He bent over a massive unburned timber lying nearby and, grunting and straining, lifted one end to commence dragging it toward the pile of reusable timbers. She marveled at his strength, regretting the limitations of her female form.

A Dhoo-Glass courier ran up, panting. Without preamble or salute, he thrust a rolled scrap of parchment toward her. She wordlessly accepted the message, hoping her glare conveyed the full measure of her displeasure. Discomfiture flashed across his face.

She broke the seal to read the dispatch and quelled a groan. According to the Dhoo-Glass harbormaster, the horse-transport ship carrying the Tanroc centurion and cavalry reinforcements had been sighted offshore and was expected to dock within the hour.

Exactly what I need: more Breatanaich who have no desire to be commanded by a Caledonach. Or a woman.

She crumpled the parchment and promptly wished she hadn't. With seven of the eight Horse Cohort alae composed of Caledonaich, odds favored the replacements being her countrymen. Of the centurion, she felt less certain. Arthur probably had appointed someone he knew well, which would rule out the Caledonaich and potentially cause more trouble in the ranks. She sighed.

"Orders, Commander?" A brief hesitation punctuated the courier's use of her rank.

She regarded the courier levelly. Orders, indeed. Longing for her husband competed with a twinge of bitterness. Arthur never would face the dual hurdles of race and gender.

"Dismissed." The junior officer rendered a passable salute and turned to leave. An idea occurred—not a strictly military one and perhaps not one Arthur would have employed, but she didn't care. "Take your midday meal with the men here, if you wish, before returning to port." She wanted no company on the ride back and no more witnesses to her meeting with the reinforcements than necessary.

He nodded once and strode toward the mess tent, which was attracting more occupants as the shadows shortened and the work crews reached sensible stopping points. As she vaulted onto her horse and spurred the animal toward the hawthorn hedge wall's main portal, she caught tantalizing whiffs of bread and roasted pork. Her stomach grumbled. She ignored it.

Ten miles of brooding left her ill prepared for what awaited her at the Dhoo-Glass docks.

The twoscore and ten Tanroc reinforcements had been culled from the best horse-warriors of Clan Argyll.

As Rhys and Conall and the others streamed by, she welcomed each with words laced with heartfelt gladness. They greeted her with respect mixed with affection before swaggering toward shore.

She felt a tug on her braid and whirled around.

The offender stood before her, hands on hips and a cocky grin painted across his face. She threw her arms around his neck, blinking back tears and releasing a long sigh.

"Missed me that much did you, dear sister?"

She let him go and swiped at her eyes, returning his grin. "Beast!" She enjoyed using the familiar epithet, but reality blunted her smile. "Yes, I did. You, and"—she glanced over her shoulder at the last of their clansmen disappearing into the crowd arrayed between the wharfside storage buildings and merchants' shops—"them."

Per clasped her hand. "And Artyr?"

She turned her head, not to look at Per but beyond him, a hundred miles north and east. "Constantly," she whispered.

"He asked me to give you this."

Per lifted her hand to his lips and bestowed a lingering kiss.

Intense longing for her consort threatened to sunder her heart.

Mercilessly, she reined in her emotions; the Breatanach soldiers would never come to respect her if they saw her in this condition.

Drawing a determined breath, she thanked him and stepped back to inspect his appearance. Over traditional Caledonach black leather battle-gear he wore a woolen mantle woven of Clan Argyll's deep blue highlighted with crossing bands of saffron and scarlet. A red-and-green-ringed copper brooch rode the cloak's folds. Its dragon winked with a sapphire eye, Per's due as an Argyll nobleman.

"You have a new legion badge," she said. To signify his status as an ala commander, the ring of his old badge had been red. Copper designated centurions—infantry, cavalry, and navy alike—but the presence of the dual colors could only mean, "Artyr put you in command of Tanroc?"

"Who else? No Breatan could hope to keep Conall and the others in line." He displayed the teasing grin she loved so well. "Your consort is smart enough to know it."

She answered him with her own smile. "And is my consort's brother-by-law smart enough to recognize who's in command here?"

Per swept her an elaborate bow. "You have always ruled my heart. Why should this arrangement be any different?"

"Beast!" As he straightened, she gave his shoulder a playful shove, and he chuckled.

They stepped off the dock to make way for the dockhands reporting to unload the ship's hold. Listening to the restless stomping and whickering of the horses, she wondered what else might be stowed in the belly of the huge cargo vessel.

Before she could voice her question, Per said, "You look wonderful, Gyan." Switching to Breatanaiche, he added, "Marriage favors you."

Without thinking, she also switched tongues. "So. I imagine Arthur told you . . ." She looked at him, astonished. "When did you learn Brytonic?"

In Caledonaiche, he said, "All of us had to learn enough to get by. Cavalry commands, where to piss, how to get meat, ale, women—"

"Peredur mac Hymar! You are terrible." She laughed. "I wager you ran right out to test that newfound knowledge of yours."

"I didn't have to run." His smile deepened. "My tutor was quite pretty and willing."

"Ha!"

"I never could keep secrets from you." Draping an arm across her shoulders, he leaned closer. "But for her, I would have been bored out of my skin. Nothing but drills, drills, drills. New tactics, new formations, and new gear, like those saddle toe-loops."

"Hard to believe something so simple can help a horseman so much." Gyan nodded pensively. "I wish I'd thought of it."

If the Caledonaich had possessed such devices, the Ròmanaich never would have troubled the Highlands.

Nor would she have met her soul's mate.

"Aye, amazing wee things they are. And I cannot forget those backbreaking stints on wall and road repair—gods!" Hand to neck, he stretched as though reliving a particularly painful event. "You have seen all the real action this summer."

"Ha." She rolled her eyes as they trod the path their clansmen had taken. "If you expect to escape repairs, think again. Tanroc's palisade is far from being finished. Not for lack of effort, either."

"Tanroc's palisade can wait." Per paused at the tavern's door. "Care to join me? The salty air has given me a powerful thirst. Besides, now that we're not caught up in bondings and joining ceremonies and cavalry games and the like, I want to hear about your battle." His gentle elbow found her ribs. "According to the latest tales, you stand ten feet tall, wear three skulls for a headdress, and wield a firebrand for a sword."

"Indeed! I don't know where people come up with these stories."

"It's the stuff legends are made of, Gyan." His abrupt seriousness banished the teasing banter.

"Me? A legend? Ha! You need that drink, Per." She tugged on his tunic sleeve. "The sun and sea have addled your wits."

He pulled open the door, and she stepped inside to a chorus of shouts and cheers. Her clansmen, grinning through foam-flecked mustaches and beards, raised flagons in salute.

"You planned this!"

"What of it? They are here and so are we. Go on in, Gyan." Per gave her a nudge. "They have saved us some seats."

Indeed they had, she observed with wry amusement, in the center of the gathering.

Conall called for her story of the Scáthinach invasion. The rest escalated the chant, punctuated by the drumming of fists upon tabletops, until the noise threatened to blow the timbers from the tavern's roof. Gyan shot her brother a teasing I'll-get-you-for-this-later look and stood. Silence descended.

"Tavernkeeper," she called, in Breatanaiche. "Please bring out the jars. Another round for everyone." Her upraised hand forestalled the cheers. "One round while I tell you my tale, mo ghaisgich." *My heroes.* And she meant it. "Then it's to work."

Good-natured groans melted into grunts of pleasure as the ale went around.

In Breatanaiche, the words rushed forth: her capture by the Scáthinaich, imprisonment on the rainy ridge, rescue by Arthur, the ensuing battle, the wound inflicted upon her by General Niall, and that duel's final result. The story unfolded easier than she'd expected, perhaps because in a month's time she'd gained enough distance from the harrowing events.

"And you may see the Scotti cù-puc," she concluded after the roaring approval had died, grinning at the association of Niall with the impossible offspring of a hound and a pig, "when you report to my workroom for your assignments. Now, to the quartermaster with you."

She shook her head at Per when he rose to join the men. He sat again, and they watched the tavern empty.

The proprietor scurried over with a jar of his best wine, demonstrating a remarkable memory for her preferences. She hadn't returned to this establishment since the day, months ago, when she had first begun to understand the depth of her folly in becoming Urien's betrothed.

Gyan accepted the wine with thanks and downed the first cupful in one breath.

"You didn't talk about the other fight," Per said quietly, in Caledonaiche.

She didn't believe Arthur would have mentioned his duel with Urien but wasn't surprised that Per had found out. "I'll defer to the storytellers," she answered, also switching to Caledonaiche.

"But you were there?"

"Oh, yes." Closing her eyes, she relived that whirlwind night, when at swordpoint Arthur had challenged Urien's right to become Àrd-Ceoigin of Clan Argyll. For the first time, she felt the full impact of how many lives had ridden on the outcome. Gyan's people, and Urien's, and Arthur's army, and those who depended upon the army for aid in peacetime and in war. "But I was too nervous about who was going to win. I don't remember many details," she confessed.

"Let it grow with the retelling. There is no harm in it."

"Not for Artyr, and no mistake." He gripped her shield arm over her consort's dragon tattoo. "He is a good man, Gyan. But Urien..."

She sighed, staring into her empty cup, half expecting to see Urien's face leering back. "I suppose this was Artyr's idea. To give me extra protection."

"What, sending some of our clansmen to Maun? In a way, it was. He gave me leave to select my men."

She debated whether to be irritated that Arthur seemed to think she couldn't take care of herself or grateful for his considerate actions. She opted for the latter. Thinking about him heightened the ache of their separation, but the harder she tried to clutch pleasant memories, the quicker her thoughts returned to the enemy of everyone she held dear.

"Do you know what Urien is doing now?" She reached for the wine jar, mulling over Angusel's accident and Urien's probable involvement. "Have there been any other incidents?"

"*Other* incidents?"

She chided herself for the slip. To the rest of the world, Urien had appeared innocent. Per was the last person to whom she'd ever confide her suspicions; the political chaos he would create by taking matters into his own hands was too disturbing to contemplate.

"At the cavalry games, he seemed... insulted." She poured more wine, took a long swallow, and stared into the cup.

"Something happened yesterday, in fact." A catch in his voice made her look up. "A Caledonach in Fourth Ala was flogged."

"What?" She felt her eyes narrow as her anger rose. "Unjustly?"

"No. The man failed to obey his decurion's orders."

She didn't want to ask her next question, afraid of how she might react to the answer, but she had to know, "Was he of Argyll?"

Per shook his head. "Clan Tarsuinn." Again that strange tone—disbelief? "Urien flogged the man himself."

Normally, a soldier's direct commander administered discipline, not an officer several ranks higher. To Gyan, Urien's involvement smacked of revenge.

Instead of sharing this troubling idea with Per, however, she asked, "Is the warrior all right?"

"He will recover. The rest of the cohort is spitting mad, but no one dares to speak out for fear of finding himself on the wrong end of the lash."

She hoped her countrymen would continue to exercise restraint. At least Per and some of her clansmen had escaped beyond Urien's reach, thanks to Arthur's thoughtfulness, which surfaced another issue. "Now that the feasting is over, what is the reaction at headquarters to our marriage?"

"To be honest, Gyan, it's mixed." He forced a smile. "The army would support Artyr's marriage to the Hag of Death, but every eligible lass within a day's ride must have died of a broken heart."

That won her chuckle. "It's more or less like that here. But they resent me because I'm not a Breatan—and not a man."

"The soldiers?"

She nodded. "They all know very well why I replaced Urien." With another sigh, she gazed into the dark depths of her wine. No reassurances swam there. She whispered, "I don't know if I can really trust any of them."

Closing his hand over hers, he said quietly, "It's only because they don't know you yet. Give them time." After a few moments, he added, "I have a surprise to show you."

"Those reports Artyr wants me to read. Thrilling."

"Aye, but that isn't the surprise."

She lifted her head. "What is it? Oh come on, Per, tell me!"

"It's in the boat," was the only information he would divulge.

After they reached the docks, he waved at the captain to have something brought from the hold. A crewman led it blindfolded, snorting and prancing, down the gangplank.

Once the white yearling stallion had found his footing on land, Gyan slipped off the blindfold. A pair of dark, intelligent eyes regarded her solemnly. She rubbed the creamy nose, and he blew a puff of moist air onto her palm.

"Oh, Per, he is magnificent!" She kissed her brother's cheek.

"Don't thank me. He's Artyr's gift. Sired of his favorite, Macsen."

"Macsen" in Breatanaiche, Gyan recalled, meant "great."

"Since he has come to me from across the sea, he shall be my Son of the Sea. Macmuir," she murmured to the stallion, patting the deeply arched neck. Macmuir's mane shimmered like liquid silver as he shook his proud head.

"Mòrdragh" would have been more accurate: big trouble.

Chapter 6

As the summer ripened, Gyan spent every free moment with Macmuir, who had been broken to bit and saddle, but in combat drills was as raw as a foal. Confronting her own weaknesses in that aspect of warfare, she practiced daily with the Argyll horsemen, though the healing wound on her sword arm limited her participation.

Angusel had insisted on remaining with Gyan at Port Dhoo-Glass. To keep him busy, she placed him on the courier roster, a duty he performed cheerfully and with an ocean of enthusiasm, even though his youth prevented him from being an official legion conscript. When not galloping messages to and from Per at Tanroc, or to the detachments at Ayr Point and Caer Rushen, he all but slept on the Dhoo-Glass practice fields.

"Has fine makings, he does, Commander Gyan. Gaining more lann-seolta by the day." Rhys, the clansman she had selected to be her aide and horse-combat mentor, stroked his ebony beard. "Another half a dozen summers, and he will be one of the best."

On the field, Angusel, spear in hand, was weaving Stonn at a hard canter through a stand of posts to retrieve the fist-size iron rings set atop each. He halted before Gyan and Rhys.

"I know, Rhys." Pride and affection warmed her tone. Every post had yielded its ring. Strictly speaking, lann-seolta referred to a swordsman's ability to anticipate his enemy's moves in hand-to-hand combat, but she suspected she might be watching an entirely new definition in the making. "Well done, Angus!"

Angusel grinned. The rings jangled a jaunty tune as he cast the spear to stick into the turf. He slid from Stonn's back and patted the glossy neck. After giving the stallion's reins to a stable hand, who began walking Stonn to cool him, Angusel grabbed a practice sword from the nearby rack. "Ready for a go, Gyan?"

"Who said you were done with cavalry drills, lad?" Rhys folded his arms and donned a scowl, although Gyan saw mirth crinkling the corners of his eyes. "And do not forget the commander's proper form of address."

"Yes, sir." Angusel transferred the sword to his other hand and saluted Gyan in the Ròmanach way, fist to chest. "Commander Gyan."

Although she and Angusel had been through too much already to let formalities stand between them, Rhys had a valid point. No sense in fostering more division by showing favoritism.

She said to Angusel, "Centurion Rhys swears your lann-seolta is improving before his very eyes, but my sword arm isn't healed enough to give you a challenging test." Massaging the spot, she glanced at her second-in-command, who nodded and selected a practice sword.

After exchanging salutes, they assumed attack stances.

The key to developing lann-seolta, "blade-cunning," lay in learning to observe the opposing warrior's elbow, which governed the sword's basic movement. When instinct and knowledge of the foe, together with superior speed, skill, and strength, alloyed with lann-seolta in the furnace of battle frenzy, devastating results occurred.

Gyan's father was a renowned lann-seolta master. She considered herself adept but still improving, though no longer by Ogryvan's hand. Having begun practicing the drills only a few months ago, Angusel faced a long road.

Yet to his credit and Rhys's, Angusel showed remarkable improvement. She caught him betraying his moves only a few times while accurately anticipating most of Rhys's. His strength, she realized as he succeeded in driving Rhys backward more than once, also was increasing dramatically.

At this rate, she wagered proudly to herself, Angusel mac Alayna of Clan Alban of Caledon would become a lann-seolta adept in half the time Rhys had predicted.

GYAN PULLED her clan mantle closer to stave off the chilly September breeze as she entered the Sanctuary of the Chalice and chose a place near the doors. Before her thronged the Breatanach bishops and archbishops who'd braved the quickening autumn seas to honor Dafydd in his formal installation as Abbot of St. Padraic's Monastery. The monks not engaged in feast preparations had crammed into the chapel along the walls and in the back with Gyan. A lucky score of musically gifted brethren occupied benches behind the gilt choir screen.

Only two other women had joined the assembly: Dafydd's wife, Katra, and Prioress Niniane. Gyan could barely make out Katra's shawl-swathed form at the forefront of the gathering as the intervening heads moved this way and that. Presumably, Dafydd the Younger accompanied her, though Gyan couldn't see the lad. Prioress Niniane stood near Merlin, who favored the name Dubricius in church, Gyan reminded herself.

The candle smoke and incense's spicy-sweet fragrance overpowered the mustiness of so many closely packed bodies, the choir's braided voices evoked a glorious sense of the divine, and the alabaster Chalice sat enthroned upon its golden platform, ever a wonder to behold. Gyan rejoiced for her friend and spiritual father, and she could think of no better man for this many-faceted job.

She watched Dafydd kneel, his white ceremonial robe flowing around him as the portly archbishop poured a ribbon of oil onto Dafydd's head from a gold-embossed silver ewer. The archbishop, a hand on Dafydd's head, commanded the congregation to join him in prayer.

Although she didn't bow her head—only Dafydd and Arthur knew of her conversion—she closed her eyes, resurrecting images of her joining ceremony, which smote her with intense longing. Merlin had delivered the regretful message that legion duties had prevented Arthur's attendance. Though immeasurably disappointed, she understood. Holding together men from such diverse cultural backgrounds surely would try the patience of the Christ Himself, to say nothing of welding those men into an effective fighting force.

She sighed, fingering the silver threads of her mantle's trim and indulging in the vain wish that she could speed the seasons' dance. Another turning of the moon would see her at her consort's side for the winter, helping him bear his burden of leadership. She chewed her lip to suppress a grin as she envisioned the days they would share, and the nights.

Especially the nights.

The rustling of robes, the muted murmur of conversation, and the stamping and shuffling of feet alerted her that the ceremony had concluded. She flicked her eyes open and glanced around. To avoid being trapped within the exodus, she quickly threaded a path to the sanctuary's main door and slipped outside.

The rich aroma of roasted pork failed to lure her to the feasting tables. She headed toward the apple orchard, where she could observe the proceedings privately. As the only secular leader present—a female foreign leader whose faith in the One God had to remain a secret—she felt as conspicuous as a snake in a rabbit warren. And, judging by some of the looks she'd already received, likely regarded as such by some of the Breatanach clergymen.

No sense in worsening the situation.

The orchard grounds had been raked of windfalls. Doubtless, the best of these had been simmered into sauce to complement the pork. She hitched her skirts and cloak, settled onto a bench beneath an apple-laden tree, and leaned back, thankful for the trunk's sturdiness after having been obliged to stand for the past hour.

On the sward defined by the church, refectory, abbot's cottage, guesthouse, and library, the new abbot intoned a blessing to inaugurate the feast and his tenure. Katra and the other monks' wives circulated among the ribbon-festooned tables, the blues and greens and yellows of their dresses bright against the men's black robes. Children either helped or played boisterously underfoot, as their ages and natures demanded. The cheery strains of reed pipes wafted on the breeze, punctuated by drums and rattling gourds and spirited clapping. Gyan silently blessed whoever had planned this merry departure from the monks' routine. After Abbot Lir's death and the horrors they'd suffered at the hands of the Scáthinaich—a portion of which had been Gyan's fault, although she'd been absolved and had forgiven herself for her involvement—these decent men and their families deserved this respite to help them trudge past their grief.

Closing her eyes, she tilted her head back against the tree to enjoy the music and succulent aromas, recalling her nuptial feast and again wishing Arthur could share this moment with her. She wondered if separation enforced by the press of duties would shape the pattern for their future. Never mind the other reason for her being on Maun, which she refused to name because she despised that Móranach bastard's siege upon her thoughts. She doubted that she and Arthur would ever be granted any time to simply enjoy each other's company without having to worry about the doings of the rest of the world.

Her heart's ache began anew, and she indulged in another sigh.

"My lady?" asked a man in Breatanaiche.

Gyan opened her eyes. Dafydd stood before her, still dressed in his ceremonial robe, one hand outstretched. She clasped it and rose.

"My lord abbot." At his look of mild discomfiture, she added with a grin, "Get accustomed to the title, Dafydd. You'll be hearing it often." Completing the journey from slave to freedman to monk to abbot in one year was nothing short of miraculous, and she could understand his unease. "How did you escape from your well-wishers?" Releasing his hand, she inclined her head toward the feast.

He smiled. "The excellent food is keeping the others occupied. For now, at least. In fact"—the smile dimmed—"some of us were wondering why you haven't joined us."

"Ah. Well, I'd planned to." She didn't think it wise to refuse Dafydd's implied request. "Now seems as good a time as any." She strolled toward the festivities, and Dafydd fell into step with her.

"You don't sound convinced, my lady."

She offered a wan smile. "I'm sorry, Dafydd. I truly am happy for you. I just needed some time alone." She never had gotten into the habit of prevaricating with him. "To think."

"About Arthur?" She must have looked as surprised as she felt, for he chuckled softly. "I know what it's like to be separated from my bride. I suspect your husband feels much the same way."

"Ha. In all this time, he hasn't visited me once."

Dafydd didn't reply. Gyan lowered her head and concentrated on the gravel path as shame burned her cheeks. Of course, Arthur loved her as much as before. Didn't he? He claimed so in his frequent letters, though words could be an easy alternative to actions.

When Dafydd stopped, she glanced up, surprised to find herself standing before the guesthouse. Pushing the door open with one hand, he motioned with the other for her to step inside. She cocked a questioning eyebrow at him, but in answer he only smiled. Curiosity propelled her across the threshold. Dafydd left the door ajar, which Gyan found even more puzzling. She voiced the question.

"I don't want anyone to get the wrong idea." He settled into one of the chairs near the common room's window and invited her to do the same. "I was hoping to continue our conversation in private."

She studied the room with its large, bare central table, chairs and benches shoved back along the walls, a sideboard laden with empty tin plates and tankards, cold hearth, and braided rugs of undyed wool covering the worn floor planks. Through the back window, she glimpsed the structure that housed the kitchen. A stairway led to the sleeping chambers. A large crucifix made of well-oiled dark oak had been affixed to the wall opposite the hearth. Gyan removed her cloak, selected a chair near Dafydd's, and sat.

"Our conversation about Arthur?"

"About you," Dafydd said. "I know the cohort keeps you busy." He shifted forward, adopting an intense expression. "Too busy to continue your studies in the faith?"

To herself, she conceded the point. While a student at the monastery, she'd enjoyed studying the Christian texts, perhaps on some level even more so than the writings of Iulius Caesar, Livy, Horace, Galen, Marcus Aurelius, Suetonius, and other authors in the monks' impressive collection. Lately, cohort duties had consumed all her time. But rather than admit it to Dafydd, she asked with a grin, "Being abbot doesn't give you enough souls to worry about?"

"I worry about whoever the Lord lays upon my heart." Concern dampened his smile. "My lady, you're young in the faith. This is a vulnerable time for any believer—for you, especially, because of Clan Argyll's prevailing religion. If you don't strengthen your faith through study and prayer, I fear it may wither."

His words made startling sense. Lack of reinforcement in her old beliefs had influenced her conversion. She reached out to pat Dafydd's hand. "I will do my best to heed what you say."

"I can help, too."

Up came Gyan's head to swivel toward the sound. Arthur descended the stairs, grinning like the hound standing over its bone trove. With an answering grin, she couldn't propel herself into his arms fast enough. The chair clattered to the floor from the force of her exit.

His arms clamped about her and his lips latched to hers with satisfying urgency. Reveling in the solid feel of his body against hers, the sharp leathery tang of his tunic and leggings, and the moist heat of his devouring lips and questing tongue, she quite forgot about Dafydd's presence.

Too long! Their separation had been much too long, as Arthur's body agreed in its own language.

She disengaged from her consort. "He lied to me!"

"Dafydd?" Arthur cocked an eyebrow at the abbot.

"No, Merlin. He told me you were too busy to come to Maun."

"He should have said that I was too busy with legion duties to attend the ceremony."

"Yes, that was it." She laughed as the subtle wording sank in. "What duties, then, Lord Pendragon?"

"Raising morale, of course, Commander." He kissed her again. "My favorite task."

"Beathach!" She cast a glance at Dafydd. "And you knew all along." When Dafydd merely grinned, she said with mock asperity, "I don't know whether to slap you or kiss you both!"

"I think our good abbot's wife would take exception to that, but I won't." Arthur kissed her with a tenderness that sent desire coursing through her. She closed her eyes, reveling in sensations her mind had nearly forgotten but her body most certainly had not.

"If my lord and lady will pardon me," she heard Dafydd murmur, "I shall leave you two alone. You are welcome to join us when you're ready. The feast should continue for quite some time."

She pulled away from Arthur long enough to thank Dafydd, which he acknowledged with a smile and a nod. He sketched a blessing and reached for the door, pulling it firmly shut behind him as he left.

Arthur lifted her off the floor to carry her up the stairs.

She laughed, wrapping her arms about his neck. "I think I can make it by myself, Artyr."

Passion smoldered in the steely depths of his eyes. "The abbot had his plans for this reunion, and I have mine." He kicked open the bedchamber door, laid her on the bed, bolted the door, and joined her.

"But the other guests—"

"Are staying at Port Dhoo-Glass, where they'll board their ships on the morrow."

"Part of the plan?"

"A well-received suggestion."

She bit her lip and frowned, hating her next question. "Will you be leaving in the morning, too?"

"Only if my lady so commands it."

She buried her fingers in his hair, guiding his head closer. "I think you know your lady won't be doing any such thing." Before he could reply, she pressed her lips to his.

He untied the laces of her gown. She had not bothered using a breastband, since the bodice performed the same function. Now, she was doubly thankful for that decision. He worked the gown off her shoulders, kissing each newly bared patch of flesh. Tingles scurried through her body. Easing her arms free of the gown, she murmured her pleasure as his fingers reacquainted themselves with her breasts, and her nipples reacquainted themselves with the discipline of standing at attention under his gentle but commanding touch. The crackling flames of desire made it difficult to think rationally, but before she could yield, she needed to learn one thing more.

"What about my cohort? They will think something has happened to me if I don't return as expected."

"Your brother is in command at Dhoo-Glass. He sends his love."

"What! Per knew, too?"

Arthur's widening grin gave the only confirmation she needed.

Per's repayment would have to wait. Arthur's didn't. She reached behind her head, freed the pillow, and swatted her consort. Laughing, he snatched another pillow to retaliate, and they battled like children until feathers burst free and flew everywhere. Still chuckling, he called for a truce.

"The great Pendragon surrenders so quickly?" she teased, brushing feathers from his hair.

"Only to the worthiest of his adversaries." Although light, his tone held no trace of mockery.

"You haven't heard my terms."

"Which are?"

"That you never leave my side." She held her fingers to his lips to hush his inevitable protest. "I know we both have duties and"—she tried her best not to think of the man who kept wedging between them—"other reasons that render the fulfillment of these terms impossible. For now. So here is what I propose." She tugged off his leather tunic and linen undertunic, and lay back onto the feather-strewn coverlet, drawing him down beside her and delighting in the feel of his chest muscles rippling beneath her fingertips. "That we make the best possible use of the time we've been given."

"Fair enough." He removed his leggings and, with her help, worked her gown the rest of the way off. Grinning, he started caressing her inner thigh in that soft, circling pattern she enjoyed, especially when his fingertips strayed over her tingling banasròn. She hitched her hips to convince him to linger in that spot. "More than fair," he whispered. As he leaned over to kiss her, his touch quickened and deepened, setting her upon the journey toward ultimate ecstasy. "And if we have a child?"

With one hand, she reached behind his head to lower his mouth to hers. She tugged at his loincloth's knot with the other. He pulled back to regard her expectantly. "I will deal with having a child when I must, Artyr."

The knot yielded, and she guided him toward fulfilling her most immediate and urgent need.

Aside from their frequent lovemaking, she and Arthur spent countless hours together talking, sometimes in the privacy of their chamber in the guest cottage but more often while strolling about the monastery's compound or sitting in a reading room on the upper floor of the library.

In this latter retreat, he began honoring his promise to help nurture her faith.

"Battles? Campaigns?" She peered at the stack of bound parchment leaves illuminated by a splash of late-afternoon sunlight, not bothering to hide her incredulity. "What have those to do with faith in the One God?"

"For the ancient Hebrews, plenty. For us, too." Arthur flipped through the stack. Finally, he tapped a Ròmanaiche passage. "Start here."

The battle she read about seemed as improbable as the concept of men striding across deep water without a bridge: a battle against tens of thousands, won by three hundred men recruited because of the way they drank water. She squinted at the text, looking for places that had been rubbed out and copied over, different handwriting styles, large gaps, or letters too close together. She found nothing of the sort. Surely, someone at some time in the manuscript's history had misrepresented the size of this force. Three thousand she could believe, not three hundred, and she said so.

"Unusual tactics," Arthur agreed. "But a small, elite unit stands a much better chance of slipping past sentries, which may not have been very many, owing to the apparent overconfidence of the enemy. Gideon's men attacked at night, when the enemy troops were no doubt sleeping the most soundly. They used sudden noise and light to create the illusion that far more Hebrews had infiltrated the camp. Perhaps the enemy troops were drunk, which would account for their turning against one another. The most important thing to remember"—Arthur looked up from the parchment to capture Gyan's gaze—"is that Gideon trusted God to make good on His promise of victory. God didn't fight Gideon's battle for him but gave him and his men the strength and courage and wits and confidence they needed to defeat the enemy by themselves."

She nodded slowly. "Explained like that, Gideon's story makes a lot more sense."

"Explained like that, one might believe that Gideon and his men had won under their own power, rather than by Almighty God's sovereign decree." Brother Stefan darkened the archway, leaning on his cane as a warrior might lean on his sword between bouts. "Did Bishop Dubricius teach you that interpretation, Lord Pendragon?"

Gyan felt her consort bristle, and she gripped his arm. "Please forgive Brother Stefan, Arthur. Being master of students—"

"Gives him no right to intrude upon a private conversation between those who are not his students." Before Gyan could diffuse the situation, Arthur said, eyes narrowed, "Bishop Dubricius taught me how to think for myself."

Stefan gave Arthur a conciliatory nod. "I'm sure that serves you well"—his eyes glinted like obsidian chips—"on the battlefield."

The tendons of Arthur's forearm writhed beneath her fingertips as he clenched and released his fist. "It serves me well everywhere."

"Perhaps," said the monk. "But I suggest you keep to your battlefields, Lord Pendragon, and leave divine matters to the theologians."

Gyan said, with as much sweetness as she could muster, "Brother Stefan is right. Battles are what you and I excel at, my love." She cocked an eyebrow at the monk. "But I believe we can all agree that Gideon's God is a good ally to have, on or off the battlefield."

"Aptly put, Chieftainess," conceded Stefan with a slight bow.

He plowed through the knot of students that had gathered to witness the exchange, brandishing his cane to herd them back to their studies like a shepherd with a wayward flock. Only after Stefan and the others had gone did Arthur visibly relax.

She caressed his sword-side forearm. "Brother Stefan is always like that," she whispered. "Pay him no mind."

"I won't." Arthur laid his hand atop hers, a grin slowly dawning. "But if you ever lead a ridiculously high-risk operation like Gideon's, you had best pray for divine help to explain it to me."

Their laughter ended in the meeting of their lips.

GYAN AND Arthur were resting in the monastery's orchard as the glowing afternoon retreated before the dusk. He lay with his head in her lap, eyes closed and looking peaceful. She sat with her back braced against an apple tree, facing west. A half-eaten apple nestled in her palm as she watched the cloud-shrouded sun stain the sky with vibrant reds, golds, and salmons as though igniting a wall of fire.

She glanced down and ran her fingers lightly through Arthur's sunset-colored hair, wishing their idyll wouldn't have to end.

The sound of a distant shout drew her attention.

"Ifrinn fuileachdach!" she whispered. It was the Caledonaiche version of an epithet her consort might have chosen: bloody hell.

A ship was closing fast upon the island. A warship.

Chapter 7

ARTHUR SCRAMBLED TO his feet. He gave Gyan a hand up, and they scanned the western horizon.

"Scotti?" she asked. The vessel's shape and direction of origin fit the guess, but she recalled that several Scáthinach-built vessels sailed in the Breatanach fleet, thanks to Bedwyr's salvage efforts. Only by its sail could they be certain of the ship's allegiance.

Arthur seemed to be having similar trouble. The sun had broken through the clouds, and he tilted his hand to shade his eyes, swearing under his breath.

"One of ours," he said at last.

"I don't know whether to be relieved or dismayed."

She had no idea how long Paradise had lasted for Adam and Eve, but for her and Arthur, it had been only three days. She looked at the apple clenched in her fist, sighed, and flung it away. It collided with the trunk of a nearby tree with a resounding thud that shook more fruit from the boughs.

Arthur caught her hand and raised it to his lips. "Let's hear the message before we leap to conclusions, my love."

The tide of her resentment rising, she yanked her hand free. "An order, Lord Pendragon?"

"Common sense."

He strode toward the gate in the monastery's wall that led to the western beach, giving her no choice but to follow or stay.

Curiosity reigned over stubbornness.

By the time she'd picked her way down the steep, sand-slick stairs to the beach, the warship had ground onto the sandbar. Foam-laced water swirled about Arthur's knees as he awaited the messenger—a Caledonach, by his battle-gear, whom she didn't recognize. The man waded through the shallows with a grim sense of purpose etched across his face. Arthur returned the messenger's salute with a nod and held out his hand to receive the leather-wrapped parcel.

Behind Arthur's back, she couldn't begin to guess the message's contents until his shoulders tightened, his head snapped up, and he faced her with an expression as grim as the messenger's had been.

Her stomach knotted.

"Gyan, I must leave." He turned to the messenger. "Optio Dileas, have two men report to the monastery's guesthouse to retrieve my gear. The rest of the oarsmen are to report to Tanroc's garrison commander for temporary reassignment. Tell Commander Conall I need twoscore soldiers to man the oars for my return voyage. I don't have time to write a dispatch." Arthur unpinned his cloak, yanked it from his shoulders, and slapped the gold dragon onto the messenger's palm. "I will send Conall's men back and recall the others within a week. Have one of the replacements return my badge." He cast a glance at the disappearing sun. "I want to be under way before full dark."

Dileas saluted with the fist that clutched the cloak-pin. "I will return it personally, my lord."

"Good." Arthur returned the salute. "Now, move!"

As the messenger began relaying the orders to the men, who'd been watching the exchange from the near rail, Arthur waded onto the beach and stormed up the stairs, his cloak draped over one arm and snapping like a battle banner.

Gyan broke into a run to catch him in the orchard, latched onto his arm, and pulled him around. "What is it, Artyr?"

She had never seen him look so furious. "A severe discipline problem at headquarters." As their gazes held, his expression softened. "Beyond that, for your sake, please don't ask."

She had intended to honor his request when its strangeness hit her. The only army problem having anything to do with her would involve her clansmen and...

"Urien." She spat the name like a mouthful of brine. "What did that machaoduin do this time?"

"What did you call him?"

"You might say 'illegitimus.' Machaoduin is much worse. What did he do?"

"In either language, it fits, then. He meted out an undeserved punishment. The soldier almost died."

Hand to mouth, Gyan gasped. "Who?"

"Mathan of Fifth Ala." Arthur's neck tendons writhed. "The unit is threatening rebellion. Merlin is doing what he can to prevent it, but he needs my help." He resumed his pace.

Like his namesake the bear, Mathan of Clan Argyll was better known for his brawn and quick temper than his wits, a deadly combination with Urien to bait him. "What did Mathan do?"

"When I get to headquarters, I will find out."

"I must go with you."

He said nothing. Upon reaching the guesthouse, he mounted its steps two at a time, dragged open the door, followed her into the building, and slammed the door behind them. He slung his cloak over one shoulder and faced her, feet planted and arms crossed.

"You will not."

"*What?*" She felt her eyebrows lower. "Who do you think you are, Artyr mac Ygrayna, to even try to stop me?"

"Your commanding officer." He snatched the cloak from his shoulder and stomped up the stairs, his boots smacking wetly against the planking.

Commanding officer, indeed!

Fury blazing, she chased him into their bedchamber, stopping in front of the chest containing his personal effects.

"First and foremost, you are my consort. That makes you answerable to me." She folded her arms and did not quench her glare. "Whether you like it or not."

He tossed the cloak onto the chest's lid and gripped her shoulders. "Mathan is my clansman now, too. If you prefer, think of it as your consort handling the matter on your behalf."

"Ha." She wrenched free of his grip to plant her hands on her hips. "This is one matter I would prefer to handle myself."

"By killing Urien? Setting Moray and Argyll at each other's throats? Getting yourself, your kin, and God knows how many others killed in the process?" He shook his head, reaching for her hands. "You know this is the response Urien wants." He searched her face.

She knew, and hated the knowing. Because knowing bred logic, and logic had to be heeded, else chaos would result.

Heartily, she wished for the freedom to act on gut instinct and let the chaos tend to itself.

A sound halfway between a scream and a growl passed her lips, and she stepped forward to bury her head against his chest, shutting her eyes against the stinging tears. Her clansman had been flogged nearly to death. Others stood poised for insurrection. The One God alone knew what that would do to Arthur's army and the people that army protected.

All this misery because she, Gyanhumara nic Hymar, had refused to marry the man to whom she first had been betrothed. A mad dog couldn't be held responsible for his fever-driven reactions, but its handler could be.

She doubted whether she could ever bring Urien map Dumarec to heel.

How many others would fall victim to his rabid attacks? How much more innocent blood would drip from his hands to spatter hers?

The tightening of Arthur's arms about her shattered the dam holding her emotions in check. He stroked her hair, murmuring words of comfort and endearment. Sobbing against his shoulder, she clung to him as if he were the only lifeline to her sanity.

She swiped at her face with a tunic sleeve, donning the best smile she could manage. "The One God be with you, Artyr. I pray He will guide you to deal with Urien in the most appropriate"—*and severest*—"way."

"So do I, my love."

He kissed the backs of her hands and released them to cup her face, covering her mouth with his.

When they parted, however, she felt compelled to say, "If Urien does something like this again, I will deal with him." She felt the full force of conviction leap to life in her gaze. "My way."

"PERMISSION FOR the Pendragon and his party to come aboard, sir?" called Dileas to the warship's captain.

"Permission granted!"

Arthur boarded the warship amid the taut salutes and even tauter expressions of the replacement crew, trailed by Dileas and the men lugging his chest. As he accepted his badge from Dileas with a word of thanks and donned his cloak, he wished for the luxury to dispose of Urien in Gyan's way. But as satisfying as that might be in the short term, it would buy far more trouble than he or Gyan or their two nations could ever afford.

The men who had rowed the warship to Maun stood in the shallows, arrayed on both sides of the prow, palms to the hull, awaiting the captain's signal to shove the vessel clear of the sandbar.

Gyan stood on the bluff above them, her form awash in the light shed by the torch she clutched in one fist. The other held Braonshaffir aloft. As the captain shouted the command and the warship scraped free of its sandy mooring, Arthur drew Caleberyllus to return Gyan's farewell.

No torture he could devise would come remotely close to the punishment Urien deserved.

Except, he mused with the barest of smiles, perhaps one thing.

It would have to wait, however, until Arthur got all the facts from Merlin, from Mathan's ala commander, and from Mathan himself.

He sat atop his chest where it had been stowed in the stern. Leaning back against a tall crate, he drew his cloak about him and glumly watched the men pull him farther from his beloved bride.

Well into the midnight watch, the warship reached Caer Lugubalion. Arthur sent Dileas ahead to tell Merlin and Fifth Ala's centurion to meet Arthur in the main infirmary, where he presumed Mathan would be recuperating.

Midway there, a winded Dileas intercepted him. Though he made a credible effort to repair his military bearing, exhaustion weighted his features. "Lord Pendragon, General Merlin requests to meet you and Centurion Airc in the prison's infirmary."

Arthur arched an eyebrow but otherwise made no comment. He clapped Dileas on the shoulder. "Have your commander remove your name from the duty roster for three days, Optio Dileas, and go get some rest."

"Thank you, sir."

With a final salute, Dileas departed for the barracks. Arthur wished he could do the same, for on the warship he'd only dozed. Suppressing a sigh, he strode in the opposite direction, toward the corner of the fortress that housed the least pleasant but no less vital functions: the slaughter yard, the tannery, and the prison.

Outside the latter, Merlin and Airc were waiting for him. Both men's faces looked haggard in the fitful torchlight, as if sleep had eluded them for weeks. He wondered whether his countenance appeared the same to them. Merlin gave him a brief nod, compassion tempering his gaze.

Arthur motioned them away from the guards, which put them closer to the tannery and its pervasive stench, before requesting their reports.

"The Fifth finished drills early that day," Airc began. "Me and Mathan and some of the other lads went to the tavern for a few rounds. We'd been there a while, when in comes Tribune Urien. He gets a flagon and passes our table at the same moment Mathan decides to visit the midden. I tried to warn him, but"—Airc sighed—"too late. Mathan jumps up without looking and knocks into Urien, and Urien spills his ale all over himself."

Arthur felt his forehead crease. "For that, Urien flogged him?"

"No, sir," Airc said. "All the men laughed—who wouldn't? Of course, that just got Urien madder. He started insulting Mathan, his looks, his swordsmanship, his horse, his lineage, anything he could think of. At first, Mathan took it—even tried to apologize. You'd have been proud of him, Lord Pendragon. But when Urien claimed that he and Mathan's sister had—"

"Never mind about that," said Merlin. "The point, Arthur, is that Urien goaded Mathan into throwing the first punch."

Naturally. "Do you have more to add, Airc?" Arthur asked.

"Aye, sir. Mathan knocked Urien clean across a table and onto the floor on the other side. But all Tribune Urien did after he got up was call for guards and a whip. I sent for General Merlin, but that didn't keep them from dragging Mathan outside to start the flogging."

"By the time I arrived"—sorrow and regret clouded Merlin's face—"the deed was already done."

Naturally! "So that's why he's in the prison's infirmary."

"As much for his own protection as for the offense itself," Merlin said.

Fighting to check his rising anger, Arthur said to Airc, "Did you and your men rebel?"

Airc looked away. "There were some ... remarks."

"And drawn swords," Merlin said.

Fists knotted and eyes flashing, Airc met Arthur's gaze. "We were angry, my lord, aye! Angry enough to chop that Breatanach macha-oduin into crow feed!"

Merlin opened his mouth, but Arthur cut him off with a slight shake of the head.

"And still angry enough to revert to Caledonian for an epithet to describe your commanding officer that means far more than 'bastard,'" Arthur offered coolly. Merlin cocked an impressed eyebrow.

Arthur's diffusion tactic worked; Airc's color rose. "I am sorry, but that is how we all feel about him." Airc relaxed his fists. "We drew but held our peace. What other choice had we? Any of us to split one hair on Tribune Urien's head would have been flayed alive too."

While Airc looked down again, Arthur and Merlin exchanged glances. Merlin's nod confirmed the truth of Airc's words.

Arthur laid a hand on Airc's shoulder, and the centurion looked up. "Forgive me, Lord Pendragon, but I wish I had run Urien through. For Mathan—and for Chieftainess Gyanhumara and you."

That sentiment Arthur well understood. He just couldn't give himself the luxury of making a public admission. Removing his hand, he said to Airc, "I appreciate your restraint, yours and your men's. I also appreciate how hard it must be for you and the other Caledonians to continue having Urien as your cohort commander."

"You are not going to replace him? One of us could easily—"

"Centurion. You serve in my army by treaty, and you will abide by my decisions. Understood?"

"Aye, sir," Airc muttered. "Doesn't mean I have to like it."

"It doesn't," Arthur allowed. "But Gyan and I, and Merlin and others are striving hard to make this alliance succeed. The Horse Cohort was always central to it, but now your ala has become the key. The other alae will be watching how the Fifth reacts."

"They already have been," Merlin said ominously. "There's been talk. One cannot walk through the mess hall without hearing it."

"So you see, Airc, I need you, Gyan needs you—Brydein and Caledonia need you and your men to put this incident behind you."

"I understand, my lord. But perhaps you will understand how hard a task we face once you see Mathan for yourself."

"I intend to. Lead on, Centurion."

He followed Airc back to the prison entrance, past the guards, and into the corridor that led to the infirmary.

Merlin kept pace beside him. "Airc has a point, Arthur," he whispered. "I don't envy you."

"Being Pendragon doesn't always mean making popular decisions, only the right ones," Arthur replied. "You taught me that, Merlin."

His mentor's only reply was a low grunt.

They fell silent but for their footfalls. Through knotholes in the floorboards rose the stink of sweat and vomit and offal, which the torches' smoke failed to mask. The prisoners' muffled moans and cries seemed to grow more urgent as Airc, Merlin, and Arthur passed overhead. Scotti warriors captured on Maun earlier in the summer accounted for most of the current inmate population, along with a large band of highwaymen and several criminals from the surrounding countryside whose offenses or belligerent natures made them too dangerous to be imprisoned anywhere else.

A legion soldier spent time incarcerated here only to wait for the convening of his military tribunal, as Urien should have done with Mathan.

Scratch that. Urien should have accepted Mathan's apology.

Passing the stairs leading to the solitary-confinement pits, Arthur wished he could bury Urien down there and melt the bloody key.

At the infirmary's door, Merlin explained their intent to the guard. The man saluted, unhitched the huge iron ring from his belt, selected a key, and unlocked the door. Once Merlin, Airc, and Arthur had stepped inside, the guard closed the door. Arthur quelled a momentary rush of panic as he heard the key turn in the lock.

Oil lamps suspended from the ceiling barely punctured the gloom. Arthur squinted at the beds, whose occupants lay chained to the frames, coughing, snoring, wheezing, thrashing, or groaning. The pungent smells of blood, urine, and valerian clotted the air.

Several burly orderlies glanced up from their tasks as Arthur and his party entered. While not garbed for guard duty, these men looked fully capable of subduing an unruly patient with martial as well as medical means.

Airc crossed the room to a bed beneath one of the barred windows. Arthur and Merlin followed him to take position on the bed's opposite side. The patient lay on his stomach, his head facing away. His breath came in short hisses, as if he'd fallen asleep while gritting his teeth against the pain. Airc bent close to Mathan's face and gently shook him awake.

"Mathan," Airc said. "Visitors."

"Go away," came the despondent murmur.

Mathan turned his head anyway, noticed Merlin and Arthur, and struggled to push himself up. The blanket fell away to reveal a mass of bandages so badly blood-soaked that Arthur couldn't tell where one whip mark ended and the next began.

Mother of God.

"Stay down, Mathan," Arthur said, curbing his fury. "Orderly!" All of them hurried to Mathan's bedside. "Why haven't this man's bandages been changed?"

"He won't let us, Lord Pendragon," the nearest orderly said.

"Every time they try, it feels like they're killing me." Mathan sighed. "Although if they did, it would be a mercy for me. And a relief for everyone else."

"Not true, Mathan." Arthur squatted to Mathan's level. "Your ala needs you. I need you. And you know Gyan would be devastated."

"Chieftainess!" Again he struggled to rise, and again Arthur bade him to stop. "Is she here, my lord?"

"No. But she wanted to be, with all her heart. Will you let these men tend you, for her sake?"

With a groan, Mathan buried his face in the pillow, his shoulders heaving. Arthur nodded to Merlin, who sent the orderlies after fresh bandages, water, salve, and a painkiller-laced sleeping draught.

When Mathan finally looked at Arthur again, his eyes were red-rimmed and wet. "I have failed. Her, you, Airc, the ala, the clan—everyone."

"You succumbed to temptation and struck a superior officer," Arthur corrected him. "You have already paid a hundredfold." *At least.* He laid a hand on Mathan's forearm and squeezed. "The only way for you to fail is to succumb to self-pity."

Surprise contorted Mathan's face. "What? You—you mean I don't have to stay here, in this prison?"

"Only for as long as it takes for your back to heal, and then you may resume your normal duties."

"Truly, sir? But Tribune Urien said—"

"Forget what Urien said, Mathan." Again Arthur's anger strained at its bonds. He stood to address Airc. "Have Tribune Urien report to my workroom in the praetorium at once."

As Airc saluted and made his way to the door to request egress, the orderlies returned. One toted a sloshing bucket of water, another balanced a load of bed linens beneath a salve pot and bandage rolls, and a third man carried a pitch-sealed leather mug and a short, smooth stick. He bent to give Mathan the draught while the other two set their burdens aside and began peeling off Mathan's bloody bandages.

Mathan grimaced; whether from the draught's bitterness or the orderlies' ministrations on his back, Arthur couldn't tell. The man with the bucket sluiced water over bandages that had become crusted to the wounds. Pale crimson streaks marred the bed linens and dripped to the floor on both sides of the cot.

After Mathan finished the brew, the orderly took the mug and offered Mathan the stick, but Mathan waved it away. "Lord Pendragon, I—I don't know how to thank you." Mathan's eyelids drooped.

"Heal yourself, Mathan," Arthur said. The last of the bloody bandages peeled away to reveal a morass of raw welts, most still oozing. *Mother of God!* Arthur sucked in a breath. "Return to your ala stronger in body and spirit, ready to give your best for me and for Gyan. That's all the thanks we need."

"Aye . . . m'lord . . ." This came no louder than a murmur as the valerian bore Mathan into its dreamless realm.

Merlin sketched the sign of the cross over Mathan's form while the orderlies bathed the wounds, gently blotted them dry, and applied fresh salve and bandages. Once they finished binding his back, two orderlies lifted him—grunting and straining against Mathan's deadweight bulk—while the third replaced the bloody linens with fresh ones.

After they eased Mathan onto the cot, Arthur drew one of the orderlies aside. "See to it that he keeps receiving the best of care." The man nodded vigorously. "Until further notice, his only visitors are to be his ala commander, the garrison commander"—Arthur aimed a glance at Merlin—"and myself."

"Understood, Lord Pendragon."

Arthur motioned for Merlin to join him. When they reached the infirmary's locked door, Arthur tried to release anger through the force of his pounding. It didn't help much. After the guard unlocked and opened the door, Arthur shouldered past him and set a grueling pace toward the praetorium, his rage and frustration mounting with each stride.

As they neared the praetorium's fountain, Merlin stopped him. "Do you want to talk to Urien alone?"

An extraordinarily tempting idea, in fact, but, "No."

Merlin frowned but didn't press for an explanation. They passed the perimeter guards, entered the building, and turned down the corridor toward Arthur's workroom. Their footfalls echoed off the marble. The oil lamps fastened to the walls guttered in their wake.

Arthur reached the workroom's antechamber and flung open the door. It hit the wall with a resounding thud.

Urien flinched. He stood with his back to the set of shelves where Arthur's aide stored the cohort reports. Nothing seemed to be amiss, either with Urien's uniform or the stacks of parchment behind him, though Urien probably had ample warning of Arthur and Merlin's arrival. Splotched across the left side of Urien's jaw, Arthur noted with secret satisfaction, was a purpling bruise.

"Explain yourself, Tribune," Arthur snapped.

"With regard to what?"

Arthur stalked closer. "Do not play games with me, Urien map Dumarec."

"Or—what?"

"Or I will kill you where you stand."

"And lose my father's support?" Urien sneered. "You don't have the ballocks."

Arthur gave Urien such a hard uppercut that he stumbled against the shelves, scattering parchment everywhere. Urien righted himself, his fists cocked and eyes blazing fury.

"Go ahead, Tribune." Grinning, Arthur jutted his jaw and pointed at his chin. "Give me an excuse to flay your back to the bone." When Urien muttered an oath and eased his stance, Arthur said, "Now look who's lacking ballocks."

"If you have a point to make," Urien growled, "then make it." He knuckled a trickle of blood from the corner of his mouth. "Sir."

"Your gambit has not earned you dismissal from the legion. You will remain at headquarters as cavalry prefect. I expect top performances from you and your men. If you so much as spit where you shouldn't, then when I'm through with you, not even the worms will be interested in what's left." Arthur folded his arms and creased his brow. "Do I make myself clear, Tribune?"

"Perfectly."

"Good." Arthur jerked a nod toward the door. "Get out of my sight."

Merlin stepped aside to let a sullen Urien pass. After the door shut, Arthur dropped into the chair behind Marcus's worktable, the emotions and lack of sleep overtaking him in a rush. He braced his forehead against his left fist and sighed.

"Was all of that really necessary, lad?" Merlin asked as he bent to retrieve the parchment Urien had knocked from the shelves.

"I'm sorry you had to see it. But I needed a witness." Arthur lifted his head and briefly massaged his right hand. "He deserves a hell of a lot more."

Merlin straightened to deposit the leaves on the table. "Have a care, Arthur. Urien will not remain your subordinate forever. When his father dies—"

"I know." Wearily, Arthur reached for ink, parchment, and a quill. Before he began writing, he spent a long moment staring at the ceiling. "May God deliver us all from that day."

Chapter 8

THE NEWS FROM Arthur, brought by courier the following day, was maddeningly vague in some ways and yet all too clear in others.

"Problem temporarily solved" was all Arthur would divulge about his confrontation with Urien. Gyan wondered what "temporarily" meant, aside from the fact that nothing could be permanently resolved with Urien until he drew his final breath and became the One God's problem.

Although her consort didn't say it in so many words, she knew better than to expect any more visits from him. And although the Sasunach threat hadn't materialized yet—the West Sasunaich were fortifying Anderida, but the scouts had not seen any signs of troop buildup—she refused to desert her post merely to satisfy the whims of her heart, however tempting those whims might be.

Arthur did report that her clansman's wounds would heal, along with the unit's morale, which made her doubly grateful. Even so, he had given her far more questions than answers, underscoring the fact that she should be at headquarters, not languishing in an extraneous command on an insignificant spit of an island a hundred miles away.

Resisting the urge to rip the parchment into oblivion, she slapped it onto the stack destined for reuse and stood. She briefly considered the idea of penning a reply but knew it would be colored by her frustration. She needed to clear her head.

She entered the antechamber, where Rhys sat at his table, copying a report from the clay work tablet to parchment.

"Commander? Something wrong?"

She paused long enough to say, "I need a sparring partner. Get some practice weapons from the armory. I'll meet you at the stables."

His obedience registered as a grunt of affirmation and the sound of his chair scraping across the tiles.

Gyan picked up a fistful of carrots from the kitchens for Macmuir and Rhys's mare. Rhys arrived at the stables as she was dispensing the treats. She took the practice sword from him and expressed her thanks. They saddled and bridled their mounts in companionable silence, which she appreciated. Angusel would have spouted a stream of questions she had no desire to answer.

They mounted and rode to the cavalry field, where First Turma was engaged in horseback javelin-casting drills. To stem rumors, Gyan had risked further estrangement between her Caledonach and Breatanach troops to inform them of the tensions at headquarters. A pity, she thought as she surveyed the turma, that the Breatanach foot soldiers trained on the north fields. Witnessing her performance might have helped bolster their confidence.

"Your turn, Commander." Winking, Rhys brandished a javelin.

She snapped out of her uneasy reverie to stare at him. He held the javelin toward her. Shorter and slimmer than its cousin the spear, the favored weapon of Caledonach horsemen was balanced for throwing rather than thrusting. A shower of these deadly missiles could send a squad of foot troops screaming for cover.

Learning to fight with her left hand had proved more difficult than she'd hoped but better than observing the proceedings, waiting for flesh to knit and strength to build. She grasped the ashwood shaft with her left hand and trotted Macmuir to the end of the field, where the turma was assembling for another charge. Rhys followed her.

He halted his mount near children who'd gathered to watch and cheer the charges. "Remember, my lady. It's no different than using your right arm. Concentrate!" His words grew fainter as she kneed Macmuir into formation. In the calm before the charge, one last shout burst through: "You can do it!"

"Come on, Macmuir." Crouching low over the creamy neck, she whispered into a swiveled-back ear, "Give me everything you've got!"

The stallion sprang toward the line of straw targets with the rest of the turma. Hefting the javelin, she took careful aim, cocked shoulder and wrist, and threw. The javelin joined its kind in the race for the targets . . . and fell harmlessly short.

The javelin's quivers seemed to accuse her of not trying hard enough.

Rhys cantered up to her as she jerked the weapon from the ground. "My lady, don't fret. It will come with time and practice."

"Ha!" She slapped at the barely healed flesh on her sword arm. "I would be doing just fine but for this."

"Aye. But think of the advantages, my lady. Not many warriors can boast of being skilled with both hands." He thumped his leather-clad chest. "I cannot."

"Neither can I."

"You will, and soon." Wheeling his snow-footed black mare around, he said, "Sword practice?"

"Gladly."

After she returned her javelin to the rack, she and Rhys spurred their mounts to a training enclosure for a bout of mounted hand-to-hand combat. They drew their swords, with Gyan again using her left hand, and closed upon one another.

Sword sparring on foot was difficult enough, but adding horses to the mix made it nigh unto impossible. Trying to kill the opponent had to be easier, by any reckoning. Curbing her stallion's battle instincts to prevent injury to her clansman and his mount while wielding her sword in directions that went counter to her basic reflexes presented a monumental challenge.

Yet she and Macmuir acquitted themselves well against the veteran Rhys and his fiery mare until a frightened woodcock darted across the field. To avoid the flapping, screeching menace, Macmuir made an abrupt sideways leap. Dropping the sword, Gyan clung to his foam-streaked neck. The bird switched directions. Macmuir swerved again. Burning pain lanced her wounded arm. Her grip loosened, and she found herself slipping, falling, yelling...

Like a candle, the world snuffed out.

NINIANE SIPPED from the plain green glass cup while the merchant looked on in hopeful expectation. The liquid's sharp taste burned her tongue, and she swallowed hard, resisting the urge to spew it out. To consider it wine required more imagination than she could summon. She set the cup on the rough-planked table.

Behind her hand, she coughed and cleared her throat. "I was hoping to find something a little easier on the palate." Though she looked forward to entering heaven one day, being poisoned by the Holy Eucharist wasn't quite the means she'd envisioned.

"Ah, yes, of course, Prioress." The swarthy merchant bobbed his head and invited her to follow him to the other side of the stall where several more amphorae stood, supported by racks specially designed for their pointed bottoms. He flashed an apologetic grin. "The better grades do cost more."

She felt her brow furrow, and she gestured at the basket looped over her arm. "I have brought the priory's best salves, blessed by the Keeper of the Chalice, Abbot Dafydd." She smiled, recalling the abbot's chagrin when she'd informed him of this duty. She didn't believe the Chalice or its Keeper's blessing enhanced the medicines' healing properties, but if the patients did, then so much the better for them—and if this merchant did, then so much the better for her.

The merchant's expression sobered as he crossed himself. "Please," he said, pointing at the tall, glazed jars, "select whichever of these suits your needs." He tossed a glance at a trio of moderately well-dressed women who were approaching the stall and leaned closer to whisper, "For you, dear Prioress, no extra charge."

She smiled her thanks, and the wine merchant turned to greet the other customers. As she gripped the handles and peered into the first amphora, her vision blurred. She closed her eyes. The odors of sweat and horses and harness leather enveloped her. Knifelike agony sliced her upper right arm. A confusion of sounds assaulted her ears: *hoofbeats, a squawking bird, terrified whinnies, and a woman's scream.*

Afraid the scream might have been hers, Niniane peered around.

The merchant was engrossed in assisting the other women, who remained focused upon tasting and discussing his wares.

The Dhoo-Glass marketplace teemed with activity, odors and noises, but the leather merchants conducted business two lanes away, and no frightened horses, raucous birds, or screaming women cavorted in the wine shop's vicinity.

Another visitation of the Sight, then. Lord in heaven, would it ever end?

Strangely, she had Seen nothing but infinite blackness.

She rubbed her arm. Though it bore no marks, the skin felt tender. Someone had been badly hurt. She couldn't ignore the anguished plea, but whose was it?

Bracing both hands against the amphora's cool rim, she drew a breath and gazed past her reflection in the wine.

The blackness surges forth with suffocating intensity.

A man shouts, his voice hoarse with fear.

Niniane couldn't understand his words. Except one.

"Gyanhumara!"

The tattered echoes waver like a sobbing sigh and dissolve into nothingness.

Her head throbbing as if caught in a vise, she released the amphora and reeled back. It tipped and would have fallen out of the rack, had the merchant not lunged to steady it. Wine splashed the dust and spattered her robe.

"Prioress, are you ill?" Wringing his hands, he looked at the amphora and back at Niniane.

Pressing fingertips to temple and blinking, she shook her head. The pain dissipated quickly, praise God. Chieftainess Gyanhumara was in danger, but when? Now, or sometime in the future? And where? Belatedly, she realized the merchant hadn't stopped regarding her worriedly. "Please forgive me for the spill."

"Take the whole measure, Prioress." When she began to protest, he said, "Please. I insist."

She had to find out what the Sight was trying to tell her. "You are most kind, good sir, but I—" A blur of movement in the lane caught her eye. She turned.

Arms pumping and chest heaving, Angusel darted between market stalls and people and animals at a dead run. He made eye contact with Niniane and came to a skidding stop. "Prioress, thank the gods!"

He gripped her hand with extraordinary strength and began running back the way he'd come. "Hurry—Gyan is hurt!"

They both broke into a dash.

In front of the apothecary's shop, she breathlessly commanded Angusel to halt. Reluctantly, he obeyed. She inhaled deeply to steady her voice and asked, "What sort of injury?"

"Her head. There's a lot of blood." He reached for her hand again. "Please, Prioress, we must hurry!"

"And I must have the right medicines." She lifted the basket of salve pots. "These are for muscle aches and sprains, not wounds. Go back and ask the wine merchant for a skin full of the first vintage he was going to sell me. He'll know what you mean. If he insists on payment, please tell him I'll settle it later." Her taste buds cringed, but the vinegary liquid would be far more suitable as a wound cleanser than a beverage. Aware that Angusel hadn't divulged their destination, she added, "Meet me back here."

While Angusel bolted away, Niniane entered the shop to barter two pots of salve for a bandage roll and bunches of dried betony, valerian, and lavender, items the priory's infirmary possessed in abundance. A pity the Sight's timing hadn't been better.

She shrugged off the irony and stepped outside with the supplies. Angusel rejoined her. "How did you know to find me at the wine merchant's?" she asked as they resumed their course.

"I didn't," he replied between breaths. "I was on my way to fetch Cynda. You were closer."

Niniane presumed this Cynda was another healer but didn't press the matter. If Angusel was as preoccupied as he appeared, staring fixedly into the distance while striding as briskly as Niniane's skirts would allow, she doubted he'd appreciate chatter.

They passed the last houses and continued through the gates. The Brytoni-uniformed guards exchanged terse greetings with Angusel, which seemed odd. With their commander injured, surely they'd have demonstrated more concern. Perhaps they didn't know, but if not, why not? For whatever reason, their behavior didn't faze her guide.

Outside the gates, he turned left onto a wide, well-trodden track hugging the wall. As they neared a field, she needed no one to tell her that the object of her worry lay in the center of the crowd of mostly Picti warriors. She couldn't help but recall a similar incident. Unlike

Angusel's accident, however, the Brytoni soldiers seemed more curious than anxious, which troubled Niniane deeply.

Angusel pulled her into a run, waving and shouting something in his native tongue. An avenue quickly opened.

The chieftainess lay on her back with arms and legs everywhere like a discarded rag doll, her lovely face whiter than sea foam. On her left temple, a bruise had begun to flower around a cut. Blood streaked her face and stained the hard-packed dirt. If her chest moved beneath her boiled-leather armor, Niniane couldn't detect it.

A wickedly sharp rock bore the crimson evidence of its role in the accident. A black-bearded warrior bent to scoop it into a gloved hand. He grunted, his sinews bulging with the effort to pulverize the rock. Failing that, he hurled it at the wall, and it shattered. When he gazed upon Gyanhumara, his eyes mirrored an emotion transcending simple concern. A swift glance at the other faces showed her that this Picti warrior didn't suffer alone.

Lord willing, she wouldn't betray their trust.

Kneeling beside Gyanhumara, Niniane asked for a dagger and got a dozen. She selected the shiniest and carefully angled the blade under Gyanhumara's nose. A slow succession of tiny clouds formed and vanished. Niniane laid the dagger aside and closed her eyes for a silent prayer of thanks.

"Prioress, is—is she...?"

Angusel's tone, his fear-rounded, golden-brown eyes, his very words sparked a memory. She had Seen him as a much older man, never far from this flame-haired lady warrior tattooed with the woad dragon and doves.

Niniane banished the future's bleak shadows to deal with present reality. "She lives!"

Relieved sighs rippled through the throng.

Palpating the neck and as much of the upper back as was not covered in armor revealed no hidden injuries. The rest of that examination would have to wait. Niniane tore a length of bandage, soaked it in wine, and dabbed dirt and blood from the head wound. Gently, she turned Gyanhumara's head to one side and sluiced the wound with more wine. Tension creased the young woman's face, but she didn't wake. She bound Gyanhumara's head and probed for more injuries. On her right arm, tender pink flesh around an older wound had torn open, probably from the fall. After finding no other sign of hurt, Niniane sent another prayer heavenward.

She said to Angusel, kneeling beside her, "She must be carried inside and kept warm."

This prompted the offering of eight shields and the saddle blanket off every horse within shouting distance.

She directed the warriors' efforts to rig a litter and accompanied the unconscious chieftainess to her quarters, where a woman who appeared to be one of Gyanhumara's personal servants met Niniane. Or rather, ignored her. Spouting a stream of anxious-sounding Picti words, the woman had eyes only for the limp form being gingerly transferred to the bed.

After Gyanhumara had been stripped of boots, weapons, and armor and settled to the woman's satisfaction, she began to shoo everyone else from the room, Niniane included.

"Angusel, tell her I'm a healer. I must stay and keep watch."

"If you stay, Prioress, then so do I." Those young eyes burned with frightening intensity.

"Very well." If he was destined to become Gyanhumara's right arm, how could Niniane deny him? "Just speak to her. Please."

While Angusel conversed with the servant, Niniane rummaged through her basket. The mild, sweet betony would make a good tea to ease the inevitable headache once Gyanhumara awoke, along with a pinch of the powerful valerian root if she complained of severe pain. Now, Niniane needed the jar of dried lavender blossoms to fold into a compress for performing their healing magic while Gyanhumara slept.

Niniane withdrew the lavender and a length of clean linen and looked up to find the servant giving her a stern appraisal. Jabbing thumb to breast, the woman spoke again to Angusel.

He translated, "Cynda agrees, but she wants the first watch."

Niniane took the older woman's measure. "Thank you, Angusel. Please tell her that I agree. It will give me a chance to prepare my medicines."

And the vigil began.

Chapter 9

ARTHUR GRIPPED THE slick rail, ignoring his cramping fingers as he mentally willed the warship to go faster. The sounds of swearing and grunting and creaking behind his back, driven by the faster-than-usual drumbeat, told him how vain a wish he'd conceived.

Another wave broke against the bow. He pulled back, but his eyes stung—not entirely from the salty spray. He couldn't do a damned thing for his wife, trapped in this endless heaving netherworld between land and sky. Or, his pragmatic inner demon taunted, once he finally reached her side.

He knew only how to end lives, not heal them.

Even his father's death hadn't made him feel this powerless, and he despised it more with each breath.

Closing his eyes and tilting his head, he allowed the westering sun to warm his face, but it gave him no comfort. By all reckoning, her accident had been his fault. Never mind that ill-trained demon-spawn of a stallion, it was his fault for letting her out of his sight and for failing to deal with her enemy—their enemy—decisively enough to render this separation unnecessary. Chin to breast, he prayed for her as fervently as he knew how.

A hand gripped his shoulder. Fewer than half a dozen people would dare such a gesture. One lay gravely injured at his destination port and another was minding the legion's affairs at headquarters for him.

Blinking, Arthur turned to regard his fleet commander. Bedwyr withdrew his hand, but his expression remained somber. He acknowledged Bedwyr's sympathy with a short but appreciative nod.

"How soon? Within the hour?" He tried to bleed the raw plea from his tone.

Bedwyr's gaze flicked out across the horizon, toward the slowly growing landmass. As he nodded at Arthur, compassion flooded his expression. "Want some company?"

"What I want is more speed. I'd grab an oar if I thought it would help." Not a bad idea, in fact. He could spell one of the men. If nothing else, the exertion might blunt his worrying. He stepped from the rail.

Bedwyr caught his arm. "Save your strength. Gyan will have greater need of it."

Scowling, Arthur pulled free, but Bedwyr had a valid point, damn him. He stared at the too-small island, resuming his prayer.

His best friend adopted a similar stance. Whether praying or not, or to which god, Arthur had no idea. Nor did he inquire. Details of faith belonged between a man and his Maker. He found it comforting that Merlin and perhaps Bedwyr, Niniane, Abbot Dafydd, and others were offering supplications on Gyan's behalf, and it strengthened his feeble, distracted efforts.

After what seemed like a millennium, the docks and buildings of Port Dhoo-Glass hove into view, growing larger by the stroke. Bedwyr excused himself to direct the crew for the journey's final leg. With each command Bedwyr shouted, Arthur felt his tension increase, as though he were a stretching bowstring.

The instant the warship docked, Arthur vaulted over the side, landed in a catlike crouch on the planking, sprang up, and sprinted toward the fort. He ignored the curious glances and queries, treating everything and everyone as either scenery or obstacles to negotiate. He tried to ignore his personal demon, who scolded him for his unseemly behavior; folks had learned to expect a calm and reserved Pendragon.

Calm and reserve could bloody well be hanged!

As the distance lessened, his mental picture intensified. Gyan lay bruised, bleeding, feverish, unconscious... dying...

God, no!

He dashed moisture from his eyes with the back of a hand and lurched onward. Across streets, through courtyards, around buildings, down corridors, up stairs, past doorways; he scarcely registered his location but let memories steer him. An ache flared in his chest.

Upon rounding a corner, he glimpsed the door to Gyan's chambers and halted, panting hard. Several of her clansmen had congregated outside. To a man, their faces and postures and hushed tones conveyed stark worry. The ache pierced Arthur's heart again, and he rubbed the spot with his fist.

He drew a breath, let it out slowly, and drew another. While he fought to regain composure, Bedwyr joined him. Arthur shot his winded friend a wan smile, tightened his jaw, and strode briskly forward, with Bedwyr gasping and trailing in his wake.

One of the men glanced their way and snapped a salute. Quickly, the others imitated his example. Wading into their midst, Arthur hunted the brambles of his memory for a Caledonian greeting and uttered it as he reached for the handle and pulled. Locked! The soldier who'd seen him first thumped on the door, shouting something. The only word Arthur could make out was the Caledonian form of his name, "Artyr." His heart clenched.

The door opened wide enough for a head to poke through, bearing the furious-looking face of Cynda. She launched into what had to be a tongue-lashing, first aimed at the one soldier, then the entire group. When she laid eyes on Arthur, she stopped and blinked once in obvious surprise. She bustled into the corridor, latched onto Arthur's wrist, and pulled him through the doorway. Over her shoulder, she gave Bedwyr and the others a final admonishment, presumably along the lines of staying put until further notice.

Inside the antechamber, she imperiously pointed at the door—or rather, Arthur surmised, the door's bolt. As he moved to secure the door, Cynda nodded sharply and turned to stride into the inner chamber without as much as a backward glance.

The grim mental images had not prepared him for the reality.

Gyan lay stretched out on the bed amid a tumble of covers, clad in an ankle-length, undyed, sweat-stained undertunic. Bandages swathed her head and upper arm, and her breathing came in labored gasps. What he could see of her hair was darkened with sweat and pasted to her head. The throes of battle frenzy had never made her cheeks appear so flushed. Bands of grief constricted his heart.

To either side, each clasping one of her hands, sat Peredur and Angusel. Cynda busied herself at a long table, preparing a salve amid the clutter of tools and herbs. To Arthur's immense relief, Niniane stood helping Cynda.

Gyan began moaning and arching her back. Peredur and Angusel tightened their grips. Her head thrashed from side to side, and she moaned louder. Niniane scurried forward with a wet cloth and swabbed Gyan's cheeks and neck while Cynda immobilized her legs.

Arthur could only watch in morbid fascination. This couldn't be happening, he told himself. This person on the bed wasn't his dear wife. It had to be some other unfortunate woman—

"Artyr!" Eyes tightly closed, she wrenched her arm from Angusel's grip and thrust it upward, fingers splayed. Her hoarse plea spurred Arthur to her side.

Angusel stood and backed away for Arthur to take his place. Her fingers tightened around Arthur's with viselike strength. He tried stroking her hand and arm and face, whispering words of endearment, to no avail. In frustration, he glanced at the others, questing for answers, but they only shrugged and shook their heads. Gyan kept crying the Caledonian form of his name and pulling on his hand . . . just like a drowning person.

"Easy, Gyan. I'm here," he murmured. Gently, he tugged on her hand, reasoning that if she were dreaming of drowning, this might bring her out of it. She clutched his hand harder, but the thrashing stopped. His hope grew. "That's it, my love. I have you, and I'm not letting you go." *Never again!* When she increased the force of her pulling, so did he.

Her body went limp. Alarmed, Arthur squeezed her hand and tugged, but she didn't respond. He felt her neck for a pulse and groaned his relief when he found it, weak but steady. He pressed the backs of his fingers to her cheek. It felt clammy; a good sign, he reminded himself. The fever had broken. He kissed her cheek, her jaw, her lips. Still no response.

"Gyan, where are you?" His whisper sounded as frayed as he felt. Losing to the assault of emotions, he laid his cheek against her chest, careful not to interfere with her breathing. "I need you so much—don't leave me. Gyan, wake up!" Tears stung his eyes. "Please!"

WAKE UP? She was awake. Drowning but awake. Wasn't she?

Her eyelids refused to budge. With effort, she willed them open. Luminous swords slaughtered the darkness. Pain assaulted her head, arm, shoulders, back. Mostly her head. She winced.

Shadows slowly gathered, resolving into a flock of worried faces: Per, Cynda, Angusel, Niniane . . . and the most precious sight this side of heaven.

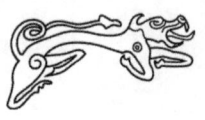

A HAND touched Arthur's hair gently. To the tune of the others' gasps and signs, he raised his head to gaze at his wife.

Her eyes had opened, and her lips wore the smile he loved so well. He couldn't kiss those sweet lips fast enough! His tongue entwined with hers, conducting its own reunion.

He nuzzled her neck, whispering, "God in heaven, Gyan, I thought I was going to lose you."

She expelled a puff of breath that might have been a sigh or a laugh. "Can't—" She coughed, cleared her throat, and swallowed. "Can't be rid of me that easily." Her voice sounded alarmingly hoarse.

He couldn't help but smile at the courage a sickbed couldn't conquer. "What makes you think I want to be rid of you?" He lifted her hand to his lips, certain she would be pleased by his decision, and bestowed a lavish kiss. "In fact, it's time you return home. I will stay here until you're well enough to travel."

"What?" She ripped her hand from his grasp. Pain-hampered fury blazed across her face as she struggled to sit up. Niniane and Cynda tried to assist her, but she waved them off and completed the movement herself. "You're ending my command here? All because of a little fall from my"—pressing her hand to her temple made her wince—"horse?" She gritted her teeth, but her glare didn't dim.

"Yes." Arthur stood. Never mind that his decision reflected sound military reasoning. Never mind that he would sooner lose his right arm than see her hurt like this. Never mind that he couldn't endure one more moment's separation from her. Wife or not, Caledonian nobility or not, she had no right to question his judgment. He said to Peredur, "You are to assume command of the Manx Cohort for the duration of the season, effective at once."

"Understood." Peredur glanced at Gyan and back at Arthur. "But are you sure it's wise to—"

Arthur felt his brow tighten. A miracle these Caledonians owned a shred of battlefield discipline. However, since Peredur was only trying to safeguard his sister's best interests—something Arthur would have done in the man's place—he refrained from delivering a rebuke. "You have your orders, Centurion. Dismissed. Both of you," he said to Angusel. They saluted and left the chamber.

GYAN COULDN'T believe what she'd heard. Though no easy task, she'd grown to enjoy the challenges of commanding one of Arthur's units. To Cynda, she said quietly in Caledonaiche, "Please leave us. I have something I must discuss privately with my consort."

"Oh, aye." Cynda's look, as she folded her arms and glanced at Arthur, could have curdled milk inside a cow. "I can just imagine."

"It's all right, Cynda. I'll be fine."

Cynda snorted and tossed another glance at Arthur. "It's himself who should be worried."

Indeed, Gyan thought, and not just from the wrath of Cynda. Arthur owed her plenty of explanations, but not in front of the prioress, either. She rephrased her request in Breatanaiche. Niniane glided toward the door.

Arthur intercepted her. "When can she travel, Prioress?"

Niniane gave Gyan a long appraisal. "Difficult to say, since she's just awakened after two days. But—"

Gyan felt the blood drain from her face. "Your pardon, Prioress." Her mouth went dry, and she swallowed hard. "Did you say two *days*?" It would explain why Arthur and Cynda and the others had looked so worried, why her voice sounded worse than a bear in heat, and why she felt like devouring an entire Lugnasadh feast.

Nodding, the prioress approached the bed and laid a cool hand on Gyan's arm. "If you eat and rest well tonight, it will be much easier to determine when you'll be recovered enough to endure the voyage."

As if she were cargo to be hauled about! She held her peace; her quarrel wasn't with the prioress. Niniane removed her hand and left the room.

After a final glance at Gyan, Cynda followed. The door swung to behind her.

Arthur stood facing the window. His hands clenched together behind that rod-stiff back. Corded muscles writhed beneath his skin. She got the distinct impression that he was waiting for her to speak.

She obliged him. "What gives you the right to order me about like one of your underlings in front of my clansmen?"

He laughed mirthlessly. "Evidently, the same right that allows you to publicly question my judgment."

"I question anything that doesn't make sense."

He faced her, his gaze alight with fiery intensity. "Just as you questioned my judgment to send you here, to protect you from further encounters with your enemy." *Your enemy.* The words ground out from between his teeth.

He blamed her for Urien.

Biting her lip, she sorted through the events of the past year, certain she could have done something to diffuse Urien's hostility.

Perhaps if she'd refused his suit at the outset...

No. He had always coveted Argyll lands. Besides, the treaty still would have obligated her to marry a Breatanach lord. If not for his arrogant insistence to show her off to Arthur... no, that wasn't true. She had insisted on meeting Arthur, and Urien had been more than happy to arrange it. Either way, she never would have discovered her soul's true mate.

And there he stood, silhouetted against the blazing golden sunset like a statue, cold and forbidding.

This shouldn't be happening! They should be celebrating the passing of her fever, not facing off like blood enemies.

Her heart ached.

Closing her eyes, she surrendered to the softness of the pillows and, as much as it galled her, to Arthur's logic. "I understand. You're doing what you think is best for me."

The swish of his cloak and the slap of his sandals on the tiles announced his approach. She caught a whiff of his leathery and altogether male scent and inhaled deeply. His lips brushed her throat, sending waves of tingles through her neck.

"Gyan, you don't know what the thought of losing you does to me. Madness can't even begin to describe it." She opened her eyes to find his face a scant handbreadth from hers. "Of course, I want to protect you. I wish you wouldn't put up a fight every time."

She couldn't resist the temptation to say, grinning, "But I like to fight."

"I know." Sighing, he shook his head. "I'd be stupid to waste your martial skills by forcing you to mind my hearth." It was his turn to grin. "Even if I thought I could get away with it."

"Ha. I'm glad you recognize the futility of trying." If she'd possessed a fraction of her normal strength, she would have swatted his shoulder.

"I hope this isn't futile." His face hovered over hers, lips to lips and tongue to tongue.

A voice nagged her not to give in so easily, but she ignored it.

PRINCE ÆLFERD mounted the gallows, set his stance, planted hands on hips, and glared at the crowd. A gust chased a handful of dead leaves across his feet and flared his cloak. Behind him, the last of the rebellious Brædan thralls had become crow bait. Before him stood their countrymen, most looking sullen and uncowed. Ælferd's troops surrounded them, weapons at the ready.

"Who shall be next?" His voice thundered across the town square. As it died, an eerie silence descended, broken only by the creaking of the ropes bearing their grisly burdens. He stabbed a finger toward a man in the front row. "You?" To Ælferd's satisfaction, the man's defiance melted into abject fear as the woman beside him tightened her grip on his waist. "You, then? Or you?" Ælferd's other random targets displayed similar transformations.

He'd have hanged the bloody lot if not for the fact that he needed their brawn and skills to turn Anderceaster into a proper staging base. From his elevated position, the lack of progress evident in the half-completed barracks and armory and sheds and silos loomed painfully clear. Ælferd didn't want to even contemplate the sorry state of the harbor defenses.

King Cissa wasn't going to be pleased.

At least, the Brædan leaders would no longer be plaguing him, encouraging the others to damage the work by night and covertly fomenting rebellion by day. New leaders doubtless would arise, but he hoped this day's example would brand their memories, because the next time he would execute the entire whore-spawned lot. Plenty of good Saxon folk in the Fatherland would leap at the chance to move to this verdant island, help him here at Anderceaster for a season, and settle rich steadings as reward for their efforts.

Ælferd stroked his chin. The idea had a lot of merit.

However, getting the word back to Saxony, recruiting volunteers, packing their belongings, and transporting them to Anderceaster would impose delays he could ill afford.

"Look to your necks, all of you!" He signaled to disperse the crowd.

Prodded by the soldiers, the Brædeas shuffled off to their various duties. Before long, the sounds of hammering and sawing, swearing and grunting penetrated the crisp autumn afternoon. Ælferd ordered the executioner to cut down the bodies and cast them, headless, into the sea. He gave a snort of derision as the executioner set to work. The collection rotting on the battlements revealed the only real progress he'd made during the last four months.

He departed the gallows and strode toward headquarters, ignoring the horsemen, wagons, people, and animals in the street, his thoughts immersed in the task of crafting a report for King Cissa. No matter how he might cloak the words, he couldn't deny the truth. Because of supply problems and these gods-cursed rebellious Brædan thralls, it had become too late to mount an invasion of Maun this year.

"Aren't you going to greet me?"

Ælferd halted, certain he'd dreamed the voice. He spun toward the sound, fully expecting to find no one there.

He couldn't have been more wrong. His beloved Camilla slid from the back of her mare and rushed to meet him as fast as dignity allowed. Gods, what a heavenly vision, her golden hair flying about her head like a sunny nimbus, her smile a silvery crescent moon, her eyes twinkling like twin stars. He quickened his pace.

They clasped hands, and he raised hers to his lips, savoring their softness and rosy scent. He marveled that she could keep them so delectable after the countless hours she devoted to training with sword and seax. Magic, he decided with a grin.

"What are you doing here?" Too late, he realized how that might sound. "I mean, I'm delighted to see you, of course, but I—you never sent word!"

Her light laughter rescued him from making an even greater fool of himself. "Father"—she nodded over her shoulder toward King Ælle, walking toward them amid a knot of bodyguards—"and I have news." Her face radiated joy. "Your uncle has agreed that we may wed!"

Ælferd's first impulse was to sweep her up in his arms, spin her around, and kiss her until all the stars fell from the sky. Her father's presence, however, restrained him to a wider grin, which disappeared as reality reasserted itself.

"Ælferd? Does this not please you?" she asked.

He couldn't bear her stricken look. He kissed her hands again. "Of course, my beloved, but there is something you must know." Upon ushering Camilla and her father into his private workroom and pouring a measure of wine for each of them, he proceeded to explain his failures.

"That is why," he concluded with a sigh as he gazed into the bloodred ripples of his wine cup, "I believe my uncle will withdraw his permission for our union, Camilla."

King Ælle cleared his throat. "You can't do anything about poor harvests, lad, or supply ships lost at sea."

Ælferd looked up, feeling bitterness well like bile in his throat. "But the thralls and their rebellion—"

"Defeated, is it not?" King Ælle asked.

"Yes, but the destruction, the delays—"

Ælle imperiously waved a hand. "Cissa will understand. I will see to that." As Ælferd began to voice his relief, Ælle continued, "On one condition."

"Name it, Your Majesty!" Ælferd would walk to the Orkneys barefoot and blindfolded if it meant Camilla would greet him at his journey's end.

A sparkle lit Ælle's eyes as he glanced first at his daughter, then at Ælferd. "Acquit yourself with honor on Maun next year. Claim it for your king, your people." His smile deepened, and he saluted Ælferd with his goblet. "Our people."

Maun. That word had become the most vulgar of epithets for him.

He shook off his apprehension and kissed Camilla's hand. "For you, my beloved, I will capture any island on earth."

Or die trying.

A chill that had nothing to do with the room's temperature shivered his spine.

Chapter 10

BRACED AGAINST THE rail at the stern of the Breatanach warship, Gyan watched Maun recede. A flock of gulls, hunting for handouts, provided noisy escort. It had been only a sennight since her accident, and her full strength hadn't yet returned. In a few short hours, the ship would arrive at Caer Lugubalion, where she and Arthur could truly begin their lives together. Yet as she felt the wind blow salt spray against her face and through her hair, a part of her didn't want to leave.

Per had insisted on accompanying her to legion headquarters rather than assuming command of the Manx Cohort. She frowned at the memory. After much persuasion, Arthur had granted Per's request but refused when she'd reiterated her desire to remain on Maun. She told herself Arthur loved her too much to want to be separated from her any longer.

Perhaps if she repeated it often enough, she might begin to believe it.

The hollow thump of boots on deck planking broke her reverie, but she knew that stride and didn't bother to turn around.

"Having second thoughts, dear sister?" Per said in Caledonaiche. An undercurrent of seriousness flowed through his tone. He joined her at the rail.

"A few." No surprise that he'd sensed her mood, but she didn't feel ready to divulge all the reasons to him. Or to herself. "I will miss the monks."

Memories stirred of the men who'd been her tutors since the spring, some of whom had been the first to die for her in combat. They had possessed a quiet courage, not the maniacal frenzy of the Caledonach way yet just as strong. The magnitude of their sacrifice still filled her heart with awe. She also would miss Dafydd, who'd awakened within her a love for the One God and His Son the Christ. This was one thing she couldn't tell her brother, who followed the Old Ones. Perhaps one day...

"You won't miss the action?" he asked.

"Yes." As she calculated the human cost of her first battle trophy, her smile disappeared. "And no." She put her back to the sea and scanned the deck for her consort. He stood near the bow, speaking with Bedwyr, while Cynda and Prioress Niniane sat huddled together near them, doing their best to stay out of the crew's way. Angusel had received permission to climb the rigging and help the lookout. "The work on Maun isn't finished. We held the Scáthinaich off, nothing more. It may take a few years, but they will return."

"I think you're right," Per said. "I also think you haven't told me what's really troubling you."

She sucked in a breath. Though the crashing waves and squealing gulls and boisterous crew provided more than enough noise, she kept her voice low. "I know how to be Artyr's warrior and leader of warriors." Sighing, she studied the cliffs on the north bank of the firth, banded by the docks and ramparts of three-sided Dùn Càrnhuilean, "Fort of the Rock-Elbows," called Caerlaverock in Breatanaiche, where the dream of a united Breatein had become flesh. Gyan wanted to help Arthur shape that dream into reality, but on her own terms.

She stared at the frothy chaos created by the warship's wake, her life seeming just as chaotic. "I don't know how to be his wife."

"It won't be easy, I suspect. With the Pendragon comes much

more than a single clan." Per leaned close. "Listen to your heart, Gyan, and you'll do fine."

She hoped he was right. Another set of footsteps made her glance up. As Arthur joined them, Per winked at her.

"What are you two plotting?" Arthur smiled, clasping her hand.

Listen to your heart.

"We were trying to decide which of us should challenge you for the Pendragonship."

He threw back his head and roared with laughter.

"And what, may I ask"—she crossed her arms, pointedly settling the Argyll Doves on her sword arm over her shield arm's dragon—"is so amusing about that?"

Her acerbity didn't extinguish his eyes' gleam. "God, I love your spirit!" She felt a tingling rush as Arthur's finger traced a line along her jaw, and she met his gaze, which had become intensely earnest. "I have no doubt, Gyanhumara nic Hymar, that you could attain whatever position you set your heart upon. Even the Pendragonship." His grin returned as he glanced at her arms. "And if you'd like to be on top next time, I'll gladly defer."

Per hooted a laugh. Gyan felt her face flush.

"Beathach!" Chuckling, she uncrossed her arms and slapped Arthur's shoulder. To his questioning look, she said, "It's not a curse." She flashed Per a grin; she couldn't count how often her brother had earned the epithet. Returning her attention to Arthur, she explained, "Just a family endearment." She kissed her consort, but a muffled cough interrupted her too soon.

They parted to discover that Bedwyr had joined them.

"We're approaching port." Bedwyr looked apologetic.

Arthur nodded, extending his hand, which Gyan clasped. Together they strode to the bow, with Per and Bedwyr following them. Cynda and the prioress rose, steadying each other as the ship kept surging forward. Gyan presumed the concern tempering their smiles was directed solely at her. Even Dafydd had demonstrated his feelings by giving Niniane permission to travel to headquarters to continue treating Gyan's injuries. Heartily she wished everyone would stop worrying so much and be more like Angusel, who had already abandoned his high perch and was leaning over the rail, every line of his stance radiating excitement.

Gyan could well understand the lad's reason. Scores of troops, infantry as well as cavalry, were lining both banks of the narrowing estuary, weapons poised in salute.

"Why this formation?" she asked her consort. "We're not returning from battle."

"I wanted my second-in-command to receive a proper welcome."

She overpowered Angusel's "Gyan!" with, "Your what?"

Arthur tapped her gold dragon, the brooch identical to his in every way save the eye's gemstone.

She tilted it to catch the light. "I thought this was just a wedding gift, like Braonshaffir." She clapped a hand to her sword's sapphire-crowned hilt.

"For now. I've made no official declaration yet. Nor can I until you've proven yourself on the battlefield and in the council chamber."

"Battlefield—ha." As she fixed her gaze upon the troops, her sole thought revolved around how precipitously he had removed her from the Manx command. "That's the last place you want me to be."

He latched onto her uninjured arm and pulled her close. "It's the last place I want *any* of my soldiers to be. War is only a means of achieving peace, and only after all other avenues have failed."

"This is how you think of me, as just one of your soldiers?" She meant it only half in jest.

"Lord God in heaven, no!" The crushing force of his lips upon hers spoke more loudly than words ever could. A level of peace she hadn't felt since the accident blanketed her heart, and she deepened the passion of her response.

On the shore, shouts erupted. Amid the chants of "Pendragon!" she could make out "Caledon!" and "Argyll!" She pulled back to grin at her consort, ignoring the giddy flutter in her chest that died as a surge of strength flooded her veins. "Some of our men know who is truly in charge."

His smile adopted the enigmatic quality that could be so maddening and so endearing. "Indeed they do."

As the warship slowed, she noticed a group of officers clustered beyond the docks. At the forefront of the unit, looking none too pleased, stood Urien. Her left hand dropped to her hilt.

"I will not let him trouble you." Arthur glared at the officers. "I promise you that."

In this she did not doubt him.

Tilting the parchment to catch the last afternoon light, Arthur stood at the window in his workroom.

Eight Brytons had been executed at Anderida for leading an attempt to overthrow their Saxon masters.

Though these people lived and died far beyond his sphere of influence, the news of their fate distressed him no less than if they'd been his own clansmen.

One day that would change. Repelling the Scots and forcing Caledonia to release all Brytoni slaves were good starts, but the task was painfully far from complete. He, Arthur map Uther, Pendragon of Brydein, would not rest until every Bryton stood free to enjoy peace and prosperity.

Permanent peace, not just the occasional respite from war.

If the Saxons and Angles and other peoples that shared Brydein chose to live in peace with their Brytoni neighbors, so much the better for everyone.

And if not, he would serve them their peace at swordpoint.

The sound of voices in the outer chamber disrupted his reverie. He wasn't expecting visitors. He crossed from the window to lay the dispatch on the table but remained standing. A knock rattled his door.

At Arthur's command, Marcus opened the door, stepped into the room, and—in a departure from routine—closed it behind him. "Sir, Tribune Urien asks to speak with you."

Arthur quelled his surprise. Urien never came to the praetorium unless summoned. "About what?"

"He wouldn't say, sir. Whatever it is, it seems to be urgent."

"Let him in."

Marcus saluted, turned, and pulled the door open. Garbed in Moray-patterned tunic, trews, and cloak, Urien marched in, strode to Arthur's table, and thrust a rolled parchment sheet toward him.

Arthur accepted the document but made no move to break the Black Boar seal. "What is this, Tribune?"

"My resignation."

When Marcus started to leave the room, Arthur ordered him to stay. To Urien, he said, "Why?"

Urien shot an irritated glance at the centurion, who was doing his best to remain inconspicuous near the door. "It's in the letter."

Arthur crushed the parchment in his fist and cast it to the floor. "Request denied." Moving from behind the table, he pinned Urien with his glare. "You are out of uniform. Correct that error at once."

Murderous rage flashed across Urien's face. He stood immobile except for his jaw, which worked back and forth. His lips pursed, and he spat. It landed squarely between Arthur's feet.

Marcus gasped. Arthur folded his arms and arched an eyebrow. "You are dismissed, Tribune. For the entire winter. Take as many of Clan Moray as you wish." He sharpened his glare. "But if you or your men fail to return to headquarters in the spring, I will send the legion to retrieve you. Understood?"

"Understood." Urien's rage dimmed but didn't die. "Sir."

He pivoted with a flare of his cloak, blustered past Marcus, and stormed from the room. Imagining that cloak with a chieftain's gold trim was far too easy—and chilling.

Marcus closed the door and stooped to retrieve the parchment wad. "Watch your back with him, sir," he whispered as he straightened.

Gyan's back concerned Arthur most, though he didn't need to share that with his aide. "Post a general order releasing all men who must attend to the harvest and other duties at home. Word it as you see fit. Just make it clear that they should expect recall at any time but no later than the ides of May."

He remained confident that Caer Lugubalion, Camboglanna, Caerglas, and the other garrisons would stay staffed above one-third strength; more than a thousand men called the legion their home. If Urien had hoped to foster division by claiming that Clan Moray had received preferential treatment, the general dismissal would rob him of that opportunity.

"The men will appreciate early release, sir." Marcus offered a rare grin. "It's been one hell of a year."

Studying the slimy glob at his feet, Arthur laughed ruefully. He couldn't have phrased it better himself.

***

"Serve yourself." The pitcher hit the tabletop with a thud. Wine sloshed over the rim. "Or have your wife do it. This should be her task, not mine." Morghe raked Gyanhumara with a sharp glare.

Arthur caught her arm before she could escape. "Caledonian noblewomen do not serve at table, Morghe. You know that better than most." She felt his grip loosen, and she wrenched her arm away. His face mirrored concern. "Tell me what troubles you."

As if he really cared how she felt.

She wanted to spit in her brother's face but wasn't in a position to show such defiance. Not yet. Not until she married Urien in a year and a half, the lengthy betrothal designed to give her enough time at Caerlaverock to learn from her mother the intricacies of clan rule. With such knowledge at her command, she planned to become indispensable to her future husband.

However, she had hoped to stay at Caer Lugubalion for a few more weeks, to become better acquainted with him before they retired to their separate homes for the winter. Arthur had stolen this opportunity from her with no regard for her feelings.

"Dismissal" was the official term describing the imminent departure of Urien and his clansmen. Morghe would have selected "banishment." Either way, it lay beyond her power to change. As usual.

She molded her countenance and posture into the image of weariness. "It's nothing, Arthur." She dragged the back of a hand across her brow. "Merely fatigue."

It wasn't a lie. She had long since wearied of being a pawn in his political gwyddbwyll game.

"Rest well, then," he said. Gyanhumara murmured a similar sentiment.

Before Arthur could change his mind, Morghe stepped down from the dais and quit the hall.

After the boisterous, smoky warmth of the fort's main dining hall, the brisk evening provided a refreshing change. Wrapping herself in her cloak's thick woolen folds, she strode down the deserted thoroughfare toward the mansio. The dignitaries' inn appeared dark and quiet, with most of the guests probably still gorging themselves at the feast.

She craved solitude, but not the whitewashed boredom of her guest chambers. Instead, she opted for the stone bench in the mansio's inner courtyard.

A tall figure stood at the rustle of her approach.

"Urien!" Pulse racing, she swallowed her surprise. "Why are you here?"

"I could ask the same of you, since I know the feast is long from being over. But I won't." Smiling, he extended a hand. "I was waiting for you, my dear."

Instinct warned her that he wanted something other than the pleasure of her company.

Curiosity flaring, she decided to play his game.

"You were? To say farewell?" She accepted his hand and squeezed it briefly. The feast's aromas clung to him: smoke, beef, and ale. Mostly ale. She forced a smile. "I'm so glad!"

He answered with a surprisingly passionate kiss. His tongue seemed to have a mind of its own as it explored the inside of her mouth. So did his fingers; they burrowed under her cloak to caress her breasts. The exquisite sensations made her fling her head back and gasp with pleasure. Urien's lips savaged her throat, and she arched closer, feeling his body's reaction between her thighs through the wool of his trews.

She realized that he might be thinking of Gyanhumara and harbored no illusions that she would ever possess his heart as long as the Picti chieftainess walked this earth.

Yet his touch had sparked her desire, and she didn't want him to stop.

"I shall miss you, Morghe," he murmured at last.

To hide her astonishment, she launched a surprise of her own. "Then why not take me to Dunadd with you? Right now."

Urien straightened, his eyes straining to become as wide as the circle formed by his mouth. Slowly, he began to laugh. "I would love to!" The laughter vanished. "But you know your brother would never permit it. Not until we are wed." His smile looked crafty, calculating. "Besides, I have need of your help here. To be my eyes and ears."

No surprise, that. "I am no man's hireling." She pushed away and folded her arms. "Get one of your men to be your spy."

He regarded her for a long time. "My men cannot frequent certain places that a lady can," he whispered.

"So! It's the Pict you're after."

"Keep your voice down."

"Am I right?"

Furtively, he glanced around. "If you think I love her, you are mistaken. My purposes lie along a different path." His brow furrowed. "One you would be well advised to accept without question."

His unspoken meaning carried a sinister implication that took her aback. She didn't dislike Arthur and Gyanhumara that much. Yet.

"What makes you think I would betray my brother and his wife?"

"Dear Morghe, who said anything of betrayal? Information is all I seek." Stepping closer, he wrapped his arms around her. "Anything"—Urien nuzzled the base of her neck—"that might be"—then her throat—"interesting." His mouth covered hers, and his tongue began making slow, gentle thrusts, matching the slow, gentle rubbing of his nethers against hers.

As much as she hated to, she broke contact to regard him critically.

What might he seek that only a woman could discover? Evidence of marital discord? Infidelity? What could he do with such information? Spread rumors? Foster suspicions? Turn loyalties?

This might prove to be an amusing wintertime diversion after all, and she wouldn't even have to abandon her plan to take up residence with her mother. Traveling across the firth was one thing, however. Dunadd—lying beyond threescore miles of lochs, glens, forests, and mountains—was quite another.

"Providing I agree to do this, how would I send news? Turn myself into a raven and fly to Dunadd?"

"And a lovely raven you would make, my dear." He chuckled, running his fingers through her unbound auburn hair. "Accolon will stay here with First Ala. News that can't wait for my return next spring can be entrusted to him." His gaze grew distant, unfocused. Finally, he gave a short toss of the head. "And I need your knowledge of herbal lore."

"Ha. Whom do you intend to poison?"

"That is not your concern." His narrowed eyes glittered in the moonlight. "Concoct something that will work slowly. I don't want to know what it is, so long as its effects mimic a natural illness."

She considered refusing, but Urien would only find someone else to give him what he wanted. Better to keep him in her debt. "And my payment?"

He fingered an auburn tress and inhaled its earthy-sweet scent of sea holly and lavender. "This." His lips fastened onto hers as he crushed her to him. His tongue and hips began their provocative dance again, rekindling her desire . . . and making a year and a half seem like a God-forsaken eternity. "And so much more."

PRINCE BADULF, son of King Colgrim of Bernicia, studied the slumbering Brædan village sprawled in the valley below and waited.

Being cramped behind cold boulders and winter-stripped thickets on the hillside, the night wind freezing one's ballocks and whipping the breath away—this part never made it into the songs.

Minstrels preferred the warm, soft luxury of the king's hall. Details gleaned from the war-bands therefore were sketchy in some places and embellished in others.

What of it, after all? No harm in heaping an extra measure of glory upon a warrior's name. If omitting the tedium won more young hearts into the war-bands, so much the better.

At least the flurries had blown off, though the obsidian sky portended a colder wait. Tucking his gloved hands under his armpits, Badulf returned his gaze to the sliver of moon, willing it to slip faster behind the dark breasts of the far hills.

There would be sentries to get past, of a sort, but farmers with pitchforks and scythes couldn't hope to outmatch warriors with longswords, especially Badulf's men. They'd amassed the highest cattle count of all his father's bands.

Like a timid maiden dipping her toe into a pool, a tip of the moon disappeared. Badulf sensed the growing restlessness of his men: a stifled cough, the stamp of a booted foot, the creak of leather. Nothing loud enough to betray their position, though even the best eventually wearied of waiting.

More of the moon slid from view. Badulf shed the gloves and cupped his hands to his mouth. An owl's cry drifted through the hills, answered by a gentle rustling like wind in dead leaves. He signaled again, and the men inched toward the village's cow byre.

The lone sentry, little more than a boy, slumped beside the byre's door, staff across his knees. As Badulf and his band crept closer, the lad's snores buzzed in Badulf's ears.

They'd almost reached the byre when a dog started barking. The Bræde came awake, screaming. Badulf's brain made the connection between the lad's cry of "Angli!" and the correct pronunciation, *Eingel*. Then his sword splintered the wooden staff and bit into the unprotected neck, and the warning drowned in a bubble of blood.

Too late; the village had been alerted, and the rush began.

"ANGLI! ANGLI!"

The stone-muffled cry wrenched Dwras map Gwyn from sleep. *Cattle raid!*

He didn't bother to weigh the odds of defeating a skilled fighting force in the dark, on the snow, armed with naught but farm tools and raw courage. After wrestling into tunic, breeches, cloak, and boots, he grabbed his pitchfork.

At the hut's door, he nearly collided with his wife.

Dressed in her thick woolen undertunic, Talya clutched their bawling infant son, Gwydion, to her chest. The gloom hid her face, but Dwras heard fear in her ragged breaths.

He stroked her hand, yanked her cloak from its peg by the door, and settled it about her shoulders, cursing the lack of time for words. Not about where to hide; he knew she'd try to cross the village, where the forest and safety lay a short dash beyond.

For what he wished to tell her, a swift kiss had to suffice.

With Talya pressing behind him and Gwydion's cries reduced to fitful whimpers, Dwras opened the door. An appalling clamor spilled through the slit: the clash of metal on metal, the baying of dogs, the lowing and stomping of cattle, the screams of the wounded, the whoops of the raiders. Dread and fear warred in Dwras's stomach.

The fight hadn't reached their hut. Dwras reached for Talya's hand. If she hurried, she still could make it to the forest...

An Angli warrior sprang at them. Pitchfork lowered, Dwras charged. The raider parried the blow, whirled, and lashed out with a booted foot as Dwras stumbled past. His knee buckled, and he fell.

Rolling onto his back, he watched the warrior close on Talya as she wailed for mercy.

Desperately, Dwras flung out a hand to catch the warrior's foot to trip him, distract him, anything to divert his attention from Talya. The sword descended with a sickening thud. She crumpled with a gurgling cry. Spurting crimson stained the pristine snow.

The warrior turned on him. He raised his pitchfork to block the blow. The sword splintered the shaft and bit into his shoulder. Agony branded his brain. He shut his eyes. Tears chilled his cheeks.

The raider's laughter mingled with the crunch of boots on the snow as he stalked off in search of other prey.

Dwras surrendered to oblivion.

OTHER VILLAGERS joined the fight, women as well as men. To Badulf, it mattered naught.

The cattle stomped and bellowed inside the byre. Stampede posed the biggest danger at this point in a raid. Badulf had witnessed the destruction wrought by spooked cows and had no stomach for it tonight, though not in pity for the Brædeas. Runaway cattle could be hard to capture, and often injured or killed themselves and others in the process. Too many Eingel womenfolk and children starved at home to allow such a disaster to occur.

At Badulf's command, a pair of men slipped into the byre to calm the beasts while Badulf led the others in search of Brædan survivors and provisions and anything else of value in this squalid village.

After the Eingel warriors had secured their bovine treasure and eaten their fill of dried beef and barley cakes, washing it down with tangy ale, their appetites turned to delicacies of a different sort. Badulf inspected the trembling, doe-eyed girls who'd been herded into one of the larger stone huts while their mothers and fathers and brothers and younger siblings lay stiffening under the stars. These girls, fated to become Eingel bed thralls, wouldn't be joining them for perhaps a very long time.

Baring his teeth in a grin, he selected the prettiest. As he ripped her tunic to the waist, exposing milk-white breasts, and fastened his mouth to the tender flesh, she cried out but didn't struggle. Nor did any of the others as his men cheerfully followed their leader's example.

This part never made it into the songs, either. Perhaps, Badulf mused as he unlaced his trews, bore the whimpering girl to the dirt, hitched up her skirts, and forced her legs apart, it was just as well. Some rewards ought to remain a secret. Fewer to share them with.

SHRILL CRIES and coarse laughter woke Dwras. The noises seemed confined to one place, mayhap another hut. Heaven only knew what his clanswomen were suffering at their captors' hands.

He resolved to find out.

Instinct goaded him to wariness. The cloud-shrouded night told him nothing of how long he'd lain unconscious. More raiders could be about. As he strained ears and eyes for signs of movement, he found none. Even the animals had fallen silent.

He pushed himself up, gritting his teeth and swallowing a scream. Black grief engulfed him. He couldn't help the survivors, for his right shoulder was a burning, bloody mess. But he was alive.

Talya and Gwydion, he learned to his horror as he gently turned his wife over, had perished, throats slashed.

Forgive me, dearest ones!

Dwras struggled to his feet, swiping at furious tears and fighting acrid nausea as his senses reported the surrounding carnage. All thoughts of burying his wife and son fled. If his wound didn't kill him, the first raider to find him lingering here surely would.

Chieftain Loth had to be told! If Loth would give him a spear, he, Dwras map Gwyn, gladly would use it to spit these murderers over a slow fire—though that fate seemed far too kind. For Talya and Gwydion and the others, vengeance remained the only burial gift he could bestow.

Clutching his useless arm to his chest, breaths birthing gray ghosts, he lurched toward the dun hills.

Chapter 11

Though the sun hadn't appeared, Gyan lay awake, and she didn't relish the idea of leaving the bed. She closed her eyes, fighting the uneasy feeling that it would only make matters worse.

Beside her, Arthur sat up. He leaned over and brushed her cheek with his lips. She released a small sigh designed to convince him that she was still asleep. Apparently, it worked. He eased out of bed and straightened the covers around her. She would have appreciated his thoughtfulness had she not been feeling so miserable.

Amazing the number of sounds he made as he prepared to face the day. Slower footfalls proved how hard he tried to be quiet, making her notice the long, metallic hiss against the privy pot, the swish of water in the wash basin, the rustling of linen, the muted slap of sandal leather on tile, the clink of metal.

Fervently, she wished for the sound of the door shutting behind him. As bodiless fingers clawed at her bowels, she didn't know how much longer she could hold out.

After what seemed like an eternity, he departed.

Rolling onto her back, she sucked in a few deep breaths, but they didn't help. She flung off the covers, bolted out of bed, and raced across the room.

Hunched in wretched misery over the basin, she succumbed to the attacks of the raging beast that dared to call itself her stomach. Heaves wracked her body until nothing remained. She braced against the washstand, panting. Sweat chilled her brow and matted her hair.

At least Arthur hadn't witnessed her deplorable weakness.

The door opened. A pair of soft-shod feet pattered behind her. The comforting warmth of wool settled about her shoulders, put there by hands that lingered after the cloak was in place.

"Gyan? Are you all right?"

"What do you think, Cynda? Do I look all right?" Her vehemence startled her. She straightened and turned to Cynda. "I mean, I—"

"Fret not, my dove. I understand." Displaying one of those infuriatingly knowing smiles, she guided Gyan back to the bed. "Rest here a moment, while I clean up."

"But, Cynda—"

"Ach now, my dove, first things first!"

Basin under one arm and privy pot under the other, Cynda marched from the room.

Gyan shook her head with a short laugh. Cynda had been growing more depressed in the weeks following Gyan's return to Caer Lugubalion, and it wasn't hard to guess why. At Arbroch, Cynda had overseen domestic duties such as obtaining and preparing food, cutting wood, cleaning, weaving, and sewing. At Arthur's garrison, other folk minded those tasks, leaving not even so much as a fireplace to tend. The heated floors robbed Cynda of that chore.

Yet she seemed much more like herself this morning. While fingering her mantle's folds, Gyan tried to solve the puzzle, but the answer remained tantalizingly out of reach.

Cynda bustled into the chamber bearing a pewter tray laden with oat bannocks and a steaming mug. Unwilling to trust her stomach with solid food, Gyan bypassed the bannocks in favor of the tea. She took a sip and recognized chamomile by its apple-like taste. Though masked with honey, the tea held a faint bitterness she couldn't identify.

"What's in this?" She gestured with the mug.

"Chamomile and lady's mantle. Drink it up, my dove. It's good for you." Cynda's grin widened. "And your bairn."

"My *what*?" Gyan fumbled the cup, sloshing hot liquid onto her fingers. Wincing, she sucked on them for a few moments. "No. No, you must be mistaken. I—I just have a bit of the flux."

"Oh, aye, Gyan, and I flew in here on Nemetona's chariot." She sat beside Gyan on the bed and patted her leg. "Think. When was the last time you had your courses?"

Gyan groaned. "September. A fortnight before Dafydd's installation as Abbot of St. Padraic's." Before those three idyllic days when Arthur had made love to her more often than she could remember. She railed at herself for being caught off guard, until another thought chilled her. "Cynda, my fall, and the fever—do you think . . .?" She couldn't bear to voice the rest of it.

Cynda firmly pressed on Gyan's belly in several places. "Did that hurt?" When Gyan shook her head, Cynda smiled. "You're young and strong, and so is your bairn. There's naught to fear." She regarded Gyan with a cocked eyebrow. "Why so glum, my dove? You'll have your bairn the moon past Belteine. Think what good fortune that will bring the clan!"

Children born near the fertility festival were greeted as heralds of prosperity. For the àrd-banoigin to bear a healthy child, especially a girl, was deemed the greatest blessing of all.

Arthur no doubt would be pleased, too. She'd given him the very excuse he sought to keep her off the battlefield forever.

No, he wouldn't do that to her. Would he?

Queasiness gripped her belly that had naught to do with the bairn.

As she gazed at the table upon which her sword and sword belt lay, depression cloaked her heart. Was the task for which she'd so diligently trained her body doomed to such a short duration?

"Gyan?"

"Yes, Cynda. It will be a boon." She managed a slim smile. "For the clan."

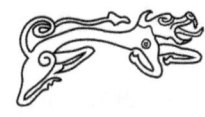

ARTHUR DREADED winter's mind-numbing boredom.

Yet this winter—coming on the heels of an enemy invasion, a

close brush with civil war, a wedding, and an accident that could have claimed the life of his bride—he welcomed. Time now to mend weapons, heal wounds, gather supplies and information on enemies, rest and regroup, and plan the upcoming campaign.

Except there would be no campaign this spring.

In one sense, this gladdened him. A year without the threat of war would imply he'd journeyed that much closer to his goal of establishing a lasting peace for his countrymen and their allies.

Peace came with a price, however, that he wasn't sure he could afford.

He pushed away from the table and stalked to the window. Hands clasped behind his back, he studied the frost-laden pines.

"What's this? Tired of reviewing scouting reports?"

Arthur pivoted to find Merlin regarding him from the doorway, arms folded and amusement playing across his craggy face.

"No," he replied quietly, returning to the frozen scene.

In the courtyard, a wagon pulled up to deliver supplies. Because of the cold, the praetorium guards helped the driver unload the crates and carry them inside. Though in the strictest sense this represented dereliction of duty, Arthur approved their initiative. These men and thousands more soon might be officially charged with such mundane tasks.

Merlin's footsteps echoed off the tiles as he joined Arthur at the window and laid a hand upon his shoulder.

"What is it, lad?"

Arthur sighed. "There won't be a campaign next season."

"Ah." The hand withdrew. "This is not good?" Merlin's question bordered on a rebuke, for he had drilled into Arthur the concept that peace was to be prized above all else.

"Of course it is." Merlin had played the role of Arthur's conscience too many times for Arthur to begrudge him that privilege now. "It would give me more time to build and train my forces. Fortify positions. Collect information on enemy defenses and activities." He faced Merlin, feeling a half-smile form. "And heaven knows the common folk wouldn't mind if the men devoted more time to road repair."

A smile flickered across Merlin's face. "And the drawbacks?"

Arthur couldn't dispel the impression of being a pupil again as he replied, "Boredom among the troops, for one." Ditch digging and drills couldn't begin to compete with battle for excitement and profit.

In peacetime, lust for action often expressed itself in brawling, which only profited the winning gamblers—if they didn't get caught.

Whether Merlin agreed or not, Arthur had no idea, for he'd turned back to the window. The outrageously expensive thick-paned glass let in the sunlight while blocking much of the cold. Nor did it obscure the view, although little existed beyond the endless stretches of white. The sense of being trapped began to clutch at his heart.

"What concerns me more, Merlin, is how the council will react."

Like his uncle and Merlin's father, Ambrosius, the first council-ratified Dux Britanniarum, Arthur possessed free rein to command the legion in Brydein's defense but had to seek council permission to initiate any offensive action.

Ambrosius's private writings revealed that he'd had to continually shore up the chieftains' supply agreements by means ranging from the currying of favor to intimidation and blackmail. Such a situation hadn't befallen Arthur... yet. But he held no illusions that it wouldn't.

His position remained secure only as long as enemy threats continued to exist, and as long as he kept winning. He despised the fact that the Council of Chieftains had him by the ballocks. Idle talk surfaced from time to time about abolishing the Pendragonship and disbanding the legion. Such words had a nasty habit of becoming reality, especially with adversaries like Urien of Dalriada, once he became Chieftain of Clan Moray, to champion the cause.

Disbanding the standing army would be a suicidal move even if peace promised to stretch into years, but Arthur couldn't tell the chieftains this. If the council so willed it, there wasn't a bloody thing he could do.

He glanced at his cousin, mentor, and friend. Merlin raised his eyebrows, but before he could speak, Arthur's aide burst into the room.

"Lord Pendragon, a messenger has arrived. From Chieftain Loth."

"Loth?" The husband of his eldest half sister was the last man Arthur had expected to hear from. What could Loth possibly want, unless... "Send him in."

Marcus ushered the man into the workroom. The messenger's skin had grayed from fatigue, hunger, and cold. Shadows circled his eyes. Muddy streaks marred his leggings, tunic, and cloak, even his hair. Arthur guessed he'd made the four-day ride in two.

"My lord, five Lothian villages have fallen to Angli raiders. More attacks are feared." The steadiness of the messenger's voice sharply contrasted his apparent physical discomfort. "Chieftain Loth requests your assistance to defend the remaining villages."

Angli raiders: Colgrim's men, no doubt. The man behind the taking of Dun Eidyn and the death of Arthur's father had stirred at last, just as Gyan had predicted half a year ago.

Conflicting emotions warred for control of Arthur's heart as he ground his knuckles into the opposite palm. A thirst for revenge flared. Because that thirst had lain dormant while he regrouped from the devastating loss at Dun Eidyn to rebuild his forces, now it smote him with vehement intensity.

Revenge was never a valid motive for military action, however, and he fought hard to suppress it.

Besides, to rouse even a few of his men from their much-deserved winter rest . . . yet the fiercely proud and self-sufficient Loth had asked for help, shouting volumes about the situation's direness. Arthur couldn't let this latest Angli outrage go unpunished.

To Marcus, Arthur said, "Get this man cleaned up and fed. Give him a bed for tonight and a fresh horse for tomorrow." Recalling the cavalry games after the wedding, he asked, "How many of Sixth Ala are in residence?"

Marcus's eyebrows lowered, and his eyes seemed to focus on a point beyond Arthur's shoulder momentarily. "Three turmae, sir."

About forty men had chosen to return to their homelands for the winter, Arthur mused, stroking his chin. No surprise there. "Assign two turmae to the Sixth to fill it out, and order the ala to pack their gear." As Marcus nodded and began to turn, Arthur briefly held up his index finger. "One of the assignees is to be infantryman Gawain map Loth."

Considering the family's history, Arthur suspected that his nephew would view the return to his birthplace as a mixed blessing, but no man with any level of equestrian ability turned down a transfer to the cavalry, and Gawain's horsemanship was better than most.

"You have a message for me to take back to Chieftain Loth, Lord Pendragon?" Weariness weighted the messenger's every syllable.

"No need. You shall ride with me and my men." Arthur clapped the drooping shoulder. "You have served Chieftain Loth well. Eat and rest. We leave at dawn."

After executing a surprisingly crisp salute, the messenger turned and followed Marcus from the workroom.

Arthur faced Merlin. "No peace this year, either."

The more he thought about the chance to avenge his father's death, the better he liked it. For Merlin's sake, however, he resisted the temptation to quip that Colgrim had penned his own execution order.

LIGHT SNOW spun out of the sky with no sign of quitting. Gyan raised the hood of her dark blue traveling cloak. Macmuir blew a riff as though in disgust, and she patted his neck. She could hardly blame the animal.

She studied her sword as it bounced against Macmuir's shoulder. The sapphire in Braonshaffir's pommel winked in the snow-dulled light. She held little hope of being able to use it anytime soon. The Angalaranach raiders probably sat safe and snug in their feast halls, gorging themselves on stolen cattle.

The child dwelling inside her would render participation in the coming summer's campaign quite impossible.

As àrd-banoigin, she held the honor of ensuring Clan Argyll's future leadership. The portion of her heart that remained loyal to Caledonach tradition looked forward to fulfilling this obligation. But having just begun to discover her way as a warrior and leader of warriors, playing a different but no less important role in ensuring her clan's future, she didn't feel ready to have these activities curtailed by motherhood.

The snowfall intensified, causing Macmuir to snort and shake his head vigorously, as if echoing her private disagreement with herself.

Female by decree of the One God, she followed the warrior's path by choice. She'd already won her first battle trophy. Death was no stranger to her. Neither was the prospect of being killed in battle. Embracing this destiny made the risks easier to accept.

Hymar had died to give Gyan life. To be brutally honest, the possibility of falling victim to her mother's fate terrified her as no legion of enemy soldiers ever could.

The realization startled her, and she inadvertently sawed on the reins. Before the pause disrupted the rest of the column, she kicked Macmuir into a walk again and shot her consort an apologetic grin.

Arthur didn't know that he would be a father before high summer. Defying the cold, he sat tall in the saddle, his cloak a scarlet blaze across Macsen's creamy flanks. This close to Angalaranach territory, he rode in alert silence. His azure gaze seemed to bore through the oak and pine trunks in search of the enemy.

Any war-band attempting to ambush a mounted unit a hundred strong would have to be not only very brave, but very foolish.

He broke his vigil to smile at her. She returned it, hoping the bairn wouldn't change the way she felt about him. Yet even as the thought formed, she had to wonder whether it was a vain one.

Perhaps she should have trusted him to believe that other than the wretched dawns, she felt as strong as ever, but she hadn't wanted to risk missing what could be her last combat opportunity for years.

The truth would have to be announced soon, though. The challenge of hiding her bairn-sickness had intensified, since she couldn't remain abed. She'd developed the habit of rising earlier than her consort to allow her body to purge itself in secret. This morning, he'd discovered her, and she shrugged it off as a reaction to the traveling. Her belly's size hadn't betrayed her yet, but that wouldn't last much longer. Nor would Arthur be fooled by loose robes and vague excuses. She was mildly surprised that he hadn't guessed already.

His smile took on that enigmatic tint. Perhaps he had guessed and was waiting for her to speak. She flirted with the idea and rejected it, vowing to select a more private moment.

Another ridge loomed, skirted by the pine-shaded track. Arthur signaled the command to head for the ridge crest. At the top of the hill, he raised a gloved hand to halt the column. As the ala spurred their mounts to the summit, he and Gyan surveyed the valley.

A Breatanach village sprawled silently below them. Although the snow still floated down, the village should have been vibrant with the sounds of axes on wood, women chatting, and the laughter of children at play. Cattle lowing, donkeys braying, chickens cackling, sheep bleating, dogs barking—all of it, missing. Even the wind had died.

Uneasiness writhed in Gyan's gut.

At Arthur's signal, the warriors of the Sixth Ala of the Horse Cohort of the Dragon Legion of Breatein cantered into the village. Upon reaching the outer ring of huts and pens, the unit divided into turmae to quicken the search.

While Arthur and the others rode off to inspect different areas, Gyan circled with Angusel and the rest of her men to the far side of the village. The snow-covered lumps that had looked like tree stumps from the hilltop revealed their identities. She halted her troop before a cluster of huts and dismounted for a closer look.

Upon dusting the snow from the nearest mound, Gyan discovered two frozen corpses that had been savaged by animals. Enough remained to identify them as a woman clutching a baby to her bosom, both with their throats slashed. Though she'd been dead more than a sennight, the cold had preserved the terror on the woman's face. The infant had died in innocent ignorance.

Pressing a hand to the bronze dragon guarding her belly, Gyan staggered away and slipped around a corner. She leaned against the cold, rough stone wall of a hut, gulping air to fight the nausea.

"Gyan, what's wrong?" Angusel gripped her shoulder.

"Leave me alone, Angus." Doubled over and losing her battle, she swatted feebly at his hand. "Please."

His receding footsteps bespoke his obedience. The remnants of her bannocks and tea burned through the snow to form a steaming puddle between her feet. She closed her eyes to blot out the carnage and failed. Her stomach began churning again.

"Gyan?"

As an arm settled across her shoulders, she turned. "You! This is all your fault!"

She used Arthur's surprise to duck past him and strode toward her horse. He caught her hand.

"What in God's name do you mean?" He glanced at their surroundings.

"Not the village, you idiot." The bile rose again. Grimacing, she spat it out. "Haven't you ever seen a woman with child?"

"Son, I'm getting old." Dumarec lifted his wine goblet with a trembling hand. "See? My body betrays me."

Urien knew what troubled his father, and it had little to do with old age. "Nonsense, Father." He hoped his smile conveyed only deepest filial devotion. "You'll lead the war-band for many years yet." He took a long pull from his ale horn to hide his smirk.

They sat at the table on the dais in Dunadd's feast hall. Their clansmen packed the lower tables, gorging themselves on pork and ale and flirting with the women who served them. A few warriors engaged in arm-wrestling bouts, and the shouts and laughter emanating from one corner announced a game of dice. Aneirin sat in his place of honor beside the hearth, softly plucking his harp. A typical winter picture for Clan Moray, but for Urien it lacked one crucial, green-eyed, flame-haired detail.

Dumarec's goblet hit the table with a dull thump, commanding his son's attention. "Lead the war-band? Against whom?" He snorted. "With the Picts as our allies—"

"You forget the Scots, Father."

The chieftain reached for a rib and with yellowed teeth stripped off the meat. "I forget nothing." He waved the denuded bone in Urien's face. "After the thrashing you and Arthur gave them, we won't be seeing their filthy faces for another five years at least."

True, Urien had to admit.

Dumarec tossed the bone over his shoulder, prompting a canine brawl. "Aneirin! Quit fondling that harp like a lover and give us a good lay!" To the chorus of warriors' guffaws, Dumarec settled into his tall-backed chair, a grin painted into the creases of his face.

Enjoy your jests while you can, Father.

Nodding toward the high table, the bard rose. Wood rasped against stone as several men shoved tables out of the way to create room for the performance. Aneirin pointed to a bench, and a servant moved it into the cleared area. Smiling brightly, a woman handed him a brimming wine goblet. He took a swallow and set it upon the bench.

"What is your pleasure this evening, Chieftain Dumarec?" Though the young man didn't shout, his clear tones reverberated throughout the timbered hall. Urien's envy rose. With a voice like that, Aneirin would have been a tremendous asset on the battlefield.

"Something to warm the blood, I think." Dumarec suppressed a shiver. When Urien's mother stepped forward to lay his cloak across his shoulders, he shrugged her away like an ill-tempered falcon.

Aneirin smiled and bowed. "For your blood, then, my lord." Lifting his foot to the bench and setting the harp on his thigh, he bent to his work.

From the first series of chords, Urien knew which song the bard had selected. The images flooded back in painful detail.

As Aneirin caroled the glories of Urien's charge against the Scotti invaders, Urien experienced anew his frustration. His battlefield brilliance had been fired by rage that Arthur had stolen what had belonged to Urien by right of treaty.

Not true. The whore had gone to Arthur willingly.

He studied the blue tattoo encircling his left wrist, hatred surging with each heartbeat. Gyanhumara's wrist bore an identical mark, but a rampant dragon covered the rest of her forearm where there should have been a boar.

The bard sang Urien's praises, but the heir of Clan Moray knew the bitter truth. If not for the arrival of Arthur's reinforcements, this song would have been Urien's dirge. Gyanhumara wouldn't have survived, either, and that thought gave him a measure of satisfaction.

The Scots had devised a clever invasion plan but failed to consider the likelihood of Arthur's swift response. To a man, they'd paid for this mistake. Arthur's Roman blood and training made him thorough in matters of war. In all matters, curse his black soul.

Urien took another pull of ale. Perhaps Dumarec wouldn't see the Scots in battle again, but his heir had conceived plans that didn't involve fighting the men from Hibernia.

With thumb and forefinger, he stroked the leather headband hiding his scar.

Dumarec, swaying snakelike to the music's rhythm, collapsed into a coughing fit. While others scurried to help, Urien eased deeper into his chair, ale horn in hand, his lips twitching into a faint smile.

His plans were budding nicely, thanks to his future wife's impressive knowledge of herbal lore. Quite nicely, indeed.

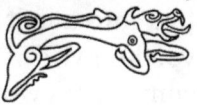

EFFORTS TO bury the villagers had to cease as a snowstorm blustered over the hills. Arthur and Gyan appropriated a hut for themselves; their soldiers occupied the remaining buildings.

Under normal circumstances, Arthur wouldn't have minded bedding down with his men. In fact, he would have preferred it, but his wife's presence hardly could be considered normal.

As she knelt beside their saddle packs, questing for rations, he wrestled with his thoughts. Initially, he hadn't been troubled by loving a warrior-woman. Their separation had been hell, but he'd assumed that once it ended, all would be set to rights.

So much for assumptions.

He didn't doubt her abilities as a warrior or leader. Her handling of the men had experienced a rocky start on Maun, but at headquarters, she'd seemed more in her element. Under her firm but fair influence, tensions between the Brytoni and Caledonian troops had begun to recede.

However, volunteering to risk herself in combat was one thing. Jeopardizing the life of her unborn child—and his—was quite another.

She unwrapped barley bannocks and dried beef strips, took a portion, and passed the rest to him, along with a measure of wine in his upturned helmet. The necessity for speed had precluded bringing the usual amenities.

He set the food on the hut's only surface elevated above the dirt and cobwebs, a squat table. After he downed the wine, the helmet followed. One of the table's legs, noticeably shorter, threatened to dump everything on the floor. He sacrificed a bannock, wedging it under the short leg to avoid disaster.

But he couldn't avoid the topic suspended between them like a drawn sword.

"Why didn't you tell me about the baby before we left?"

"So you could treat me like a broken piece of battle-gear?"

"That's unfair, Gyan."

She left her uneaten supper on the table, paced to the hearth, and whirled to face him. The fire at her back put her face in shadow, but he knew the heat of her glare. He parried it with his.

"Is it?" Her voice dropped into a half whisper. "Would you have brought me with you, had you known?"

Only in the direst of circumstances would he ever order a wounded man to fight. All other considerations aside, she was one of his soldiers. Yet he also had vowed never to be parted from her.

He shrugged under the burden of truth. "Probably not."

"Ha!" She faced the fire. "I suspected as much."

"Gyan—"

"I do not need your excuses." The flames popped and sizzled and belched smoke, as though goaded by her words.

He crossed to her side, grasped her arms, and spun her around.

"By God's holy wounds, woman, don't you know that I care for you more than life itself? What if we encounter Angli raiders while we're still miles from Dunpeldyr?"

Incredulity froze her face. "*What?* Is the mighty Pendragon worried about that diseased, heathen rabble?"

"I'm worried about you!"

"Bring them on!" She shrugged out of his grip and slapped her bronze scabbard. "Braonshaffir craves the taste of enemy blood."

"You would risk our child—"

"I am a warrior first. The bairn hasn't changed that." Again she reverted to that low, dangerous tone. "Are you suggesting otherwise?"

Am I? Should I?

He waded through memories of tales to a mist-shrouded time before his mother's people had settled the Island of the Mighty, when they'd clashed with the ancestors of his father in the lands beyond the Narrow Sea. Greek and Roman writers had reported the strength and ferocity of these barbarian women, who fought alongside their husbands.

Presumably, these women had had children, too.

Who was he to gainsay his wife, an adept warrior?

"I'm not suggesting anything of the kind, Gyan." A smile lit her face. "I just hate seeing you hurt. Or sick."

The smile vanished. "I am not sick."

"Then what do you call what happened at daybreak? Or later, when we first got here?"

"It comes with the territory."

"I may not be privy to the secrets of womanhood, but I suspect what happened outside the hut had nothing to do with your child."

She folded her arms and looked down. Her prolonged silence heralded a private battle he couldn't help her with no matter how much he wished to.

"In a way, it does," she said quietly.

"What do you mean?"

She uncrossed her arms and slumped against his chest. He circled his arms around her and ran his fingers through her long, silken hair.

"Seeing that baby..." she whispered, shuddering, into the folds of his tunic. "I kept imagining it was my child."

Her child—their child. Accustomed to ending life, creating it filled him with unending awe. He lifted her chin to kiss his warrior, his wife, and the mother of his son. Their son. "I won't let that happen to our son."

She sighed and moved away. Seated cross-legged on the thin straw pallet they had spread before the hearth, she propped chin on fist and stared toward the leaping golden flames. "I almost wish it will be a boy-child."

A gust of wind howled down the chimney, toying with the fire. He fed it another lump of peat and joined her on the pallet. He put an arm around her shoulders, and she leaned against him. "Does it matter so much?"

"Bearing a girl-child first portends good fortune for the clan." Drawing her knees up, she sighed again. "I was Hymar's second bairn."

Arthur knew Caledonians traced descent through the mother, and their women shared in clan rule. This differed from Brytoni tradition, wherein children bore their father's name and women rarely ruled. Beyond that, he could cite few customs of his wife's people and knew little of their language—lacks he needed to remedy.

"Peredur's birth couldn't have brought bad fortune to Argyll."

She shrugged. "That year's harvest was lean."

"And when you were born?"

"I killed my mother." She stopped his protest with an upraised hand. "When she took my father as consort, the priests foretold that a girl-child would be born to them, a child that would be her death. No specifics were mentioned, but when Hymar learned that her confinement would occur at Samhainn, she knew she hadn't long to live."

"Why?"

"Caledonians believe that a kinsman—or woman—of a child born at Samhainn shall die within the coming year..." She trembled, and he hugged her closer. "It's all too often true."

No provision in Arthur's Christian upbringing allowed him to believe such a superstition. Not wishing to belittle the beliefs of Gyan's people, however, he pursued the topic closest to his heart. "What of our child if it's a boy?"

"By Caledonian law, the children of the àrd-banoigin must be raised at her clan seat. If this bairn is a boy, my father can see to his rearing and training. It is not a common practice, but the law permits it." She glanced down at her belly, as if trying to glimpse the child, before staring at the fire.

Not a common Brytoni practice, either, but sometimes dictated by necessity. Arthur wondered what his childhood would have been like under his mother's influence. Yet he also found himself imagining how Ygraine might have felt, forced to give up her infant son with no assurance that she would ever see him alive again.

He whispered, "Would you be able to do such a thing, Gyan?"

"I—" Her neck and shoulders tensed. "I think so. If I must."

"And if we have a girl?"

"If it's a girl, I must stay at Arbroch with her until she reaches womanhood."

Though no louder than the patter of a summer evening shower, her words struck him with the force of a thunderclap. Arbroch lay well north of the Antonine Wall, a day's ride from the nearest navigable firth, to say nothing of the dearth of good Roman roads. The Brytoni border wouldn't be close enough to satisfy the council, making the prospect of moving legion headquarters to Arbroch political as well as military suicide.

How in heaven's name could he honor his vow—his heart's fervent desire—to stay with his wife if her people's laws barred his way?

No answers swam in the swirl of smoke and flame. She leaned her head against his shoulder, breathing a sigh. Arthur lowered his hand to rest lightly upon her belly, where his child grew. Their child.

God willing, their son.

Chapter 12

LOTH PACED THE rush-strewn flagstones of his family's living quarters. His sharp oaths punctuated the fading afternoon, the subjects cycling between the raw weather, the Angli, and his brother-by-marriage.

Annamar glanced up. "Patience, my husband. It's been only a week and a day since your messenger left. Any number of things can delay travel at this time of year." She refrained from mentioning that some delays could well become permanent.

This sparked a fresh round of curses against the snow. Sighing, she gazed at their daughter, Cundre. Sated at last, the baby had begun to drift into milky slumber. Annamar shifted Cundre to the other side and adjusted a fold of the floor-length amber tunic to cover the feeding slit, then wrapped her in the lamb's-wool blanket and settled her into the cradle. Cundre did not wake.

Medraut, almost four, wandered over from his game of sticks and stones. Smiling, Annamar let him control the cradle. It always amazed her how gently he treated his newborn sister.

Eleven-year-old Gareth doubtless could be found where most boys his age liked to be: in the kennels, the stables, or the mews.

The eldest of Loth's brood though no longer his heir, Gawain, lived much farther away. The latest news had mentioned a battle on the Isle of Maun. Arthur had spoken of Gawain's fighting prowess with highest praise and assured her that her son hadn't been seriously wounded, but it did little to salve her worry.

The baby woke with a cry, as if echoing her mother's distress. Medraut pushed the cradle harder. Cundre's whimpers grew into lusty wails. Annamar laid a firm hand on the cradle's edge.

Medraut cast his gaze around the room and with a delighted squeal toddled toward Brigid, a deerhound bitch, who lay sprawled in the fire's glow. Tangling stubby fingers in her black coat, he tried to interest her in a wrestling match. Brigid suffered the boy's attentions with silent canine patience. Medraut gave up to pillow his head on a shaggy flank. Brigid's sigh sounded decidedly relieved.

As Annamar bent to pick up Cundre, the tresses bequeathed to her by her father, Gorlas, swept down in a chestnut curtain. She lingered over her daughter, composing herself. Loth hated displays of weakness, especially over the young man he refused to acknowledge as his firstborn son.

"Dash it, he must come," Loth muttered. "No telling where those Angli bastards will strike next. Or when."

"If Arthur can help, he will."

With Cundre burped and quietly nestled against her shoulder, Annamar glided to her husband's side. His face looked ruddier than usual in the firelight, and she wondered when the worry lines had furrowed so deeply. Her free arm wrapped around his waist, and she leaned her cheek against his broad chest. He returned the embrace with a fiercely possessive hug.

"He'd better, if the council's agreement means anything to him."

The door crashed open, and Gareth hurtled into the room. Arms windmilling in exuberant haste, he slid to a stop in front of his parents. His rumpled tunic and breeches reeked of the stables, and his face radiated joy.

Annamar gazed at her son with amused affection.

Loth scowled. "I trust you have a good excuse for bursting in here like this."

Gareth squared his shoulders, but the excitement splashed across his face didn't ebb. "Sir, the hunting party is back!"

Medraut joined the group and fastened his short arms about Gareth's legs, happily oblivious to the horsy smell. Grinning, Gareth dropped a hand to ruffle his brother's shock of pale blond hair.

Loth cleared his throat. "And?"

"They found a cavalry troop at one of the raided villages this morning. The horsemen were digging graves for the dead."

"I'd rather they put their backs to better use," Loth grumbled. "Who's their leader?"

Gareth's grin widened. "Uncle Arthur!"

Annamar shot her husband a didn't-I-tell-you glance, but he paid no heed. "Hmph. I gather Arthur's troop didn't come in with our hunting party. Why?"

"Sir, they—" The abrupt clamor of activity outside overpowered their son's words.

Loth strode to the window, shoved out the shutter, and looked down. "Arthur and his men are here. Anna, see that they are shown our best hospitality." From the back of a chair he snatched his clan mantle, a forest-green cloak woven with crossing strands of dark blue and gold by Annamar's own hands. He flung it across his shoulders and pinned it with his gold Lothian Bear brooch without breaking stride. "Son, attend me." He disappeared into the corridor before anyone else had twitched a muscle.

As Gareth moved to follow, Annamar caught his wrist. "Find yourself a clean tunic and trews first." Nodding, Gareth tried to pull away, but Annamar held him fast. "Is Gawain here?"

"I didn't ask, Mother. He's infantry, remember?"

"I just thought that mayhap . . ." She released Gareth with a sigh, and he ran toward the sleeping chamber he shared with his younger brother.

Annamar laid Cundre in the cradle and crossed to the window. The courtyard teemed with horses and men, with more arriving by the minute. *Lord, have mercy! Feeding and sheltering all these guests, and with no notice! Thank God for the huntsmen. Perhaps they'd taken several stags.* Although Dunpeldyr had enough fresh meat for a few days, a prolonged stay would seriously strain the stores.

To say nothing of tempers.

Mentally reviewing the list of bedding and other supplies Arthur's men would need, she studied the activity. Loth and Arthur stood talking in the center of the courtyard while the cavalrymen eddied around them, dismounting and leading horses to the stables. Including... Gawain! Thank God. More or less. Loth turned pointedly away as his son and mount passed by. Annamar shook her head but dispelled her irritation to wave cheerfully when Gawain glanced up at her window. Even at this distance, she saw sadness and regret dampen his answering smile. Her heart ached for him. For Loth, too.

As Gawain moved from view, another figure joined the brothers-by-marriage, wearing a cloak of midnight blue over leather-and-bronze armor. The warrior removed the helmet and shook loose long coppery braids in a decidedly feminine gesture. The way her hand lingered at her belly as she brushed dried mud from her sword belt spoke its own story.

So. Arthur had brought his bride... and his unborn child.

Annamar felt her lips slowly curl into a smile as she speculated about how Loth was handling this turn of events.

"Women!" Loth snapped. "This is no operation for women!"

Gyan laid a hand on Arthur's forearm as he readied a retort. "Chieftain Loth, perhaps you haven't heard. Dunpeldyr is, after all, a wee bit removed from events." As Loth spluttered an impotent protest, Arthur suppressed a laugh. She continued, "I defeated the Scotti invasion commander in single combat."

"Gyan, you're being too modest." Arthur captured Loth's gaze. "By that one act, she probably prevented scores more casualties on both sides. My wife is fully capable of holding her own against Angli cattle thieves." Arthur hoped she understood how deeply he meant it.

"Hmph. Let's get out of this blasted snow and into my private council chambers, Arthur, where we can continue our discussion in comfort. Gyanhumara, my wife should be down shortly to conduct you to the guest chambers."

"Gyanhumara comes with us."

"Are you mad, Arthur? Are all the affairs of men to become women's work?"

"I respect my wife's judgment." He sharpened his tone. "I suggest you do the same."

The two men glared at each other. Being much shorter put Loth at a disadvantage. He relented, but not at the sacrifice of his pride. As the chieftain whirled, his cloak flared behind him.

"Follow me." He didn't look back. "Both of you."

Arthur and Gyan exchanged amused glances as they started after their brother-by-marriage.

"Is he always like this?" she whispered.

Arthur shook his head. "I think Loth fears the Angli threat has grown beyond his control." Gazing at nothing in particular, he saw only the bodies of murdered Brytoni villagers. So much waste of life, and for what? A few head of beef that could have been purchased for a fair price, had Brytoni-Angli relations rested on better footing. Small chance of that ever happening now. "He may be right."

Hammering footfalls drew his attention. Gareth came pelting down the colonnade, his Lothian-patterned cloak streaming behind him like a green wing.

"About time you got here." Loth gave his son a stern appraisal. "Your mother had you clean up, I see. Good. We don't need the council chambers smelling like a midden."

By this time, Arthur and Gyan had caught up with Loth and his son. Mischief gathered on Gyan's face. "So, Loth, are the affairs of adults to become children's work?" she said with a teasing grin.

"Permit me to remind you, Chieftainess, that as my heir, Gareth has as much right to be present as you do." The stare he fixed on her was frostier than the snow underfoot. "Perhaps even more so."

Arthur wondered what she'd choose for her verbal parry but never found out. Anna approached them from across the inner courtyard.

"My husband, where are your manners? Keeping our kin out in the cold." She embraced Arthur and gave Gyan a warm handclasp. "Well come, both of you. If Loth hasn't the grace to thank you for arriving so quickly, I will. We appreciate it very much."

"Aye." Reluctance and gratitude warred in Loth's tone. "We do."

As the sky spat more snow, Anna fussed with her cloak to shake off the flakes. "Let's get inside before we all catch our deaths!"

THE PRIVATE council chambers of the Chieftain of Clan Lùthean easily could have been mistaken for an armory. A legion of swords, war-knives, hammers, axes, pikes, spears, and javelins marched across the timber-ribbed stone walls. The oil lamps illuminated shields of various sizes and designs: the chest-high, oval, leather-bound oaken style favored by Caledonaich; the curved, shoulder-high, rectangular tin Ròmanach infantry type; and the small, round, ashwood version with its wickedly sharp bronze boss, which Gyan recognized from Arthur's scouting reports as a Sasunach design. Of the many others, their origins she could only guess.

Enshrined over the hearth, which housed an inferno that roared like a raging dragon, hung a weapon whose owner had to be the chieftain himself. Subordinate only to Braonshaffir in beauty and Caleberyllus in length, this double-bladed sword boasted a pommel inlaid with polished amber. Had she not possessed such a magnificent weapon, her heart would have been ablaze with envy.

Servants scurried everywhere, carrying pitchers of wine and uisge, bearing platters heaped with fragrant beef and bread, moving the massive oak table to the center of the room, arranging chairs around it, filling and lighting the lamps, securing the window-coverings, prodding the fire.

A wonder they didn't collide.

Like a rock in a wind-whipped sea stood Loth's wife to direct the work. When they finished, she herded the servants from the room. On her way past Gareth, she paused to bestow a kiss on his brow. The lad bore it with a half-pleased, half-disgusted look.

"Loth, send Gareth to bed if he gets sleepy. Don't forget about him."

Absorbed in the task of spreading a large hide map across the table, the chieftain grunted.

As Gyan stepped toward the table, Annamar caught her hand. The steadiness of the older woman's gaze was much like Arthur's yet softer, as though worn by the march of years.

"Your sleeping quarters will be ready soon, Gyanhumara. Any of the servants can conduct you there, if you decide to retire early." Annamar's smile reminded Gyan of the absent Cynda.

Loth's wife glided from the chambers. The double doors swung to with a resounding thump. Gyan spent several moments staring at the ornately enameled Lùthean Bears that appeared to growl at each another from opposite doors.

Could her sister-by-law have guessed about her bairn? Would

this jeopardize Gyan's already tenuous relationship with Loth? Affect the outcome of this mission and her participation in it?

"Gyan?" Arthur's voice carried across the chamber. "Joining us?"

Warding off her uneasiness with a toss of her braids, she strode briskly to her consort's side.

Loth didn't look up at her approach. "My people were hit here." With a quill dripping crimson ink, he marked five *X*s on the map, each a day's ride from the nearest Angalaranach settlement.

"Have you retaliated?" Arthur asked.

"Not yet." Loth tapped the map with the quill's gray-feathered tip. "They left only one survivor, which is why I found out when I did. The bastards probably were too drunk to realize their mistake."

"Then we must capitalize on it." Arthur's tone blew as cold as the snow-chilled winds rattling the windows' shutters.

"Aye! Then you'll help me hunt them down?"

"Certainly. This spring, after—"

"But—"

Arthur silenced Loth with a glare. "After the troops return, and supplies are replenished, and the roads and tracks are passable again. Not one day sooner. A winter campaign with a third of the legion is suicide."

"To the devil with risk, Arthur!" Loth smashed his fist to the tabletop. The goblets rocked, slopping wine. "Those murdering Angli thieves must be punished!" He gave Arthur a pointed look. "I'd have expected you to be the first in line."

It seemed an odd comment until Gyan recalled that Arthur's father had died fighting the Angalaranaich. She tried to divine her consort's thoughts. Sorrow, perhaps, or revenge? Impossible to tell. His face may as well have been chiseled in granite.

"They will be punished, Loth." Arthur gave a solemn nod. "You have my word."

"I don't want your bloody word." Loth's lip curled into a snarl. "I want results!"

"Gentlemen, please." Gyan held up her hands. "Our task is to solve problems. Not to create new ones." With their full attention, she forged on. "Loth, you are concerned that more villages will be raided this winter?"

"Aye," he muttered.

She faced her consort. "Arthur, you need time to devise and implement a detailed campaign plan, correct?" He nodded. "Then I propose we take some of our men, dress them as villagers, and send them to defend the villages standing in the greatest danger."

"Impossible!" Loth made a dismissive gesture. "It can't work."

"Why not?" Arthur grinned at Gyan. "It's an excellent plan."

"Too hard to implement," declared Loth. "An influx of men would be noticed. The Angles are probably watching the other villages."

Arthur said, "We can send in the men under cover of darkness, perhaps during a new moon."

"Or during a snowstorm," Gyan suggested. "Even the hardiest spies must take cover from the weather."

"Very well. Let's assume we can get them into the villages unnoticed. We're talking—what? A dozen men per village? A score?" Loth's eyes issued a glittering challenge. "In a village of a hundred, how long do you think these men will stay unnoticed?"

Arthur parried Loth's glare. "If we time their arrival with a snowstorm, they could easily be taken for travelers or huntsmen seeking emergency shelter."

"They'd have to be well provisioned. I will not impose undue hardship on my people."

"God's wounds, Loth!" Gyan glanced at Arthur, surprised by his outburst. He clenched his jaw. "Every element of this plan can be worked out to everyone's satisfaction."

"Hmph. It would never fool the Angles." Loth shook his head. "Doesn't matter what manner of trappings you hang on a warrior, you can always spot one a mile off. But the point is moot, Arthur. Most of the men you brought are Picts."

"They are men!" Gyan fought down a surge of battle frenzy as she rounded on Loth. To her satisfaction, he backed up a pace. "Fine, honorable *Caledonian* men who have learned to speak your tongue."

Loth's gaze didn't waver. "I meant no offense, Chieftainess."

She let her crossed arms and arched eyebrow answer for her.

"I think Uncle Arthur is right. It's a great plan, Father!"

Loth whirled toward his son. "My own flesh turns against me, eh?"

Wide-eyed, Gareth shrank back. Gyan laid a reassuring hand on his shoulder. He whipped his head around. Recognition spread across his face, and he relaxed visibly. She gave him a brief smile.

"Your flesh, Loth," and she sharpened her words to sting like icy needles, "possesses a good deal more sense than you do."

She spun and strode toward the door. Neither Loth nor Arthur moved to stop her. It would have mattered naught had they tried.

GARETH RACED ahead to open the doors and followed Gyan from Loth's council chambers.

In the corridor, she stopped to take her first real measure of this sister-son-by-law. Gareth favored his father and older brother in coloring, with dark brown hair and eyes and a hale complexion. But his lean limbs and boat-size feet promised greater height. Like most boys his age, his freckled face held no trace of guile. The glimmer of intelligence provided a welcome antidote to Loth's attitude.

"Gareth, can you please show me to my quarters?"

"Aye." He trotted down the corridor without checking to see whether she kept up. "This way!"

Chuckling softly, she lengthened her stride.

The torchlit passage was deserted, and no sounds emanated from within the rooms they passed. Gyan gave voice to her curiosity.

"This wing is for special guests. You and Uncle Arthur are the only ones at Dunpeldyr right now."

"Gawain and the rest of our men? Where are they sleeping?"

"With the clan warriors in the Great Hall." Gyan wondered how they could find space without resting their heads upon one another. As if reading her thoughts, Gareth added, "There's plenty of room."

His assurance satisfied her. The last thing she and Arthur needed was discord between their men and Loth's.

Gareth halted before a door. It yielded to his push, revealing a comfortably large set of rooms. Her saddle packs and Arthur's slouched between a worktable and a pair of tall-backed chairs. The fire lent its cheery glow. Freshly crushed lavender competed with the piney smoke to sweeten the air.

From beyond the inner door leading to the sleeping chamber, the fur-covered bed seemed to beckon invitingly, making her body feel wearier than ever.

"Can you tell me about your fights?" A hopeful look spread across his face. "Please, Aunt Ganora?"

"It's Ghee-an-huh-mah-rah." She grinned. "But only my enemies call me that." Swatting his shoulder won her a lopsided if embarrassed smile. "Someone as brave as you can call me whatever you like!" Any other time, she'd have been delighted to honor Gareth's request, but this evening her priorities lay elsewhere. She cast a longing glance at the bed, a much more comfortable elsewhere. "We will talk on the morrow, Gareth." She nudged him toward the corridor. "Thank you. You have been most helpful."

His lips twisted into a pout. "Just one story? A short one?"

"I think not, young man." Gareth turned on the intruder.

In the corridor, hefting a tray laden with bread, cheese, and two steaming mugs, stood his mother. With her free hand, Annamar motioned Gareth out of the way. He obeyed, none too swiftly.

"We shall talk, Gareth." Gyan raised an open hand. "I promise."

Visibly happier, the lad scampered down the corridor.

"Please forgive him, Gyanhumara." Annamar balanced the tray on one hand to close the door. "Men and children don't understand certain things."

Wearing that same enigmatic smile as before, she bustled into the room, set the tray on the table, and began checking the shutters for drafts.

Some women didn't understand, either. Gyan hunted for civil words. "Really, Annamar, you needn't trouble yourself."

"No trouble." Annamar glanced up from her inspection of the floor rushes. "Please try the tisane. It should help you sleep. And my kinfolk call me Anna."

Gyan reached for one of the mugs as Annamar disappeared into the bedchamber. Pleasant warmth flowed into her palms. She perched on the thickly cushioned couch near the fire, studying Arthur's elder half sister. Instinct told her Annamar's welcome wasn't feigned. Not as the welcome of another sister of Arthur's might have been.

Suppressing thoughts of Morghe with a mental shudder, Gyan gazed at Annamar's serenely smiling face as she returned from her tour of the sleeping chamber.

"Mine call me Gyan." Annamar's smile deepened, but she remained silent, waiting, Gyan thought, for her to say—what? Gyan pondered her cup. An apple-like fragrance rode the tendrils of steam. She took a sip. The tea tasted hauntingly familiar. "What is in this, Anna?"

Annamar picked up the other mug and joined Gyan on the couch. "Nothing special, just chamomile, rose petals, lady's mantle. And a dollop of honey, of course. You looked a mite tired, and I thought this might help you feel better."

The same ingredients Cynda used; no wonder it tasted so familiar. Gyan gave her sister-by-law a questioning glance, but the other woman had set her cup down to stir the fire's embers.

"The journey has been more tiring than I expected." A safe enough answer, Gyan hoped.

"I shouldn't wonder, Gyan, in your condition."

My condition, indeed! "Excuse me?"

"Come, my dear, let's not play games." Annamar laid the poker aside and caught Gyan's hand. "Don't try to fool a woman who has four babes of her own."

Gyan pulled it free. "I don't know what you're talking about." She couldn't run the risk of Loth finding out. It would destroy any sliver of credibility she might possess with the man.

"As you wish." Annamar plucked at her tunic's neckline. "I ought to look in on my youngest. She should be waking for a feeding soon."

As Loth's wife rose and started for the door, another thought occurred to Gyan. What if Annamar told Loth her suspicions anyway? The One God alone knew what Loth's reaction would be.

Were Gyan to refuse Annamar's hand of friendship, she might never get another opportunity to forge a bond with a Breatan that went beyond battlefields and bedchambers.

Furthermore, here stood a Breatanach mother not bound by Caledonach strictures. Perhaps Annamar could help.

"Anna, wait. Please. Yes, I am with child." Annamar again settled herself beside the fire, nodding slowly. "Is it that obvious already? Do you think others might suspect?"

"Oh, no. Certainly no man would guess." Annamar's laugh tinkled like silvery bells. "Why, Gyan, you look positively relieved. Haven't you told Arthur yet?"

Gyan stared at the shimmering depths of the tea before taking another sip, wondering how far to trust this woman.

"He knows. But—" A bigger sip this time. "Anna, it's too soon."

Annamar's slender eyebrows rose in graceful arches. "You've been married since July, and you can't possibly be farther along than that, yet." The eyebrows lowered to cap her frown. "Arthur doesn't think the child is his?"

"No, no. Of course he does, and rightly so. I have lain with no other man." Clutching the mug, Gyan stood and paced across the antechamber. She couldn't possibly explain everything to this stranger. But to remain silent when so many doubts and—yes, even fears—assailed her heart... surely that would be worse. After setting the mug on the table, she faced Annamar. "I am not ready to be a mother." Sighing, she dropped her voice to a whisper. "I—I don't even know if I really want to be one."

"Ah." A world of understanding lived in her level gaze.

Annamar retrieved the mug from the table, pressed it into Gyan's hands, clasped her shoulders, and gently but firmly propelled her back to the couch.

"My dear Gyan, every sane woman questions this. Never mind the pain of childbirth; it's over quickly enough and soon forgotten, thank God, or mankind would have ceased to walk this earth long ago." Seriousness overcame Annamar's mirth. "What I'm talking about is when you give a score of your best years to raising your children, nurturing them, teaching them, shielding them from famine and war only to see them run off one by one to perpetuate the starving and the killing." Her eyes glistened. "And maybe fall victim to it, too."

Gyan pondered the words in silence. Preoccupied with what changes motherhood would make in her own life, this aspect had eluded her. Her heart began to throb with shame.

"Anna." Gyan didn't look up. "Are you happy as a mother?"

"It's not all milky spittle and soiled swaddling bands. There will be adjustments in your life, yes. I'd be lying to deny that. But it's not a prison."

Gyan felt Annamar's fingers sweep a stray lock from her forehead. She lifted her head, and Annamar's hand withdrew. "But are you happy?" Gyan persisted.

Annamar's sigh sounded wistful, and Gyan wondered what had prompted it. "There is a special joy in watching your children challenge the world in their unique ways and knowing that you've had a hand in it. A hand in shaping the future." She rested her hand lightly on Gyan's shoulder. "You will know that joy, too, Gyan."

Annamar bade her good night and left the chamber.

Gyan stared at her hands, rubbing them. Callused from a sword's hilt, they knew the slick, hot feel of the blood of other women's sons. These hands already had begun to shape the future. Their way.

Would the motherly joy Annamar had described counterbalance

the pain of being denied the chance to pursue the life for which she'd been trained? The life she'd chosen and desired above all else?

Arthur and Loth sat at the table in the council chamber, the deerhide map of Dunpeldyr and surrounding territory stretched between them. Painted with blue ink to mark Brytoni holdings and red for Angli, it depicted the land extending to the north bank of the Fiorth River, west to Senaudon, to the southern border between Brytoni Gododdin and the Angli kingdom of Bernicia, and east to Berwych and the sea. Crimson marked the five obliterated Gododdin villages.

Like a pair of jaws, the Angli forces were pushing east from Dun Eidyn and west from Berwych, devouring all Brytoni land in between.

"In a year or two, the bastards will be at my bloody doorstep."

A miracle Dunpeldyr hadn't fallen already. "Hiding soldiers in the villages will slow the advance." God willing. Arthur took a swallow of the amber uisge, brewed by the monks at Glaschu Monastery at the western end of the Antonine Wall, threescore and ten miles distant. He welcomed the potent barley liquor's warmth.

"Hmph. If I'm lucky."

The only luck Arthur believed in took the form of three feet of tempered steel called Caleberyllus. "It will buy me time to move the troops." Never mind gathering provisions for men and mounts, erecting temporary shelters, workshops, and storage sheds, forging weapons and armor and horseshoes and harness fittings, and the myriad other details that went into implementing a campaign of this magnitude.

"The entire legion?" Hope flared in Loth's eyes.

Arthur shook his head. "Most of the cavalry. Half the foot—"

"Only half?" A thick fist thumped the tabletop. "How the devil do you expect to defeat the Angli with only half the infantry?"

After Loth's arrogant verbal posturing, especially toward Gyan, the temptation to bait him was too great to resist. "Have you already forgotten the fierceness of Caledonian horsemen? It's been only a year and a half since Abar-Gleann." He took another searing swallow. A quick glance rewarded him with a view of Loth's surprise. "Of course, as late as you arrived to the battlefield, you missed most of the cavalry action."

Loth wisely let the jibe pass. He had expressed his disagreement with Arthur's election to the Pendragonship by withholding support at Abar-Gleann. Afterward, while everyone cheered Arthur's brilliant win, Loth salvaged his reputation by claiming unanticipated delays in having to skirt Angli territory. Arthur hadn't believed him but, because he'd felt generous in the wake of his first major victory, he had chosen not to call Loth to account. Not publicly, anyway.

Loth appeared subdued as he pushed from the table and rose to approach the fire. Holding palms to the dying flames, he said quietly, "Are you sure it will be enough?"

"It will have to be. I cannot leave the western garrisons empty, and it takes time to recruit and train men."

"Hmph. Don't think about coercing any more of my children into joining you."

"I do not coerce anyone. Gawain made his choice, passed the enlistment training, and has become an asset to the legion. Anyone else who thinks he can do the same is welcome to try."

Loth turned toward Arthur, eyes alight. "Then take Dwras."

"Dwras?"

"Dwras map Gwyn, the farmer lad who survived one of the raids. By God's holy, bleeding wounds, Arthur, I have never seen such anger in my life. Perhaps you can use that anger against the Angli bastards who destroyed his family."

"Perhaps." A man of deep anger, however, seldom made a good soldier. "But it might be hard for him to live at another village."

"I don't care what you do with him. He can't stay here much longer. His temper has gotten him into trouble twice already. I don't need someone like that haunting my hall, picking fights."

That Arthur could sympathize with. Drink in hand, he joined Loth at the hearth. "I will speak with him on the morrow."

Loth stooped to swipe a fistful of rushes from the floor. One by one, he snapped them in half and flung the pieces into the flames. "You didn't assign yourself or your wife to a village." Another woody stem flared into oblivion. "You are welcome to winter here, of course." Two more broken pieces joined their kin. "Both of you."

Arthur wondered whether the welcome extended to Loth's firstborn—someone else not assigned to a border village—but that discussion could wait for daylight. He clapped Loth's shoulder. "I appreciate the offer, but it will depend on what Gyan wants to do."

Loth chuckled. "The man whose wife rules him begs for trouble."

"No danger there. I'm only concerned for her happiness."

He gave Arthur a measuring stare. "You really do love her. I thought it was an arranged match."

"Of course. I arranged it." Arthur smiled briefly. "We both did. I never would have challenged Urien if I hadn't been certain of Gyan's heart."

Loth sacrificed the remaining rushes to the fire. "Is she really as good as they say?" Arthur felt his eyebrows lift. With a rueful grin, Loth added, "In battle, I mean."

"I wouldn't entrust my life to many people." The truth smote him with abrupt clarity. "But Gyanhumara of Caledonia is one of them."

AIDED BY a half-dozing servant, Arthur found the guest quarters. After making a quick survey of the layout, he bade the girl to take the oil lamp with her. He had no wish to disturb his sleeping wife.

While he groped toward the bed, the sound of her peaceful, even breathing greeted him. He stripped off cloak, boots, tunic, and trews and eased under the furs. Gyan lay on her side, facing away. Nestling against her warm back, he slipped his arm across her waist. His hand came to rest against her belly. He wondered when it would begin to show evidence of the child within. Their child.

Her fingertips drifted over his. "Mmm . . . Artyr?"

"Forgive me, Gyan. I didn't mean to wake you."

"Never mind . . ." She shifted onto her back and reached up to caress his cheek. "Did you and Loth finish?"

"Yes. First Turma will winter here as reinforcements. Fourth and Fifth I'm keeping as escort. The rest of our men have been assigned to border villages, along with some of Loth's. On the morrow, we gather peasant clothing and—"

"Ha! So Loth liked my idea. He could have admitted it to me. I ought to change Dunpeldyr's Caledonaiche name from Dùn Pildìrach, Fort of the Turning Ascent"—an apt description of the easily defended approach to the summit, Arthur privately agreed—"to Dùn Pildìoras."

"And that means the Fort of—?"

"The Fort of He Who Has Turned Stubborn."

Arthur barked a laugh. But despite all of Loth's blustering, he could think of no man he'd rather see as an ally in this dangerous corner of Brydein. "Loth isn't a bad sort, Gyan. And he's smart enough to recognize good counsel, even if he's not accustomed to the source."

He heard the faint, low growl of her dissent and cut off any further disagreement with a long kiss. Her lips were warmly inviting. He brushed his fingertips across the swell of her breasts.

She caught his hand. "What about me, Artyr? Do I stay here? Or go back to Caer Lugubalion? And what will you do?"

"Those are two options, of course. You could also winter at one of the Gododdin villages. And ..." He kissed the side of her neck lightly, lingeringly. "Arbroch is only a few days away."

Her sharp intake of breath told him her decision. No surprise. His lips worked around to her throat, and she let out a slow sigh.

"Can you send someone to fetch Cynda?"

"Consider it done." After another kiss, he added, "Morghe, too."

"Morghe?" She pushed herself onto her elbows. "Why?"

"She's a healer, for one thing."

"Arbroch has healers and midwives aplenty."

He couldn't fathom her reluctance but had no patience for ferreting out the answer. It was late, the morrow promised to be quite busy, and he needed to put this matter to rest. He countered with logic to which Gyan surely could relate: "The birth of a Brytoni nobleman's child must be witnessed by a female member of his family. In the strictest sense, I'm not a nobleman, since the Clan Cwrnwyll elders refuse to waive the illegitimacy of my birth—"

"But you are Chieftainess Ygraine's son, and the protocol must be observed," Gyan finished for him. She eased back down. "And Morghe's knowledge of Caledonaiche makes her the logical choice."

"Exactly." As the silence stretched between them, he wished he hadn't sent the servant away with the light. Into the blackness, he offered, "I'm glad you understand, Gyan."

She sighed. "I suppose you will be leaving for headquarters."

Under normal circumstances, yes. A thousand details awaited him regarding the selection, equipping, provisioning, movement, and quartering of the troops to be assigned to the Angli campaign. Details that could be handled quite competently by Cai, Merlin, Marcus, and other officers. He suspected his wife needed him more than they did. Come morning, he'd send a message telling them so.

He covered her mouth with his and found it pliant yet... reserved. "My love," he whispered, "I will stay with you for as long as I can. If that's what you want."

She reached up with both hands and pulled his head to hers. Their lips met in an explosion of ravenous passion. Working her hands toward his hips, she arched her body against his and delivered a silent invitation he was altogether delighted to accept.

Chapter 13

Trencher balanced across his good forearm, Dwras map Gwyn returned to the eating area of Dunpeldyr's Great Hall to find another man seated on his bench. Empty seats abounded, but Dwras was sick unto death of having things stolen from him, especially by arrogant warriors who wielded their status as an excuse to abuse decent, honest, hardworking folk.

He jabbed the offending warrior on the shoulder. With a grunt, the man swung his head around to fix narrow eyes upon him.

"What d'ye want?"

"My seat. I want it back." Dwras lowered his eyebrows. "Now!"

"You—what?" The Lothian warrior's laughter nearly made him choke. A grinning companion slapped his back.

"Oho, Farmer Dwras thinks he's one of us, lads," chortled another warrior, making a shooing motion. "Be off with you! Back to your pigs, farmer boy."

They burst into cackles, hoots, and hog calls. Dwras felt his cheeks flush.

The warrior in Dwras's seat found himself buried under sops and ale.

"My mistake, sir." He grinned devilishly. "I thought this was the sty."

Bellowing, the warrior shot to his feet. Soggy bread flew everywhere. Dwras ducked the blow. Upon connecting with a bony chin, he sent the man sprawling across the cluttered table. The warrior's humiliation more than balanced the pain lancing Dwras's healing shoulder. The audience's jeers redoubled with vicious glee.

The warrior stood, ale-streaked face darkened with rage and fist cocked. "You filthy whore's son, I'll—"

"Halt! Everyone!"

Trailed by a detachment of guards, Chieftain Loth strode across the hall, toppling benches and shoving servants from his path. Fists lowering, the adversaries stepped apart.

Dwras bowed his head to accept the chieftain's harsh judgment. From the corner of his eye, he saw the warrior reacting in much the same manner, and it gave him a perverse surge of satisfaction.

"You." Loth thrust a finger close to Dwras's face. "Your doing?"

The truth died in his throat. Surely Chieftain Loth would believe his own warrior over a mere farmer.

He sighed. "Aye, my lord." Perchance the end would come quick and painless. On the other hand, he'd never been that lucky.

"Hmph." The chieftain turned to address someone behind him. "This is the farmer who brought me word of the raid. I told you he's too much trouble to keep here."

Here it comes, Dwras mused, banishment. Mayhap the chance to join his wife and son sooner, a fate for which he dared not hope. He certainly had nothing left on this side of eternity.

The man Chieftain Loth had addressed stepped to the forefront of the gathering. Dwras felt his jaw go slack.

If any woman's son had ever claimed divine descent, this one ought. To call him fair of face would be a gross injustice when his countenance radiated strength, confidence, and intelligence in equally great measures. His face seemed both young and old at once, accustomed to receiving instant respect and obedience: the face of a god.

"I think he has more to tell." Even the man's voice resounded godlike in its commanding yet compassionate authority. Profound sympathy shone from his intense blue eyes. "Don't you, lad?"

"What's to tell, Arthur? Dwras was causing trouble." Loth nailed Dwras with his stare. "Again."

"I want his story."

As he loosened his tongue to describe the brawl, his head reeled like a drunkard's. What name had Chieftain Loth given this man? Arthur? Loth's brother-by-marriage, the Pendragon himself, here in remote Dunpeldyr? In the dead of winter?

Impossible!

This warrior came dressed for the part, aye, sporting more finely spun linen, well-tooled leather, and freshly polished bronze than Dwras had seen in his entire score of years. Scars adorned those hard-muscled arms and legs, too, thin white ribbons left by only the sharpest blades.

The Pendragon, indeed.

He couldn't believe his fortune. Rather, his misfortune, for he felt utterly foolish for boring Arthur with such a trivial matter. He dropped his gaze to the floor rushes.

"Dwras, I commend your courage for alerting Chieftain Loth, as badly wounded as you were." Arthur's hand rested lightly upon Dwras's uninjured shoulder. "This may be cold comfort, but you helped spare many more villages. And I like your spirit. Even if it's a bit—misdirected." Dwras dared to meet those unwavering eyes. Their fire branded his soul. "I would like to put that spirit to better use."

For the second time in as many minutes, he thanked God that his jaw was hinged to his head, else it surely would have hit the floor. Had he heard aright? Was the Pendragon asking him to trade his pitchfork for a spear? Giving him a chance to avenge his loved ones? A chance his own chieftain had denied him?

More to the point, was he, Dwras map Gwyn, a simple son of the earth, truly capable of doing such a thing?

If grief for his family and friends had begun to ebb, hatred for their Angli murderers would smolder as long as blood flooded his veins. Now, icy conviction tempered the molten hatred.

Thrusting out his chin, he raked the astounded Clan Lothian warriors with a defiant glare.

"When do we leave, Lord Pendragon?"

"Can you ride?" Arthur asked.

Placid farm beasts, aye, not the fearsome dervishes warriors favored, but no power in heaven or on earth could force him to confess that to Arthur. "Aye, my lord."

Arthur nodded slowly, as if pondering the truth of the claim. For one terrifying moment, he believed the Pendragon could read his thoughts and discover the lie.

"Pack your gear. We depart at dawn."

Dwras felt smitten by an intense wave of unworthiness. Who was he that the mighty Pendragon would take a personal interest in him?

One glance into those intense yet compassionate eyes told him all he needed to know. Mimicking the Pendragon's warriors, he squared his shoulders and raised his fist to his chest in an unspoken pledge to devote himself to Arthur's service to the very best of his ability.

ANGUSEL WOKE to a familiar pressure in his vitals and sat up. His wolfskin wrap slid off, and cold smote his shoulders. He pushed aside the tent flap to discover what else had invaded the camp.

Trees, ground, tents, supply packs, nothing had escaped winter's snowy touch. Even the stars had vanished behind a vast shroud.

An icy wind prickled his bare arms and echoed down his spine. Taking care not to disturb his tentmate, he tugged on his long-sleeved undertunic and boots and shrugged into his battle-tunic. He retrieved his cloak and gloves, parted the tent flap as little as possible, and crawled outside.

After standing, he pinned his cloak in place, donned the gloves, and dusted snow from his leggings. The Pendragon had ordered half the men to stand watch while the others slept, and the four at the firepit belonged to the second watch. Angusel gazed eastward but couldn't discern any lightening of the sky.

This sojourn boded ill for getting any more sleep.

The central campfire had been built within a three-course-high ring of stones designed more to contain the light than the flames. This meant less heat for the occupants of the tents ranged around the firepit like a wheel's spokes, obliging everyone to double up. The cold made it foolhardy to risk doing without fire, but being this close to Angalaranach territory carried its own deadly risks. Shielding the light also helped reduce night blindness.

Thus, his eyes adjusted quickly in the half gloom, and he noticed that the Pendragon, who with Gyan had taken first inner-perimeter watch, was already awake. He sat hunkered and silent under his heavy black cloak with his back to the fire beside one of the soldiers. Both men faced the narrow path that connected the thicket to the stream.

The only other access into the camp's center—unless an enemy wished to alert every soul within half a league by hacking through dense brambles—was by way of the logs where the company had tethered the horses, on the opposite side of the camp from the burn that provided their water supply. The Pendragon had divided the watch between the horses, the burn, and the outer and inner perimeters.

During his watch, which had begun at sundown and seemed to end half a lifetime later, Angusel had been posted to the inner perimeter. He thought it odd that Arthur would go to such lengths to defend a traveling camp; they were twoscore and three of the legion's finest horse-warriors and likely to defeat a force five times their number.

However, he knew his place was not to argue but to serve the Pendragon and Gyan to his utmost. Especially Gyan.

A latrine trench had been dug between the inner perimeter and the horses. As Angusel exchanged a whispered greeting with the Pendragon and the guard, Gyan emerged from the tent she and her consort shared. Clutching her cloak to her chest, she hurried for the latrine. Angusel would have stayed until her return if his own needs hadn't been so acute. The trench was long enough to accommodate half the camp. But as he moved to follow her, Arthur stopped him.

"Give her a few moments alone," whispered the Pendragon.

Angusel gritted his teeth. "But, my lord, I—" The unmistakable sound of retching cut off his protest. He squatted to meet Arthur's gaze. He couldn't be sure in the fickle light, but he thought Gyan's consort looked concerned. "Is she all right?"

The Pendragon lifted a shoulder noncommittally. From beneath his cloak came the creak of leather and scrape of metal. "It's a female matter."

When Angusel would have voiced his next question, Gyan returned. Her stride, as purposeful as ever, displayed none of the urgency she'd shown only a few minutes before. She thrust a hand toward her consort, who gave her a wine skin he and the guard had been sharing. She swilled a mouthful, turned her head, spat, and swallowed several gulps.

Satisfied that she seemed no worse for her bout of the flux, Angusel excused himself and headed for the latrine.

In spite of the snow, saddle sores, stiff muscles, and lack of sleep, life looked far better after he'd finished the task at hand.

As he tied his breeches and smoothed his tunic, he studied the horses. They seemed more restless than they ought: tossing their heads, whickering uneasily, stamping, and snorting. The loudest noises, he realized with alarm, were coming from his own mount.

Angusel hurdled the smelly trench and landed lightly on the other side. Slowly, he approached the limb attached to the log where Stonn's reins were tied, offering pats to other horses along the way.

The area had been selected for being relatively clear of brambles, stumps, roots, holes, and anything else that might harm the horses. The march of trees resumed another ten paces beyond, where the outer perimeter guards had been posted.

Angusel found his stallion standing with all four hooves stiffly planted, ears pinned back, and tugging at the reins.

"Steady, boy." The tugging stopped, but when he reached for Stonn's cheek, the horse jerked away. He persisted and finally was able to lay a hand on Stonn's neck. "What is it, Stonn?"

As if in answer, the stallion blew a loud snort and was answered by other horses in the line. Angusel strained his ears and squinted at the tree line but couldn't sense any predators.

The cloud cover thinned enough to let the half-moon illuminate what appeared to be a fallen log beyond the first line of trees, which in itself wasn't unusual. But the company had spent the waning twilight scouring the woods for deadfall to use for the horses' tethers as well as the fire, and he suspected that the log—or whatever it was, for its shape didn't look right—hadn't been there before.

Ignoring the warning prickle and wishing he'd brought his dagger, he gave Stonn a final pat and set off to investigate.

Clouds shrouded the moon, and the path dimmed. Cautiously, he crept forward and toed the log. It felt far too soft for wood.

An arm flopped onto the snow.

In a burst of moonlight, he saw blood beneath the body.

One of the sentries! His throat had been slashed. He was armed, but only because he'd trapped his sword between his body and the ground when he fell. Who had killed him—raiders or an Angalaranach patrol or bandits—Angusel couldn't begin to guess. Nor did it matter.

He whirled, stuck two fingers in his mouth, and blew a shrill blast. An arrow grazed his shield-side shoulder as he rolled the sentry's body and stooped to snatch the sword.

More arrows arced over his head and sped toward the firepit.

The forest erupted with unholy whoops and screams, as though all the Otherworld's ifrinnaich were invading the camp.

Swift as lightning, he felt his battle frenzy ignite. He ran at Stonn, wrenched the reins free, and scrambled onto his back, brandishing the sword and yelling his challenge at the enemy.

ARTHUR HEARD the whistle and dived away from the fire. Gyan followed—not a heartbeat too soon; arrows riddled the ground where they'd been sitting. One caught their guard in the throat. He fell with a wet gurgle. Someone across the camp gave an agonized cry, but whether his wound was mortal, Arthur had no time to assess.

"Sentries, report!" he shouted in Latin, as the men who'd been asleep began bursting from the tents, swords drawn.

Only four of the eight outer-perimeter sentries responded. The men posted nearest the horses and the stream were either dead or too close to the enemy to reveal themselves. Either way, it told Arthur that the enemy forces were arrayed to attack both access points.

A smart ploy, he grudgingly conceded.

Thankful for having divided the men into just two watches, Arthur sent the second watch to the horses, where Angusel had freed and mounted his stallion and was engaged in close combat with one of the raiders. Arthur sent the men of the first watch to reinforce those already fending off the attack from the stream side. He regretted having no way to direct the surviving outer-perimeter sentries but trusted them to join the battle wherever they might.

When Gyan drew her sword and moved toward the horses, Arthur caught her wrist. "You're with me. To the stream."

Her eyes glittered fiercely in the flickering light. "So I can hide behind your sword?" She wrenched her arm free. The crimson flush that signaled her battle frenzy began staining her cheeks. She drew a deep breath. "I think not. They're after the horses."

"I know. But, Gyan, it's too—" He stopped himself, suspecting how she'd perceive his protest.

"Too dangerous?" she finished for him. "Ha." She shook her head and pointed with her sword toward the stream, where the enemy was hacking through the brambles to widen the line of attack. "Here comes the biggest threat. I will secure the horses and lead the men back to reinforce you."

Without waiting for his agreement—or argument—she bounded off, cocking her sword overhead and adding her Caledonian battle cry to the din, leaving no time to be furious with her as the raiders broke through the thicket and his battle began.

GYAN JERKED her sword from the man she'd gutted and glanced up to watch in horror as one of the raiders pulled Angusel from Stonn's back. She whipped her head around. The rest of her men lay dead, injured, or were putting other raiders to flight.

"A'mi!" she called in Caledonaiche, and in Ròmanaiche, "To me!"

The fighting had spooked the horses, and most were trying to free themselves, rocking the tether logs violently.

Angusel and his assailant disappeared behind a log. A yelp of pain rang out. No time to wait for the other men to return. Gyan gauged the distance around the log: too far. She sheathed her sword, ran toward Angusel's last known position, jumped on top of the log, and vaulted onto the raider's back. Together they tumbled, one over the other, across the hard-packed dirt toward the trees.

As she grappled with the raider, he worked his dagger free. She rolled before he struck, but not far enough to avoid a hard blow in the stomach. The dragon on her wide bronze belt deflected it, but pain bolted through her midsection.

My bairn!

Grimly, she thrust aside concern for her unborn child to concentrate on her own survival.

She gathered her feet to her chest and shoved with all her strength. The enemy warrior stumbled backward, giving her time to scramble to her feet, doubled over and panting heavily. The man had to be twice her size. Her arms felt like deadweights; she could scarcely hold her sword, never mind using it with deadly force.

Muscles quivering, she gripped it with both hands and braced herself for the raider's assault. Sword lowered, he charged.

A dark blur slammed into him from the side. Bellowing, the raider lost his balance and fell with a heavy thud. Gyan hurried over to finish what her benefactor had started. She thrust Braonshaffir through the enemy's neck, and he drowned in his own blood.

The horses seemed safe, but by the shouts and clamor of steel on steel, she knew Arthur's battle at the burn was far from over.

"A'mi!" she cried as the first of her men emerged from the trees.

Of the fifteen that returned, one was clutching a bloody sword arm to his chest and another was limping badly. She glanced around in the graying dawn and saw a shape crumpled nearby, groaning. As she approached, the shape rolled and sat up, hand to head.

"Angusel!" Gyan dropped to her knees beside him. He had several wounds, though none looked mortal. "Are you all right?" she asked in Caledonaiche.

A bewildered expression crossed his face, and he shook his head, apparently less in answer to her question than to collect his wits. "Where is the hellion? Did I get him?"

She grinned at his choice of epithets, ifrinnach. "Hellion, indeed." She stood and offered her hand, and he hauled himself to his feet, swaying slightly. "You saved my life, Angus. I"—*and my bairn*—"thank you. But we must help Artyr. Can you fight?"

"Aye."

Angusel raised his sword before his face in salute, prompting the other men to do the same. Gyan couldn't help but notice the winces, grimaces, and oozing wounds.

She nodded sharply and appointed two soldiers to guard the remaining horses and any men too injured to fight. The rest she ordered to mount up. Whooping to wake the dead, they careened through the camp.

Chapter 14

Wading calf-deep in the frigid waters, Arthur had just dispatched another enemy warrior when he heard the thundering from within the thicket. He whirled, Caleberyllus at the ready, to behold what had to be the most glorious sight under heaven.

The surviving raiders must have thought otherwise, for they broke off and bolted into the woods, howling as if the devil himself were chasing them.

Arthur regarded his wife—braids flying, breath steaming, eyes glowing, cloak billowing, sword flashing—and understood their terror.

He had never felt more relieved in his life.

"Halt!" he shouted hoarsely as Gyan and her men spurred their horses through the stream. "Do not pursue." He slogged onto the bank and gave the regroup order to all within earshot.

Gyan and her troop sheathed their swords, wheeled their mounts about, and splashed back to Arthur's side of the stream. She kicked Macmuir close to him, her arched eyebrow issuing a challenge.

Arthur didn't need to explain orders to a subordinate, but he needed an argument with his wife even less. "They know this land better than we do. And they know our number. I suspect the attacks covered the archers' retreat. If they have an outpost nearby, they will return with reinforcements."

The night's events seemed to overtake her, for she gave a heavy sigh and slid from her mount, steadying herself against Macmuir's neck. "You do not believe these were brigands."

"Not bloody likely. These men were clever and well organized." Arthur didn't see any potential captives in the immediate vicinity, though that didn't mean they wouldn't find any later. He strode to the corpse of the last man he'd killed, which was lying facedown on the bank, head in the water. He rolled it over to reveal the man's badge, a snarling leopard's head. "Colgrim's men. Either a raiding party or a patrol." He ordered the others to collect the dead, help the wounded, secure any injured Angli prisoners, and move everyone back into camp.

"If they do have an outpost in this district, don't you want to look for it?" she asked.

Not with his gravid wife in the troop, though Arthur knew better than to make that announcement. "Our best course," he said as activity bustled around them, "is to put as much distance between us and this location as possible."

For once, she didn't disagree. One look at her face in the advancing dawn told him why. Fatigue and pain had etched their marks. She staggered to him, threw her arms around his neck, and sagged against his chest. He held her tightly, wishing he never had to let her go.

The force of her lips against his proclaimed the same wish.

ANGUSEL WORKED with the rest of the company to help recover the wounded and dead of both sides, collect weapons and other valuable items, bind wounds, dig graves, fill the latrine, gnaw on bannocks and dried beef, swill ale, strike camp, and try to make sense of having lost eight to death, five to disabling injuries—and all the wounded

Angalaranaich, before they could be securely guarded, to suicide.

Absent a priest, it fell to the Pendragon to commend the departed souls to the One God. "Or whichever gods they followed in life," he added diplomatically.

While the entire company saluted their fallen companions with raised swords, Gyan led the Caledonaich in singing the warrior's lament. Angusel saw unshed tears brimming in her eyes and heard the catch in her lovely voice. In this she wasn't alone.

They had dug the two mass graves on a low rise overlooking the burn where they'd repelled the bulk of the attack.

"Abar-Bhàis," Gyan named the battlefield, drawing her cloak close, as if it could shield her from what she'd invoked.

"What does that mean?" asked her consort as they picked their way toward the horses. "River Mouth—something."

"Mouth of the River of Death," she replied reverently.

A fitting tribute, Angusel silently agreed. The Pendragon's seannachaidh would have a fine time crafting songs from that theme for the living as well as the dead.

THE REST of that day passed in taut silence. A man died of his wounds in the night, so the next day had to begin with digging another grave and singing another tearstained lament. This was followed by more subdued words and oppressive stretches of silence as they ate, broke camp, and rode on. No one spoke of the skirmish, as though fearing that a careless word might invite another attack. Normally, Angusel might have tried lifting his companions' spirits with jests, but the exhausted, pain-wracked, dour faces bespoke the need to be left alone.

With the exception of Gyan, her consort, and the worst of the wounded, everyone took turns as outriders, flanking the column in all four directions at a hundred paces. At regular intervals, the outriders reported back, and other men took their places.

After Abar-Bhàis, no one scoffed at the precautions.

Yet Angusel brooded less upon the recent past than upon what would happen later this evening. For the Pendragon expected the troop to reach Senaudon by dusk, and Gyan expected Angusel to remain there while she and her consort and the others traveled on to Arbroch.

Conflicting desires battled within him.

After a year's absence, he eagerly anticipated watching the sun rise from atop Senaudon's battlements, sparring with his clansmen, renewing his friendship with his mother's cats, even seeing her again—in spite of the less than pleasant memories they shared.

But now his heart was Gyan's to command. His oath meant more to him than life itself. He'd known it from the first moment the idea had entered his mind in her quarters after the Scáthinach battle. Even without his sword with which to make the pledge, no decision had ever felt so right. He, Angusel mac Alayna, deserved a place at Gyan's side no less than her clansmen did.

By midmorning, his fretting had bested him. He broke rank and nudged Stonn forward.

"Angusel—" began the Pendragon sternly.

Gyan cut him off with a sharp glance. "Something wrong, Angus?"

"Can we talk, Gyan?" Angusel pleaded, in Caledonaiche. "Alone?" He shivered as he uttered the last word, "aonar," but dismissed it as a reaction to the cold.

She relayed the request in Breatanaiche. Her consort didn't seem pleased but nodded his consent. Angusel gave him a look of thanks that went unacknowledged. The Pendragon continued his course, motioning the troop to do the same as Gyan and Angusel reined their mounts out of formation. Once the last rank had pulled several horselengths ahead, they kneed their horses forward.

"What's this about?"

"I think you know." She raised an eyebrow but didn't answer. He drew a deep breath. "Why can't I stay at Arbroch with you?"

"Don't you want to winter at your home? See your mother again?"

"See her, aye." He ran a gloved finger over his fealty-mark. "Winter with her, nay. My place is with you."

She stared into the distance, and Angusel tried to follow her line of sight. Her consort's gold-tipped scarlet horsehair crest floated above the heads of the other riders. The Pendragon also bore the dìleas-tì, the Caledonach symbol of a warrior's fealty. Angusel felt proud that he and Arthur shared this kinship . . . but he couldn't ignore the twinge of jealousy.

"If that is your wish." She flashed a smile that looked more like her usual self. "But I fear you will be bored."

"It's only for the winter."

"I go to Arbroch to bear Artyr's bairn," she whispered.

His jaw dropped, and he stared at her. "What? Nay, you can't be—" He snapped his mouth shut to collect his whirling thoughts. "Wait. You two have been together only since, what, October? How—" He felt his cheeks heat. "I mean, when—"

"In September, during his visit to Maun."

"But you fought the Angalaranaich!"

"And you saved two lives that night." Her fingertips strayed to the fresh dent in her bronze sword belt, and she bowed her head.

"I saw the raider's war-knife hit you." Angusel sucked in a breath. "Is—is your bairn all right?"

"I think so." Slowly, she shook her head. "One thing is certain. I am done with battles for a long time." She leaned over to grip his arm. "Only Artyr and a few others know. Until Arbroch's walls surround me, I plan to keep it that way, understood?" Straightening, she let go of him.

"Aye. But what about me? Do I have to stay at Senaudon?"

A short laugh burst from her lips. "If you fret about being left behind when Artyr joins his troops in the spring, I will make sure he doesn't forget you."

"That's not it." A tide of memories threatened to overwhelm him. "How well do you know my mother?"

She shrugged. "We have met."

Absently scratching the bandage on his shield arm, he studied Stonn's coaly mane, speckled with snowflakes. As he brushed them away, deciding what to say, more floated down. "When the Pendragon took me as hostage after Abar-Gleann, I—" He looked up. "I was glad to go."

"Forgive me, Angus. I thought, since you hadn't been home in a long time . . . I didn't realize—" Her smile conveyed the warmth of their deepening friendship. "Of course, you will be welcome at Arbroch." Her eyes lit with a mischievous glow. "But at the first jest about how fat I get, it's out into the snow with you!"

GEREINT MAP Erbin, commander of the Brytoni occupation force at Senaudon, had spent the afternoon whisking from inspection to inspection. Troops, barracks, horses, fortifications, sentries, armory, supplies: everything had to be perfect for the Pendragon. Fortunately, Gereint's vigilant command had borne fruit. The discrepancies—a careless uniform here, a cracked harness there—were easily set aright. For the first time all day, he stretched his feet to the fire, pewter mug of mulled wine nestled warmly in one hand, and let his heart slow to a more decorous pace.

It didn't last.

"Enter," he responded to the impatient rap on the door.

The angular form of Centurion Ulfyn strode into the workroom. He thumped fist to bronze-clad breast. "Sir, the Pendragon is here."

Gereint's wine sloshed as he stood. "Here? In my antechamber?" He set the mug down and, tugging at his gleaming cuirass, made a swift check of his uniform.

"No, sir. The feast hall. With Chieftainess Alayna."

The prefect of the Badger Cohort downed his wine without tasting it. Who did that woman think she was? This was her fortress, and her clan's doings remained hers to govern, but the latitude Arthur had granted her didn't include the right to play hostess to Gereint's commander as if Gereint himself didn't exist.

"Eleven of the Pendragon's escort," Ulfyn continued somberly, "have reported to the infirmary. Most of the rest have minor, field-dressed wounds. They lost nine men: eight in action and one from his wounds the following night."

"Bandits?" Only a village-size band could have inflicted that much damage on one of the Pendragon's vaunted cavalry squads, but the alternative...

"An Angli ambush, sir, two days to the south."

For Ulfyn's sake, Gereint squelched his surprise. Two days was far too close for comfort. He resolved to ask Arthur for reinforcements. "Very well, Ulfyn." He abandoned his mug on the table, snatched his scarlet cloak from the back of a chair, flung it about his shoulders, and pinned on the red-and-green-ringed silver dragon. "Let's go."

Gereint found the Pendragon and a score of his men—Picts, to judge by their armor—standing just beyond the feast hall's tall oaken doors. They concentrated on the stately progress of Chieftainess Gyanhumara as she passed the many-tiered niches containing skulls and embalmed heads representing generations of vanquished foes. Without sparing a glance for her surroundings, Gyanhumara marched to the dais, where the Chieftainess of Clan Alban reclined in languid anticipation.

Alayna looked absurd, her raven hair wound in elaborate braids atop her head, plaited with strands of silvery thread that sparkled in the torchlight. Gereint would have wagered a wagonload of heather beer that she was wearing too much face-paint, as usual. The gold lions of her torc snarled at each other across the hollow of her throat. Her bosom threatened to burst free of the scarlet gown.

Squelching his amusement, Gereint turned to his commander, squared his shoulders, and cleared his throat. "Lord Pendragon, I have conducted a thorough—"

"Everything I've seen so far looks excellent, Gereint. I will hear your full report later." The Pendragon directed his attention toward the far end of the hall.

Gyanhumara reached the dais, and her sapphire-pommeled sword hissed free of its bronze scabbard. She stooped to lay it on the flagstones and took a step backward. Alayna nodded once. Gyanhumara raised her right hand, fingers knotted into a fist. From his angle, Gereint could see blue wing tips of one bird and the tail feathers of another. The older woman responded with a similar gesture, displaying a rearing, roaring, grayish-blue lion.

"Argyll is well come to the Seat of Alban." Alayna spoke Pictish, which Gereint and his men had learned to facilitate their duties.

"Alban is most gracious," Gyanhumara replied, lowering the arm.

Alayna's lips pursed. "Identify Argyll's àrd-ceoigin."

Gereint gave his head a slight shake; he'd never heard that term during the past eighteen months and had no clue what to make of it.

Gyanhumara raised her other arm. The spread wing tips and lashing tail of this creature were decidedly draconic.

Alayna leaned forward in her chair, animosity—but not surprise—etched into every line of her face. "State his name and titles."

"Ròmanach Artyr mac Ygrayna"—*Roman Arthur son of Ygraine*, Gereint mentally translated—"Càrnhuileanach Rhioghachd agus Àrd-Ceann Teine-Beathach Mór"—*Man of Clan Cwrnwyll of Rheged and... High-Chief Great Fire-Beast?*—"Bhreatein." *Of Brydein.* He had never heard anyone render "Pendragon" in Pictish; they always uttered the word with their quaint accent. After listening to that mouthful, he understood why.

The Chieftainess of Clan Alban shifted her gaze past Gyanhumara. "Let him approach."

Gereint had witnessed plenty of bizarre behavior at Senaudon, but Alayna's treating her conqueror like a piece of property vaulted to the top of the list.

Yet Arthur looked as unperturbed as ever. At his wife's nod, he signaled a young Picti warrior, who strode with him to Gyanhumara's side. Arthur made no move to disarm, though the Picti lad did.

Alayna scrutinized the trio. "This man does not wear the Doves of Argyll. By what sign can you prove that he is your consort?"

"Artyr mac Ygrayna wears the fealty-mark," declared Gyanhumara, "sworn unto Argyll and sanctified in the rite of bonding the moon before Lugnasadh."

Arthur unwound and removed the short white stole that served as neck padding. With his fingers, he shifted his armor and undertunic toward his left shoulder far enough to reveal a thin red scar at the base of his neck. Gereint couldn't fully suppress a shudder.

Alayna's eyebrows lowered. "Chieftainess Gyanhumara, have you not instructed your consort in our ways?"

Gyanhumara and Arthur exchanged a nod. Arthur grasped the Picti warrior's shoulder and urged him forward.

"Chieftainess Alayna, I am advised that I may display a different sign of friendship. To that end, I restore your son, Angusel mac Alayna, to you." In Brytonic, that commanding voice rang throughout the feast hall. "His courage and loyalty have proven to me that the honor of Alban need not be enforced by retaining him as a hostage."

Gyanhumara rendered his remarks in Pictish. Smiling, Alayna extended an open hand. Angusel mounted the dais, clasped her hand, knelt, and bowed until his forehead touched her hand.

"Well come, Àrd-Oighre h'Albainaich." Another term Gereint had never heard, but it was much easier to grasp: *Exalted Heir of Clan Alban.* The fingertips of Alayna's other hand brushed Angusel's shoulder bandage. "What did they do to you, son?"

"Not them, Mother," Angusel said with a nod toward Arthur and Gyanhumara. "Angalaranach warriors." He gave a lopsided grin. "Nothing we couldn't handle."

Gereint pursed his lips to restrain a laugh, wondering at what point during their history the Picts had started calling the Angli "the Diseased People."

Alayna accepted Angusel's news with a thoughtful nod. Abruptly, her face clouded with a scowl. "Angusel, which clan has claimed your fealty?"

"Argyll!"

"Argyll." Alayna extracted her hand from her son's. "Chieftainess Gyanhumara, I hope you appreciate the treasure you have won from me."

"Indeed I do. Angusel mac Alayna has saved my life and the future of Clan Argyll. He is a credit to his clan." Pride rang from each syllable. "And mine."

ANGUSEL SAT on a bench near the round stone firepit in the center of Alayna's private reception chamber, her sleek black cat Eala curled in his lap. If he'd ever worried about how his mother fared since Abar-Gleann, one glance around the room served to allay those fears. True to her name, which meant "splendid," she never had been one to scorn luxury, but Angusel could have sworn that her pillows, furs, tapestries, and furnishings had doubled. He ran his fingertips over the nubby, brocaded cover of the bench's cushion.

"Argyll." On his mother's lips, it sounded like a curse. "Must I lose everything to Argyll?"

Bronze mirror in hand, Alayna perched on an ornately carved stool while a maid finished unwinding her braids, extracted the silver threads, and wrapped them around a stubby pine spool. The woad Lion of Alban prowled along one lean forearm. Wings splayed and beak split in a screech and talons flexed for the kill, the Falcon of Tarsuinn swept across the other. Her shoulders, swathed in her clan mantle, trembled with barely leashed fury.

"First the Pendragon and now you! What will Gyanhumara steal from me next?" The girl made a careless movement with the jeweled comb, catching an ebony tangle and making his mother wince. "One more slip, and it's back to kitchen drudge duty for you." She cut off the maid's stuttering apology with an impatient wave of the mirror.

Angusel held his peace. It didn't matter that the Pendragon never had been Alayna's to begin with or that Angusel's decision to swear allegiance to Argyll had been his alone. Once she latched onto an idea, she never let go.

As he stroked the silken fur, Eala began purring. When his hand stilled, she butted it imperiously. Smiling, Angusel resumed his duty.

"What if this new loyalty conflicts with the good of Alban? What will you do then, my buck?"

"I—I don't know, Mother. I hadn't really thought—"

"I suggest you give it some attention."

He stared at her in astonishment. Caledonach warriors had been swearing fealty to the leaders of other clans for generations. While hostilities flared occasionally between member-clans, the Confederacy prided itself in the strength of its unity—unlike the ever-feuding Breatanach clans. He failed to recall any stories of a Caledonach trapped in a clash of loyalties.

Yet this didn't mean it couldn't happen.

Why was she so concerned about his reactions? Did she suspect neighboring Argyll of planning to snatch Alban lands? Or was she hatching a similar plan? For revenge, perhaps, because Gyan had won the Pendragon's affections? Angusel fervently hoped not. Gyan and her consort had trouble aplenty from enemies like Urien and Colgrim without Alayna tainting the mix.

On the other hand, what if desperate need drove a move against Argyll, say, during a plague or famine? What would he do then? Under whose banner would he fight?

His gut clenched as the desire to stay home challenged his oath.

"And look at you, Angusel," she said, switching topics as blithely as a butterfly flits from thistle to clover. "Fighting in battles, and not even a proper man yet." Cocking her head to survey herself from a different angle, she fingered a lock that framed her face. "When will you take care of that little detail, hmmm? Once you complete the trial, I can petition the elders to name you chieftain. Your combat experience will make ratification quick and easy."

He scratched the wound left by the Angalaranach arrow.

Becoming a man by Caledonach law meant passing the deuchainn na fala, a test of courage, stamina, and wits. Not even battle was considered a substitute for the "trial of blood" prescribed by law for the warrior-born.

While a hostage and later, after the Pendragon had granted his freedom, there'd been neither the time nor the place to conduct the trial. The Isle of Maun offered many wonders, but a forest wild enough for the test didn't number among them.

There was, however, an overriding issue.

Eala stood, stretched, mewed, and touched her nose to his face.

"Gods, I don't want to be chieftain," he whispered into the twitching ear. She settled into his lap as if in agreement.

"What was that, son?"

"This summer, Mother. Mayhap before Lugnasadh." With luck, the delay would give him time to figure out how to avoid the destiny she had chosen for him.

"At Arbroch, I suppose?"

"Makes sense. I know our lands too well."

"Just like your father. He preferred to do things the hard way." Her lips thinned into a grim line. "Look where it got him."

In his first battle, Guilbach mac Leanag of Clan Tarsuinn had earned the Breatanach title *Gwalchafed*, "Summer Hawk," the name he bore proudly for the rest of his life. Gwalchafed died in a border skirmish against Uther's troops when Angusel was four.

He tried to summon his father's face, but it remained blurred, colorless. The only detail he could recall with any clarity was the Alban Lion tattoo roaring across Gwalchafed's shield arm. Angusel had loved to touch that tattoo; it always seemed as if he were petting a real lion. His mother wore the same pattern, of course, but it had never felt the same—physically or emotionally.

Tears stung his eyes, and he blinked them away. Had he been alone, he wouldn't have bothered.

The keening over Gwalchafed's body, his mother's as well as his own, he never would forget. He suspected revenge had driven her attack on Abar-Gleann. With Uther's son untried as a leader of men . . .

How wrong she had been.

"Mother, I just—" His voice caught, and he cleared his throat. "I want to make you proud of me."

After thrusting the mirror into the maid's hand, Alayna turned, smiling, and stretched her arms toward him. Gently, he dislodged Eala from his lap. She bore the treatment with casual feline indifference as she leaped onto the cushions of a nearby couch to begin grooming her hinter parts. Angusel rose and stepped into his mother's embrace.

"I know, son." Her sigh warmed his neck. "Whatever happens, you always will."

Chapter 15

Morghe sat on the curved, backless gilt Roman curule chair beside her mother, looking down upon their clansmen and doing her best to appear at ease. The judgment session had stretched into hours, and Morghe needed to take a walk, preferably toward the midden. She rapped her nails on the chair.

Ygraine cocked an eyebrow. "Patience, daughter." She gave Morghe a slim smile reminiscent of Arthur's. "Above all, a lady must cultivate patience."

The next case involved a pair of farmers and a dead cow. Fingertips tented, Ygraine listened to both accounts. Owen claimed Liam had stolen the cow from him and planned to butcher it before he could discover his loss, which Liam protested vehemently. According to Liam's story, the unfortunate animal had died near the shared border of their pastures, and Owen had dragged the carcass through a gap in the wall to make it appear as if Liam had stolen it. Owen, of course, denied Liam's accusation.

Ygraine questioned both men on the size and health of their herds, and the condition of the border wall. According to Owen, the wall needed repair, but the rubble made it too difficult to pass from one side to the other, especially when burdened with a dead cow. Liam claimed a wide enough gap existed to commit the deed.

Ygraine leaned toward Morghe, lowering her voice. "What say you, daughter? How would you resolve this dilemma?"

Morghe eyed the farmers. Both men appeared equally sincere; both stories equally plausible. Confidently pitching her voice for the farmers to hear, she told Ygraine, "I would inspect the wall. The men's stories are at odds on this point, and it's easy to verify."

"Perhaps too easy." Ygraine's gaze hardened upon the farmers. "Don't you agree, Owen?"

A startled look crossed the farmer's face. He began fidgeting with the cap in his hands, turning it like a wheel. "Begging your pardon, Chieftainess, I do not understand your meaning."

"Do you not?" Ygraine rose, and so did her voice. "Which of you," she asked the assembly, "journeyed here with this man, Owen, to hear my judgment and then act upon it?"

The people looked around, murmuring. When no one confessed, Morghe's doubts increased, but she'd seen her mother use this tactic often enough to prevent her skepticism from taking over quite yet.

She noticed a man at the back of the hall, edging toward the doors. Ygraine ordered the guards to bring him forward. Owen blanched as his accomplice blurted out that he had agreed to return to the wall's gap with a cartload of rubble to make it appear as Owen had described.

"Mercy, my lady!" Owen cried. "Your wisdom stopped me."

"True enough. Your intent, however, was clear. You swore false testimony. That is a crime against your neighbor, your chieftainess, and your God. You must make peace with God however you might, but you shall make restitution to Liam of the best cow of your herd. As for your chieftainess"—she tapped a finger on her chin—"add one-fourth again as much to your next tax levy." Ygraine waited while the scribes completed their notations. Later, this would be calculated and entered into the rolls, and the district's tax collector would verify that Liam had received the cow. "I pray this will help you resist such temptations in the future."

Owen bowed. "My lady is most gracious." Oddly, he sounded relieved. Morghe had expected him to be resentful.

She turned to her mother as Owen, trailed by Liam, threaded through the crowd. "You were within your rights to imprison him. Why didn't you?"

"He has a farm to manage and a family to feed. They'd have been sore-pressed to do it without him." Ygraine inclined her head at a group huddled near one of the firepits, the widows and orphans being sheltered at Caerlaverock. "I don't need to increase their numbers."

That Morghe understood. "But how did you know Owen was lying?"

Her mother chuckled as she sat and arranged the folds of her gown and clan mantle. "Experience. Knowing my people in a way that comes only by being out among them as often as I can. No," she said as Morghe drew a breath to speak. "I didn't know about that section of wall, but I know Liam is a tidy farmer. He must have cleared the rubble, perhaps intending to mend the gap later that day." She patted Morghe's hand. "The best thing you can do for yourself and your people, daughter, is to get to know them."

Morghe nodded thoughtfully. "No wonder your popularity waxes by the year, Mother." She meant it.

Ygraine uttered a rueful laugh. "Fate robbed me of the chance to teach Arthur about life. I'm thankful this didn't happen with you."

As Ygraine prepared to call for the next case, the doors burst open, and a Picti-garbed messenger strode into the hall. He thumped fist to breast in a legion salute. The Brytoni crowd shrank from him, exhibiting emotions ranging from dislike to revulsion. The courier ignored them.

Ygraine bade him approach, and he obeyed.

Rather than presenting a scroll, the messenger said in good Brytonic, "Chieftainess Ygraine, your son, the Pendragon, requests the presence of his sister, Lady Morghe"—he gave a respectful nod in her direction—"at Arbroch, Seat of Argyll, until June."

"Arbroch? Until June! But why—"

Ygraine waved Morghe into silence. "Did Arthur state a reason?"

"Nay, my lady." He said to Morghe, "The Pendragon did instruct me to tell you that all will be made clear when you arrive."

Not *if* she arrived, but *when*. Resentment reared. She gazed imploringly at Ygraine. "Please, Mother, don't—"

Don't—what? Don't let Arthur order her about? Don't let him take her from Ygraine's tutoring, as when she had been Merlin's pupil? Don't let him keep using her as a political pawn? She sighed.

Ygraine gave her a reassuring smile. "June isn't even six months off. Is that so bad? You can spend time getting to know your sister-by-marriage and resume your wedding preparations when you return. In fact, I will look forward to it."

Six months! Not now! Not when she was learning so much, with more yet to learn. Then the reason for Arthur's summons and its secrecy smote her.

She abolished her resentment with a slow smile. "No, Mother. It shan't be bad at all."

FINGERS GRIPPING the cold pewter tray, Niniane sighted her destination, wishing she could keep as tight a grip on her emotions.

Any soldier or servant in the praetorium could have delivered the message and the uisge, his favorite beverage. She wondered why she'd volunteered. A simple desire to help, yes, nothing more.

She chided her foolishness and quickened her step.

From down the hall came a series of clicks, each followed by a muted exclamation; whether of triumph or defeat, she couldn't tell. The sounds originated from the chamber she sought. Its door faced her as she tried to face how she felt about the man inside.

After balancing the tray, bearing a carved pewter pitcher and a pair of matching cups, on the palm of her left hand, she took a deep breath and knocked.

"Ave," said a voice from within.

As bidden, she pushed open the door and stepped across the threshold, glancing around with a physician's eye for detail.

Upon initial inspection, a visitor to the spacious workroom might offer a reasonable guess regarding its occupant's vocation. A jet crucifix as long as a man's arm gleamed starkly against one lime-washed stone wall. Before the glazed, unshuttered window stood a scribe's easel and vacant stool. The easel displayed a scroll opened to a section Niniane recognized as a half-finished Latin prayer. The untutored might admire its illustration: monks scything a wheat field. Dust motes swam in the stream of late-afternoon sunlight as it splashed against the manuscript. An orderly array of goose quills and inkpots covered the small table nearby.

The much larger table in the room's center hosted several damp clay tablets and iron styli of varying lengths and thicknesses, as well as stacks of parchment, a knife, and more quills and ink. A brass platter of bread crusts, cheese rinds, an apple core, and an empty amber-colored glass goblet crowded into one corner. The goblet's color announced its nobility, for the vast majority of glassware to be found in Brydein was green—so much so that the Brytoni words for "green" and "glass" differed by the addition of a single letter. A cluster of unlit bronze lamps hung on a chain from the beam overhead.

The workroom of a high-ranking clergyman, indeed, but that assessment represented only the partial truth.

Scrolls peered from tall willow baskets and competed for space on shelves lining the walls. While many contained treatises of Christian doctrine, others described architecture, astronomy, history, mathematics, medicine, philosophy.

And warfare. On the worktable, a tiny wheeled catapult stood atop a sketch of its counterpart, its finger-size firing arm erect. Pebbles littered the tiles at Niniane's feet.

The siege engine's designer hunched over the drawing, tapping quill to chin. Softly, she cleared her throat.

Bishop Dubricius favored her with a warm smile. No lust, no passion, not even a hint of desire, exactly the sort of smile she found attractive... and terrifying. Thank God he couldn't hear the stuttering of her pulse.

"Come in, come in. And please mind the stones." He waved his quill at the floor and, mercifully, returned to his notations.

Upbraiding herself for acting like a moonstruck maiden, she picked her way around the stones. She set the tray on the table and poured two rounds of uisge. One she gave to Bishop Dubricius, along with the sealed parchment. His fingertips brushed hers, and she felt warmth rush to her cheeks. She left the other cup beside the pitcher.

"Cai will arrive soon, Your Grace. He's seeing to his horse." She hugged the tray to her chest. "I thought you and he might like something to warm the blood."

"Ah, Niniane, many thanks." He opened the message. After studying it briefly, he set it on top of a stack of parchment leaves and drained the cup. "You're a blessing to this household."

"You are most kind, Your Grace." Lowering her eyes, she couldn't stop her smile. "As always."

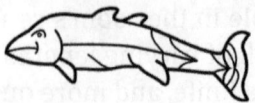

Merlin heartily wished she'd quit acting so bloody formal. Bad enough to use his ecclesiastical honorific in public, but even in private . . . why, he knew for a fact Arthur didn't get that sort of treatment from her.

Such incomprehensible creatures, women.

Perhaps a different approach might relax her manner.

He fingered the rim of his cup, trying not to dwell upon the fetching way in which a few chestnut curls had escaped her wimple to frame her angelic face. "How are your studies progressing?"

"Very well, thank you. Especially the writings of Hippocrates and Galen." Sadness stole the wistful yearning from her expression.

"But?"

She sighed. "A touch of homesickness. It's nothing, Your Grace."

"I understand, Niniane."

She had journeyed to Caer Lugubalion to nurse Gyanhumara's head wound and stayed to help treat men—even prisoners—recovering from injuries received during the Scotti invasion. Early winter storms had trapped her at headquarters until spring.

Merlin had offered her lodgings and access to his personal library in exchange for her healing skills, which she'd accepted readily enough. For him, the arrangement couldn't have been better. Niniane's herbal teas could cure everything from a bellyache to a hangnail, and her salves worked blessed marvels upon overworked muscles.

How he'd survive after she returned to Maun and her priory, he didn't care to contemplate.

The door flew open and hit the wall with a resounding thump. In paced a stocky man, crunching heedlessly across the pebbles, trailed by a Scotti slave carrying an oil ewer.

"What's this all about, Merlin?" Cai glared at him. "Dragging a man from his hearth in the dead of winter—bloody indecent, it is!"

Merlin chuckled. "Good evening to you, too, Cai. Please forgive my insensitivity. In addition to the original reason for asking you here"—he lifted the parchment Niniane had brought him from atop a pile of scouting reports—"I have word from Arthur."

Cai's face brightened. "Well? When does he return?"

"I should leave." Tray in hand, Niniane started for the door.

"No, stay, Prioress. Please." Merlin gestured to a chair. "This may interest you too." As she perched on the chair with the tray in her lap, he said, "Arthur plans to winter with Gyanhumara."

"What?" Cai roared. Standing on tiptoe to reach the hanging lamps, the slave shuddered. The ewer almost slipped from his three-fingered right hand. A few drops splattered the documents beneath. "Watch what you're doing, you stupid oaf!"

Cai cuffed the man's ear. Stammering an apology, the slave clutched the ewer to his chest and lurched from the room.

Merlin frowned.

"Cai, the man's hand is not whole!" Niniane protested.

Camboglanna's garrison commander shook his sandy mane. "If he can hold a jug, Prioress, he can do it carefully."

"Still," she said, "it hurts nothing to show compassion."

"Did he and his companions show any compassion when they attacked Maun?" Cai retorted. "When they slaughtered more than half the Tanroc garrison soldiers and civilians? And flogged all the rest of the surviving soldiers, including the wounded? Is that your idea of compassion?"

"Did the Lord Iesu command us to love only those who love us?" Her gaze melted from righteous indignation to humble appeal. "We are all precious to God, Cai, and should treat each other accordingly."

"Amen." Merlin gave her an appreciative nod.

Cai rolled his eyes. He said to Merlin, "Did Arthur give details?"

"Some." He shoved the parchment across the table. "You read it."

Cai regarded the dispatch, nodding slowly. "Arbroch. Why on God's earth would Arthur want to winter at Arbroch?"

"Why, indeed?" Merlin pointed to the uisge. "Here, Cai. I suspect you may need it."

Cai tossed it down and held out the cup for another round.

Refilling it, Merlin said, "Arthur has a wife to think about now." He set the pitcher down, picked up his cup, took a sip, and peered over the rim at his guests. "And a child."

Caught with a mouthful, Cai nearly spewed it. He swallowed hard and coughed. "You think she's with child? Already? That wasn't in the letter."

"Of course!" The prioress clapped her hands once. "It makes perfect sense—and explains why Gyanhumara seemed so edgy."

"And why they declined to stay at Dunpeldyr or return here. Most women prefer to be with their kinfolk at that time." Merlin laughed, not unkindly. "You ought to know that, Cai."

The young man with the legendary sexual appetite merely shrugged. "Wanting to see her there safely, perhaps even staying a few days, I can understand. But the whole bloody winter?"

"Come, now." Merlin smiled. "What were you two planning to do here? Hunt together? Arm wrestle? Play gwyddbwyll?"

"Lay out next season's campaign, dash it!" Cai drained his cup, and again, Merlin poured more. "Just as we've always done."

Gripping the tray, Niniane rose. "Forgive me, Your Grace, Cai, but I really must be going. You must have much to discuss."

As much as Merlin would have liked her to remain, he didn't disagree. "Thank you for the uisge, Prioress. And the dispatch."

"My pleasure, Your Grace."

"One thing more," added Merlin. The way she regarded him in innocent expectation sent a thrill coursing through his soul. He rebuked himself, hoping he'd shown no outward sign. "Gyanhumara's servant, Cynda, has been summoned to Arbroch. I will detail an escort. Can you please convey this to her so she can make the necessary preparations?"

After murmuring her acquiescence and bobbing a curtsey, Niniane slipped from the room. Merlin kept staring at the door after it had swung to.

Cai uttered a low whistle. "Saints preserve us. Not you, too, Merlin?"

"Hmmm?" He reached for the model catapult. "Let me show you my latest design."

"Don't try to change the subject. That tactic didn't work for Arthur, either. He refused to heed my advice, and look where it got him."

"What in heaven's name are you talking about?"

"What, indeed?" Cai rendered a credible imitation of Merlin's tone and inflection, the primary difference being that Cai's face had split into a wide grin. "I saw the way you were looking at Niniane, you sly old dog."

"This dog isn't too old to box the ears of an overcurious whelp." He smacked the tabletop.

"Point taken." Cai laughed. "So, what are we going to do about that wayward brother of mine?"

"Do?"

"You know what I mean. Now that he's saddled with a wife and a child."

Cai's acerbity surprised Merlin. "You don't like Chieftainess Gyanhumara. Why?"

If the question's directness surprised him, he hid it. "She's too aggressive. I've known the type. They want everything their way. Complete control."

"Admirable qualities in a warrior and leader."

"But not in a woman! Women were never meant to lead."

"Ah. Then you wouldn't mind telling that to Cleopatra, Boudicca, Vennolandua . . . or Alayna? Even though she lost, she fought an excellent battle."

Cai expelled a noisy sigh. Tipping his chair onto its rear legs, he thumbed his cup's intricate carving. "I don't know, Merlin. It's just a feeling, but . . ." He looked up, settling the chair onto all fours. "I think Arthur should have let Urien keep that woman."

Merlin shook his head, as much in disagreement as to dispel his own nagging instincts. "He couldn't run the risk of Urien—or any of the other chieftains, for that matter—growing too strong."

"Good point." Cai finished his uisge and set the cup down. Merlin moved to refill it, but Cai waved him away. "Then he should have waited to marry her, especially with the Scots and Saxons and Angles riddling our arses with their spears and arrows."

"I don't agree, Cai, for two reasons. Arthur has free access to Gyanhumara's wealth—which is, as I understand, quite considerable. This will be a great boon to the legion." Merlin downed his drink.

Cai nodded. "And the other reason?"

"The advice of the Apostle Paul, that it's better to marry than to suffer the flames of passion." Merlin's lips curved into a smile. "Advice you would do well to heed yourself, Cai."

"You too, my friend." Chuckling, he made a show of protecting his hands from Merlin's favorite punishment for insolence by tucking them into his armpits. The rod had gone the way of kindling long ago, of course, but Merlin appreciated the jest. Cai said, "If I'm ever that far gone, I'll let you sing my wedding mass."

The aging man who controlled swords and shaped minds and shepherded souls displayed a smile of paternal affection.

"Cai, nothing would please me more!"

BRACING HERSELF against the door, Niniane closed her eyes and blew out a slow sigh.

How long can I keep fighting destiny? Mine . . . and the bishop's?

Thinking of him in that manner helped. She couldn't fall to the temptation of referring to him by his familiar name, even in her deepest thoughts.

She'd grown accustomed to the Sight's intrusion upon her life, until she arrived at Caer Lugubalion and the new visions began. Visions of herself and Mer—Bishop Dubricius, alone.

Curiously, she couldn't discern what they were doing, except that he seemed to be teaching her something. The object in his fist remained maddeningly out of focus to her dream-eye. In each vision, they sat in the same room, remarkable by the profusion of light spilling in from its many tall windows. No such chamber existed in the praetorium of Caer Lugubalion or anywhere else she'd ever visited, in flesh or in spirit.

The scene appeared perfectly innocent, yet she couldn't mistake the love that softened his sharp gaze, or the tenderness with which he clasped her hands. When she woke from these visions, her roiling emotions came dangerously close to being a natural response to what she'd Seen.

Therein lay the dilemma. When she'd first donned her plain robe and wimple in the service of the Lord, she vowed to ignore fleshly promptings. Her order didn't require this; the Church of Brydein differed from its continental counterpart by permitting its servants to marry and raise families, but how could one dedicate oneself fully to the Lord with a family to consider?

The Sight might not reveal the whole truth, but it had not lied to her yet. Nor had she any reason to believe it ever would.

But how long can I hold my destiny at bay?

Her answer took the form of a soft moan.

URIEN STOOD on the Dunadd battlements, buffeted by gales and squinting through the swirling snow at the frozen river that lent its name to the valley and fort.

The Add Valley boasted mild winters. Not even the most grizzled Clan Moray elder could recall a worse storm. This demonically strong wind shrieked through chinks, rattled loose stones as though they were a child's playthings, and could rip a man's cloak from his back in a thrice. Urien glanced at the nearest guardsman, who'd muffled his head and face with a fold of his cloak. After giving the man a sympathetic nod and making a mental note to advise his father to shorten the duty shifts until the wind calmed, he headed for the stairs leading down into the inner courtyard. Vigilance be damned; the feast hall was the only sensible place to be.

Not an original idea.

The firepits at either end of the hall labored to perform their dual duties of providing heat and food, and warmth enveloped him like a favorite quilt. Folk not involved with meal preparations stayed well clear of those stone-bellied monsters.

The primary disadvantage to passing the afternoon in the hall lay with the feast itself. The rewards of the hunting party's labor, a wild boar and a score of conies and partridges, perfumed the smoky air. His stomach rumbled. The commencement of the feast seemed an eternity away.

He stopped inside the doors to survey the riot of activity. Women gossiped gaily while wielding needle or distaff. Children wrestled and tumbled and raced with each other and the hounds. Men amused themselves with various pursuits. The younger bucks, ale in hand and silly grins painted across their faces, flirted with the maidens. Dicing and arm wrestling occupied many a married man.

A sizable area had been cleared of benches and tables. To this impromptu arena he made his way. Amid a lively chorus of shouts and cheers, the men wielded staffs to sharpen eyes and wits and reflexes while vying for the "hero's portion," a haunch carved from the feast's main attraction.

He grabbed a staff from the collection leaning against the wall and entered the friendly competition. After a few minutes on the defensive, his muscles had shed enough of that devilish cold to press an attack. An unguarded opening allowed him to trip his opponent. The warrior went sprawling. Urien pinned him beneath the staff's butt.

"My lord, I yield!" To discourage any thought of trickery, he applied more pressure to his adversary's chest. "I yield!"

Urien removed the staff. The warrior rolled to his feet and staggered off, probably to drown his disappointment in a brimming ale horn.

An excellent idea, in fact. As much as it rankled him to admit it, that bout, compounded by having fought the gales on the battlements, had left him a bit winded. Declining the challenges that flew his way, he embarked upon his new quest.

Every man in the hall knew he could capture the hero's portion any night he chose. Gorging himself interested him far less than feeding his men's loyalties.

A keg stood near the main entrance. He bypassed a closer keg in favor of the position affording a better view of the hall.

And a prettier serving-maid. The slender, raven-haired wench with a saucy smile and even saucier curves managed her task with cool efficiency, not becoming flustered as other women did when Urien bestowed his favor. Winking, he accepted her ale. At a more appropriate time and place, he planned to discover just how well those nimble hands could perform other tasks.

After taking a generous swallow, he dragged the back of a hand across his lips and peered over the horn's rim at his father. Dumarec hunched in his tall-backed chair on the dais, the gold-trimmed black clan mantle draped about his stooped shoulders. He looked more like a crone than the chieftain of Dalriada's most powerful clan.

A few generations earlier, the clan's druids would have ordered Dumarec's sacrifice when he had grown too weak to lead the warband. Now, Christian priests legislated morality, forcing Urien to seek more creative means of accelerating his rise to power.

His gaze met Dumarec's across the hazy gap. Urien raised his horn in salute. Dumarec responded with a gesture that might have been a nod or, more likely, a cough.

With any luck, Urien map Dumarec would be sitting in his father's seat, swathed in the mantle of Clan Moray, before spring planting. Then the real work could begin.

"Lord Urien?" A hand dropped to his shoulder.

He whirled, preparing a rebuke. Annoyance evaporated into surprise as he beheld a mud-splashed, snow-dusted Accolon. Shadows beneath his eyes and the weary slope of his powerful shoulders proclaimed the length of his journey.

"Accolon, well met!"

Accolon's presence could only mean news from Morghe too important to share in public. As Accolon dropped his hand to the pouch at his belt, Urien subtly shook his head.

"Later, my friend," he whispered. Other clansmen had noticed the warrior's arrival and were approaching fast. Grinning, Urien thrust his ale horn at Accolon. "First, let's thaw you out!"

Chapter 16

"I SHALL ACCOMPANY THE work party." Gyan's announcement won instant, open-mouthed attention among those clustered around her in the courtyard near Arbroch's main gate. Her eyes flashed a challenge at anyone daring to meet her gaze.

The work party in question had been tasked to clear a path for the following night's religious celebration to honor the advent of spring. Although how these folk could envision spring when snow still piled knee-high went beyond Arthur's ken.

As near as he could gather, a clan ruler was required to oversee the priests' handling of the workers, slave as well as free. Because of the Abar-Gleann treaty, no Brytons stood in the slaves' ranks. Some had remained at Arbroch as free citizens, however, and had chosen to help with the day's work. Of their compensation Arthur hadn't a clue, perhaps their choice of lambs.

He studied his pregnant wife, proud of her devotion to her clan yet questioning her insistence to volunteer for the league-long hike.

Bad enough that she'd have to make the journey during the ritual; as quickly as she tired lately, he didn't like the idea of her making two such trips in as many days. But he held his peace, curious to see how this internal clan matter would play out.

One by one, the others remembered their tongues.

The High Priest said: "Is this wise, my lady?"

Cynda said: "Out of the question!"

Ogryvan said: "Have you gone daft, lass?"

Peredur said: "Aye, the bairn has addled her wits."

Morghe said: "More than your wits will suffer if you insist on trudging about in this God-forsaken snow."

Fists on hips, Gyan frowned. "You." She stabbed a finger at Angusel's chest. "I suppose you're with them?"

Kicking at a lump of snow, he shrugged. "I think they're right."

"Ha." Eyes narrowed, she faced Arthur. "What say you, husband?"

"What would you have me say? That you have my blessing to endanger our child?"

"Our child!" The words clotted into a ball of mist in the dim dawn. "That's all anyone ever thinks about. *Our child* is about to drive me out of my skull!"

With a swish of her white rabbit-fur cloak, she stalked toward the living quarters. Clucking like a grouchy hen, Cynda set off after her, with Morghe not far behind.

Arthur, too, made to follow.

Ogryvan caught his arm. "This is women's business."

"She is my wife! I must—I want to—" He wanted to enfold her in his arms and never let go, but the Caledonian words danced maddeningly beyond reach.

"My wife acted the same way, and it's not just the bairn." He punched Arthur's fur-swathed shoulder. "Gyan needs to be alone. Leave her be. You too, Angusel." Ogryvan flung the command at the lad as he tried to edge away.

"In the feast hall, Angusel," said Arthur. "I'll join you for sword practice."

"Not now!" Ogryvan's thundering dissent surprised everyone. "Artyr comes to the Nemeton with me."

"My lord," began one of the priests, "no outsider may—"

Scowling, Ogryvan rounded on the man. The priest shrank back and winced as his shoulders grazed the snow-covered stone wall.

"In case that incense you snort all day has made you forgetful, Priest, Artyr mac Ygrayna is my son-by-law and father of the next heir to the Seat of Argyll."

"Aye," Peredur put in. "How can he learn our ways unless he participates?"

"What says the exalted heir-begetter?" asked Vergul, the priest who had presided when Gyan received Arthur's dragon tattoo and Arthur swore his oath to her. His frosty stare sent a chill down Arthur's spine. "Does he wish to join us?"

Arthur turned his gaze from person to person. The priests didn't want him present; his wife's kin did. So be it.

He answered, "I do."

"Good, good!" Ogryvan clapped his gloved hands twice. "Then let us begin."

Vergul cast Arthur a venomous glance before helping his brethren organize the workers. Arthur ignored him. He wasn't about to let one sour-faced bigot jeopardize the hard work he and Gyan had invested to encourage unity between their peoples.

The High Priest selected another priest to accompany the work party. To Vergul's credit and Arthur's surprise, he did not argue with his superior.

Logic dictated the procession's order. Those wielding picks and shovels worked in front, followed by the food and ale bearers, and behind them, the priest. Arthur and Ogryvan walked side by side to guard the rear.

Although accustomed to leading, Arthur recognized the position's advantages. It let him watch the proceedings closely enough to step in quickly, yet far enough away to maintain privacy. The workers talked and sang among themselves, and the priest kept his own counsel, speaking only to direct the work.

This left Arthur and Ogryvan to each other's company, which suited Arthur perfectly. As the work progressed across Arbroch's meadows, he pressed his father-by-marriage for tales of Argyll's history. Though claiming to be no bard—the word Ogryvan used sounded like "shawn-ah-kee"—he fulfilled Arthur's request. Stories of battles and raids, famines and plagues, as well as periods of peace and prosperity, poured forth in Ogryvan's booming bass tones. Arthur's vocabulary expanded as he questioned unfamiliar phrases or concepts.

When the steepening path became treacherous with roots and

ruts and rocks, however, he devoted more attention to how he might help Gyan navigate this route the following evening.

"Your turn, lad."

He directed a quizzical glance at Ogryvan, who regarded him with amusement. The work party had halted, and the men, the priest included, were straining to lever a downed pine off the trail.

"Sir?" He wasn't sure whether Ogryvan meant for him to help move the tree, or if he'd missed something Gyan's father had said.

"I've told you about Argyll. Now, you speak." He tapped Arthur's chest. "About yourself. How did you come to lead the Breatanach army at such a young age?"

Arthur thinned his lips. Gyan didn't know the whole story of Dun Eidyn. Hell, not even Merlin knew. "I could ask you the same of Gyan. She has much responsibility for clan rule."

A shout went up, followed by a series of crashes and thuds as the tree rolled off the path and into the ravine, startling dozens of crows, sparrows, and grouse into flight.

As forward progress resumed and the birds' squawks died down, Ogryvan stroked his graying beard. "Aye, that she does. It's been so ever since she reached womanhood." The chieftain gazed up the path. "My dear wife died birthing her."

"And you still miss her."

"Aye." More a sigh than a word.

"You're not afraid you'll lose Gyan like that, too?"

"Gods, I hope not." Ogryvan uttered a rueful laugh. "But I'd be a liar if I said I never thought about it."

"So would I," Arthur admitted. "But I believe she will be in good hands." In death as well as in life, though he felt ill equipped to explain this to someone who worshipped other gods.

"Aye, lad. That she will." After striding in silence for a while, Ogryvan said, "You haven't answered my question."

Since Ogryvan had chosen to bare his soul, fairness demanded the same of Arthur. He willed the guilt to stay submerged.

"Dun Eidyn—the fort you call Dùn Éideann—was my first battle. Colgrim had lain siege, and my father led the standing army to relieve the fort. He promoted me to lead the reserve troops. I wanted to fight in the main division, at his side, but command of the reserves was too great an honor to refuse."

Arthur snorted, recalling everyone's reaction, including his. "I never questioned my father's judgment, even though most of his generals did. I thought I could do damn near anything."

"Surely Uther had good reason to trust your abilities."

"Only Merlin's word." In response to Ogryvan's puzzled look, Arthur added, "Merlin, the priest who performed our wedding, was one of my father's best generals, and he trained me."

"Ah." Ogryvan's smile turned cryptic. "Then I imagine your father had good reason indeed to trust the man's word."

"I don't know." Memories rushed back, unwelcome but unchecked. "When we got to Dùn Éideann, we had no idea..." The Angli-infested scene returned as vividly as the accursed reality had been.

"That there were so many enemy troops?"

Arthur nodded, reliving his shock and fear as the Angli forces, outnumbering the Brytons by ten to one, had pulsed around Dun Eidyn's walls. He forced himself to continue. "My father fought in the unit behind the phalanx." With his hands, he formed a wedge to explain the formation. "A strong phalanx will open the enemy's line for the main body. He posted many of his best men to the phalanx." *Where I should have been.* Arthur grimaced at another bloody memory. "Against those odds, they didn't stand a chance. Neither did his unit." His chest ached as though the Angli spear that had taken his father's life had struck him instead. Briefly, he ground his knuckles into the spot.

There were still days he wished it had.

"And your unit?" Ogryvan asked. "What did you do?"

"Nothing." Arthur laughed mirthlessly. "That's the hell of it. I was too surprised by the enemy's numbers. I should have ordered my men to help my father's troops, instead of holding them back."

"As you were ordered to do."

Arthur had never considered it that way before and told Ogryvan so. "Still, under the circumstances, I—"

Not even Merlin had heard this confession. He could scarcely admit it to himself. But here walked a man who might not feel the sting of disappointment upon learning of Arthur's failure. He wished he could leave it unspoken but knew he couldn't.

He regarded Ogryvan squarely. "I should have overcome my fears, sir, and reacted quicker. Maybe then my father would have lived."

"Or maybe not." Arthur started to protest, but Ogryvan put up a hand. "A similar quandary faced me at Abar-Gleann. The battle might have gone differently if I had beaten Urien in that race to the dike." Arthur raised an eyebrow, and the chieftain laughed. "And don't go abusing that notion, you whelp! Leave this old man a shred of pride." His expression sobered. "Of course, that might not have changed anything. In battle, you never know when an insignificant event will turn the tide."

True enough. One thrown horseshoe, one miscommunicated order, one ill-aimed arrow might rob victory from the winning side.

The chieftain said, "You feel badly about your father's death, perhaps even responsible. Anyone would, lad." Ogryvan gripped Arthur's shoulder. "I'll wager your guilt is undeserved."

Arthur shrugged the hand away. Guilt he deserved, not what had happened after Uther's death. "The men insisted on following me. Heaven only knows why, when Merlin and other officers had survived."

"Because you transformed the rout into an orderly retreat to save countless lives. No mean feat, that. Panic is a vicious plague."

"You heard about that, sir?"

"And the main details of the battle, aye. Word does get around, even up here." Ogryvan smiled. "But I wanted to hear it from you. A man reveals his true measure by how he handles defeat." The smile vanished. "Having guilt is natural, but if you let it consume you, Artyr, you will be of no use to anyone. Gyan included. I'd rather not see that happen to her. Or"—affection crinkled the corners of his mouth and eyes—"to the man she loves."

The procession stopped. The priest ordered silence while he intoned a prayer. A blessing, Arthur surmised, even though he didn't recognize all the words.

"You're right," he told Ogryvan after the priest had concluded.

Two stark choices reared up like the monoliths of the nearby circle where the workers resumed their shoveling. He could forever wonder how he might have saved his father's life. Or he could bid Uther farewell and put the matter behind him, laying it, and his father, to rest.

He drew a breath and chose.

Fist to chest, Arthur said, as much to himself as to his father-by-marriage, "I swear I will not let guilt best me."

PROPPED ON a bench in Arbroch's feast hall, shoulders to the wall and feet buried in a cushion atop a stool, a cup of heather beer in hand and sweltering under her ceremonial robe, Gyan felt like an outsider in more ways than one.

Tables and benches had been shoved aside to make room for the Dance of the Sun. Revelers leaped and kicked and shouted and clapped and whirled in a double-ringed blur. The frenzied rhythm couldn't be hampered by the injured or ill, those too far gone in their cups, or any woman with child. The sun had to return to full strength to assure another year of bounty, and this dance, madly spinning in every feast hall across Caledon, was believed to ensure success.

Gyan knew better. The One God had revealed the Old Ones as mere hunks of granite. By infinite contrast, He was mighty enough to weave the fabric of heaven and earth, yet compassionate enough to fold to His eternal bosom the soul of a bairn.

This knowledge turned bittersweet in the face of her clansmen's beliefs. Upon the word of the clan priests swung the pendulum of life and death. Not even rulers could claim immunity.

A reasonable man like Argyll's High Priest might be swayed to the One God, but he'd need a miracle to see another Àmbholc. Several priests, Vergul included, were already vying for succession, straining to prove their worthiness by adhering to the least jot of the law, regardless of whether it served the greater good.

Gyan shuddered to think what would happen to the clan under the spiritual control of an intolerant man like Vergul. Earnestly, she prayed that, should it come to pass, she would be politically, emotionally, and spiritually strong enough to beard that lion in its den without being mauled. Dafydd's occasional letters provided her only training in the faith, and she had far more to learn before undertaking such a crucial task.

Fortunately, the priests were occupied at the temple, preparing for the evening ritual. Common wisdom dictated that they could divine a person's most secret thoughts. It wouldn't have surprised her.

Within the last few days, she'd begun to notice the stirrings of the life that dwelt within her. She felt another nudge and studied the swell of her belly beneath her gray-feathered robe, recalling how precipitously Arthur had relieved her of command following her accident with Macmuir, citing love as the reason. Perhaps it had been merely a convenient excuse.

Their child constantly reminded her of that love. Arthur hadn't seemed overly pleased that she wouldn't be wielding Braonshaffir for a long time, but, knowing how much this meant to her, he might have been exercising diplomacy. On the other hand, she couldn't blame him for wanting to keep her safe. She'd do the same for him without hesitation.

Denying her nature to satisfy Arthur's concerns, however, was rapidly becoming too expensive a cost to bear.

She kicked aside the stool and rose. The room started spinning. She braced her hand against the wall, closed her eyes, and bowed her head, praying for strength, guidance, wisdom, answers, anything that could ease her turmoil.

With a sigh, she opened her eyes, wishing for better company than her thoughts, but Per and Angusel were dancing. Cynda had disappeared to find Gyan more heather beer. Ogryvan sat in his usual corner, challenging all comers to arm wrestling. Arthur, looking regal in Caledonach ebony leather beneath his gold-trimmed scarlet legion cloak, was—

She blinked hard, but the scene didn't change.

Arthur was sitting down to Ogryvan's challenge. The Ogre never lost. This Arthur knew as well as anyone, having witnessed countless bouts over the past several weeks, though never as a contestant. Why he'd decided to try his luck tonight, she could only guess. Her misgivings yielded to pride and love.

"Artyr, wait!" Although she tried to pitch her voice over the din as if on a battlefield, the bairn had dampened this ability, too.

Miraculously, Arthur glanced at her. She waved and began to pick her way toward her father and her consort.

"I had to see this," she confessed to both of them as she drew near.

Ogryvan chuckled. "Who will you be cheering for, lass?"

"I think this hall needs a new champion." The kiss she bestowed upon her consort underscored her hope. "Good luck," she whispered, grinning, "my little champion."

Arthur beamed at her.

"Ha!" roared the Ogre. "Then let us see what this demon-whelp husband of yours can do!"

Gyan helped Arthur remove his cloak, marveling at the crowd the event had already attracted. She could hear the measured handclaps and pounding of feet as the dance whirled behind them, but anyone not dancing was either standing near Ogryvan's small, square table or hastening there with all possible speed.

The combatants greeted each other with a stately nod as though meeting on the field of blood.

Elbow to table and arm cocked and fingers flexed, hand met opposing hand with a resounding slap. Sinews writhed, lips curled, jaws clenched, knuckles whitened. The advantage teetered like a pine battling the wind. Perspiration beaded upon furrowed brows.

A chant intruded, quiet but intense.

"Ar-tyr... Ar-tyr... Ar-tyr..." Her consort's Caledonaiche name danced upon the lips of many Argyll warriors. Hugging his cloak to her bosom, she raised her voice with them as the battle raged.

An arm weakened. The opponent pressed the advantage. His adversary fended off the attack. Stalemate again.

"Ar-tyr! Ar-tyr! Ar-tyr!" More onlookers hurled the name toward the rafters.

A surge of strength proved too much for the other. Both arms crashed to the tabletop. Fist thrust upward, the victor stood and surveyed his realm. His fiery smile rivaled the sun.

The Dance of the Sun froze.

"Artyr!"

Every man and woman in the hall joined the chorus.

"Ar*tyr*!"

Even the Ogre.

"*Artyr!*"

MORGHE HUNCHED over the scroll drooping across the too-small table in the too-cold anteroom of her too-Spartan chambers, squinting under the too-dim candlelight while the barbaric Picti form of her brother's name blew the roof off the feast hall.

Jamming hands to ears, she jumped down and paced to the hole in the wall that had the audacity to call itself a hearth. Just like everything else in this God-forsaken barbarian stronghold, the fire's warmth failed to lend comfort.

Mercifully, the noise ceased. She heaved a log onto the glowing heap. Summoning Arthur's face, she jabbed the embers. Flames roared to life. Gasping, she stepped back.

With a toss of her auburn braids, she chuckled softly. She could take a hint.

If she didn't exercise care, Arthur would devour her as he devoured anyone he deemed of use. Just as he'd devoured these Picts: horsemen, lands, wealth, women, and their very hearts. And the poor fools had no idea what he'd done to them.

A tentative knock disrupted her thoughts.

"Enter," she snapped.

The door opened to reveal a slave bearing an oil ewer. She recognized him by his maimed right hand. Winter's bite had chapped the stumps where two of his fingers should have been.

"Ah, Lughann, well come!" She didn't have to force a smile. "The days don't lengthen quickly enough for me."

"Aye, me lady." He bobbed a bow and set to work.

This man and several of his Scotti brethren, captured during the failed invasion of Maun, had accompanied Morghe to Arbroch to replace freed Brytons who'd returned to their villages.

Lughann's half-hand didn't prevent him from working efficiently, first filling the lamps, and then using the candle to light each wick. He turned the logs in the fireplace and added several more.

Experience had taught Morghe to cultivate allies everywhere. Even if she had no intention of being true, she deemed it wiser to appear so, as with Gyanhumara and her kin, until necessity dictated otherwise. A slave, whose presence commanded no more attention than would a chair, could prove useful.

"Thank you, Lughann. Wait." As he paused to regard her expectantly, she glided to the shelves bearing her herbs and medicines. "I have another task for you." Scanning the rows of neatly labeled clay jars, she asked, "Would you happen to know why my brother's name was being shouted in the feast hall?"

"Oh, aye, me lady, that I do!" His face split into a crooked grin. "The Pendragon arm wrestled the Ogre and won."

Arm wrestling Gyanhumara's father—that was all? These Picts were even more gullible than she'd given them credit for. Suppressing a laugh, she selected a small jar and passed it to the slave.

"Apply a dollop twice each day, upon rising and before retiring.

Mind that it gets rubbed in well."

"Who's to be receiving this, me lady?"

"Why, Lughann, it's for you. For your hand."

Ewer tucked under one arm, he cradled the jar as though it were the most precious gift on earth.

"Many thanks, Lady Morghe! A true angel, 'tis what ye be."

Bowing repeatedly, he shuffled backward from the room. She closed the door, latched it, and faced the fire. By the time she'd collapsed into her chair, tears of laughter coursed down her cheeks.

An angel? Not bloody likely. The word wasn't in her vocabulary.

"Well done, lad!" Ogryvan's dove-feathered ceremonial robe added to the cacophony as he thumped Arthur's back. "Even the Dance of the Sun stops for you."

Gyan glanced behind her and gasped. "Father, shouldn't we order it to begin again?"

Arthur shot her a questioning glance. As a Christian, even a covert one, the pagan rituals should hold no import for her. Then the truth smote him with awful clarity. Caledonian priests held as much power over their devotees as the Church of Brydein did over theirs and for the same reason: control of the masses.

He reached for her hand. Relief dominated her expression.

Ogryvan gazed at the feast hall's double doors, propped open to allow winter's chill to combat the heat. The westering sun's rays filtered through the trees, bestowing a golden glow.

"Nay, lass. The priests are due at any moment." He returned his attention to Arthur. "Although another bout like that, Artyr, and Clan Argyll will be clamoring for you to replace me as chieftain."

This prompted more cheers.

Arthur's heart lurched. A Caledonian prophecy had decreed that a Brytoni chieftain would bring Gyan great joy and great sorrow... and death. He banished the thought. Even if it were possible for him one day to wear a chieftain's mantle, no power in heaven or on earth could ever force him to bring sorrow to his beloved Gyan.

That he would cause her death was obscenely ludicrous.

"Surely, sir, you cannot mean—"

"Nay. But you are my son-by-law. It's time you started acting like it," Ogryvan declared. Arthur cocked an eyebrow. "Call me Father, as does Per, the son of my heart. Or Ogryvan." His grin radiated pure mischief. "Or Ogre, if my name proves too much for your feeble Ròmanach-Breatanach tongue."

If only half the rulers of the Caledonians, Scots, Saxons, Angles, and Brytons—especially the Brytons—would wield humor rather than swords, Brydein wouldn't suffer half its problems.

"If my tongue is so feeble, Ogryvan"—Arthur matched the Ogre's grin—"then perhaps your daughter can help me strengthen it."

He bent to kiss Gyan. The hoots, shouts, and claps intensified as she yielded to his touch. His conscience scolded him for indulging in such an emotional public display. Cheerfully, he ignored it.

"Children, please!" Although Arthur couldn't see Ogryvan's face, the warm affection rang clear. "Save it for after the Nemeton."

"He's right, Artyr," Gyan murmured. "We must join the procession."

He obeyed without surrendering her hand. Priests had begun to herd folk outside, where more priests awaited to direct them this way or that. As Arthur moved with the crowd, he tried to decipher the priests' actions, but even after he crossed the threshold and everything should have started making sense, it didn't.

In Brytonic, he voiced his question to Gyan.

"As each man and woman has a rightful place in life," she replied, also reverting to Brytonic, "so it is reflected in the Àmbholc procession. Farmers are ranked by the bounty of the year's harvest, herdsmen by the increase of their stock. Warriors by their success in battle. Craftsmen by their skills, and so on. The clan rulers—Father, Per, me, and you, my consort—share the third highest place."

She frowned, her gaze fleeing into the distance, and Arthur wondered what sorrow had invaded her mind.

"The third highest place," she continued, "behind the couples to be wed this night." Her emerald eyes focused sharply upon him. "Caledonians value the shared trust of a man and a woman."

He nodded, praying for a way to demonstrate his trust in her.

That the priests occupied the procession's head, Gyan didn't have to voice. Arthur paused to survey the column before taking his place. While this was no trained unit, neither was it an unruly mob. Even the children waited in reverent silence. The column contained uneven ranks, as few as one and as many as four abreast. Family groupings, Arthur presumed. The shoveled path dictated the column's width.

He and Peredur took the outer positions of their rank, with Gyan and Ogryvan in the middle. Three couples stood ahead of them, preceded by two ranks of four priests.

As a foreign sister-by-marriage, with no function in Caledonian society, Morghe had been excluded from this event. He doubted that she would have participated even if she'd been invited. But he found it odd that Gyan's frequent shadow was missing.

"No outsider may enter the Nemeton," Gyan whispered in response to his query.

Ogryvan had made it abundantly clear that marriage to Argyll's àrd-banoigin nullified Arthur's "outsider" status. What, then, of the non-Argyll spouses of other clan members? Was this why some ranks had only one person? Or were only the rulers permitted to marry outside the clan?

Before he could ask anything else, the line moved. Years of military training took over, and he remained silent. The procession snaked past the feast hall and armory, between the long buildings of living quarters and several beehive-shaped structures, across the market square, and on toward an open wooden pavilion near the fortress's wall. While he'd had no need to visit this area of the settlement, he recognized the structure as the temple of their gods. Under its high, peaked roof stood a huge, shallow, bronze dish supported by four clawed feet. Smoke billowed, and flames hissed and spat sparks. A stack of torch butts flanked the dish.

As they neared the temple, one of the priests, his face veiled by the shadows cast by his hood, broke rank to stand near the torches. To a silent rhythm, he stooped, snatched a dead torch, thrust it into the flaming dish, and offered it to the next person in line. Everyone received a torch.

Everyone except Arthur.

"You shall not defile the Sacred Flame," the priest snarled in a harsh whisper. "The Old Ones do not welcome heretics." He aimed the barb at Gyan, and Arthur didn't need the warning prickle to recognize the priest's identity.

"I suggest you treat the exalted heir-begetter with a wee bit more respect, Vergul." Her voice thrummed low and deadly.

They locked gazes. The chill in Arthur's gut predicted this wouldn't be the last time Gyan would engage Vergul in a battle of wills.

"Please forgive my zeal, Chieftainess, Exalted Heir-Begetter. I was merely defending my faith." Arthur noticed Vergul's subtle emphasis on the word "my." The priest dipped his head, lit a torch, and thrust it at Gyan. "The Old Ones punish those who defile the Sacred Flame."

Gyan snatched the torch from Vergul's hand and stepped off the platform.

The exchange had forged a gap in the procession. Gyan strode to catch the others without waiting for her father and brother to reform the rank.

"What can I do, Gyan?" Arthur whispered, in Brytonic. The set of her jaw and shoulders betrayed that inner battle again, and he wanted so much to help her fight it.

The gap closed, and Ogryvan and Peredur joined them.

Glancing at Arthur, she shook her head. If only he could find a way to help her bear her burden. If she trusted him enough.

These thoughts kept nagging him as the procession moved through the gates of Arbroch and out across the meadows, silent but for the crunch of booted feet on packed snow, an occasional muffled cough or sneeze, and the constant snap of wind-whipped flames. Neither brisk nor sluggish, the pace gave Gyan no difficulty.

That changed with the trail's slope. Arthur reached for her hand. Her smile conveyed gratitude, and she seemed to draw strength from his touch. As the trail steepened, her breath started escaping in ragged gasps, and her head and shoulders bowed.

Ogryvan also had been watching her, his distress plainly etched across his face. Arthur signaled for his attention, stepped closer to her, and extended his arm toward Ogryvan across her back.

This time, arm gripped arm not to compete but to help.

With a sigh, she leaned against their support and allowed them to assist her up the path.

At last, the stone sentinels loomed into view. With nods of thanks to Ogryvan and Arthur, she pushed away to walk the final steps unaided. Arthur smiled at her determination.

As the priests took positions inside the Nemeton, the rest of the procession coiled around the outermost ring of stones. The High Priest raised his oak staff, and the betrothed couples stepped forward. Like spokes on a wheel, the men fanned out, their brides facing them across the circle. At the High Priest's command, they approached the brush-smothered altar, one pair at a time, to feed the altar fire with their torches in the Caledonian gesture of marital unity.

It reminded Arthur of the rite he and Gyan had performed during their wedding mass, using candles instead of torches. Though Merlin had never spoken of it, Arthur wondered whether that pagan deviation from the established order of worship had raised a few eyebrows among Merlin's clerical peers.

He rebuked himself for engaging in speculation.

The last war Arthur ever wanted to fight was a "holy" one.

His mind snapped to the present when the crowd cheered the kissing couples. Then the High Priest called all couples married last Àmbholc who sought annulment to come forward. No one did. Another round of cheers burst forth.

The couples lined up to kneel before the High Priest. Ogryvan strode into place behind them, followed by Gyan and Arthur and Peredur. A hush settled over the clearing as the rest of Clan Argyll prepared for the ritual's final stage.

THE NIGHT before, Gyan had prepared Arthur for this moment. When their turn came, she didn't kneel but bowed her head in the customary manner for a gravid woman to receive the High Priest's prophecy about her unborn child.

Arthur also remained standing. She understood his choice; the priests of the One God wouldn't have tolerated any other behavior from him. The attention of Clan Argyll's High Priest stayed focused upon Gyan, which was fortunate for Arthur but stymied her silent prayer to the One God for forgiveness of her involvement in this rite. She could not risk revealing such thoughts to the one person on earth possessing the power to strip her of her rank and conduct her execution.

The old man entrusted his staff to an attendant. With one hand resting on her head and the other on her belly, his words crackled softly, like dead leaves. "Chieftainess Gyanhumara, your son will be a great warrior." Certain he was finished, she lifted her head.

The High Priest drew a rasping breath. In the torchlight, his eyes blazed like Lord Annaomh incarnate, a look she would never forget. She gasped and fought not to retreat. "And you shall possess his soul."

Numbness enveloped her.

Not from cold, although the wind had picked up. Not from fatigue, although her body would gladly embrace her bed this night. Not from hunger, thirst, or any other physical discomfort.

She would have welcomed any of those things—and a mortal wound—over the shock of the High Priest's words.

Bowing, she accepted the torch, rekindled from the Sacred Flame. As if of their own accord, her feet carried her from the Most Sacred Ground and the Nemeton, a few paces behind her father and the newly married couples. She sensed Arthur beside her as a presence only; he didn't seem real. The trees, the snow, the wind, the stinking bundle of tarred twigs burning in her fist, nothing seemed real. Nothing except the words echoing in her mind.

"What did he mean, Gyan?"

Arthur's question startled her, and she sought to devise an answer to soften the truth. Yet a lie would serve no purpose.

Though the ranks of the procession had spread out on the trail and no one walked within earshot, she took no chances. Arthur had whispered his question in Caledonaiche, but she answered in Breatanaiche. "Caledonians who worship the Old Ones believe in the idea of an immortal soul just as those who worship the One God do. They also believe there's a way to prevent the soul from leaving the body at the moment of death."

"Almighty God." He squeezed her hand. "The heads in the feast hall."

She nodded slowly, marveling that the broken, frosty ground passing beneath her feet felt as insubstantial as everything else.

"My son, destined to become a great warrior, will someday become my enemy. And I—I will—" She couldn't finish.

"Gyan, you cannot believe this."

Though they were no louder than the rest, the urgency in his words compelled her to meet his gaze. There she found no rebuke, as she'd feared, only deepest concern.

"I—" Belief in the One God freed her from the shackles of pagan prophecies. Or so she'd thought, but apparently a lifetime of Caledonach traditions couldn't be cast off so easily. "Artyr, I—I don't know."

"Could there be another meaning?"

She shook her head.

"A possibility for error, then? Or could this be a chance to guard against what might happen and prevent it?"

Another day, she'd have answered yes to at least one of his questions. Now, she couldn't be sure about anything.

Chapter 17

BRIGHT AS DAY, the moon lit the ice-crusted rocks and brush where Prince Badulf and his band hid in shivering misery. The valley stretched below in an endless swath of white, broken only by the stone huts, byres, sheds, and pens of the Brædan village. The stillness, the snow and ice, the cold, the full moon—alone, any of these factors would challenge the hardiest warband. Together, they added up to one conclusion.

He'd chosen an evil night for a raid.

These factors could be overcome by courage, skill, self-discipline, and luck. The first three, Badulf's men owned in abundance. He hoped luck wouldn't prove to be in short supply.

For the past fortnight, a host of omens had fueled Badulf's foreboding: a rope coiled like a striking snake, a raven-shaped puddle of spilled ale, a cloud piercing the heart of the moon like a spear, the sky blackened by an enormous flock of crows, a pack of starving dogs devouring each other in bloody desperation.

Badulf pulled his cloak tighter about him, a thin shield against the cold.

Nothing could shield him from his dread.

For his men's sake, he buried his feelings behind a brave mask. None of them had seen the omens, as if the gods had penned their message for him alone.

His death he could face. The possibility of leading his friends to theirs made his gut writhe, as if he'd downed a vat of poison.

He glanced skyward and spat a curse; the moon seemed determined to stay above the ridge. Instead of cutting across the meadows under cover of darkness, his band would have to hug the tree line, a much longer distance, to be sure, but much safer.

Badulf signaled his men, and they began the tedious process of moving from tree to rock to bush. Sometimes running, sometimes crawling, sometimes slithering, always trying to keep something between themselves and the village. At least it kept them warmer.

The famine that had sprouted from the stubble of the ruined harvest had begun to gnaw at the bellies of even the thriftiest Eingels. The success of Badulf's mission—indeed, the success of all Colgrim's war-bands—was crucial.

DWRAS MAP Gwyn chafed his arms beneath the wolfskin wrap and stomped his feet, but nothing could dispel this blasted cold.

Life in the Pendragon's service bore no resemblance to what he had expected.

He'd expected action. At the very least, he'd hoped to be trained by the other warriors to one day send the accursed Angli raiders to their gods.

Expectations held no truck with reality.

Reality meant being posted with a handful of Arthur's men to guard another Lothian village, one so deep in Brytoni territory that the Angli threat had to be slim at best. Reality meant enduring the endless pitying glances of the villagers, who knew he'd witnessed his family's slaughter. Reality meant helping with their winter chores—chopping wood, tending livestock, mending tools—not from a sense of duty or kinship, but to combat mind-murdering boredom.

Reality meant knowing the Angli never would raid this God-forsaken village.

Occasionally, the guard captain deigned to show him a few tricks with sword or spear. Spear, mostly, as if he didn't believe Dwras capable of mastering the art of swordsmanship. Usually, Dwras cleaned armor and weapons, fetching this and hauling that and doing whatever chores the soldiers deemed unworthy of their station.

Including nightwatch sentry duty. The others took their turns, true enough, but it seemed he stood at this post much more often.

A warning prickle froze his mental complaints.

The moon-bathed meadows gleamed serenely before him. Not even a stray leaf stirred. Abruptly, the night seemed eerily quiet. Something had invaded the valley. A wolf?

He studied the frost-bound birches and pines at the valley's fringes. No movement there—wait. That tumble of boulders and broom far off to his left... somehow didn't seem... right. Nothing he could describe, exactly, just a feeling that refused to abate.

The shadows shifted and stopped. After a handful of breaths, another shifting—a bit closer—then stillness again.

Raiders!

His fingers curled around his horn. If he blew it now, the soldiers and villagers would have time aplenty to respond. The thrice-cursed Angli whores' sons wouldn't set one bloody foot in this village!

But if he acted too soon, the raiders might flee, and he wanted nothing more than to take his spear and spit as many as he could. If the raiders escaped unseen, he'd be rebuked for sounding a "false" alarm. Imagining the taunts, he groaned softly. The soldiers would never let him live it down.

He chewed a gloved knuckle. Each silent moment brought his chance for revenge that much closer, but too great a delay might cost him his life and the entire village with him.

Inspiration hit. If he feigned sleep, the raiders might show themselves sooner. Not a sure wager, but a better plan than playing this damned guessing game.

Dwras map Gwyn felt astonishingly calm as he inched down the byre wall and let his head slump. With one eye closed, he kept the other half open upon the valley. The spear slowly came to rest across his lap. His other hand, hidden in the wolfskin's shaggy folds, clutched the horn. He gripped the spear and waited.

Without doubt, he'd never done anything as hard as pretending to be asleep while judging when the raiders had crept far enough from the forest. He feared his hammering heart would wake everyone by itself.

A few more steps... just a few... more...

As Badulf and his men left cover to approach the village and its lone, dozing sentry, the man jumped up, bleating the alarm. The huts spewed shouting men and women brandishing scythes, axes, pitchforks, and staves. Surprisingly, many of the men wielded swords. The sentry raced toward them, howling to wake the dead, spear leveled.

Warriors!

But not Loth's. These men fought with skill and discipline the likes of which Badulf had never seen. As the sentry neared, the moonlight bouncing off his cloak-pin revealed not the rearing Bear of Lothian, but a raging dragon. The omens, Badulf realized with bowel-loosening despair, had been true!

Killing came to Dwras with incredible ease. The first foe tasted the spear point through the throat. *That, for Talya!* The second died with the spear sprouting from his belly. *For Gwydion!* As he yanked it free, he caught another warrior in the chin with the spear's sharpened butt. He whirled to see the man staggering backward, arms flailing. Dwras gladly helped him enter the realm of the Angli gods.

He lost count after that, remaining oblivious to how the others were faring. Everything melded into a blur of snow churned with mud and blood in dawn's ashen netherlight. Sometime during the skirmish, his spear shaft broke. He didn't recall picking up a dead man's sword, yet there it lay in his fist, and just as useful as his spear had been.

Passion for vengeance flourished within him. Each man he felled spawned the lust to kill two more. To his fierce joy, there seemed to be an endless supply.

IN ANGUISH, Badulf watched another man fall beneath the sentry's spear before his sword became too busy trying to save his own skin. Hoarsely, he bellowed retreat, fervently praying that his surviving men could hear him.

He broke away from the skirmish line. As he lumbered across the meadow, with the enemies' pursuit thundering in his ears, he drank hope from the sight that some of the others had escaped.

THE REMAINING Angli warriors bolted for the woods.

No! They have no right! I want them all dead around me!

As Dwras began to follow, something snagged his heel. He glanced down and laughed. A fallen raider was feebly attempting to hinder his pursuit. Smirking, he raised his sword for the finishing blow.

The man blurted a single word that sounded a lot like...

Mercy.

He pressed the sword to the wounded warrior's throat. The captive looked up at him through pain-hazed yet hopeful eyes.

Mercy?

Talya had begged for mercy. Had this man's companions shown mercy to her or Gwydion or the others? Would they have shown mercy to him, had they found him alive that night? Or tonight? Fresh hatred gusted through him. Did this Angli dog deserve what had been denied to Dwras's loved ones?

Could this be the man who had murdered Talya and Gwydion?

He stared at his enemy's grimy, blood-smeared face, racking his brains for the tiniest trace of recollection.

But it had been so dark, and the warrior had struck so quickly... Dwras abandoned the effort. Proof or no, it mattered naught. If this man hadn't killed them, another Angli warrior had. By heaven, he, Dwras map Gwyn, would make them pay! Every last stinking fatherless son!

He tightened his grip. The captive's eyes squeezed shut.

I like your spirit. The memory of that voice surged forth as real as if the Pendragon were standing beside him, ankle-deep in the icy mud and gore. *I would like to put it to better use.*

Surely there could be no better purpose than to help Arthur rid Brydein of these Angli vermin.

Yet he couldn't forget the fathomless compassion welling in those eyes. When Chieftain Loth had been prepared to pass sentence, Arthur the Pendragon had bestowed mercy.

The man at his feet lay wounded, unarmed, and helpless. Killing him would make Dwras no better than his family's murderers.

So be it. He cocked his sword.

Talya never would have approved.

"No!" Stiffness seized Dwras's newly healed shoulder as he flung the weapon away. Arcing across the sky, the sword flashed golden in the sun's first rays before plunging into a clump of heather.

Conflicting emotions collided within him. Feeling faint, he cast about for something on which to brace himself, but no tree or boulder or building stood close enough. He bent double, hands to trembling knees, panting. His gaze fell upon the warrior he'd spared, who was regarding him with tearful gratitude. Dwras's vision misted.

His mind's eye beheld his beloved wife standing before him, not—thank God—as on that fatal night, but smiling broadly, arms outstretched in loving welcome. How he ached for her touch! For the assurance that she'd forgiven him for failing to protect her and Gwydion—and for the ability to forgive himself. Face in hands, he dropped to his knees, heedless of the slushy chill soaking his leggings, his shoulders shaking from the force of his sobs.

Invisible warmth enveloped him in tingling waves. After his salty well had run dry and the warmth dissipated, he inventoried his emotions, amazed to find that his rage and hatred and frustration had yielded to new sensations of lightness, of cleansing, of deliverance. And forgiveness.

"Well done, Dwras map Gwyn!" A hand clapped his shoulder. Wiping his eyes, Dwras scrambled to his feet to gape at the grinning unit commander. "Or should I say, Dwras Gwyn Peldyr?"

Dwras Gwyn Peldyr? Surveying the pale heavens, he pondered the name... and liked it.

Farmer Dwras, son of Gwyn, had died with his village. This day had witnessed the birth of a warrior, Dwras White Spear.

He saluted his commander and gave the wounded Angli captive a hand up. The blood-price for Talya and Gwydion had been paid in full. Dwras Gwyn Peldyr vowed to spend the rest of his life in the Pendragon's service, honoring their memories with deeds of valor.

VICTORY CHEERS replaced the sound of pursuit. Badulf didn't care. Though his desperately pumping arms and legs felt like stone weights, the shame of being caught in the trap goaded him. It took nigh unto forever before he found the horses. Another age passed as he waited for the rest of his men. Fewer than half had escaped.

Shouting the order to mount and retreat, his thoughts centered upon home and revenge. First, he had to usher his war-band home.

Revenge against Arthur the Dragon King of Brædæn would come in good time. And he, Badulf Colgrimsson, Prince of Einglaland, would lead the assault.

Chapter 18

ARTHUR TILTED THE parchment to catch the oil lamp's glow. An afternoon mid-April snowstorm had driven Arbroch residents to the safety of stone, timber, and the hide window-coverings that sealed out the weather as well as what daylight might have ventured into the room.

Bedwyr's report detailed damage wrought to the fleet at Caerglas by an earlier storm. Extra mooring lines hadn't kept a warship from colliding with its neighbor. Other ships had suffered less debilitating damage. Repairs were under way, so the news easily could have been much worse.

While thankful for his best friend's expertise, it did little to put him at ease.

Glancing at the closed door leading to the sleeping chamber, he sighed. He didn't regret his choice to winter with Gyan, for the knowledge he was gaining daily about Caledonians and their language counterbalanced the sacrifice of separation from Bedwyr, Cai, Merlin, and the rest of his companions.

But he felt as if his limbs were tied to four horses, each straining to race in a different direction.

Someone knocked purposefully on the door but not hard enough to rattle the timbers. After setting down the report, Arthur rose from behind the table, crossed to the door, and opened it, grateful that its well-oiled hinges didn't thwart his efforts to be quiet.

In the hallway stood Per, a sealed parchment roll in one hand. Finger to lips, Arthur motioned him into the antechamber.

Per cast a worried glance at the sleeping-chamber door. "How is she today?" he whispered.

Had this been legion headquarters, the Pendragon would have delivered a rebuke for the breach of discipline. Yet at headquarters, where the living quarters and workrooms existed in separate wings of the praetorium, Per's question never would have arisen.

His wife's half brother looked troubled. The message could wait.

Arthur shrugged. "Napping. She needs it." Since Per had initiated the conversation in Caledonian, and Arthur didn't mind the practice, he answered in kind.

"Aye." This sounded less like a word than a grunt as Per sank into a chair by the hearth. "I will be glad to see this bairn safely birthed. Then mayhap I'll get my real sister back."

Arthur laid a sympathetic hand on Per's shoulder. "Cynda says this is normal."

"She would know. She helped birth both of us, and the gods alone know how many other bairns besides." Per sighed as Arthur withdrew to the other fireside seat. "But Gyan seems even more changed lately. Less talkative, more broody, ever since—" The copper head jerked up, emerald eyes aglitter in the leaping firelight. "Artyr, what did the High Priest tell her Àmbholc night?"

What to say? She hadn't sworn Arthur to secrecy, either then or at any time during the past six weeks, but the prophecy's nature demanded silence. And Per deserved an explanation.

Arthur made a choice. Not a particularly good one, for an intentional omission was a lie, but he hoped this time the end could justify the means. "Our child will be a boy." Slowly, Per nodded. Into the protracted silence, Arthur offered, "I understand Caledonaich do not interpret this as a good omen." Per's shrug failed to hide the flicker of pain. Too late, Arthur remembered that here sat an "omen" in the flesh. "I meant no offense, Per."

The pain yielded to Per's customary grin. "What do mumbling old mages know? The omens pointed to Caledonach victory at Abar-Gleann!"

As the shared chuckle died, Arthur asked, "Dispatch?" He pointed at the parchment clutched in Per's fist.

"Gods! I almost forgot." He thrust it at Arthur. "From Loth of Dùn Pildìrach."

Arthur read the message that heralded the moment he'd both hoped for and dreaded.

"Three more raids on the same night. All repelled with the help of our men." He didn't mention Loth's footnote about farmer Dwras map Gwyn, whose efforts had earned him the respect of his unit and the appellation "Dwras White Spear." Arthur felt a nudge of satisfaction.

"Your next move?" Per asked.

Arthur rose and crossed to a parchment-laden shelf. As he separated the leaves, he identified aloud each dispatch's purpose.

"To Dumarec, Alain, Ygraine, Bann, and the other members of the Council of Chieftains of Breatein, to notify them that the campaign begins. Loth, of course, doesn't need one." Arthur fanned the stack and set it aside.

Per's eyes widened. "So many? What if even one falls into the wrong hands?"

"If Arbroch were any closer to Angalaranach territory, I would be more concerned. But as a precaution, I have coded each message." Arthur picked up the next pile. "To Cai at Camboglanna, to mobilize the foot troops." A brief smile formed at the thought of Cai's reaction. He slapped the parchment onto the table.

"To Gereint, to begin organizing the staging area at Senaudon and prepare for the troops' arrival." Alayna probably wouldn't like this, but she had no choice. The message joined Cai's.

"To Merlin, to appoint a temporary garrison commander at headquarters, issue the legion recall order, and gather supplies to help Gereint." Normally, Arthur wouldn't remove a senior officer from his post, especially one who also shouldered pastoral duties, but for overseeing the troop-staging efforts, Merlin carried the best qualifications in the legion.

"To Bedwyr at Caerglas—sorry, you call it Dùn Ghlas—to increase fleet patrols." A necessary precaution, even though Arthur expected no trouble from the Scots. The last time they had defied his expectations it had almost ended in disaster.

The final message he liked least: "To Urien at Dùn At, recalling him to Senaudon to head the cavalry."

"The whole cohort, Artyr?"

Arthur read concern in Per's eyes and appreciated the sentiment.

He'd have preferred to rely on someone whose loyalty he could trust—someone like Peredur mac Hymar of Argyll—but keeping Urien busy with the Horse Cohort would prevent him from troubling Gyan. He hoped.

"The whole cohort," echoed the Pendragon. He shuffled the sheets into a stack, leaving them on the table beside the oil lamp, a scarlet wax stick, and his dragon seal. "Today's snow should melt quickly. Find men to carry these dispatches—"

"What dispatches?"

Gyan stood framed in the sleeping chamber's doorway, her once-slim form all but filling it. Her gaze lit on the parchment, and she extended her hand.

Arthur gave her the dispatches and shot Per a glance.

Per stood. "I'll be in the feast hall, recruiting couriers." To Gyan he said, "You look wonderful! Did you sleep well?"

Grunting noncommittally, she lumbered into the antechamber. "As well as I ever do these days." Her smile seemed forced.

If her brother noticed, he made no comment. He planted a kiss on her cheek and left the room. Arthur secured the door.

He turned to his wife. She had taken a seat by the fire to read the dispatches; he had taught her his encoding scheme so they could share private messages, too. "So. It begins, then."

Arthur nodded toward the scroll on the table. "More raids were attempted a few days ago. Our men helped repel them."

"Our men!" She spat the words at the fire. "Ha. I have nothing to do with this." She slapped the dispatches. "Only this." Her hand settled upon her belly.

Arthur dropped to one knee at her side, his hand gripping hers. With the fingers of his other hand, he reached for her chin.

"Gyanhumara nic Hymar, I love you, no matter what happens."

As though to emphasize the truth of his words, the baby kicked. Grimacing as she glanced down, she massaged the spot. Arthur helped her. She did not resist.

"And I love you, Artyr." Her hand stilled as she contemplated the flames. "But you can't understand what I'm going through."

"I'm isolated here, too—isolated and useless. Me, Arturus Aurelius Vetarus, Dux bloody Britanniarum! Playing the pampered prince in my wife's stronghold while everyone else does my work."

She blew derision through pursed lips. "Spare me. You can remedy that any time you damned well please." Her gaze sharpened upon him. "You consider me *useless*?"

Clenching a fist, he studied the rafters. His hand relaxed with his sigh. "God, no. Gyan, if this"—he gently pried the dispatches from her fingers—"is your heart's desire, you will find a way to come back to it. I know you will."

He leaned in to kiss her. She didn't refuse—or react. His redoubled efforts yielded only the barest response, as if she had given up on life. On him.

It disturbed him to the core of his soul.

SYMBOLIC OF the vast, glittering fabric of the heavens, the Arbroch meadows glowed under a thousand Belteine fires. Each had been banked within a small circle of dirt and stones with plenty of wood at hand. These fires would claim more attention as the night's celebration waxed to its climax. Now, they burned low and untended.

Gyan watched the central bonfire, progeny of the Sacred Flame, with mounting dread.

The bonfire flared ever higher with each offering. A tithe of harvest stubble invoked blessings upon the fields for the coming year. The bones of livestock that had fallen victim to disease or accident or predator summoned protection for the flocks and herds. Women brought winterkill from their kitchen gardens for ritual cleansing of the home. Warriors sacrificed shields, split and irreparable, as a vow to improve fighting skills. Married couples offered damaged household items in pledge to repair broken relationships.

She studied the progress of one man and woman as they struggled toward the bonfire with a large, boxy structure—a table or perhaps a bed frame. The fickle light made it hard to ascertain. Since custom dictated offering an object in proportion to the size of the problem, she wondered about the nature of this couple's difficulty. As the fire consumed their sacrifice, they twined their arms about each other in a long embrace and rejoined their clansmen, hand in hand.

Gyan's tears welled. As short-tempered as she'd been toward Arthur, especially during his final days at Arbroch, it was a miracle he had tolerated her presence. Most days, she couldn't tolerate herself.

After the bonfire had claimed the last purification offerings, two-score young women stepped up to prance around its perimeter while the rest of the clan shouted and clapped.

Swiping at her eyes, she remained silent in the face of more evidence that her life had forever changed. All maidens old enough to bear children joined the Dance of the Virgins to consecrate the people's offerings. Gyan would have danced in this circle for the past three Beltean, had she not been living on Maun last year, though she doubted whether the One God would have approved.

Even so, she missed not being able to join her clanswomen.

As the Dance of the Virgins drew to its frenzied close, she labored to her feet and trudged down the grassy knoll toward the arc of pregnant women forming around the maidens. Some had borne other children; some, like Gyan, had not. Some had recently conceived and looked as slender as reeds. Others, like Gyan, bore robe-shrouded proof of milk-swollen breasts and bairn-rounded bellies. These women had come to present their unborn children to the clan for all to partake in the natal blessings.

Partaking of the blessing meant laying hands upon the belly of the mother-to-be. Typically, a woman received attention only from her kin and friends, but at Belteine bonfires all across Caledon, everyone sought their gravid àrd-banoigin for a special blessing.

Gyan tried to imagine what it must have been like for her mother to have been touched by so many hopeful hands and glumly wondered whether her frightful moodiness would keep her clansfolk away.

And she fretted that the One God might not take kindly to a mortal attempting to dispense blessings. If she'd been early in her term, she might have opted to deal with this concern another year. Today, she had no choice.

Yet, she reluctantly admitted to herself, the central issue had naught to do with her doubts about religious practices.

Caledonaich believed a woman would bear as many children as the number of Beltean she had danced with the virgins. If this proved true, Gyan's return to the world of swords and spears would be short-lived at best. When the Doves of Argyll had first adorned her sword arm, bearing children hadn't ranked highly on her list of priorities. But she firmly believed in taking all her responsibilities seriously.

A chilly gust made her reach for the edges of Arthur's heavy black traveling cloak. She'd felt a wee bit silly when she'd asked him to leave it with her, wielding the excuse that as the weather warmed, it would be excess baggage. She inhaled deeply of its masculine scent, regretting not having told him that she needed it as a reminder of his presence. In the next breath, she despised the circumstances that birthed that need—and in the breath after that, she despised her resentment.

Her bairn squirmed, as if sensing her turmoil.

She laid a hand over the spot and squeezed her moist, stinging eyes shut. *Please forgive me, my son! This is not your fault. Or your father's.*

The fault lay with her chosen response.

She still loved Arthur, she insisted to herself, fingering the cloak's edge. During the past few months, the character of her love had changed; gone was the unbridled passion they'd enjoyed. Cynda called it normal and temporary. Gyan hoped both would prove true.

Yet this hope, coupled with her remaining shreds of love, had failed to prevent her from lashing out against Arthur, her father, her brother, Cynda, Angusel, and anyone else unlucky enough to cross her path whenever her mood darkened.

If Arthur's absence stretched into years, she wouldn't blame him. She'd bid Per and Angusel farewell, but her parting gift to her consort had been stony silence. Arthur had looked back after the column had started moving, and she'd glimpsed his hurt. More than anything, she wished she could live that day over again. She didn't know how to repair the damage her behavior had wrought.

Affixing a smile to her lips to mask the guilt smothering her heart, she joined her clanswomen.

A place opened between Bryalla, huge with her fourth, and Mardha, who showed no sign of being with child. Though Mardha never boasted, Ogryvan made no secret that she warmed his bed.

Did she carry Gyan's half sibling, perhaps conceived during the March storm that had immobilized Arbroch for a week? A child who might become playmate and friend and companion-at-arms to

Gyan's son? Mardha's radiant smile told Gyan everything. The mothers clasped hands, and Gyan gave Mardha's an extra squeeze.

As the virgins stepped forward to receive the blessing of new birth, Gyan recalled her feelings from prior years. Even before putting her life into the hands of the One God, she'd never approached her gravid clanswomen with the desire to receive blessings for any future children she might bear. Still, she'd always taken care to lay hands upon each one, a happy duty to conduct.

The first approached, a shy lass not long out of swaddling bands herself. Mentally, Gyan braced herself for the touch. The maiden's fingertips barely brushed Gyan's belly, but her surprised giggle announced that she'd felt the bairn's nudge.

Gyan's smile felt more relaxed and genuine than any she'd given in months. A tingling raced from crown to soles.

The rest of the clan followed the maidens. Mardha, Bryalla, Gyan's father, Cynda . . . the surprisingly long parade of faces blurred in the firelight. As each pair of reverent hands sought her blessing of renewal, the tingling intensified. The clan's support had always boosted her spirits, but never like this, as if blessings—and forgiveness—poured upon her instead.

Perhaps that wasn't far from the truth.

For her heart felt as if it had shed invisible shackles. She had no idea what was happening to her or why, and didn't want to know lest this sensation die before it could bear fruit.

The tingling ebbed at the end of the blessing ritual. Her newfound peace remained.

As she returned to the grassy rise overlooking the Belteine bonfire and its myriad tiny brethren being stoked for the evening's conclusion, she thanked the One God for using her clan to bestow His precious gift.

Chapter 19

ARTHUR WATCHED GAWAIN—Sixth Ala's newest member—spur his mount after five cows that had decided to bolt rather than step onto the path that led up to Dunpeldyr's summit. Angusel drew rein to follow.

"Hold, Angusel," ordered the Pendragon.

The lad obeyed, none too happily, and nudged Stonn over to where Arthur sat astride Macsen, overseeing the final leg of the final drive to recover Clan Lothian's stolen cattle. Questions and disappointment paraded across Angusel's face, but to his credit, he remained silent. Life with First Turma, Sixth Ala these past seven weeks since leaving Arbroch—not as an official conscript because of his youth but rather more of a unit mascot as an unspoken favor to Gyan—had at least taught the young Caledonian warrior not to argue every order.

Though Arthur had several reasons for wanting Gawain to handle the wayward cattle solo, none of which were Angusel's concern and not the least of which being that Arthur's nephew had all but cut his first tooth on a cattle raid, he rewarded Angusel with, "Watch. If Gawain needs help, then we'll act."

"Aye, Lord Pendragon," Angusel replied evenly.

True to form, Gawain had already headed off the strays and turned them back toward the herd. Angusel kneed Stonn to a position estimated to prevent Gawain's charges from bolting in other directions and looked back at Arthur for approval. He bestowed it with a short nod.

As the other horsemen kept the rest of the herd moving up the steep, rocky switchback path that had earned Dunpeldyr the Caledonian name Dùn Pildìrach, Arthur swatted at the hundredth fly to circle his grimy face in the past hour. A score of its brethren were pestering Macsen; his beleaguered horse tossed his head and shook his mane and fretted and fidgeted like nothing Arthur had ever seen— except during other cattle drives. In silent apology, he reached down to brush a buzzing, biting swarm from Macsen's neck and gave it a reassuring pat. The damned flies returned moments later.

On his list of military operations, cattle raiding ranked dead last.

Never mind the moral ambiguity of stealing property that had been stolen from his countrymen at the outset—people who, because of that same property, lay long past the need for its return; thus, their chieftain reaped the benefits. Never mind that the unfenced summer pastures made guarding the animals nigh impossible, even for veteran Angli warriors. Never mind the minimal casualties. Never mind the fact that Arthur's men and Loth's treated each raid like a cavalry-games competition, whooping and yelling and guiding their mounts with speed and precision to encircle the herds and stampede them past any hope of pursuit . . . and keeping a tally among themselves that stopped mattering after the first half dozen pints of the night.

At this stage in every raid, Arthur chose the rear position to make sure no man or beast got lost on the return ride, and the view—along with the stench, dust, flies, and his mood—never improved.

Gawain drove all five rogues back into the herd and would have joined Arthur had he not signaled Gawain and Angusel to ride farther ahead as moving buffers between the cattle and the sheer drop. Two raids back, a bull had plunged to its death. At Loth's insistence, the man whose inattention made him responsible for the loss had received ten stripes, which Arthur had negotiated down from twenty, and he'd wielded the whip himself to make sure that was all the soldier got.

God, he hated cattle raids.

He was thankful when this herd passed through the upper rampart without incident, and the men secured all threescore and two head in the market pens.

Loth was waiting for him at the cattle gate, looking as unappreciative—and free of sweat, flies, dust, and dung—as ever.

"A word, Arthur..." Loth began.

Arthur could well imagine what that word would be. He ignored Loth and rode to where his men were dismounting in front of the stables.

"Fine work today, all of you. The first round is on me." Their cheers buoyed Arthur's spirits some. He felt even better to see his brother-by-marriage puffing to join the gathering. Suppressing a wicked grin, Arthur called his nephew forward. "You may put an extra pint on my tab, Gawain, for preventing those rogues from escaping."

Any day Arthur could needle Loth for the despicable indifference he showed his firstborn was a good day, cattle raid or no.

Arthur dismissed the men. As he dismounted and handed Macsen's reins to Angusel, he noticed Gawain collecting good-natured ribbing from his envious companions and a frosty look from his father. Arthur stepped in front of Loth to eclipse it.

"You wanted to speak with me?" Behind him, he heard the diminishing sounds of men and horses moving away and heartily wished he could join them.

Loth glanced toward the pens. Most of the cattle had found the feed and water troughs, though a few stood at the fence, looking decidedly wistful. Arthur knew exactly how they felt.

"Good haul today, Arthur. Thank you."

He covered his surprise with a nod. "My last haul."

"Are you sure you don't want to—"

"Hell, no." Tugging off his gloves, he turned to stride toward the stables, where the last of his men were disappearing with their horses inside. "I have more important work to do."

"More important than punishing Colgrim?" Loth called after him.

Arthur halted, clenching his jaw. Mucking a midden was more important than lining his brother-by-marriage's pockets for no more compensation than room and board for him and his unit. He faced about. Loth had made no move to close the gap. That suited Arthur just fine.

He pitched his voice to battlefield timbre. "If you want to conduct punitive raids and strengthen that royal Angli bastard's resolve, you go right ahead. I'll start writing your eulogy."

Horror cascaded over Loth's face. He hurried closer to Arthur. "But your sister, our children—you would refuse to help us? You can't! You swore—" Abject fear leached through the harsh whisper.

His pity for the man went only as far as lowering his voice. "I swore to defend the northern Brytoni clans from foreign threats. Don't stretch that oath to cover defending your stupidity."

Loth's cheeks flushed crimson. "Punitive raids will weaken King Colgrim, not make him stronger! Maybe even destroy him!"

"Loth, if you truly believe that—"

The sound of cantering hoofbeats cut off Arthur's retort. He looked past Loth to see a lone armor-clad horseman in a legion officer's cloak emerge through the rampart's gates and follow the invisible line drawn by the settlement's guards straight toward Arthur and Loth's position. The courier, noncommand optio rank, halted his horse, dismounted, and saluted Arthur while Loth stood scowling, arms folded. After Arthur accepted the small scroll and broke the seal to begin reading it, the optio acknowledged the chieftain with a polite nod.

Arthur closed the scroll and regarded Loth. "My service here is done." He dismissed the courier and resumed course for the stables.

Loth lengthened his stride to match Arthur's. "The message?"

"Merlin needs me," was all Loth needed to know. Arthur intercepted Angusel as the lad emerged from the shadows of the stables' central aisle. "Find Lord Peredur. He and ten men of his choosing shall accompany me to Senaudon. You and Gawain, too. Everyone is to wear battle-gear, pack light, and meet me in front of the tavern. We depart soon thereafter."

Angusel rendered a sharp legion salute, but life with Sixth Ala hadn't erased his grin. Arthur felt like grinning, too. Merlin had not supplied a reason for the summons, but anything short of administering corporal punishment was better than dealing with Loth.

Or Gyan.

The pain of their parting surged again. He set a brutal pace for the living quarters but knew he'd need Mercury's wings to outdistance the ache. He wasn't sure even that would work.

Loth caught up with him in his quarters. Arthur had finished sluicing the remnants of the raid off his face and was stripping out of his riding leathers.

"You're not taking all your men with you."

Arthur chose to interpret the statement as an observation, not a command, though Loth stood within his rights to make it one. After wrapping his neck with a light linen stole, he lifted a neatly folded scarlet tunic from the clothes chest. "The soldiers guarding Lothian villages may stay as long as necessary. Send them to the Senaudon staging area when you have no more need of them." As he pulled on the tunic, he regretted having to wear a clean one over his unwashed body. So be it. He donned the double-fringed, metal-studded battle-kilt, strapped on his footgear, and reached for his torso armor.

"Humph. In this you trust my judgment. But—"

"I trust you to do the right thing for Clan Lothian in every decision you make. I hope that trust isn't misplaced." Arthur finished buckling one side of the breastplate to the backplate and shrugged on the heavy bronze rig. "The courier and the rest of my men quartered here can expect recall within the week."

"Fair enough." Delivering his second surprise of the day, Loth helped Arthur adjust the armor and buckled the other side. After they got it sitting comfortably enough across Arthur's shoulders, Loth grinned at him. "Thank God you're not a chieftain, or we'd all be in trouble." He handed Arthur his helmet and retrieved Arthur's scarlet cloak—to which Arthur had left his dragon badge attached—from the back of a chair.

Arthur chuckled as he settled the helmet into place. "You most especially, my brother. Please express to Anna my affection and thanks." He hoisted on his sword belt, cinched it, and tucked his gloves into their usual spot. With his left hand, he picked up the sheathed Caleberyllus, which would be secured to his saddlebow for travel. Pursing his lips, he glanced at the sweaty riding gear and other items haste was forcing him to leave behind. "And my regrets."

He accepted the cloak and badge from Loth. Through their firm armgrip, he felt Loth's earnestness and sincerely hoped Loth could feel his.

An hour from Senaudon, Arthur and his troop encountered the outer perimeter. Though the legion didn't possess the manpower to establish a heavy presence this far out, it encouraged him to see soldiers stationed at the major roads leading into the staging area. Angli operatives would have to negotiate miles of dense forests and rugged hills. Only the River Fiorth provided easy access, and its surrounding land lay so unprotected that sheep could be counted from a mile away.

What he didn't expect was to find Merlin waiting for him. The darkness of Merlin's countenance boded ill.

Arthur ordered his men to halt and dismount for a ration break. His gut's tightness warned him that whatever Merlin had to say would take at least that long.

He left Macsen with a sentry as the men began rummaging through their saddle packs for food and wine before leading their mounts off to graze. Merlin beckoned Arthur to follow him toward a stand of trees well removed from the picket area.

"Lord Peredur should join us too," Merlin said.

Per heard and strove to catch them.

"What's this about, Artyr?" His whisper carried anxiety. His resemblance to Gyan made Arthur's heart ache anew, yet he welcomed that pain as a reminder of how much he loved her.

In answer to Per, Arthur shrugged. He expected the news to center on either the staging plans or Gyan. Because Merlin had requested Per's presence, Arthur wagered on the latter, squelching speculations about what sort of news would involve Gyan and yet require this much urgency and secrecy.

"Well?" Arthur demanded of Merlin after the thick, leafy screen shielded them from view. "Is she all right?"

"She?" Merlin cocked an eyebrow. "Ah, Chieftainess Gyanhumara. I hear she is very near her time but hasn't given birth yet. That's not why I asked you here."

Arthur tried to hide his relief but, judging from Merlin's faintly amused smile, he didn't succeed. "The staging preparations, then. What has gone wrong?" The invisible fist clenching his gut squeezed harder.

"Illness will prevent most of the troops from moving east this summer. A pox has struck Caer Lugubalion."

"What!" Per verbalized Arthur's reaction.

However, interruptions were neither appropriate nor appreciated. Arthur shot Per a stern glance and bade Merlin to continue.

"Not the killing pox, Lord Peredur." Arthur silently shared Per's relief. Merlin added, "This pox usually strikes children, but they're well again in a week or so. Adults aren't nearly as fortunate."

"Are you certain we cannot launch the campaign?" Arthur asked Merlin. The supplies required to sustain men and mounts through the winter wouldn't be cheap, even with help from Clan Argyll. Another damned contingency he didn't need.

Merlin nodded. "It's not as dangerous as its cousin, but we still cannot risk spreading this plague."

"What about you, Merlin, and the men you brought? Aren't you taking the chance of spreading it yourselves?" Arthur didn't believe Merlin would have made such a foolhardy decision, but he'd have been a greater fool not to ask.

"Praise God, no. We left before the outbreak."

Praise God, indeed. "How many have this pox?"

"A fifth of the legion, by last report, not counting townsfolk. That number may well double before summer's end." Merlin's frown deepened. "And you no longer have a cavalry prefect."

"Dumarec is dead?" Arthur asked bleakly.

"Not yet. But he's not expected to last the month."

"And Urien has taken all Clan Moray troops back to Dunadd." *God's holy, bloody wounds!*

"That's actually the good news, Arthur. He took only a score of cavalrymen. Handpicked, not all from a single turma. Moray foot and the rest of their cavalry contingent are here and healthy, since they'd reported straight from their homes."

Arthur's thankfulness died under the blade of a larger concern. "The Moray alliance?"

"No official word," Merlin replied, "but Urien cannot change anything until he becomes chieftain."

It wouldn't surprise him if Urien dissolved the betrothal to Morghe as well as the alliance.

Glancing heavenward, he offered a quick prayer for Dumarec's recovery. Sick troops at headquarters, a leaderless cavalry cohort at Senaudon, and a very pregnant wife at Arbroch gave him more than enough crises to juggle across the breadth of his world.

One crisis, however, he could resolve immediately.

He solemnly regarded his Caledonian brother-by-marriage, thankful that Per had proven to be someone he could trust and doubly thankful that he was not enmeshed in Brytoni politics. "Centurion Peredur mac Hymar, you are hereby promoted to the post of Praefectus Cohortis Equitum. As a nobleman, you may use the title of 'tribune,' if you wish. Or 'commander' . . ." Per flashed a smile that reminded Arthur even more of Gyan than recalling her preferred method of address did. "But before we get you settled into your new command, you and I have other business awaiting us a day's ride from here."

Arthur faced Merlin. "I trust you can do without the Horse Cohort prefect for a few days?"

Merlin nodded.

"Good. Per, let's pay a visit to your sister."

Per grinned. "Take Angusel. He will nay forgive you if you left him here. Nor would Gyan."

As Arthur voiced his agreement, a brief chill taunted his spine. He dismissed it as a reaction to all the news.

GYAN MOVED slowly along the line of swords inside the large timber building that served as Arbroch's armory. Her ponderous bulk and the mounting daytime heat as summer marched toward its annual climax obligated her to do everything slowly these days. Here, she possessed an excuse beyond the obvious: inspecting the clan's weapons hoard.

Warriors wealthy enough to commission special arms and armor kept those items in their quarters; the armory housed weapons and shields that were distributed in times of attack to arm a greater segment of the populace. Most of these items had been crafted more cheaply—no ornamentation, thinner and shorter blades, less attention to detail and quality—thus, it was essential to ensure their usefulness should the worst come to pass.

She waddled to the wall where the shields hung and stood sideways to better see any cracks lurking in the wood. This late in her term, she didn't dare attempt to heft them, and handling the swords was out of the question. That was the condition to which she'd agreed in order to buy this blessed respite from the hovering-hen fussiness of Cynda and Ogryvan's ever-escalating worry.

While pondering the inevitable conclusion that only the safe birthing of this bairn would deliver everyone from their fears—Gyan included—she felt a twinge in her belly and absently massaged the spot. Like its handful of predecessors, it barely deserved notice and was gone in moments. She pivoted and crossed to the rack of spears.

They looked adequate, as far as she could tell, standing upright around the rack's curved central core made from a massive, knotty oak log that had defied all efforts to split it for firewood. The spears formed an orderly cone with the heads crossing at its apex. A warrior could grab one and stab his attacker in one fluid movement. *Except, perhaps, with . . . that one.* Gyan peered closer at a spearhead whose leather wrapping-thong appeared to have loosened.

She stretched to grasp the dangling tail—if the wrap felt secure, its repair could wait for another day—and regretted it. A pain more fierce than all its brethren combined hit her with startling force. She staggered back. Too late, she let go of the spear's wrap, and the shaft shifted and collided with its neighbors, knocking down a dozen spears with a fearsome clatter.

Expecting half the clan to burst into the armory at any moment, she bent as much as her body would permit, hands to thighs and gritting her teeth to will away the pain. It obeyed. Panting softly, she lingered in that position to be certain it would stay banished.

"Cousin Gyan?"

Iomar mac Morra, Ogryvan's much younger and as-yet-unmarried cousin, son of the Àrd-Banoigin of Clan Rioghail, must have entered through the armory door behind Gyan's back. He and Morra were visiting Arbroch ostensibly to buy breeding stock . . . though the àrd-banoigin carrying the child of the Caledonach Confederacy's conqueror had to be the prime topic of conversation at every clan seat across Caledon, making any news of her condition coveted information.

She grasped Iomar's hands to let him help her straighten. "I am fine, Iomar, truly." She grinned, lightly squeezing his hands. "My bairn has started his training early."

Iomar bowed his forehead to her hands before releasing them. "I would expect nothing less of the son of the Warrior-Chieftainess of Clan Argyll and the Pendragon of Breatein." Though he quickly stooped to retrieve the fallen spears, she detected the honest flash of envy in his eyes. He replaced all but the spear that had sparked the mishap. "You must have been examining this one."

"Yes. Do you think it requires repair?"

Iomar yanked on the leather tail so hard his knuckles whitened. The wrapping remained secure. Bracing the spear against the wall, he used his dagger to trim the loose end. The offending piece fell to the floor for a servant to sweep away later. "It will do, for now." He returned the spear to the collection.

"Thank you." They moved at her pace to the rack of javelins. "Did you find what you needed for Rioghail's breeders?"

"Aye. Mother and Cousin Ogryvan are working out the payment details. They only needed my eye for horseflesh." He began pulling javelins one by one from the rack, testing each point carefully with his thumb and testing the shaft's flexibility with both hands before replacing it—something Gyan would have done herself had she not made a mess of the spears. Before reaching for another javelin, Iomar gave her a sidelong glance. "You do realize that every exalted heir in Caledon cried to see you marry the Pendragon?"

Chuckling, she shook her head, not in answer but in self-deprecation. "Every exalted heir in Caledon should have far better things to do, or I will personally take them all to task. And they should be thankful that Artyr chose to ally with our people in such a"—her hand pressed the side of her belly, where another pain, brief and less intense, flourished—"meaningful way."

She gauged his face for a reaction. If not for Arthur's treaty, she might have entertained a suit from Iomar mac Morra, whose huge frame and darkly handsome looks reminded her uncannily of her father, even though Iomar's relation to Ogryvan was a generation removed. Noble Caledonach cousins of differing clans sometimes married to strengthen alliances and consolidate wealth.

She felt a rush of wet warmth between her legs and watched Iomar's grudging agreement transform into wide-eyed astonishment. Following the line of his gaze, she looked down. A puddle was oozing across the floorboards from beneath the hem of her robe. Another pain hit her, weakening her legs, and she clutched at Iomar for support, grateful for his ready strength. He carefully began ushering her from her world of swords and spears. The idea didn't bother her as much as she'd expected it to.

It was time, she realized with calm, determined, and blessedly fear-free certainty, for an entirely different battle to commence.

URIEN HAD never set foot inside his parents' chambers. As a child, there'd been no need. In the care of first his nursemaid and later, his tutors, he saw his parents often enough as his activities intersected theirs in the feast hall, practice fields, chapel, hunting runs, or elsewhere around the settlement. After joining the army, he'd not been home long enough to see much of his own chambers, never mind anyone else's.

It felt odd to view these rooms for the first time upon the cusp of them becoming his.

There wasn't much to see except people. Physicians, guards, couriers, advisers, clerics, servants, and errand boys packed every span of floor space. What little talk they shared sounded subdued and impossible to overhear.

Regretting his decision to await the ferry and not to swim Talarf across the last loch, he wondered whether Dumarec had already died.

Slowly, folk noticed him standing in the doorway. In moments, everyone's gaze turned upon him. As though directed by an unseen hand, they bowed. He quelled his surprise. This treatment he could become accustomed to very quickly.

An avenue formed leading to the bedchamber's door.

Squaring his shoulders, he strode to that door. A guard opened it, and Urien caught a blast of fetid air. Eyes watering, he stepped inside. The door thumped shut behind him.

Heavy draperies shrouded the tall windows. The few oil lamps scattered about the room did little to alleviate the gloom. It took a few moments for his eyes to adjust. The air reeked of herbs and incense.

Urien's mother, a physician, and a priest stood near the canopied bed. A few servants hovered beside a table laden with food, drink, and medicines.

Dumarec lay on the bed, propped by pillows. The clan mantle covered his thin body, its black folds lending stark contrast to his ghostly pale flesh.

As Urien drew near, one of Dumarec's hands feebly waved.

"Urien, my son." The crackling whisper barely bore a resemblance to his father's voice.

He dropped to one knee beside the bed. "Father. I have come, as you asked."

In Dumarec's eyes, mirth struggled past the pain. "I can see that, lad. My body may be failing me, but my eyesight hasn't. Yet." The cold, leathery hand clutched Urien's. "You will be chieftain soon. Swear to me you shall always do what is best for the clan." Though the bony fingers shook, they wielded surprising strength. "Swear it!"

Leaning closer, Urien locked his gaze with Dumarec's. "I swear, Father." The heir of Clan Moray had never felt more sincere. Since the chieftain embodied the clan, what was best for the chieftain was best for all. "Before God and these witnesses, I do so swear."

Dumarec's head twitched in a parody of a nod. The hand holding Urien's relaxed its grip. He sucked in a rattling breath and blew it out slowly. His eyes, fixed upon Urien, glazed. His chest stilled.

As he studied Dumarec's face, the frozen stare seemed to adopt an accusatory cast. Urien blinked hard, but the disquieting sensation didn't ebb. Surely he'd imagined it. He forced himself to slowly rise and back away, letting the physician take his place. It didn't take long for the man to confirm the truth.

While Urien's mother gently lifted the lifeless arms, the priest took the clan mantle from the bed. One by one, she removed the pillows so Dumarec could lie flat, and she folded his arms across his chest. She didn't weep as she performed this final service for her husband.

She bent to kiss Dumarec's brow and joined the priest, who still held the clan mantle. They draped it around Urien's shoulders.

Urien gazed at his father's body as the cloak's weight enfolded him within the moment he'd desired with all his being. Yet he couldn't suppress a twinge of remorse for the man who had shaped his life by teaching him about warfare and leadership.

Nothing he couldn't live with, however.

Head high, the new Chieftain of Clan Moray threw open the doors, stepped into the light, and greeted his clan.

Arbroch's atmosphere crackled with hopeful expectation.

After receiving a hearty greeting from the gate sentries, who'd been pleased to report that Gyan had gone into confinement that morning, Arthur, Per, Angusel, and the rest of the escort were summarily ignored—which suited Arthur perfectly. No sense wasting time fawning upon them.

The men stabled their horses, and Arthur sent Angusel racing ahead for the latest report about Gyan. The lad met him and Per outside the ruling family's living quarters.

"They say she's doing fine," Angusel blurted as breathlessly as if he'd run from Marathon.

"Did you see her?" Per asked. "When will the bairn arrive?"

"I don't know." Angusel shook his head, clearly frustrated. "Cynda won't let me into the birthing chamber. She won't let any man enter. Chieftain Ogryvan tried, too." He leveled his golden-brown gaze at Arthur. "I'll wager she won't even let you in, my lord."

Arthur chuckled. "I may just take that wager, Angusel."

If excitement among the folk outside ran high, inside they bordered on ecstatic. Women paraded through the doors to Gyan's chambers carrying linens, bathing implements, buckets of water, firewood, and other necessities. Each chatted gaily with her neighbor.

Without breaking stride, Arthur made for the door.

"Oh, no, you don't, my lord." Cynda seemed to appear from nowhere to block his path, arms crossed and eyes flashing.

He donned his most charming smile. "Cynda, my wife is in there. And my child. I would like to be with them, if it's all the same to you."

"It most certainly is not the same to me, Lord Artyr. Men have no business here."

"My family is my business." Still smiling, he charged his tone with warning. Then a better idea occurred. "If you prefer, I'll pick you up and carry you in with me. Do you think Gyan would be jealous?"

She shook her head with a short laugh. "Very well. You may go in. Only the exalted heir-begetter," she announced to the other men. They answered with a chorus of disappointed groans. She said to Arthur, "But if you get in the way, my lord, I guarantee you will regret it."

"Careful, Artyr," advised Per, grinning. "Our little tyrant does not make empty threats."

Arthur believed him all the more when he saw Cynda in her element, barking orders as crisply as a veteran centurion. Like well-trained troops, the women swiftly obeyed, but he had little care for their work. He didn't even wish to speak with Morghe, already stationed at the bed's foot to witness the birth.

Only the figure on the bed held his full attention.

Gyan was half lying, half sitting against a mountain of pillows. Naked from her swollen waist down, her knees were drawn up and apart. As the flesh of her abdomen rippled, her sweat-streaked face contorted in the most excruciating agony he'd ever witnessed.

To his immense relief, her face relaxed and her hands unclenched, but the spasm left her gasping. Cynda bent over with a damp cloth to swab Gyan's brow. When Cynda moved back, Gyan turned to look his way, but another spasm caught her as she tried to speak.

He dashed across the room to her side.

"If you plan to stay there, my lord"—amusement and affection warmed Cynda's tone—"then I suggest you make yourself useful." She pressed the cloth into his hand.

Arthur dabbed Gyan's flaming cheeks. She managed a weak smile. "Artyr. You—you're here. Why?"

He took her hand, surprised by how hot it felt. "Stampeding cattle couldn't keep me from you, my love." Smiling, he inclined his head toward Cynda. "Neither could she."

Gyan tried to laugh, but her body succumbed to another convulsion. Her hand gripped his with Amazonian strength. He groaned through gritted teeth as the pain shot all the way up his arm.

"Ah," cooed Cynda at his shoulder. "Forgive me for not warning you, my lord. That's one of the hazards of this type of combat."

"Oh, Artyr, I hope I didn't—"

He silenced her with a quick kiss. After flexing his fingers to get the blood circulating, he took her hand again. "Don't worry. I'll be ready this time."

A good thing, too, for her next spasm lasted a lot longer.

Morghe let out a delighted squeal. "The crown! I see the crown!"

A host of pleased murmurs sprang up around the chamber as the other women jostled for a better view.

Cynda shouldered them aside to look for herself, nodded, and quickly moved to Gyan's other side. "Your bairn is almost here, my dove." Gyan sighed softly as Cynda said, "Remember what I told you?"

"Yes, Cynda. I remember." She sounded much stronger, which heartened him. "Push for all I'm worth. And breathe."

"Good lass." Cynda glanced at Arthur, reaching for Gyan's shoulders. "Quickly, my lord, before this next pain comes upon her. We must hold her up. It'll make things go a wee bit easier."

He'd have cut off his right arm and beaten himself with it if he thought it might help. They supported her shoulders and back through waves of pain as Gyan gasped and moaned, and the child wrestled into the world.

At last, their efforts earned the sweetest sound under heaven: an infant's first cry. His child... their child. Their son!

Thankfulness flooded Arthur's soul.

Cynda produced a knife and cut the cord. She sheathed the knife and handed the sticky, squalling infant to another woman. As the servants cleaned the baby, Cynda instructed Gyan to push out the afterbirth. Once the bloody mass was removed, Cynda cleaned Gyan's legs, bound her loins with sphagnum moss and bandages, and ordered Arthur to lift her so the linens could be changed. Eyes closed, Gyan submitted meekly to their ministrations. After Cynda finished, Arthur settled her against the pillows and blotted her sweat with a dry cloth. Her eyes flickered open to reveal exhaustion beyond measure.

"We have a boy, my love," he whispered. The first stage of the prophecy had come to pass, but he had no intention of broaching that subject. Ever. He couldn't begin to fathom Gyan's agony, but he felt as if he'd just defeated an entire enemy army with only a cudgel. "What shall we name him?"

"Loholt," she replied. "It means 'for terror.' One day, he shall strike terror in the hearts of his foes."

Scrubbed and swaddled, this tiny terror nestled sleepily in a blanket of Argyll-patterned lamb's wool. Gingerly, Arthur took his son from a beaming Cynda, who showed him how to cradle the baby's head. Eyes misting, he gazed in sheer awe at the red, wrinkled mite. "Loholt," he whispered. "Loholt mac Gyanhumara." His son yawned.

"No." Gyan reached up to take him from Arthur's arms, pushed aside a fold of her tunic to expose the feeding-slit, and with her free hand gently brushed her nipple against the baby's mouth. It took only moments for Loholt to figure out what to do. As the perfect little lips flexed and tugged, Gyan's smile lit the entire room. She said, "Loholt mac Artyr."

Chapter 20

LOHOLT MAC ARTYR.

The bairn had haunted Angusel's thoughts for three maddeningly interminable days.

He paused over his half-devoured mound of ham, cheese, and bread, grinning to recall the Pendragon's face when he'd finally emerged from the birthing chamber, looking as if he'd just spent a night in Lugh's feast hall, dazed yet smitten by the joyous wonder of it all. To questions about Gyan and the bairn, he divulged only that Gyan had borne a son and named him Loholt, and that both mother and child had survived the ordeal commendably well.

Probably, Angusel thought with a broader grin, much better than the father had.

Chieftain Ogryvan, favoring the Pendragon with a hearty laugh and backslap, had vowed to melt his son-by-law's tongue with liquid fire. Nobody saw either of them until late the following morning.

Clan Argyll didn't seem disappointed that their àrd-banoigin had borne a boy-child. Gyan was young, healthy, and strong, ran the general opinion, with time aplenty to bear a daughter for the clan. Angusel knew Breatanaich prized their boys and held their girls in little regard.

Barbarians. He took a swig of ale.

Did Gyan hope to forestall ill sentiments from Arthur's kin by naming Loholt for his father? Did she believe she needed to?

Naturally, her choice had raised eyebrows among her clansmen, but any real trouble would come from the jealous guardians of the law. If the Argyll priests were even half as stubborn as Alban's, Gyan's fight against the ancient tradition of naming the child for his mother would be fierce indeed.

But the woman to whom he'd pledged his sword and soul could defeat any man on his own turf.

The aromas wafting from his plate reminded him of his unfinished business, which he attended to until the food had disappeared to the last crumb. He pushed himself up from the bench, handed the trencher to the nearest servant, and strode toward the feast-hall doors.

As with the last three days, Angusel resolved to present himself at Gyan's antechamber. If Cynda again refused entry, he planned to remain with Lord Peredur and Chieftain Ogryvan in case Cynda experienced a change of heart. A slim chance, granted, but better than doing nothing.

He understood the reasons for Gyan's seclusion. She needed time to heal and marshal her strength, and Loholt needed to grow accustomed to his new world of light and noise.

To say naught of the possibility of treachery.

He slapped his dagger's hilt. No treachery would come within a hundred leagues if he, Angusel mac Alayna of Clan Alban, had any say.

Upon entering the antechamber, he greeted Gyan's father and brother.

Today, miracle of miracles, Cynda let him enter!

Gyan looked more beautiful than ever. Her hair, freshly brushed and braided, shone like burnished copper. Gone were all traces of the haggard lines that had creased her face, and the dark circles beneath her eyes had lightened.

At her bosom she cradled a bundle of blankets.

The bairn was feeding, Angusel slowly realized, for her tunic's design made it hard to tell at first glance. One tiny hand won free of the blankets to curl around her finger. With a smile, she began to hum a warrior's victory song, softened for small ears.

He had no wish to disturb this peaceful, private moment. Curiosity sated, he turned to depart and almost collided with Arthur.

As he stammered an apology, the Pendragon waved him silent, his smile suffused with pride. The plain tunic and trews made it easy to mistake the man for any other pleased new father, rather than the stern warlord Angusel had come to know.

"Come, Angusel, and meet our son," he said.

Gyan glanced up at Angusel's approach, and her smile deepened. She'd adjusted her tunic and was holding Loholt to her shoulder, rubbing his back. After he uttered a milky burp, she cradled him in her arms.

"Well come, Angus," she murmured. "Hold your new sword-brother."

She placed Loholt into Angusel's outstretched arms, and he did his best to imitate how she'd held him. Angusel's sword was heavier.

My new sword-brother!

Peering past the layers of blanket at the sleepy infant's face, Angusel tried to imagine that future. Whose looks would Loholt favor? He appeared to have his father's square jaw and sapphire eyes and high cheekbones, and his mother's delicate nose and mouth, but any of that could change with time—and injury. The hair, hidden by the blankets, was anyone's guess. Would Loholt stand as tall as his father to one day wield the mighty Caleberyllus? Or his mother's Braonshaffir?

Angusel had no idea. But he would do all within his power to escort Loholt mac Artyr to his destiny.

Steadied by her consort's hand, Gyan swung her legs over the side of the bed and stood. She lifted the sleeping bairn from Angusel's arms and crossed to the hearth, where Loholt's cradle had been set well back from the danger of stray sparks but close enough to the warmth. While Gyan settled Loholt into his cozy bed, tucking a silver-trimmed Argyll-patterned blanket about him and placing a new rag doll at his side, her consort thrust his head into the antechamber to speak to Cynda. The woman bustled in, needlework in hand, and beelined for the chair beside the cradle.

For the first time, Angusel realized that no other servants worked in the room. Most strange.

"We're taking no risks," Gyan whispered in response to his question as she eased back onto the bed. "Until the naming ceremony, Loholt must be seen by as few people as possible."

The naming ceremony, conducted a sennight after birth for children of the àrd-banoigin, was the rite for presenting the àrd-oighre to the clan. At this time, the child received a simple version of the clan-mark on the right heel to signify his status as exalted heir.

Angusel pondered his mark, the outline of a rampant Alban Lion. Until the naming ceremony could be performed, the àrd-oighre might be mistaken for any other child. Down the turbulent centuries, more trouble had befallen Caledonach children during this vulnerable sennight than at any other time during their youth.

He wasn't sure which concerned him more: Gyan's quietly ominous words or the fact that her brief walk about the chamber had taxed her strength. Yet rather than embarrass his sword-sister, he stayed with the topic she had broached.

"Risks? Arbroch is secure. Isn't it?"

"As secure as possible, Angusel. But there has been a new development." The Pendragon's visage darkened. "Dumarec is dead."

"Which means..." The ugliest of pictures flashed to mind. "Gods help us, Urien is a chieftain now." Angusel's hand went to the absent sword hilt. Realizing his mistake, he sighed and asked, "Why tell me?"

Gyan laid a hand on Angusel's forearm. "Because, Angus, I—" She glanced at her consort with a smile and said, "*We* know your heart. We have no doubt of your devotion to us or to our son, and we believe you can serve us in a way no one else can."

Her emerald eyes ignited with their old fiery glow. Though the reason might be unpleasant, Angusel rejoiced to see the Gyan he knew and loved best return.

"Anything, Gyan!"

Even if it meant confronting Urien in that cù-puc's own stronghold. In fact, Angusel wished for it with his entire being.

Morghe's lips curved into a smile as she blew on the parchment. The endless months of pretending to be amiable toward Gyanhumara and her clan while enduring their weird ways finally had borne fruit.

She folded the sheaf, dripped wax onto the top flap in two places, and flattened both scarlet splotches with her seal. After a few moments, she tested the raven imprints with a fingernail.

"This will help you tell the messages apart, Sichuan." She gave them to the waiting courier, one of Ygraine's men assigned as part of Morghe's escort at Arbroch. "The one with the single seal gets delivered first." More importantly, the double seal would alert its recipient to the message's significance. "Change horses at Caerglas and Caer Lugubalion." She dropped three gold filigree brooches into his upturned palm with a delicate *clink*. "Use these to buy bed and board and whatever else you need along the way."

Sichuan tucked the parchment and brooches into the pouch at his belt. He bowed and left the antechamber.

Her smile widened as the door swung shut behind the most loyal and capable man of her entourage.

With Sichuan's return to Arbroch—within the month, if the Fates deigned to grant him swift passage—she could start arranging her long-awaited departure from this God-forsaken Picti outpost. She hoped to be ensconced at her mother's fortress before the end of hay-making season, then the planning for her wedding to Urien could commence. Chieftain Urien, she amended with a surge of pride.

Morghe ferch Uther, Chieftainess of Clan Moray of Dalriada.

Such a poetic ring . . . and so close to becoming reality she could almost feel the cool gold circlet against her brow. The Feast of Christ's Passion never had held significance for her. Next year's celebration, ten months hence, with Urien at her side and his people fawning at her feet, promised to be an entirely different story.

As she moved the quills, inkpot, sealing wax, and parchment to the shelf overhead, she started to hum a popular wedding dance tune.

Someone knocked on the door. Ordinarily, the intrusion would have irritated her. Today, she'd happily dance with the devil himself.

She opened the door to find Angusel standing in the corridor, glancing over his shoulder and looking perplexed.

"Angus? Something wrong?"

He gave her a startled look. "Wrong?" He met her gaze, looked over his shoulder again, and stared at his foot as he scuffed it against the flagstones. "Nothing, Morghe. I passed Sichuan and was just curious . . ." When his eyes met hers, they burned with abrupt intensity. "Where is he going? He was dressed for travel but seemed to be in too much of a hurry to talk about it."

While she displayed a smile as innocent as Gyanhumara's son, she pondered Angusel's motives. She'd never seen him act suspicious about anything. He didn't exactly seem suspicious now, either. Curiosity, then, as he'd claimed. And who was she to deny his wish?

"Why, I've sent him to my mother with news of her grandson's birth." This was perfectly true. She grinned. "If you see Arthur before I do, can you please tell him I've done this?"

That won an answering grin. "I will! I'm sure he'll appreciate having one less detail to arrange." Angusel turned and strode down the corridor, his Clan Alban cloak flaring in a sky-blue billow.

As URIEN moved at a mind-numbing plod astride Talarf, his senses sharpened to the creaking and jingling of harnesses, the snapping of the procession's torches, and the smoke's tarry tang; to every hoofbeat and footfall and murmured prayer, which escalated as folk joined the crowd from each farmstead and crofter's hut along the way; to the squeaking wheels and groaning timbers and flapping fabric on his father's bier; and to his mother's sobs, muffled against the shoulder of one of her women as they sat beside the bier's driver.

The heightened awareness reminded him of riding into battle.

The bier hit a rut and lurched to a stop. He started, sawing the reins, and Talarf reared. The column halted. Bringing his horse down with a soothing word, the Chieftain of Clan Moray berated himself for his foolish nervousness.

The coffin had shifted, but the bier remained undamaged. He ordered the procession forward, casting a glance over his right shoulder. Dawn tinted the sky with streaks of gray, although an hour would pass before the sun breasted the hills.

They crossed the remaining fields, tromped over the bridge crossing the River Add, and streamed into the forest. As Urien reached the clearing, he could still hear people on the bridge. He wheeled Talarf about and marveled at the procession's length. With a stab of remorse, he hoped his death would prompt such an outpouring of respect.

Licking his dry lips, he returned his attention to the clearing. The two stone-paved, stone-studded circles had been built centuries earlier to honor gods as old as the hills. Although the Lord God Almighty could move those hills with a single stroke, He couldn't move the people's hearts to abandon their ties to this place. Rather, Urien amended lest he incur divine wrath upon himself, God's priests had failed to sway the people to accept such radical changes and therefore had adapted some of them into the worship of the Almighty.

Perfumed by the priests' censers, the clearing thrummed with Christian music and prayers to speed Dumarec's soul to his eternal rest. Whether or not this was true, the son of Dumarec dared not guess, but the mourners' rapt faces revealed the ritual's comforting effect.

Urien's mother, red-eyed and pale as she rested a hand against Dumarec's coffin, had stopped crying. The sight gladdened her son. As often as he'd tried during the past few days, he'd been unable to offer her any words that didn't sound trite or insincere... or weren't a downright lie. Instead, he'd let gestures—a handclasp, a hug, a sympathetic glance—speak for him. Across the gap, he sent her another of those glances, and she answered with a wan smile.

More musical prayers accompanied the work as Dumarec's honor guard slid the coffin from the bier, bore it to the freshly dug hole between the stone rings, and lowered it into place. Cries escalated to wails as workers filled the grave. Even Urien wasn't immune to tears.

Blinking hard, he raised his arms and drew a breath. "My clansmen!" He ignored the priests' stares. "Good people of Moray, I am certain my father would have been honored—as I am honored—by your demonstration of love and respect for him." Silence settled over the clearing, punctuated by discreet movements as people wiped their faces on cloaks and tunic sleeves and anything else at hand. "I am also certain Chieftain Dumarec would have wanted us to celebrate his passing into a better world"—this he spoke for the benefit of his mother and others whose beliefs outpaced his—"and not mourn it overmuch." A few heads nodded. "I can envision no better way to celebrate his life than to acknowledge the fact that his beloved memory remains with us through the embodiment of his seed to lead you." Urien drew his sword and thrust it skyward, letting Talarf dance a little. Every eye tracked him now; more heads nodded, and some of the soldiers cheered. "Therefore, my clansmen, let us adjourn to Dunadd without further delay, thence to conduct the fealty-swearing ceremony."

Amid the claps and shouts of approval, the chief priest scurried to Urien's side and motioned for a private word. He sheathed his sword and leaned over.

"Forgive me, my lord, but it is customary to wait a full week. The clan needs time to mourn."

"And they shall have all the time they require." Urien lowered his eyebrows. "After the ceremony."

"But the chapel isn't ready, and the choir hasn't—"

Smiling, Urien clapped the priest on the shoulder, straightened, and raised his voice. "Holy Father, there shall be time aplenty to conduct the funeral mass, and I heartily encourage you and your brethren to continue your preparations." This drew appreciative murmurs from the crowd. "Today, let us ask our people to bring naught but their devoted hearts as we conduct the rite in the ancient way."

Cheers flew heavenward.

"With holy water," interjected his mother into the lull.

Urien gave her a measuring glance. He could count on one hand the number of times he'd heard her express an opinion to Dumarec in public. Yet his father had always given her words due consideration—apparently with good reason. He inclined his head. "As you will, my beloved Lady Mother. Your wisdom honors the clan."

FOR THE first time in too many months, Gyan perched atop Macmuir. Since her body hadn't yet recovered from the birthing, forcing her to wear loin bindings stuffed with sphagnum moss to stanch the flow, she sat sideways on Macmuir's back, both legs dangling over one side. This was especially awkward while trying to hold the squirming bundle otherwise known as her son. Why some women habitually rode in this manner by choice, she had no earthly idea.

Arthur and Angusel strode at Macmuir's head, each gripping the bridle. Her father and brother flanked her to keep her balanced. Not even Angusel had been pleased with her insistence to ride, but she cared naught for anyone else's opinion. She hadn't strength enough to make the journey afoot, and for a warrior and mother of a warrior, her war-horse presented the only acceptable choice.

Ahead, torches ablaze with the Sacred Flame, marched the priests of Argyll. The rest of the clan streamed down the path behind Gyan.

The predawn chill couldn't dampen soaring spirits. Snippets of excited banter wafted her way.

She wished she could share their enthusiasm.

Urien map Dumarec, Chieftain of Clan Moray, had become wealthier and stronger... and far more dangerous than ever.

He had sent Arthur a formal letter stating his intention to continue supporting the legion, no huge surprise. A declaration of withdrawal would have announced his plans louder than a chorus of war-pipes. Silence would have spoken volumes, too. Urien wasn't ready to make his move.

Thanks be to the One God.

Gyan gazed at her son, lulled asleep by Macmuir's gait. Worry clawed at her heart. A military campaign took a great deal of time and wealth to prepare. An attack against one person did not.

Yet Angusel hadn't discovered evidence of a plot against Loholt. Apparently, she thought with a thin smile as she recalled his report of the sundry places he'd visited, not for want of trying. The only thing even remotely unusual was Morghe's decision to send one of her men to Ygraine with the news of Loholt's birth, rather than letting Arthur dispatch one of his soldiers.

To assume Urien didn't already know about Loholt would be a grave mistake. Surely, if he sought revenge on Gyan through her son, he'd have arranged for something to occur before the naming ceremony.

The increased guard might have thwarted Urien's plan, but it wouldn't prevent him from trying again. The Arbroch guard couldn't remain doubled forever.

She tossed her braids with an impatient shake. Whether she ever wielded a sword again, she would remain a warrior at heart. A warrior dealt with the realities of the present and left the ghosts of the past and shades of the future to fend for themselves. She smiled at Loholt. Present reality took the form of this precious little incarnation of the love she and Arthur shared.

The procession stopped, and a priest approached Angusel.

"Angusel mac Alayna of Clan Alban," intoned the hooded figure with a bow, "you must wait here until Clan Argyll returns."

Angusel nodded his reluctant acceptance, though his eyes bespoke his desire to continue with the rest of the procession. Gyan wished she had the power to grant it, but this tradition couldn't be broken. Arthur, as àrd-ceoigin, was a rare exception. No other person outside the clan could learn the hidden way to the sacred Nemeton of Argyll.

"I'm sorry, Angus," she murmured. "This shouldn't take long."

She read the disappointment in his eyes as he released Macmuir's bridle and withdrew to the edge of the path. Disappointment yielded to fierce pride as he honored her and her son with the warrior's salute. It pleased her to return the salute on Loholt's behalf: an appropriate gesture, for her next battle loomed.

DISARMED AND stripped to the waist, Urien stood atop the long, flat, white Chieftain's Rock outside Dunadd's innermost gate while Clan Moray packed into the courtyard around him. Symbols had been carved into the rock ages ago: a basin, a footprint, and notches whose meaning not even the bards could recall. Another, more recent symbol adorned the rock's face: the Boar of Clan Moray. At the chief priest's signal, Urien knelt beside the basin. The priest dipped his fingers into the sanctified water to anoint Urien's brow, chest, and both shoulders in the name of the Triune God. Tingling erupted at each point of contact.

Urien resisted the urge to wipe the water away.

He rose for the arming, which symbolized divine allotment of the chieftain's power, whether performed by a Christian priest or one of another faith. No stranger to the trappings of war, the chief priest completed the donning of Urien's padded undertunic, breastplate, backplate, belt, sword, helmet, and clan mantle efficiently.

The priest bowed to Urien and jumped down from the knee-high rock, his part in the proceedings finished save for the closing prayer. The final step was Urien's to take alone.

Swallowing convulsively, he stared first at the hollowed-out footprint, then at his own foot, trying to gauge the sizes and wishing he had tested the fit beforehand. The depression accommodated an average-size foot against which Urien's foot and, symbolically, his ability to rule would be judged. A smaller foot was viewed as a positive sign that the chieftain would grow into his responsibilities. A larger one portended an ill fit between the chieftain and the clan. No one would swear fealty to such a man.

Urien drew a deep breath, strode forward, and crammed his foot into the hollow. A surge of relief dispelled the discomfort wrought by pinching rock.

Planting fists on hips, he stared across the sea of smiling, cheering faces as the men lined up for the fealty-swearing, searching for anyone who might dispute his claim upon the hearts of Clan Moray.

He had no takers.

THE PROCESSION halted before the stone sentinels ringing the Nemeton's Sacred Ground. While a beaming Ogryvan held his grandson, Arthur helped Gyan dismount. As the rest of the clan entered the clearing, she lingered in his arms, drawing upon his strength. She'd told him what would transpire, but this battle he couldn't help her fight.

She collected Loholt from her father, tucked a soft fold of the Argyll-patterned blanket around his wee face, and strode onto the Sacred Ground.

"By what name is the Exalted Heir of Clan Argyll to be known?" The High Priest's crackling tone carried across the hush descending upon the clearing.

"Loholt." Gyan readied her arguments like an archer collecting arrows. "Loholt mac Artyr."

The High Priest cocked an eyebrow, opened his mouth as if to speak, then seemed to think better of it and merely nodded. When Vergul began to voice disagreement, the High Priest silenced him with a glare. This seemed decidedly odd, but she wasn't about to question her good fortune. She swallowed her relief as she entrusted her son into the High Priest's care.

After entering the inner stone circle guarding the Most Sacred Ground, he gently laid Loholt on a cushion atop the altar, unwrapped the blanket, and freed his right foot. The graying priest who had applied Per and Gyan's tattoos stepped forward to perform the same service for her son. Loholt whimpered at the first prick of the knife on the back of his heel. She stood poised to rush to his side.

The priest worked quickly yet carefully. Loholt didn't make another sound. Gyan grinned. Her son had borne his ordeal like the true warrior he was fated to become.

Recalling the rest of his prophesied fate, she suppressed a shiver. She would sooner take her own life than cause him to lose his.

The High Priest picked up Loholt and wrapped the silver-trimmed blanket around him. "I present the Exalted Heir of Clan Argyll, lawful firstborn son of Chieftainess Gyanhumara nic Hymar and her consort, Artyr mac Ygrayna. This child is part Breatanach by blood. His name represents this fact—and rightly so." Loholt cooed as the High Priest freed the newly marked foot and angled it for the crowd. Bright blue dye glistened in the outline of two tiny doves. "By the Mark of Argyll, let it be forever known to all that he is Caledonach in heart, mind, and spirit."

He kissed the bairn's forehead and placed him into Gyan's arms. "Clan Argyll," he continued, the pride in his aged voice undisguised, "I present to you Loholt mac Artyr."

Chapter 21

URIEN TRIED TO block out the noises and movements of the soldiers around him on Dunadd's practice range to focus down the arrow's shaft, his emotions as tight as the bowstring between his fingers. Chieftainship bore no resemblance to what he'd imagined.

Certainly, he'd expected decisions to be made upon his father's death: dismissing old advisers and appointing new ones; renewing trade agreements; assessing clan holdings, livestock, tax levies, and other assets; inspecting the war-band; forging alliances. He hadn't expected these tasks to leave no time for plans of a more personal nature.

His arrow sped toward the target and nicked the center's edge. *Damn.*

Having to send that thrice-cursed letter of support galled him like badly tanned breeches, but silence would have aroused Arthur's suspicions.

He pulled another arrow from his quiver. As he nocked and drew it, he imagined a different target, one surmounted by a scarlet-crested helmet. He released the arrow.

It struck dead center.

"Well done, my lord."

Urien turned, resisting the urge to train an arrow upon the intruder. He had ordered Accolon, his new aide, not to disturb him except with matters of utmost urgency.

Accolon stood a dozen paces away, flanked by a man in travel-stained clothes. A leather pouch hung at the man's belt under his dagger sheath. The courier's Cwrnwyll-patterned cloak bore the Ivory Unicorn badge, but either Ygraine or Morghe could have sent him.

Lowering his bow, he invited the men to approach.

They bowed. "My apologies for this intrusion, my lord," began Accolon, "but—"

Urien waved Accolon silent and extended his hand to accept the letter from the messenger. As he examined the seals, he pursed his lips. The raven imprint identified it as a message from Morghe, but why the double seal? Urgency? Or some other meaning?

He broke the seals and read about how she'd sent the messenger to Ygraine first, using the double seal to make sure the man didn't deliver the wrong letter to her. Apparently, Morghe believed that traveling by way of Caerlaverock decreased the likelihood of the messenger being followed to Dunadd.

Her plan didn't account for the possibility of interception, but he was impressed that she'd taken a precaution that he might have ordered under similar circumstances. He grinned. Perhaps he shared more in common with his future bride than he had believed.

"Get ready, Accolon." He clapped his friend's shoulder. "At first light, you embark on a journey as my envoy." Triumph swelled Urien's chest. "Of sorts."

LOHOLT WAS crying.

Gyan pulled the covers up to her ears. Sometimes if she waited a few moments, he quieted on his own.

Another angry squeal pierced the gloom.

Groaning, she rolled out of bed. Even now at the height of summer, the flagstones chilled her feet as she crossed to the cradle. She picked him up, murmuring his name. His cries calmed and his lips puckered. She moved him into position. He latched onto her breast and began tugging furiously. She smiled at him, caressing his cheek, awed that she could meet his needs in such a primal, intimate way.

He seemed content to feed while nestled in the crook of her arm. She paced to the window and swept aside the covering. The brisk morning spilled into the chamber, carrying with it the aromas of fresh bread and roasting beef. Beyond the guards' crossed spears, some of the residents had already begun their day's tasks. Most of the activity flowed toward the market square: wagons bearing casks and crates, tall covered carts laden with clanking pots and flowery bunches of herbs swinging against the sides, youngsters driving squawking flocks between the vehicles. Dogs cavorted everywhere, adding their barks to the commotion as cats languidly observed the proceedings from doorsteps and windowsills. Of sheep and pigs and goats and larger animals, Gyan saw no sign, nor did this surprise her. The Lugnasadh festival and livestock show was only a fortnight away, and these animals would be moved to the meadows once the sale pens were built.

She gazed beyond the thoroughfare to a training enclosure where one warrior—Seumas, she guessed, or perhaps Torr—towered over a circle of younger warriors. They stared in rapt attention as he used one of their companions to demonstrate what appeared to be a type of feint, judging by the quickness of his movements.

Gyan ached to be with them, to grip the leather-wrapped hilt in her fist and know she could swing her sword with even a wee bit of her usual strength. Better still to be at her consort's side, helping him recruit and train men for the Angalaranach campaign.

Loholt finished his meal. After adjusting her tunic for modesty and patting his back, she held him up to watch his future sword-brothers. He made such a fuss that she had to step back from the window and pull the covering closed.

She sighed. One day, she'd introduce Loholt to the warrior's arts, but she heartily wished that time would come before she forgot them herself.

Cynda bustled into the room, took Loholt, and proceeded with her usual efficiency to change his swaddling cloth. Cleaned and covered and cuddled, happily mouthing the head of his favorite rag doll, he settled down in Cynda's arms.

Gyan gazed longingly at the sword belt she was still too big to wear and the sword she was too weak to wield. Argyll's smith had wrought wonders to obliterate all traces of the Angalaranach raider's blow. Too bad he couldn't repair her body as easily.

"Go ahead, Gyan."

Startled, she spun toward Cynda. The woman was rocking, full attention upon the sleeping Loholt. She couldn't be sure whether she'd heard Cynda or the prompting of her heart.

Cynda glanced up, smiling. "You're much thinner. Try the belt."

Gyan donned tunic and trews, pulled on her boots, and strode to the shelf where the belt had lain, carefully dusted and polished—and idle—for more than half a year. She delighted in the feel of its cool bronze ridges and valleys. The belt slid into place easily enough. Her joy evaporated when she failed to fasten the thongs.

With an exasperated sigh, she glared at Cynda, who laid Loholt in his cradle and approached her.

"Ach, I said you were thinner, my dove. I made no claim that it would be easy."

By the time Cynda managed to secure the thongs, Gyan could scarcely breathe, but she wouldn't have traded the sensation for all the gold in Caledon.

"You could get longer thongs."

"No!" Gyan experimented with a few kicks and lunges. Each movement eased the pinching. "No. These will stretch."

She regarded her sword, couched in its elaborate bronze scabbard, hanging above the belt's shelf. The pommel's sapphire shone invitingly in the lamplight. She gripped the hilt, sucked in a breath, and lifted the sword.

Miraculously, it didn't feel as heavy as she'd expected. As the blade sang free of the scabbard and she reacquainted herself with its balance, a tingle raced up her arm. She handed the scabbard to Cynda, who backed away to give Gyan room.

She ripped the air with cuts and thrusts. Her form felt awkward, but that would improve with practice. Reflexes, too, sorely needed honing, but she had to start somewhere.

"Why don't you go down to the practice arena for a while?"

An extraordinarily tempting idea... but reality lay cloaked in the form of a creature weighing half a stone who depended upon her for his very survival. "I can't leave him, Cynda."

Cynda stepped forward, holding out the scabbard. "Nonsense, my dove. Of course you can. You should." Cynda's eyes glittered with a warrior's fierceness. "You must."

Must? She longed to believe that. Cynda's presence in the chamber and guards stationed at every door and window assured Loholt's safety. However, his protection comprised only one facet of the issue. She took the scabbard and sheathed her sword.

"What if he wakes up hungry while I'm gone?" Holding the scabbard in one hand, she held up the other to forestall the obvious answer. "The training arena isn't that far away, and I can be sent for easily enough, but what if something happens and I must go somewhere else? What if—"

Cynda chuckled. "What if we find him a wet nurse? That's how Per was suckled."

"Really?" Gyan couldn't curb her surprise. Every other clanswoman suckled her own bairns. It always seemed so natural, so right . . . and so unavoidable.

"Oh, aye. Your mother was a busy lady, what with seeing after the affairs of the clan. Her consort was more interested in gaming and hunting and fighting. Chieftainess Hymar couldn't afford to let a bairn slow her down."

Gyan gazed at her sword. All she knew of Per's father, Byrn mac Lorana, was that he'd lost the challenge by Ogryvan mac Glynnis for the right to be Hymar's consort. If Byrn had declined to share the responsibilities of clan rule, it was easy to imagine Hymar seeking a more capable partner and, in the meantime, a wet nurse for her son.

"I suppose you have someone in mind already, Cynda."

Cynda grinned and scurried from the chamber.

Gyan shook her head with a laugh. Cynda probably knew more about the daily workings of Arbroch than any hundred residents combined. As she settled into the chair beside the cradle, foot to the runner and sheathed sword lying across her lap, she wondered what she'd ever do without her.

Cynda returned with a brown-haired slip of a lass. One of the freed Breatanach slaves, if Gyan read the scars on her neck aright, and a kitchen servant, judging by the old knife nicks on her hands and the odors that followed her into the chamber. The young woman glanced at Gyan nervously before lowering her gaze. Gyan's gut lurched. Was this lass capable of meeting Loholt's needs and ensuring his safety?

"This is Tira." Cynda urged her forward. "Her bairn died not a sennight past."

Cynda's confident endorsement satisfied Gyan. She grasped her sword and stood. Gasping, Tira shrank back. Gyan gave Braonshaffir to Cynda and spread empty palms toward the lass. "No need to fear, Tira," she said gently, in Breatanaiche. "I am very sorry for your loss." Into the threatening silence, inspiration descended. "If you serve me and my son well, then once he is weaned, I will provide you with the means to return to your village. Would you like that?"

Gyan scarcely needed to hear the profuse thanks that followed. The happiness mirrored in Tira's pale blue eyes was payment enough.

Tira assumed her post beside the cradle. Gyan kissed Loholt's reddish-gold head. He stirred, uttering a squeaky sigh, but didn't wake. Gyan's heart surged with love for him and his father.

Straightening, she faced the woman who'd suckled her, kissed her bruises, bandaged her scrapes, and listened to her joys and fears. Cynda fastened the scabbard to Gyan's belt and stepped back, nodding her approval.

Gyan snatched her cloak from its peg by the door. Flinging it about her shoulders and feeling much more like her old self, she left the chamber.

A BABY cries and squirms in the arms of a peasant woman. The woman coos and rocks the child, to no avail. Another woman takes the baby. The cries cease. A foot kicks free of the blankets. The flickering firelight reveals the heel's tiny blue mark.

Over the older woman's shoulder hovers a hulking bear of a man. "How do we pay for his keeping, eh?" He looks at the woman holding the baby. "Hers, too, for all that."

The man holds out a broken-nailed hand. Into the callused palm drops a plain silver ring. "Ho! You take us for fools? This scrap of silver won't last a month."

"Take the wagon and harness, then," says a third woman.

"Your horse, too."

"No. She is my way home." With an angry grunt, the man folds his arms. "Very well. I shall return with another in a day or two."

The man nods, grinning. "Done."

An earring appears, a golden loop strung with three pearls: white, silver, and black.

Avarice ignites in the man's eyes.

"Do not give the child to anyone who cannot show you its mate." *The pearls seem to glow of their own accord before being swallowed by the peasant man's grubby fist. "If you sell or lose this token, your lives are forfeit."*

Niniane woke with a start. She pressed a hand to her throbbing temple and glanced around. By the full darkness, she guessed the time to be sometime between matins and lauds. The sparse but familiar furnishings of her quarters in Caer Lugubalion's praetorium, silhouetted by starlight, met her eyes. She'd spent all these weeks ministering to the hundreds of pox victims but would have to pack today, for she was due to return to her priory on the morrow.

Normally, she Saw snatches of battles, accidents, alliances, the forging of Arthur's sword: events that shaped the future of Brydein. Why in heaven's name had the Sight shown her a peasant baby?

She felt perspiration bead on her brow. As she touched the spot, she dismissed the warmth as a reaction to the vision.

Perhaps the child wasn't a peasant.

She closed her eyes and tried to recall details.

Niniane had Seen through the eyes of the woman who had offered the jewelry, but she recognized neither the woman's voice nor the items—not that this greatly surprised her. In an abduction, servants often performed the act.

The child's identity remained another mystery. The peasant's hut had been too dark to make out faces. The blanket might have been dark blue or black. No features distinguished the baby from any other. The peasant man referred to the child as a boy, but that was all—

There had been something, Niniane realized: a mark on the heel of one foot, too regular in shape to be a natural one. A Caledonian child, although the people had spoken Brytonic? Niniane hadn't heard of Caledonians tattooing infants, but Brytons never wore tattoos.

Rubbing her eyes, she again conjured the vision, concentrating on the baby's heel. Not one mark but two. Two birds, wings spread.

Loholt of Argyll!

Queasiness gripped Niniane's stomach. The baby hadn't seemed very old. Her return to Rushen Priory would have to wait until after she had warned Arthur and Gyanhumara.

As Niniane rose and reached for her robe, her eyesight blurred and the room began to spin. She flailed her arms, trying to find something to grab for support. A bedpost, a chair, a wall, anything.

She couldn't see. Her legs buckled. Gasping, she tried to cry out, but she couldn't summon enough breath for sound. Pain hammered her head as she collapsed.

As Angusel neared the living quarters of the rulers of Clan Argyll, he shook his head in astounded disbelief.

"Gyan!" Grinning, he ran toward the doorway where she stood. "You look great!"

He clattered to a halt, and she pulled him into a brief embrace. "Thank you, Angus." She released him and glanced around, inhaling deeply and flexing her arms. "I feel great." A smile lit her face as she regarded him again. "Ready for a practice session?"

"You mean, with you? But aren't you—I mean, your strength—"

She chuckled. "Of course, I won't be in top form yet. I won't break, either, if that's what worries you. I don't stand a chance of returning to top form without practice." Her smile deepened. "Exercising my tongue is the last thing I need to do."

As she headed toward the practice grounds, Angusel broke into a trot to catch her.

"But Loholt—"

"Will be well taken care of. Even if he gets hungry in my absence."

Angusel nodded his approval as Gyan bypassed the racks of practice weapons and drew her sword to begin a solo routine of slashes and thrusts. Angusel selected a pair of swords and shields and joined her.

"Here, Gyan." He held out a shield and a blunted, weighted sword when she paused to rest. "Let's have a go with these."

Her mouth bent in amusement. "Loholt may have stretched my body, but he hasn't addled my wits. I was going to get a practice sword before sparring with you." She sheathed Braonshaffir, unhooked the scabbard from her belt, and laid the sword aside. "Thank you for saving me the trouble."

He barely had time to ready his sword before she shifted into attack posture and lunged at him.

As he studied her face, aglow with fierce joy, he couldn't suppress his happiness. What she lacked in strength she made up in sheer determination. Several times, she drove him back a pace or two. Yet she was tiring quickly. He could see it in the runnels of sweat on her face, the graying look around her eyes, and the laboring of her breath. But she refused to quit.

Saluting her with his sword, he ended the match.

She stuck her sword point-down into the dirt and leaned against the hilt, panting and smiling.

"I can see," she said between breaths, "that I have much work before me." She straightened, lifted the sword, and pressed its rounded point against Angusel's chest. "So do you."

"What?" He dropped his sword and shield, and raised both hands in mock surrender. "Me?"

"Absolutely. You need more battle experience."

That argument again. "But, Gyan, my place—"

"Your place is where you will do me and Clan Argyll the most good." She lowered the sword, but her gaze didn't dim. "Loholt and I are well guarded here. I want you to join Arthur."

Although he hated to admit it, she had a valid point. He never would become a great warrior fighting on practice grounds all his life. For her sake, he wanted—nay, *needed* to become the best.

Going to Senaudon presented two problems, though he shoved from his mind the one matter over which he had no control. His deuchainn na fala, however, he could control.

"I will join the army at Senaudon." Angusel challenged her with a gaze every bit as intense as hers. "As a true warrior." Grinning, he added, "Wearing the finest pelt-purse you've ever seen!"

Chapter 22

MORGHE HAD TO admit the Picts knew how to stage a celebration.

The occasion in question, Lugnasadh, started on the calends of August and would run for a week to honor the bull-god Lugh with such activities as horse racing, cavalry drills, animal exhibitions, and sales—not only sales of livestock, but clothing, jewelry, weapons, tools, food, drink, medicines, and anything else that could be piled onto a wagon or stuffed into a crate, barrel, or sack. The meadows surrounding Arbroch had grown tents and booths and pens by the score, rendering it impossible to walk in a straight line from one end to the other. Music and haggling and laughter abounded, often masked by roars of approval as a race ended.

The odors of live animals clashed with roasting meat, making it hard to decide upon the more pervasive. Since a mare stood closest at the moment, Morghe opted for the former.

What a sleek animal, too: black as midnight, with a white blaze and three white-stockinged feet. While the owner held the halter, Morghe rubbed her hand over the velvety nose.

"Looks can tell you only so much, my lady." The voice behind her sounded vaguely familiar. She turned. A stranger casually bestrode a chestnut horse. "If you're serious about buying that mare, I suggest you try her paces first. I shall be honored to provide escort."

"Indeed." Morghe planted a hand on her hip. "Why, may I ask, should you be wanting to do that? And why should I be wanting to let you?"

His face split into an impudent grin. "You really don't recognize me, do you, Lady Morghe?"

Recognize him? She wanted to slap that grin off his face, whether she knew him or not. Narrowing her eyes, she studied his bearded face.

"Accolon! Why are you here? And why the disguise?" Not only had he sprouted facial hair, but he wore a plain tunic and trews and an equally plain cloak. He carried no weapons that she could see, and no clan or army badge betrayed him. Her suspicion ignited.

He made a sweeping gesture with one arm. "Traveling clothes." To the horse's owner, he said, "A saddle and bridle, if you please, good man. We won't be long, I assure you. This should allay your fears." He dropped a silver buckle into the man's outstretched palm. As the owner bowed and disappeared into a nearby tent, Accolon nudged his mount closer to Morghe. "I promise, my lady"—a chill crept up her spine at his quiet menace—"you shall have your answers soon."

He said nothing of consequence while the owner saddled and bridled the mare, nor as they trotted their mounts into the forest west of Arbroch. Once the trees had screened them from view, he kicked his horse into a fast canter. She urged the mare to keep up. Normally, she would have enjoyed the mare's smooth gait and the fact that the animal didn't seem taxed by the pace.

After what felt like an eternity, he reined his horse to a halt, and she followed his example.

"Accolon of Dalriada, explain yourself."

"Take a look around you." His voice hardened in a manner she didn't like. "A good look. You must remember this place."

She laughed. No one told Morghe ferch Uther what she must and mustn't do. No one save her brother, but she ignored that niggling thought. However, she would never discover the nature of Accolon's game unless she played along. She maneuvered the mare in a tight circle, taking in a full view of her surroundings.

This strip looked much like any other ill-built Pictish road, little better than a parallel pair of cow tracks, grassy down the center and flanked to either side by oak and elm trees and undergrowth, lush in the fullness of summer. A few paces ahead, the road bent sharply to the left around an outcropping of rock. Nearby stood a shattered, lightning-charred oaken monument to the capricious ravages of nature.

"Why should this place be important to me?"

"Loholt mac Artyr." Accolon's eyes took on a sinister glint. "Bring him to me here in three days, and I will handle the rest."

Hand to mouth, Morghe stifled a gasp. That was low even for Urien. Abruptly, Accolon's disguise made terrible sense.

She drew a breath to steady her voice. "This is madness. Surely you can see that. I cannot spirit the baby past the gate guards at night. And I can't believe you expect me to accomplish it in full daylight."

He leaned toward her in the saddle, leering. "Oh, but I do, my lady. What better time than when the gates stand wide open for the festival, and everyone is buried in their own petty distractions?"

"Loholt is never left unguarded. If Gyanhumara isn't with him, you can wager that her servant is. Or his wet nurse. Trying to slip past any of them would be impossible."

His grin widened. "Not for someone of your talents."

"Talents?" Her heart twisted. "Whatever do you mean?"

"Ha. Let's just say that I am aware of the part you played in Urien becoming chieftain when he did."

She struggled to keep her expression neutral. So that's what had become of the aconitum. The enormity of her actions dragged at her heart. Perhaps marrying Urien wasn't so wise . . . no. He would bestow upon her the only worthwhile thing in life: power. She just needed to stay on his good side, which wouldn't happen if she didn't cooperate with his war-hound.

"Someone with your knowledge of medicines," Accolon whispered, "can doubtless concoct something to help you smuggle a baby from his mother."

The mare snorted and shook her head. Morghe stroked the glossy neck, thinking less of the risks than of the innocent baby who had not asked to become Urien's enemy, the baby who always gave her a smile.

Regardless of how much she wanted to please her future husband, in this act she would take no part.

She met Accolon's gaze unflinchingly. "And if I refuse?"

"Then I will find another accomplice." He parted his cloak to reveal a cavalry sword. "The brat has a wet nurse, you said."

She felt her eyes widen. "You wouldn't dare kill me!"

"Oh, but an accident would be so tragic, don't you agree?" He laughed harshly. "And so pathetically easy to arrange."

"I'm betrothed to Urien!" She couldn't help the shrillness of her voice or the thrashing of her heart.

"You were not his first choice."

And may all the gods of all the people on earth damn Urien to hell and back for that! After he made her Chieftainess of Clan Moray.

As she scanned the tangled tree branches, she glimpsed a woodcutter's hut set well back from the road, and an idea formed.

"Very well, Accolon." She looked down, sighing and slumping her shoulders to feign resignation. "Three days."

ANGUSEL FELT something crawling on his leg and groggily batted it away, hoping to get back to sleep. His head throbbed, and his body felt stiff and chilled as if he'd spent all night on the—

Ground?

His fingers dug into what should have been his bed and pulled up a fistful of dirt and musty leaves.

He sat up, instantly awake. A circle of oaks towered overhead, their intertwined branches forming a thick canopy lost in the tendrils of mist. The forest stretched in every direction.

Which forest? And why?

He snorted at his slow wits. His deuchainn na fala, of course.

Someone must have drugged his wine at the feast. His last recollection ended after Seannachaidh Reuel had begun to sing.

He scratched his chest and glanced at his loincloth. A quick check nearby turned up his sheathed dagger, a water skin, and a sack containing a day's ration of dried beef, bread, and cheese, exactly as prescribed by law. Everything else he needed to survive his hike to Arbroch he'd have to find, hunt, or fashion himself.

The trial had to take at least three days or the candidate suffered allegations of having received help. Whether true or not, such warriors bore the stigma of cowardice and were never accepted into the clan's war-band. The law prohibited overly mourning youths who never returned.

Angusel shinned up the nearest tree and peered through the branches. If he could determine his location and close some of the distance, it would be a simple matter to camp, hidden, near Arbroch until enough time had passed for his trial to be declared valid. The sun warmed his skin, but he could only tell that he was in a hollow. No wisps of smoke curled above the trees or beyond the ridge crests. Just as well, since even speaking to other people was forbidden.

After climbing down, he kicked through the deadfall for a stout and nearly straight branch. He unsheathed his dagger and sat on the cool ground beneath the tree. With the branch balanced on his lap, he made quick work of stripping off the twigs and set to work sharpening the narrow end.

By law, he'd been left a day's walk from Arbroch, but in which direction? He could make a guess and walk for half a day. If nothing started to look familiar, he could return to this spot by nightfall and pick another direction on the morrow . . . and on and on until he finally stumbled on the right way. That presumed he could recognize the land within a half-day's walk of Arbroch. Or he could improve his chances by reason.

A day's walk east would put him close to the coast, but this place bore none of the usual signs: no gulls, no trees stunted by a diet of salt spray, no fishy or tarry tang in the air, no restless murmur of the waves.

He could rule out being south of Arbroch, because that would have left him near the northern bank of the mighty Ab Fhorchu, within shouting distance of Senaudon. He'd climbed every rock and explored every deer path surrounding his birthplace. This wasn't Senaudon.

Since candidates had to travel in one of the four primary directions—the deuchainn na fala was designed to be challenging, not impossible—this left north and west. Due west of Arbroch lay the border of the Breatanach Clan Móran; going north would thrust him deeper into Clan Argyll territory.

Both seemed equally likely.

He preferred to do things the hard way, his mother had said of his dead father. *And look where it got him.* Angusel rubbed his chin, questioning the wisdom of his choice to conduct the deuchainn na fala here rather than at Senaudon.

Too late now.

He sheathed the dagger. Upon testing the spear's point with his thumb, he deemed it serviceable and far better to have on hand in case trouble attacked him in the shape of a wild cat, bear, or boar.

As he gazed southward, instinct made its suggestion. Failing this test would bring shame not only upon Clan Alban but upon Gyan and Clan Argyll, which, gods help him, he'd never willingly do.

He stowed the dagger with the rations, shouldered the sack and water skin, and gripped the spear as a walking staff. Upon turning to put the rising sun over his left shoulder, he began his trek.

"Get down. Now!" A sword glints in the man's hand.

Beyond the brush stands a wagon drawn by a lathered horse. Three figures sit in the wagon, two in front. The person sitting in the rear holds a bundle in both arms. A riderless horse stands nearby, foam-flecked sides heaving. Shadows obscure the faces.

A scream rings out, followed by a piercing cry. The scream belongs to a woman; the cry, an infant.

One by one, the people abandon the wagon. The figure holding the sword moves slowly, inexorably toward the others...

Niniane gasped. The vision vanished.

Worse than Seeing someone's imminent death came the certainty that these visions described an attempt to abduct Loholt. Illness had kept her confined to her chambers for most of the past fortnight. She'd been too ill to even send a message.

Not that a written warning would have helped. Niniane found it best to speak privately to the parties involved. Besides, too many things could happen to the message or its bearer, even if the courier were one of Arthur's most trusted soldiers.

Illness be hanged, she'd have to make the journey herself.

She swung her legs over the side of the bed and stood. Her balance failed, and her flailing arms knocked the pitcher from the washstand. It hit the tiled floor and shattered with a resounding crash.

Groaning, Niniane slumped back onto the bed. She didn't need the Sight to forewarn her of what would happen next.

As if on cue, the door banged open, and an older woman rushed in, tongue clucking and head wagging. Sister Dorcas picked up the shards and set them on the side table. She planted her fists on her ample hips and surveyed Niniane with a scowl.

"Prioress! What are you doing out of bed? You are not well enough—"

"I must try, Dorcas." Niniane massaged her temple, willing away the pain. The visions she could do nothing about. They wouldn't leave her mind until the events had passed. "Lives may depend on it." With Dorcas's help, she tried her legs again.

While Niniane steadied herself, Dorcas retrieved Niniane's robe from the back of a chair. "Lives? Whose lives? What in heaven's name are you prattling on about?"

Niniane sighed and ran her fingers through her unbound hair. She didn't know Sister Dorcas well, but the woman seemed forthright and hardworking, if her zealous nursing was any indication.

Again, pain speared her head. To even contemplate a journey to Arbroch, she'd need help.

"The son of Arthur and Gyanhumara is in danger." As Niniane watched Dorcas's face transform into an expression of horror, she added, "Perhaps others are, too."

Niniane lifted her arms, and Dorcas slipped the robe over her head. As the prioress moved toward the door, Dorcas stepped in front of her, arms crossed. "You could have had a fever dream."

"My fever is gone. Feel for yourself." Dorcas pressed her hand to Niniane's forehead but didn't look convinced. "I can't tell you how I know. I just do. Please, Sister, I must hurry. I don't know how much time is left."

Dorcas's sternness evaporated. "You mean 'we,' Prioress."

"What?"

Dorcas stabbed a gnarled finger at her breast. "I will go with you. We will need an armed escort, too."

Niniane couldn't deny it. Sitting down, fingering her cross's chain, she considered her options. She could prevail upon her brethren in the clergy, but they would never provide enough protection if the party encountered brigands or wild animals. Not to mention the risk of them asking questions about her mission that she had no desire to answer. The last thing she—or Arthur or Gyanhumara or Loholt, for that matter—needed was for the wrong person to find out about her gift of foreknowledge.

She looked up into Dorcas's questioning gaze. "Sister, how fare General Cai's troops? Have they recovered from the pox yet?"

"Why send to Camboglanna? Why not ask for an escort here?"

"Bishop Dubricius wouldn't refuse my request, but isn't he at Senaudon?" Niniane asked, and Dorcas nodded. "I don't know his replacement." Fever stunted her recollection of the man's name. She shook off that disturbing thought with a toss of her head and reached for the wimple lying on the bedside table. She said, "I've known Cai for many years. How are his men? Has their quarantine been lifted yet?" Camboglanna lay less than a mile distant, and Niniane hoped that Dorcas hadn't been too busy to hear the latest reports.

"A few cases are still recovering." Dorcas stroked her chin. "They opened the gates yestermorn, so it's likely safe enough."

Niniane offered a silent prayer of thanksgiving, fixed the wimple in place, and stood. "Sister Dorcas, would you please take my request to General Cai while I pack?" As Dorcas drew a breath for what Niniane suspected would be a protest, she held up an open-palmed hand. "Fret not, I won't tire myself." Not too much.

"Very well, Prioress." Dorcas sighed. "Will there be a letter?"

"No need. Tell him you represent me, and that we'd like some guards for a journey to Arbroch and Senaudon. If he asks about the nature of my business, please make arrangements for he and I to discuss it privately." Niniane prayed Cai would grant her request without pressing for answers. Half a legion she didn't need.

Yet that was exactly what she'd get if Cai learned that the son of his foster brother might be in danger.

Chapter 23

MORGHE SURVEYED THE trio of maidservants standing before her. "See that you get a good price for everything," she admonished. Though not particularly intelligent, they could be relied upon to carry out explicit instructions. She adopted a tolerant smile. "Once the wagons are loaded, you are all dismissed to enjoy the festival for the remainder of the day."

The women lifted their heads, a puzzled expression furrowing each brow, and for good reason: Morghe rarely bestowed free time. Today, however, she needed to conduct her business without a gaggle of servants asking questions she didn't care to answer.

Her smile deepened. "Yes, you heard me. Now, off with you!" She made a shooing motion with her hands.

After a flurry of curtseys and thank-yous, the maidservants scurried from the room. She noted their excited responses. Perhaps generosity wouldn't be such a bad habit to cultivate. Within reason, of course.

Alone at last in the anteroom of her guest chambers, she hugged her arms to her chest, reviewing her plans.

At last night's feast, Gyanhumara had revealed that she'd have a busy day at the festival today, judging races and livestock. Morghe had suggested that Cynda join Gyanhumara. Cynda would have refused, but to Morghe's secret delight, Gyanhumara seemed enchanted by the idea and convinced Cynda to enjoy a respite from nursery duty. The powdered valerian root Morghe had slipped into the wet nurse's customary evening brew would, in theory, also make Loholt drowsier and easier to handle.

Morghe hoped.

The fact that she didn't have a choice rankled her, but as much as she disliked her brother and his wife, she simply couldn't idly watch Urien succeed with her innocent nephew's murder. Nor could she risk her life or her relationship with Urien by informing Loholt's parents. She possessed no guarantee of her plan's success, but no other solution stood a better chance of ensuring the child's safety as well as her own while keeping her primary goals intact.

The question of when—or whether—to reunite Loholt with his parents, she hadn't given much thought except to recognize the potential benefits inherent in both options. With the baby safely hidden, there'd be time aplenty to reach that decision later. Perhaps even years later. She grinned at the irony that Arthur's son also would be reared in ignorance of his illustrious parentage.

The grin died as she envisioned the consequences of her failure.

Footsteps and muted talking in the corridor shattered her musings. A knock on the door made her flinch.

She flung her cloak about her shoulders, holding the edges closed across her chest and attempting to don a serene expression completely at odds with her swelling panic. "Enter."

A familiar figure shuffled into the antechamber.

"Lughann!" His name shot from her lips like the snap of a branch. More calmly, she asked, "What do you want?"

"Begging your pardon, me lady, but last night you told me to stop by this morning." He ducked his head as if expecting a blow.

Of course! She berated herself for allowing her nerves to make her forget this small yet vital element of her plan.

"I've ordered Astarte to be hitched to one of my carts, and I need you to drive it for me." She gazed speculatively at his half-hand, suppressing another rush of panic as she realized she'd forgotten to take his disability into consideration. "That is, if you can."

To his credit, he didn't hesitate. "Aye, me lady." He broke into a shy grin. "'Twill be me pleasure!"

"Good." She swallowed her relief. "Wait for me and my traveling companion behind the granary."

If her choice of meeting places surprised him, he hid it well. "Aye, me lady." Lughann bowed and turned toward the door.

Only after he'd left did she permit herself the luxury of a sigh, again cursing her nerves.

She wanted the fastest creature on four legs to help her reach her destination and, with any luck, return her to Arbroch before Loholt's disappearance could be discovered. Naming her new black mare after an ancient Phoenician goddess was perhaps a bit superstitious, but Morghe wouldn't refuse aid from any quarter. She regretted the necessity of having to use a cart, but Tira couldn't ride. Besides, a cart would draw far less attention than two women and a baby astride one horse. Having a male driver would appear even more ordinary.

Morghe hoped.

With the sounds of Lughann's footfalls fading into silence, she shed her cloak and drew a deep breath.

Bent over the bathing tub, she poured a strong chamomile tonic over her hair several times, working it into every strand. She heartily wished one of her maidservants could help her, but by now, they'd be so deep into the maze of market stalls that a pack of hounds would take hours to find them.

She wound a towel around her head, stepped out of her shift, and donned her plainest riding gear. Not exactly peasant garb, but the light brown tunic and breeches would have to suffice. She rubbed cold charcoal into a few places on a frayed gray cloak to make it appear more aged, set the lump aside, and, as an afterthought, brushed her sooty fingers lightly across her cheekbones and forehead. She removed the towel from her head and felt her hair. Almost dry. In front of the full-length bronze mirror, she grinned.

The face looking back at her seemed haggard and much older, framed by dark blonde hair, not her usual lush auburn. She fastened her hair behind her head with an undyed leather thong. Since she normally wore it unbound, this simple trick completed the disguise nicely. Her own mother would have been hard-pressed to recognize her.

Into a pouch suspended by a cord around her neck went a silver ring to be used to purchase Loholt's safety, an inexpensive bauble and no great loss to her. The means of securing his release, however, required something special.

She poked through the shallow, velvet-lined cedar box containing her favorite jewelry and decided upon a pair of earrings made from exquisite pearls, three on each golden loop. The earrings had been a natal-day gift from her mother, and breaking up the set gave Morghe pause, but they'd serve her purposes perfectly. With one earring staying with the child, the other would serve as proof of—she grinned—guardianship. An earring joined the ring in the pouch. She tied it shut and tucked it into her tunic.

Morghe draped the cloak across her shoulders, pinned it with an unadorned, circular iron brooch, and pulled up the hood. Someone would have to look closely to see her sooty face and altered hair color. She would have preferred to be recognized by no one, but keeping everyone away would have been impossible to arrange, and she couldn't give the impression of a stranger leaving the ruling family's living quarters. Fortunately, the guards who normally stood the day watch around the building had been reassigned to the festival grounds.

She grabbed an empty canvas sack, eased open the door, and peered into the hallway. Her luck held; no one was about. She hurried to Gyanhumara's chambers to reduce the risk of being seen and to stimulate the urgency she'd need to convey to Tira. As the planned words whirled in her mind, her heart began to race.

Without knocking, she tested the door. It wasn't bolted. Praising her luck, she slipped into the antechamber and gently pulled the door closed.

The door to the sleeping chamber was shut but, as with the outer door, not locked. With her hand resting on the handle, she pressed her ear to the crack between the door and its frame. The muffled sound of sleep-heavy breathing came from within.

She eased open the door, grateful for its well-oiled hinges. Quickly, she surveyed the chamber. Tira and the baby lay sleeping, Loholt in his cradle near the hearth and his wet nurse on a mat beside him. The baby was snugly wrapped in a distinctive Argyll-patterned blanket that would have to be discarded at some point. She couldn't permit her plans to unravel because of a stupid scrap of fabric.

Tira stirred. Morghe crossed the room and bent down to shake Tira's shoulder. "Tira! Tira, wake up!" She kept her voice low. Tira looked up through groggy, uncomprehending eyes. "Loholt is in danger!"

The woman sat up, one hand at her mouth and the other clutching her blanket to her chest, her eyes round in fear.

"Who—who are y-you?" The words tumbled out in a strangled gasp.

Morghe smiled less to reassure the wet nurse than in realization that her disguise was more convincing than she'd hoped. "Lady Morghe." She beckoned. "Come, Tira, you must hurry and dress."

"M-my lady? It is you! But your face, your hair—"

Though Morghe chafed at the delay, she spared a moment to explain, "Someone wants Loholt dead, and I need your help. This must be done in absolute secrecy, or he won't be the only one to die." Morghe hid her satisfaction with Tira's shocked response; partial truths always worked so much more effectively than bald-faced lies. "Hurry and dress, then help me gather the baby's things."

As Morghe rifled through the chest containing Loholt's blankets and swaddling cloths, the swish of fabric told her Tira was dressing.

"Does Chieftainess Gyanhumara know about this?"

Perspiration trickled down Morghe's spine. Clutching a handful of folded swaddling cloths, she slowly straightened and pivoted to face Tira. She arched an eyebrow and placed her free hand on her hip. "What do you think?"

Tira looked away, murmuring, "Of course, my lady."

While the wet nurse stooped to retrieve her cloak, Morghe silently expelled a breath.

"Here." Morghe thrust the sack at Tira and stepped briskly to the hearth. "Make sure we have enough."

"For how long?"

Morghe paused in her quest for a cool piece of burnt wood. "A week," she decided. The fabric could be washed easily enough. That detail wouldn't be her concern, anyway. As Morghe latched onto a suitable candidate, she noticed Tira stuffing more swaddling cloths into the sack.

As Tira finished, Morghe rose from the hearth. Apologetically, Tira held out the bulging sack, which Morghe accepted with a nod.

"I don't have time to color your hair." Tira's common mouse-brown color rendered the precaution unnecessary. "This will have to suffice for your disguise."

Morghe applied several ashen streaks across the forehead and cheekbones of a surprised Tira and brushed away the excess. Crude, Morghe realized, but good enough to pass a cursory inspection. She settled Tira's hood over her head, and the shadows it cast over Tira's face completed the effect.

Morghe nodded once in satisfaction and gazed into the cradle. Loholt hadn't moved, probably still sleeping off the valerian he'd ingested through Tira's milk. Normally an active, happy, curious baby, he looked especially vulnerable and innocent.

She swallowed, her resolve wavering. Arthur should be dealing with this threat. That's what he bloody well had been bred for.

If she warned Arthur and Gyanhumara, however, Accolon might try to kill her, forcing her to beg protection for herself, as well. Morghe ferch Uther begged nothing from no one. Besides, if she told Arthur about Urien's plan, he'd terminate the betrothal—and in spite of all this, she still wanted to marry Urien. No sensible woman would jeopardize the chance to acquire that much power.

Tira picked up the baby. He yawned but otherwise didn't stir. Morghe adjusted the folds of Tira's cloak to hide the child, taking care to keep the fabric from touching his mouth or nose. Tira again reached into the cradle and pulled up a rag doll of indeterminate gender but well beloved, to judge by its tattered and stained visage.

"Put it back." Morghe motioned impatiently at the full sack. "We don't have room."

"But, my lady, it's his favorite toy."

"I can tell." She smiled wryly. "Leave it here, where it will be waiting for him. We wouldn't want to risk losing it, would we?"

Tira looked at the floor. "No, my lady." She drew a breath, lifted her head, and met Morghe's gaze. "But he's never been without it. If he wakes up and finds it missing, he will cry, and—"

"And we can't have that happen." Morghe stuffed the toy into the sack, tied it shut, hefted it over her shoulder, and spirited her charges from the room.

Gyan's boots squelched as she tromped down the corridor toward her quarters. Her trews, soaked to midthigh, chilled her legs.

Cynda scurried beside her, chuckling. "You should have seen the look on your face when that rider came flying at you. Priceless!"

For the first time since the incident, Gyan smiled.

She'd been judging horse races, standing inside one of the course's curves to spot fouls. A rider had failed to navigate the turn and was thrown from his horse. His momentum carried him straight at her. She darted aside, and the rider crashed into a nearby water barrel. He'd escaped with only scrapes, bruises, splinters, and a thorough soaking. Water had sloshed onto her, too.

Gyan hated having to leave her post, but she had no wish to spend the rest of the day pretending to be wading a river.

Besides, it would be good to look in on Loholt. Her smile deepened.

As they reached the door, she could hear no sounds within. Odd; Loholt usually played quite noisily at this time of day. A chill shuddered through her that had naught to do with her sodden state.

She pounded on the door, calling Tira's name. No response. Nor was the door bolted; also odd. Tira had strict orders in this regard. The only exception had occurred this morning, when Gyan and Cynda had left while Tira was sleeping. Tira should have lowered the bolt as soon as she woke up. Readying a rebuke, Gyan stormed into the room.

Empty! So was the sleeping chamber. She glanced at Cynda, her worry escalating. "Where could they be?"

"Ach, it's a fine day, my dove." Cynda bustled to the chest containing Gyan's clothing. "Likely Tira took Loholt out for some fresh air." She pulled out a pair of linen trews and gave them a shake.

Gyan wrestled off her wet boots and trews and accepted the dry garment. As she pulled it on, she couldn't dispel her apprehension. "Without telling me?"

Cynda shrugged. "Your guards have festival duty. Who else could she have—"

"Anybody!" No. She mustn't worry. There had to be a logical explanation. "You're right. She probably forgot." Gyan resolved to have a talk with Tira later.

Carrying the dry boots, Cynda passed the cradle and glanced down. "Oh and look. His favorite toy is gone." She handed the boots to Gyan with a grin. "Maybe she's taken him to the festival. She knows he'll fuss if he's without it for very long."

Gyan sat on the bed to don the boots. "Then let's find them."

TREES PASSED in a blur. The cart's wheels jounced over roots and rocks, forcing Morghe to clench her jaw. Her arms ached from bracing herself.

She glanced back. Tira, one white-knuckled hand clutching the cart's side and the other arm wrapped tightly around the baby, looked terrified. Loholt screeched and grinned as though this was the most fun he'd ever had.

Morghe turned to Lughann as they approached Accolon's meeting place. "Can't you make this rig go any faster?"

Lughann flicked the reins, but the pace didn't quicken enough for her liking. She closed her eyes and sighed.

"Hold on!" Lughann yelled.

The cart lurched, and Astarte let out a startled neigh. Morghe's eyes flew open to see Lughann straining to halt the mare. A man in plain-looking clothes, astride a plain-looking horse and gripping a not-so-plain-looking sword blocked the road. With boulders encroaching on one side and a wall of trees on the other, Lughann had no choice but to try to stop.

Fates be thanked, he did, but Morghe wished she'd ordered her driver to plow right through the man.

Accolon clucked his tongue, grinning, as he nudged his horse closer. "Lady Morghe, this is not our appointed day."

"Indeed?" She tried to slow her racing heart. "I must have confused the dates."

He grunted. "I must say, I've seen you look prettier."

The soot! As calmly as she could, she replied, "I didn't have an opportunity to bathe this morning."

"Ah, of course. Obviously, you were in a great deal of haste."

Before she could protest, Loholt let out a wail, followed by Tira's frantic but futile efforts to shush him.

"Well, now." Accolon peered into the cart. "What have we here?"

Morghe snatched the reins from Lughann's hands and slapped them across Astarte's back. Horse and cart leaped forward. Tira yelped, but the baby didn't even whimper. Morghe hoped he was all right but had no way to be certain.

In minutes, Accolon had caught up. Face contorted in fury, he drew abreast, crouched on his horse's back, and jumped. Tira screamed. Morghe urged Astarte on, hoping the burst of speed would disrupt Accolon's balance.

No such luck.

Accolon pushed Lughann off the cart and wrested the reins from her. Accolon's horse kept pace as Accolon pulled Astarte to a halt.

Drawing his sword, Accolon ordered Morghe down. Tira shrieked and Loholt cried, but they seemed unhurt. How long they'd remain thus was anyone's guess. Accolon ordered them out, too, before jumping down. Morghe glanced down the road, but Lughann had vanished.

"I am not in the habit of killing women." Accolon leveled his sword at Morghe and Tira. Still clutching the struggling Loholt, Tira shrank behind Morghe. "But now is a fine time to begin."

ANGUSEL STRADDLED the log, bending over the trophy while scraping his dagger across its surface. Though he was no closer to identifying his location, at least he'd have something to show for it.

Grinning, he ran his fingers through the beautifully speckled fur, reliving the pleasure, after having endured countless wild onions, dandelions, strawberries, and toasted grasshoppers—which, amazingly, tasted like nuts—of roasting and eating his meaty catch.

He flipped the hide to begin the onerous task of rubbing in the paste he'd made of the creature's brains, thanking the gods he hadn't become a tanner by trade. The very thought made his skin crawl.

Ideally, he'd have snared the rabbit on the eve of his return to Arbroch, eliminating the need for this step, but he didn't want to risk either not catching another rabbit or letting this pelt dry out. Neither possibility boded disaster, but he wanted with all his heart to pass this trial brilliantly. Hence the need to—his lips stretched into another grin despite his dislike of the job—use the brains the gods had given him.

Rumbling drew Angusel's attention, and he swiveled his head, knotting his eyebrows. Distant thunder? Nay, the sound was closer, and he heard the creaking of wood, too.

Wagons! His spirits soared. He had to be near the Arbroch road!

He stuffed his dagger and pelt into the sack, along with what remained of the preserving paste in its oak-leaf wrapping. After shouldering the sack, he dismounted the log, snatched his spear, and set off. He'd have to avoid the other travelers lest his deuchainn na fala become nullified. He didn't think that would be a problem from that caravan, since it seemed to be headed the opposite way.

A woman's scream froze Angusel's soul.

Clenching his fists, he glared up at the towering oaks. Why pass a ritual test, he challenged the gods, if someone he could have helped got hurt or even killed?

His answer came not from the trees but from his heart.

Spear in one hand and dagger in the other, he ran toward the wagons and more screams, praying to catch up and fearing he harbored a futile wish.

He came upon a stopped cart hitched to a foam-lathered black mare with heaving sides and quivering limbs. A man stood near the horse's flank, sword pointed at two smaller, hooded figures huddled beside the cart. From his hiding place, Angusel couldn't see their faces, but by their stature and bearing, he guessed they were women, likely the same women whose screams he'd heard. He fervently hoped he hadn't arrived too late. The swordsman's intent as he neared the others, like a cat toying with a cornered mouse, was hideously obvious.

Another figure burst from behind an outcropping and attacked the swordsman. Though garbed and collared like a slave, he displayed the courage and grace of a warrior, but he was unarmed. A thrust of the other's sword, and the would-be rescuer crumpled to the ground. The swordsman stepped over the body to approach the women again.

One of the women shrieked. Another cry mingled with hers, higher and more persistent.

Dear gods, a bairn!

The woman shrank from her attacker, and her cloak shifted. A shaft of late-afternoon sunlight slanted through the trees, making silver threads flash in the hem of the child's blanket.

The pattern was . . . oh, gods.

Loholt!

Questions flooded his brain, but he had no time to ponder them. He stood, aimed, and flung his spear at the swordsman. The spear pierced the man's leather-clad shoulder. Cursing, he dropped his sword to paw at the shaft.

No time, either, to weigh the odds of defeating someone who, though wounded, was much bigger and better armed than he. Angusel drew his dagger, burst through the bushes, and charged at the swordsman.

GYAN DID her best to banish her worry as she watched the race.

Rounding the curve, one of the riders let his horse drift a little too far to the outside, crowding another contestant's horse, whose stride faltered. The second rider flailed his arm to ward the first away, catching him on the shoulder to make him sway in the saddle. They exchanged glares, but both riders returned their attention to the race without further incident, as if the contact had never occurred.

"My lady, did you see that?"

She gave a small shake of the head, not in answer but to clear her mind. She'd witnessed the fouls, but initially they'd failed to register as such when all she could see was Loholt's face. She regarded her fellow judge. "What? I—yes. Disqualify them."

As he waved the red flag to signal the finish-line judges, she cast a glance at the sky, where the sun stood at well past its zenith. Tira and Loholt remained at large. This, she reminded herself, might mean nothing. The grounds were packed with people and animals. Cynda had suggested that Gyan return to judging races to take her mind from the problem. She'd reluctantly agreed and had sent Cynda to await Tira and Loholt in Gyan's quarters.

She wished she'd kept searching.

Donning a rueful smile, she faced her companion. "I'm sorry. You'll have to carry on without me. I have other business to attend to."

Gyan's judging partner, a merchant who understood the necessity of maintaining one's privacy regarding business ventures, merely smiled, bowed, and shifted his attention to the start of the next race.

Feeling better for her decision, she strode off to find the festival's captain of the guard, Rhys, stationed in Arbroch's main gate tower. As she dodged past revelers, children, musicians, and other performers, crafters' and merchants' stalls, livestock pens, and the occasional loose dog, cat, pig, or chicken, she devised a simple plan. She would order the guards to check for the Argyll clan-mark on the foot of every male child, within Arbroch's walls and without.

No, better to make it every babe in arms.

At the base of the guard tower, she stopped. What if this resolved into a simple misunderstanding? Wasn't she overreacting? Wouldn't she feel foolish for having mobilized all of Arbroch to find her son?

"Chieftainess? Something wrong?"

Gyan looked up to see Rhys descending as she stood poised to ascend the steps.

Was something wrong? Gyan hoped with all her heart there wasn't. Yet she had to be sure.

In the privacy of the guardroom, she explained the situation to Rhys. Compassion softened his gruff features. When she finished, he saluted smartly.

"Fret not, my lady. If they're here, we will find them."

If. Rhys unintentionally had voiced her doubts, but she couldn't let them cripple her.

Trying to sound calm, she said, "The warrior who does shall escort them to the guard tower without delay."

"As you command, Chieftainess." With another salute, Rhys left.

She stood at the slotted window and braced both hands against the ledge. As she formed a prayer for the safety of her son, her gaze roved not heavenward but toward the festival grounds. She squinted at the fingernail-size people and animals scurrying about. Rhys's men, recognizable by their identical black battle-gear and clan cloaks, fanned out among the crowd. Tira and Loholt had to be down there.

And Tira's explanation for running off with the bairn without a by-your-leave, Gyan thought darkly, had better be a good one.

WHILE THE swordsman tried to yank the spear shaft free, Angusel dived for his legs. The spear came out. Both weapons flew from the man's grasp as he fell with a yelp onto his wounded shoulder.

Angusel rolled to his feet and spat a curse; he'd lost his dagger. The swordsman lay on his back, motionless. Angusel didn't dare hope the fall had killed him. He had to do something to finish his foe, but without a weapon, what?

As he looked about, he saw no sign of the women or Loholt. Mayhap his diversion had helped them escape. He spied the spear and sword, nearly obscured by grass tufts in the road. The spear lay closer, but the sword would give Angusel a better advantage if he could reach it before his adversary stirred. Its hilt lay just beyond the man's fingertips.

Angusel crouched, gauged the distance, and sprang.

He never made it.

In midair, Angusel watched in horror as the man's eyes snapped open and he grabbed his sword. The point came up. Angusel steeled himself against certain agony.

LUGHANN WOKE to a nightmare of pain and blood. Gingerly, he touched his abdomen, where most of both seemed to be concentrated. With the stuff that oozed onto his hand he could have painted a picture, but he lived. Barely.

He heard a struggle nearby. Never mind his condition; Lady Morghe needed help!

Galvanized by that thought, he stripped off his tunic and tied it about his midsection to stanch the blood. Standing presented another problem altogether, but fighting off dizziness and nausea, he made it. The divine Lugh Longarm favored him, for the nearby rock mass lent him balance, strength, and concealment.

As he inched around the rock, a glint of metal caught his eye. A dagger lay at his feet. Another stroke of fortune! Hand upon the rock, he stooped to retrieve the weapon, scarcely daring to hope Lord Lugh would grant him a warrior's death.

Gripping the dagger's hilt with his unmaimed left hand was a new experience, but he managed well enough. He straightened to peer past the rock. The man Lady Morghe had called Accolon lay sprawled on the ground. Another stood panting nearby, a well-muscled youth clad, strangely, in naught but a dirty loincloth. The good Lord Lugh alone knew what had become of Lady Morghe, her companion, and the babe. His gut churned.

The lad turned toward him, and Lughann gasped. *Lord Angusel!*

Lughann stepped from behind the rock. The lad's head moved, catlike, as if gauging a distance. Accolon's foot twitched. Angusel would die unless Lughann acted fast.

Gritting his teeth against the eye-popping pain, he lunged for Angusel, connected with him in midair, and shoved him beyond reach of Accolon's sword. The sword sliced into Lughann's gut and back out. Pain burned a fiery trail. Lughann collapsed. Accolon kicked him, and he rolled down and down, over rocks and roots and dirt. He fell with a splash into a stream. The water enveloped him.

The fire in his gut yielded to cool numbness. The world's reddish haze dimmed to black, then flared to dazzling silver. Lughann felt his lips relax into a smile. Blessed Lugh Longarm had granted his wish.

DEAD SILENCE dominated the forest.

Skirts hitched, Morghe crossed the stream in three wet leaps and ran back toward the road, knees trembling and tears streaming. Angusel lay near the cart, blood oozing from a head wound. His arms and torso bore several crimson cuts. Accolon stood over him, panting and swaying, sword poised to deliver the killing blow.

"Accolon, hold!"

He turned, revealing the bloody mess of his left shoulder. "Kind of you to save me the trouble of hunting you down, my lady."

Angusel, eyes closed, moaned. Accolon pressed his sword to Angusel's throat.

"Please—no!"

Not moving his sword, he twisted his head to regard her. "Why should you care if this whelp lives or dies? Better he died. One less witness."

The fate of Loholt and Tira was too great a secret to bear without the added burden of Angusel's death. She whispered, "He was—is—my friend."

"Bah. This friend"—his lips made the word a curse—"will betray you to Arthur and Gyanhumara."

"He wouldn't! No, he couldn't have—he didn't recognize us." She hated herself for the dithering fool she must sound like. Hands on hips, she said, "I'm sure of it."

"Are you?" Up swung his sword as he pivoted to face her. His eyes glinted as hard as the blade. "Care to stake your life on it?"

She refused to flinch. Although Accolon's face looked drawn and pale from pain and loss of blood, it didn't make staring down the length of his sword any easier. She sucked in a breath. "A compromise, then. We leave him here, untreated, and let the Fates do what they will." She glanced at Angusel and sighed. "If he dies, he dies."

"What if he lives and remembers?"

"If he lives, I doubt he'll remember much." She injected her words with a confident tone. "I've seen many soldiers forget how they'd gotten injured."

"It's a stupid risk. I'll be better off without him." He tightened his grip on the sword and advanced on her. "And you."

As she watched with a runaway heart, his eyes widened and lost focus. His stride faltered. The sword slipped from his grasp as he fell against the side of the cart. The jolt revived him, and he clawed at the wood for support.

Morghe snatched up his sword. Gasping and clinging to the cart, he could only watch her. She pointed it at him and grinned. "It seems you do need me after all, Lord Accolon."

He gritted his teeth and groaned. "Just kill me and be done."

"I need you to tell Urien that his orders have been followed." She tried not to dwell upon the fact that she could scarcely heft the weapon, never mind her chances of wielding it lethally.

"I'll be lucky to make it to the next village."

She surprised herself by saying, "I'll bind your shoulder." Her eyebrows lowered. "Only if you promise not to move while I get something to use as a bandage."

Accolon regarded her with suspicion but didn't refuse. She moved to the opposite side of the cart and opened the sack containing Loholt's effects. Sword in one hand, she rummaged awkwardly through the sack for a swaddling cloth and returned to him.

He winced and extended a hand. "My sword, if you please?"

"So you can kill me?" She kept the sword's point leveled at him. "I think not."

He laughed harshly. "As you've observed, Lady Morghe, I'm in no shape to do anything to anyone. I've field-dressed enough battle wounds to know you'll need both hands for this one."

She despised having to give up her advantage, but, Fates curse him all the way to Hades's realm, he was right. Nodding her agreement, she said, "Besides, if you kill me, you're too weak to hide my body. Someone will link me to Loholt and, through us, trace this whole bloody business back to Urien. If your chieftain doesn't kill you, my brother surely will." She grinned triumphantly. "Have I your word that you won't harm me?"

He sighed. "My word."

After cleaning the sword on Loholt's blanket, she gave it to him. Grimacing, he sheathed it.

She drew closer to get a better look at his shoulder, but the mangled leather obscured her view. "Dagger?" she asked.

"Is it that bad, then, that you'll have to put me out of my misery?" He smiled wanly, but she chose to ignore the jest. Smile fading, he presented his dagger to her, hilt first.

She cut away the bloody fabric and leather to expose the wound. Splinters stuck out at odd angles. The surrounding flesh looked inflamed between the purple and blue mottling, and blood seeped from the gash.

With the dagger's point, she pried out the largest splinters. His frequent gasps suggested she was doing more harm than good. She surprised herself again by regretting she had no valerian for him.

She stopped to regard him frankly. "Except for the bandaging, I've done all I can with this. Without my salves, I can't prevent infection from setting in," she admitted. "You'll have to find a physician as soon as possible."

He inclined his head. "My compliments, my lady." As she wrapped his shoulder with strips torn from the swaddling cloth, he continued, gruffly, "And my thanks."

She tied off the final strip, helped him climb into the saddle, and handed over his dagger. "Just remember our agreement."

Tersely, he nodded and nudged his horse's flanks. As the animal started forward, he reeled, pressing a hand to his temple, but didn't fall. He disappeared around the bend.

She clutched Loholt's torn, bloody blanket and picked her way down to the stream. It snagged on a bush and pulled from her hand. An edge settled to trail in the water. She crouched beside her distorted reflection. Tears brimming, she bowed her head and bid farewell to Lughann and Angusel.

Chapter 24

At the sound of footsteps, Gyan leaped from her chair and all but flew to meet her visitors. Her father entered the chamber, followed by Rhys. Both wore grim expressions. Her heart twisted.

Yet she had to ask, "What word?"

Rhys bowed his head. "Loholt and his nurse are not within Arbroch proper." He met Gyan's gaze. "Nor on the festival grounds."

Fists clenched so hard that her nails stabbed her palms, she spun and returned to the window. Not to look down but up, to ask the One God where her son could be found, why Tira had taken him, and how, and when. She glared at the peaceful heavens, willing them to divulge their answers, feeling anything but peace.

Ogryvan's arm settled across her shoulders and squeezed, but for the first time in her life, she drew no comfort from the gesture.

Your son will be a great warrior. Her tears failed to wash away the prophecy's dreadful conclusion: *and you shall posses his soul.*

Maybe the High Priest had been wrong... and maybe it was better this way. Her battle trophy flashed to mind. As a proven enemy of Caledon and Breatein, Niall the Scáth had deserved his fate.

Her son did not.

Loholt's wee face appeared in her mind's eye: smiling, crying, laughing, and sleeping. All his moods seemed infinitely precious, and now she feared they would be lost to her forever.

"*No!*" Gyan pounded the window ledge, ignoring the sting and shrugging off her father's arm. Death couldn't be the only way to defeat this prophecy. Life begat hope. It was all she possessed. "He must be alive!"

"Gyan, we'll widen the search," said Ogryvan.

"We must! Tira doesn't know how to ride. She can't have gotten far in less than a day." That, at least, lent some comfort. "But with all the woods and hills, glens and burns..." Hands on hips, she regarded Rhys levelly. "This is nothing against our men; the territory is just too big. We must request a detachment from Artyr to help."

"Aye." Ogryvan said to Rhys, "Send Seumas."

His most trusted bodyguard? Yet it made sense. Seumas could escort a burning candle through a blizzard, and he certainly knew how to be discreet. She gave her father a grateful glance and turned her thoughts to composing Arthur's message. But the idea of committing the terrible reality to parchment nauseated her. She clutched her belly.

"Rhys, please see that Artyr gets an accurate report."

"Aye, Chieftainess." Instead of saluting, he briefly clasped her hand. A breach of protocol, and everyone in the chamber knew it, but she hoped Rhys could read the gratitude in her eyes.

As Ogryvan and Rhys left, she wished with all her heart that she could join one of the search parties, but her place was at Arbroch to coordinate the search, to be here for her son the moment he returned, and to bear the agony of waiting.

Agony no prayer could relieve.

ANGUSEL WOKE to a chilling breeze and dragged a hand across his eyes. The memory of the fight slammed into his mind, followed by intense pain. He tried to curl up and will it away, but nausea forced him to hands and knees, leaving him weak and gasping. His stomach heaved and heaved, but nothing came up.

How long had he lain unconscious?

More important, was anyone lurking about to finish him off? For he doubted he could defeat anything more deadly than a fawn.

He pushed to a crouch and peered into the gloom. The fight might have occurred hours ago or days. Enough moonlight filtered through the trees to show he was alone. The silence, complete save for the leaves' rattling and the burn's *plash*, confirmed it. No cart, no swordsman, no women. No Loholt.

Not caring which god heard him, he fervently prayed Loholt was safe in Gyan's arms.

While assessing his injuries, his mind returned to the fight.

The assailant had outweighed Angusel by several stones, armed with a sword to Angusel's dagger. Angusel had evened those odds somewhat with his spear; while he hadn't delivered a mortal blow, the wound had rendered his adversary's sword arm all but useless.

Yet not useless enough. He would have spitted Angusel in mid-dive if another man hadn't taken the blow.

Angusel glanced around again, but of his savior no sign remained. Had he survived somehow, too? Impossible. He'd seen the sword slice through the man's gut. No one could walk away with a wound like that.

He wished he could have done something to help the man who'd sacrificed his life for him. During the fight, it hadn't even entered his mind. All too soon, the enraged swordsman had borne down on Angusel as he dived for his spear. The man fought past Angusel's guard to clout him in the head with the sword's pommel.

After the initial explosion of pain, the memories stopped.

Carefully, he touched the side of his head where the ache felt greatest. The stickiness confirmed the wound still seeped blood. Why hadn't the swordsman killed him?

Maybe he planned to return. To ifrinn with pain, weakness, and nausea! Angusel wouldn't give up without a fight.

Dizziness overtook him as he tried to stand. The wind seemed determined to chill him to the bone. Kneeling, he rubbed his arms. The possibility of his surviving the night, to say nothing of more combat, became increasingly remote. On hands and knees, he groped for his dagger, clinging to the hope that he'd provided the distraction the women had needed to carry Loholt to safety.

At last, Angusel's fingers found the smooth, cool surface of his blade. Fumbling to sheathe it, he breathed a prayer of thanks. The stream's whisper seduced his thirst, and he half slid, half stumbled down the bank. He eased onto his stomach and plunged his hands into one of the burn's deep pools. As he greedily sucked water from his cupped palms, he felt the brush of fabric against his leg. He sat up and pulled the cloth from the bush.

His heart lurched.

He fingered a small, soft blanket, slashed and crusted with blood. Moonlight glinted off its silver threads. Though shadows hid the pattern, he knew which clan had created the fabric.

Cursing the darkness and pain, he searched for Loholt's body. The nearness of the burn—a convenient disposal place, especially for such a tiny body—killed the hope that Loholt was, by some miracle, still alive.

He widened his search to the road, where he found his spear and sack but no trace of Loholt. Unutterably weary, he sank to his knees on the hard-packed dirt, bowed his head, and wept. Not for himself, but for his lost sword-brother.

Rain woke him. Angusel had no idea how much of the night had passed. He clutched the blanket to his chest, gripped his spear, and braced himself on the shaft to gain his footing. After picking up the sack, he began trudging toward Arbroch. The pain, hunger, fatigue, cold, and wet he ignored, driven only by the desire to share Gyan's grief.

By all the gods, he would not fail her in that.

ACCOMPANIED BY his cavalry prefect and infantry commander, Arthur rode Macsen up the column's length at a slow trot, wrestling with his own nerves as much as his stallion's.

The Angli, at last, had gone on the offensive.

As Arthur inspected the troops prior to departure, he mentally reviewed Loth's dispatch. Several more villages had fallen, some practically within sight of Dunpeldyr, and a unit of Loth's men had been lost except a few who'd escaped to report the disaster. Even now, Loth's scouts were attempting to assess the strength, location, and composition of Colgrim's army. Arthur's decision to commit half the Horse Cohort and two cohorts of infantry to Dunpeldyr's relief had been based on gut instinct alone.

No, he corrected himself. Goaded by the Dun Eidyn nightmare, his gut had demanded he throw all available men into the fray. Merlin had advised holding half the force in reserve. Alayna's fishing and merchant vessels could transport them down the firth, should it come to that.

Arthur, Per, and Gereint had reached the column's head when a shouted challenge rang out from Senaudon's gate tower. The rider entered without further delay and kicked his mount into a canter, straight toward Arthur.

"Seumas," he acknowledged as the man halted his mare and rendered the Caledonian salute. Why in God's name had Ogryvan sent his most trusted warrior? Arthur's gut churned its prophecy.

"Chieftainess needs your help, Lord Artyr," Seumas said, in Caledonian. "Your son is missing."

Seumas may as well have run Arthur through.

"What?" said Per. "How—?"

Arthur curbed his panic to silence him with a glare and asked Seumas, "Did she send a message?"

Seumas pulled a folded parchment sheet from his pouch and handed it to Arthur, who broke the dark blue Argyll Doves seal and read.

Bloody hell!

His wife and child needed him desperately.

So did Loth's wife and children, and the wives and children of every man who looked to Dunpeldyr for protection.

He tightened his jaw and gazed at the billowing gray clouds, loathing his decision. With a jerk of his head, he motioned Per and Gereint out of the formation, and they nudged their mounts to a discreet distance.

In Brytonic, Arthur said, "Gereint, appoint your second to head the infantry cohorts. You have command of the cavalry." Since Gereint knew the Caledonian tongue and ways, Arthur hoped the change wouldn't strain everyone's tempers too greatly. "Per, take one of the reserve alae, and—"

"Go, Artyr. For your son." Determination conquered Per's worry. "I will lead the army."

Arthur's paternal instincts declared war on his military logic, and it took every shred of self-control to keep from surrendering to the extraordinarily tempting offer. Finally, he shook his head and reverted to Caledonian. "Thank you, Per. But I cannot." Arthur forestalled Per's protest with a brief grin. "Help your sister. Tell her I will arrive as soon as I can. I depend upon you to have Loholt waiting there for me."

"I understand, Artyr." Per wheeled Rukh about and exchanged a few words with Seumas before heading toward the cavalry barracks to begin recruiting for his grim mission. Seumas followed him.

Arthur wished his brother-by-marriage Godspeed with all his heart.

"Why not recall Peredur to the cavalry and let me take your place?" Gereint asked.

Why not, indeed? The Pendragon gave Gereint a long appraisal. The suggestion made perfectly logical sense . . . if the enemy were anyone other than the Angli. Lust for vengeance iced his tone as he said, "You have your orders, Tribune."

Gereint regarded him stonily behind his salute and rode off to implement the change of command. Arthur kneed Macsen back toward the formation's head. After Gereint returned, Arthur drew Caleberyllus and held it aloft, and the column surged forward as one.

By midday, cloaked in cold drizzle, he was beginning to regret his choice as he waited on the Brytoni side of the Antonine Wall, watching the cavalry guide their skittish mounts over the temporary wooden bridges and ramps built to span the ditches and dike. At this rate, the infantry was going to catch up soon. This was the most direct route, and to rush the crossing in this weather would invite disaster, but Arthur chafed at how much the delay might cost Dunpeldyr.

Or Loholt.

As the rain slackened, the wind blew the tantalizing smells of the nearby village's cooking fires toward him. His stomach rumbled. He ignored it. No time to indulge those needs until after establishing the disposition of Colgrim's force. A measuring glance at the faint glow where the sun was bravely trying to burn through the clouds told him the cavalry could make Dunpeldyr by sundown if the rest of the journey went without incident.

If. He snorted. Only a fool put stock in an estimate containing that damned word.

"Lord Pendragon!"

Arthur wheeled Macsen toward the hail. A detachment of Clan Lothian warriors trailed one of Arthur's forward scouts at a hard canter. In their midst rode one very red-faced Loth. Quelling his puzzlement, Arthur spurred Macsen to meet them.

"Thank God!" Loth blurted. "Arthur, you must go back."

He couldn't fathom how Loth had heard about Loholt. "Not until I've assessed the Angli threat."

Loth shook his head, his color deepening. "There is no Angli threat. But there will be soon if you don't return to Senaudon."

"What the bloody—" Arthur cut himself off and said to the scout, "Tell Tribune Gereint to halt the column and report to me." As the soldier sped away, he faced Loth, brow knotting. "Explain."

"I lost most of a unit in a skirmish, and the survivors found three deserted villages on their way back to Dunpeldyr. That's when I dispatched the message requesting your help." Loth shifted in the saddle and hunched a shoulder to wipe a rivulet from his cheek. "The villagers weren't killed. They'd gotten wind of the skirmish and evacuated. By the time my scouts arrived, everyone had returned."

Like a summer brushfire, Arthur's fury ignited. "Let me make sure I understand this." He maneuvered Macsen closer, making Loth's mount whinny and shy. "You had me mobilize based on an unconfirmed report?" *When I should have been searching for my son?*

"Aye." Loth had the grace to look humbled. "Forgive me."

Two words Arthur never expected to hear from this brother-by-marriage on this side of hell, but he had no time to savor them. "You owe me food for two thousand men and fodder for five hundred horses. Two days' worth."

Loth grimaced. "Expect the wagons within a fortnight."

"And when you get back to Dunpeldyr, you'd best start digging in," Arthur advised. "We must assume the Angli scouts know about this blunder. Even with the withdrawal, you may have an invasion on your hands soon."

"By God," Loth said, shaking a fist, "let's take the bloody war to them now, on our terms!"

Arthur wished he could. "Even if I had the council's approval—"

"I'll make sure you get it."

"Loth, I don't have the troop strength. Not enough men have recovered from the pox." Gereint joined them, and Arthur said to him,

"Sixth Ala's First Turma accompanies me to Arbroch. Withdraw the rest of the force behind the wall and camp here overnight. Return to Senaudon at dawn and put the men back to work on the staging effort."

Gereint acknowledged the orders with a salute and rode off.

"Arbroch, Arthur?" Loth smirked. "So. The mighty Pendragon can't stay away from his lovely bride."

"My lovely bride," Arthur grated out, "needs help finding our abducted son. Something I should have been doing instead of chasing a phantom Angli army and stirring up trouble neither of us can afford."

As Loth stammered an impotent apology, Arthur set heels to Macsen's flanks to collect his escort for the ride back to the decision he should have made at the outset.

NINIANE FELT both thankful and irritated that illness had forced her to ride in a litter. As much as she hated to admit it, her strength hadn't fully returned. She never would have completed the journey astride horse or donkey, and the litter's canopy sheltered her from sun and rain. Even if the wind blew the rain at an angle, the canvas sides could be let down and secured for additional protection.

The pace, however, dragged unbearably. Interminable stretches of trees and bushes and rocks seemed to crawl past the litter. The closer she and her Clan Argyll volunteer escort came to Arbroch, the slower they seemed to travel.

She tried to dismiss her feelings as a product of her overanxious imagination. Asking the escort's captain to increase the pace wouldn't happen unless she planned to explain why, which remained out of the question.

Leaning against the backrest, she closed her eyes, reminding herself of the Lord's command not to be anxious about anything. Easier said than done.

An order rang out. Though given in Caledonian, of which Niniane knew little, she had learned to recognize it as the command to halt and dismount. The litter came to a swaying stop. Bracing a hand against the frame, she peered outside, expecting to find signs of Arbroch, but the forest still enveloped them.

Not more than an hour had passed since they'd stopped to feed and water the horses, and it was too early for a ration break. Her impatience grew. Any delay, however slight, might prove costly. She quelled the pernicious thought that it might already be too late.

She turned to her companion, dozing on the opposite bench, and patted the woman's knee. "Sister Dorcas." An eyelid flicked open. "Please find out what's happening. Hurry!"

That brought Dorcas fully awake. She nodded her assent. The litter driver helped her down, and she scurried from view.

The look on the older woman's face when she returned Niniane never would forget.

"Prioress! There's a—a body in the road!"

Illness or no, Niniane had never moved so fast in her life. She scrambled from the litter and hurried past a startled-looking Dorcas. The soldiers, standing beside their mounts in two neat columns, regarded her curiously but said nothing as she dashed past them.

Dear Lord, not the baby!

The commander and a few of Niniane's escort had formed a loose semicircle around somebody lying on his stomach in the middle of the road, face turned to one side. He was much larger than an infant yet just as pitifully ill equipped for travel: almost naked and bearing recent, untreated sword wounds. She mouthed a quick prayer of thanks that it wasn't Arthur's baby, followed by a prayer for the well-being of the fallen traveler.

Another armed group, she realized belatedly, had joined her escort. These men wore the same saffron, scarlet, and dark blue patterned cloaks. Judging by their position on the road, they had not overtaken her group from behind.

Although she couldn't understand their conversation, she thought it odd that none showed interest in helping the traveler. Perhaps he'd been injured so badly that no one knew what to do. Surely, then, someone would have summoned her. Her prophetic gift might be a secret, but her skill as a physician certainly was not.

She shrugged off her perplexity and sidled between the men. No one stopped her as she knelt and pushed the curly black hair away from the bloody temple, revealing a deep gash the length of her finger... and the youth's identity.

"Angusel!"

The color had leached from his face. Cuts covered his arms and torso, the dried blood blackened with grime. Numerous leg scratches suggested a battle through dense brush. He wore a loincloth, and one hand clutched a small sack. An oak staff lay nearby. Its sharp end bore dark stains that could only be blood.

His chest moved with each breath, but he'd need help. Soon.

She stood to tear strips from the hem of her robe, and knelt beside Angusel's head. Before she could wipe dirt from the wound, she felt a hand grip her shoulder. "Nay, Prioress." Not Caledonian but accented Brytonic. Eyebrows raised, she glanced up to find herself staring into the green eyes of Gyanhumara's brother. "Ye cannot interfere."

"What?" Niniane rocked back onto her heels, trying to dispel her astonishment. "Why? What's happened?" She had a sick feeling she knew the answer but asked, "What has he done?"

Grief flashed across Peredur's face. "My sister's son is missing." She could hear his quiet despair as clearly as a thunderclap.

She closed her eyes, swallowing a sigh. *Too late!* A hundred questions bombarded her about how it had happened, and when, and who was responsible... and why God had caused her to fail.

Immediately, she rebuked herself. Misfortune had made her too ill to attempt this journey sooner, not an act of God. She clung to His promise that He could make all things turn out for the best, bad as well as good, for those who loved Him.

But what good could possibly come of this travesty?

Peredur continued, "Angusel mac Alayna may be involved." His tone made it clear what part he thought Angusel had played.

Dizziness overcame her, and she bowed her head.

She had failed everyone.

Angusel hadn't been one of Loholt's kidnappers, but Niniane couldn't share this without divulging her secret and exposing herself to allegations of witchcraft.

She studied the prone figure, profoundly wishing she could do more for him, and whispered, "I don't believe that, Lord Peredur. He has no reason to betray Clan Argyll."

"Strange, aye, Prioress." Sympathy softened his features' rigid mask. "He is death-loyal to Gyan." Peredur snorted. "He was."

Death-loyal? She banished her curiosity in the face of her most pressing concern—and Angusel's. "Let me bind his wounds."

He shook his head. "During the deuchainn na fala, he speaks to no one." He slammed his gloved fists together. "I cannot question him."

She staved off more confusion to lock her gaze with Peredur's, her gesture indicating Angusel's unconscious form. "Obviously, he can't speak. If I could treat him—"

"Nay. Caledonian law forbids it." As Niniane tried to form a counterargument to this bizarre custom, Peredur's hand went to his chin, and his expression grew pensive. "But he may die. We need answers." He stood and backed away a pace. "Help him, Prioress." No compassion thawed his words.

She thrust Peredur's attitude from her mind to concentrate on her work. At her request, one of the soldiers brought her water in an upturned helmet. As she took the offering, the memory of treating the lad at the cavalry games smote her. That day, Angusel had been a fallen hero. Today, he may as well have been a condemned criminal.

With a sigh, she moistened a cloth and carefully cleaned off the blood and dirt. He moaned and jerked his head but didn't wake. She rued the haste that had caused her to forget to pack her usual array of salves. Several of Angusel's wounds, the head gash in particular, looked as if an infection had already flared. She hoped they would let her correct this once they arrived at Arbroch.

As she bound the bandage around Angusel's head and tied it in place, she asked Peredur, "Why do you believe he might be—involved?"

Peredur reached under his cloak and drew out a tattered length of fabric. "He held this."

Niniane gasped. Across Peredur's outstretched palm lay the blanket of her visions, but she had never Seen it torn and stained with blood. She watched in stunned silence as Peredur allowed his nephew's blanket to slip to the ground.

She tried to deny the evidence of her eyes; she had Seen the child alive in a peasant's hut while someone bartered for his future. Her visions never lied.

Something terrible must have happened to change all that. Something she had failed to See.

Dear God, no!

"I—" Tears left cold tracks on her face. "Lord Peredur, I am so very sorry." Sorrier than he could ever know. Unable to say more and unwilling to meet his gaze, she buried her face in her hands.

"Not your fault," Peredur whispered.

Not true!

"You—you found the—the child's—" She couldn't finish. More tears coursed down her cheeks, and she stanched them with the back of her hand.

"Nay." But only a matter of time, apparently.

Gently, he helped her to her feet. She felt guilty for accepting even that small kindness.

A weak groan drew her attention. Angusel moved his head, flailing his arms and kicking as if fighting for his life. His eyelids fluttered open. No fever-madness glowed in his eyes, only despair.

He rolled to his feet. Although he made no sound, winces and stilted movements betrayed his suffering. He grabbed his staff to support himself.

Pressing his free hand to his head, his eyebrows shot up as his fingers encountered the bandage. He started to remove it, but Niniane firmly shook her head. She answered his inquiring look with an encouraging smile.

With a sigh, he let his hand drop to his side. Slowly, he turned in a full circle. When he saw the blanket lying on the ground, he gave a small cry and stooped to snatch it up. The sudden motion must have made him dizzy, for he kept his neck bent, head supported by one hand, as he straightened. Sorrow seemed permanently etched into his face and sagging shoulders, but when he beheld Peredur, his anguish deepened. He clutched the tattered blanket to his chest. Niniane felt tears burn her eyes.

Emotionlessly, Peredur thrust a hand toward Angusel. Angusel looked at the blanket, then back at Peredur, before yielding to the unspoken demand. Peredur's fist closed over the bloody fabric, and he turned to address, in Caledonian, one of the horsemen. The warrior mounted, took the blanket, and spurred his horse toward Arbroch. Peredur called another warrior to him and again uttered a Caledonian command. This time, Niniane discerned one word: Senaudon. The man directed his horse into the woods, heading south.

No one hindered Angusel as he left Peredur and the other soldiers. Their faces remained impassive.

Angusel shuffled away, head bowed and looking as if he'd lost his last friend on earth.

Niniane ached to console him, walk with him, anything to let him know he wasn't alone.

She despised the Sight for rendering her powerless to help.

Chapter 25

ARTHUR FOUGHT FOR patience as he rode with his escort through the crowds leaving Arbroch. People, dogs, livestock, carts, and wagons created a flood of activity, and he and his men were bucking the current like salmon returning to spawn.

Thank God Loth had stopped him at the Antonine Wall.

As they crossed Arbroch's meadows, Arthur gauged the greetings. Some waved and cheered as if nary a thing in the world were amiss. Others gave nods laden with concern and sympathy. Apparently, Loholt's disappearance wasn't yet widely known. Nor was he about to change that. Even his men didn't know the reason behind this abrupt mission. Arthur hoped for a happy resolution, but his gut's tautness cautioned him against indulging in too much optimism.

While he returned the people's gestures with an occasional nod or salute, he tried to think through the situation.

According to Gyan's message—not penned in her hand, which

fueled his worry—Loholt's wet nurse had taken him past Arbroch's gates. To judge by the number of festival participants, a lion could have stalked among them unremarked, never mind one woman with a baby.

Still, to have disappeared so quickly, she must have had help, but from whom, and why?

Only one name made sense.

He ground his teeth. If any harm befell Loholt, and Urien could be linked to the deed, then to the devil with politics. Arthur would personally crush Urien's bones to powder.

Near Arbroch's outermost rampart, the turma met a convoy of horsemen and wagons. The decurion, riding on Arthur's right flank, gave the command to move aside. When the crimson banners flown by the other group came close enough to identify, Arthur lifted an eyebrow at his own clan's symbol, the Ivory Unicorn.

He recalled Morghe's plan to return to Caerlaverock and finish preparing for her wedding. So today was the day.

Guilt warred with revulsion at the thought of Urien becoming his brother-by-marriage next spring. Guilt won. Not only had he lost the chance to speak with his sister, but if he'd been here instead of pursuing nonexistent Angli threats, Loholt might be safe.

Ruthlessly, he clamped off that reasoning. Loholt must be safe. It was simply a matter of finding him.

The lead rider of Morghe's escort recognized Arthur and saluted. The others followed his example. Arthur felt both amused and irritated by the men's comical attempts to straighten in the saddle, but he had no time to waste rebuking a lax unit. As they passed, he armed his glare with disapproval.

In its center, Morghe rode a spirited black mare, looking regal in her traveling garb. When she met Arthur's gaze, her face contorted with a flash of—what, fear? No. He must have imagined it. She drew nearer, and her lips curved into a smile.

He considered stopping to question her about Loholt. However, anything she knew, Gyan should know.

"God grant you a safe journey, Morghe," he said as she rode by.

She nodded once. "Thank you, Arthur."

Fingering his chin, he watched her until the wagons and the escort's rear ranks obscured her form. Why should she display fear toward him, even for a moment? And why the smile? If she knew Loholt was missing, she ought to have realized Arthur would be worried. Her smile hadn't been one of reassurance, but—what?

Perhaps she didn't know about Loholt's disappearance and was trying to be friendly. If so, then why the fear?

He turned to address Gawain. "Did Morghe's behavior seem strange?"

"You're asking me?" Gawain shrugged, grinning. "All women's behavior seems strange, kin or not!"

As the shared laughter trailed off, Arthur studied the fortress. His most acute concerns lay not with his sister but inside the gates. He kicked Macsen into a canter. The decurion shouted the corresponding command, and they thundered past the last ramparts.

Gyan must have seen them coming. Waiting at the base of the gate tower, she looked as if she hadn't slept in a fortnight, God help her. Arthur's heart ached. He halted, dismounted, and shoved the reins into Gawain's hands. While the decurion snapped orders to stable the mounts, Arthur strode to her. They embraced, and she pressed her face against his breastplate.

"What news, my love?" he whispered, stroking her disheveled braid.

Beneath his hand, she shook her head. "Nothing." Although he'd spoken in Brytonic, she responded in Caledonian. When she looked up, grief flooded her gaze. With all his heart, he wished he could bear it for her. "Artyr, I—" She slumped against his chest. "I am so sorry!"

As he hugged her tightly, one thought consumed his mind. Those who had abducted Loholt were going to be sorry. If he allowed them to live long enough to feel anything other than the most excruciating pain this side of hell.

For her benefit, he switched to Caledonian. "Gyan, I will summon the legion, and—"

"Your pardon, Chieftainess, Lord Artyr, but I do not believe that will be necessary."

He released his wife and turned toward the unknown voice. A soldier in Caledonian armor stood a few paces away. He wore an Argyll-patterned cloak fastened with a badge bearing the Argyll Doves rather than the legion's dragon.

Arthur waited for Gyan to order her man to deliver his report. Activity in the yard dwindled as more people stopped to watch.

"Gyan?" Arthur nudged her. She seemed to be staring at a length of silver-edged Argyll wool clutched in the warrior's hand. "Shouldn't we hear his report? Perhaps somewhere more private?"

"No need." Her tone sounded bleak, and her eyes adopted a haunted look. "The clan will find out soon enough. Torr?" She nodded at the warrior.

Torr approached, went to one knee in front of her, bowed his head, and offered her the fabric. As she unfurled it, her eyes widened. The material was slashed in several places and stained with blood.

"Wh-what—" Her chin began trembling violently. She clamped her mouth shut and covered her eyes with one hand. With the other, she held the fabric to her chest.

"What does this mean?" Arthur finished for her, gesturing at the cloth.

Torr rose, shaking his head. "My lord, it belongs—belonged—to your son."

"His . . . his favorite b-blanket," she whispered. The trembling of her lips and chin returned.

Arthur wrapped his arm around her and asked Torr, "Where did you find it?"

"The search party found Angusel mac Alayna on the west road. He was wounded, unconscious, and"—Torr nodded toward the blanket—"holding that."

"Angusel?" Arthur felt his eyebrows knot. "Is he all right?"

"He awakened in our presence, my lord, and is on his way here. He limps but should arrive within the watch."

"What? Alone and wounded? Why did you not help him?" This sounded too strange, even for Caledonians. "What was Angusel doing out on that road? Was he questioned?"

Torr spread his hands. "He finishes his trial of blood."

A singularly unhelpful answer. "His—what?"

"A ritual required of every Caledonian warrior. The youth must not accept help or speak to anyone." Gyan's words sounded soft and hollow, and her gaze seemed leagues away.

She shrugged out from under Arthur's arm, spun, and headed toward the feast hall. He strode to catch up and grabbed her hand. The fury in her glare made him recoil in surprise.

"Gyan?" Even pregnant, her mood swings couldn't compare. "Do you think Angusel is involved in Loholt's abduction?"

"I know not what to think." She resumed her course. "Torr," she called without bothering to look back, "escort Angusel to the feast hall the moment he arrives."

Arthur didn't know what to think, either. Or feel. Their son could be dead, if he took the meaning of that accursed cloth aright, but he couldn't permit himself the luxury of succumbing to his grief. Not while he stood on the verge of losing his wife to hers.

Trailing after her, he vowed not to let that happen.

GYAN SAT with her back not touching the elaborately carved judgment chair on the dais, clenching and unclenching her fists. Her consort, her father, her brother, and the High Priest surrounded her, clucking meaningless syllables like a flock of witless biddy hens.

The hall teemed with clansfolk come to witness the proceedings. Chieftainess Alayna entered with her entourage and stormed up to the dais. Perfunctorily, Gyan performed the rite of welcome. How Angusel's mother had found out—and how she had managed to arrive so quickly—Gyan didn't know and didn't care. She wished everyone would leave her alone. Arthur and Ogryvan included.

Loholt was dead.

Even without the proof of his body, her heart screamed the truth. She would never see her beloved bairn again.

Her tears had been seared by anger: at Tira, for obvious reasons, and at Urien. With sickening certainty, she knew he'd devised the plan. She also nursed anger toward Cynda for initially insisting nothing was amiss.

Behind it all smoldered fury toward herself for heeding Cynda rather than her own instincts.

Regardless of who had planned or committed the crime, she, Gyanhumara nic Hymar, had failed her son. She had been elsewhere when he needed her most, indulging in foolish, self-centered frivolities. The admission's pain hurt as acutely as a sword thrust.

The doors opened. A hush descended. The crowd parted.

A lone youth approached the dais, limping, with head and shoulders sagging like a prisoner being led to the executioner's block. His arms, legs, and torso bore several fresh scratches, and he leaned heavily on a crudely fashioned spear. A clean bandage bound his head. His sack hung half-open at a crazy angle across his chest, and his soles left bloody traces on the flagstones.

Feeling as if someone had wrapped up her compassion and hidden it away, Gyan could only observe Angusel's progress with detached interest, caring for naught save what he knew about her son.

Although if he had seen the deed, she wasn't sure she wanted to hear his report. Having her awful mental pictures augmented by the truth could only make them worse.

First, however, the prescribed ending to Angusel's deuchainn na fala had to be enacted.

Angusel played his part, going to one knee below the dais. He slid the sack from his shoulder, reached in and pulled out a supple rabbit skin. The High Priest took it from Angusel's uplifted hand. Upon examination, he pronounced it suitable for Angusel's bian-sporan. Normally, the candidate greeted this announcement with elation. Angusel merely accepted the hide and thrust it into his sack.

"Angusel mac Alayna, Exalted Heir of Clan Alban," said the High Priest, "your trial of blood is complete once you answer these questions." His ancient knuckles whitened as he gripped his carved staff, and he leaned forward. "By law, I must remind you that you are honor-bound to answer truthfully. Lies are punishable by banishment. Do you understand?"

Angusel nodded limply, like a rag doll. The association brought to mind Loholt's favorite toy. Gyan jammed her fist against her mouth.

"Very well," the High Priest said. "Did you speak with anyone during your journey?"

"Nay."

She felt her eyes widen. If he had witnessed her son's murder, he would have spoken out to try to save him. Wouldn't he? Or did his deuchainn na fala matter more than Loholt's life?

"Did you receive help from anyone?"

"Aye."

"The bandages?"

"Aye."

"Yet you did not speak to the person or request aid in any way?"

"Nay. I was unconscious."

While the High Priest stroked his snowy beard, speculative whispers skittered about the hall.

Gyan's ideas fit the facts all too well.

Even armed, a servant girl couldn't have wounded Angusel that badly. If Tira had been alone, he probably would have brought her and Loholt back to Arbroch with scarcely a struggle, his Oath of Fealty prompting him to act to preserve Loholt's life. There had to have been at least one other person with Tira, probably a man. Possibly Urien, although Gyan doubted it. Urien might have ordered the deed, but she didn't believe he would have sullied himself with its implementation. Angusel must have discovered Loholt's murderers, possibly while her son still lived, and tried to fight them.

Tried... and failed so utterly that the murderers left him alive as punishment to forever bear witness to his failure.

Her fury still smoldered against Urien, Tira, and Cynda. Cynda she'd deal with soon enough. The other two lay beyond her reach. Her anger acquired a new focus.

"Since the aid was rendered without Angusel's knowledge or consent, I rule that it does not invalidate his trial of blood." The High Priest raised both arms over his head. "If there are no other objections—"

Gyan rose. "I object."

Using the staff, Angusel stood, confusion furrowing his brow.

"Explain your reasons, Chieftainess." The priest lowered his arms and his eyebrows.

"Yes, Gyanhumara," added Alayna, eyes glittering. "Please do."

Unconcerned with the menace in Alayna's voice, Gyan announced her theory. "Therefore, Angusel mac Alayna, you must have seen the—" She gulped, struggling to marshal courage. "The murderers. Am I correct?"

"Almost. I saw two women and one man." He shook his head. "Two men. One attacked the other, but he was killed right away."

"Four!" One, maybe two people Gyan could believe, but four? And why would one attack the others? An outlaw, maybe? Or a difference of opinion regarding Loholt's fate? "Did you recognize them?"

"Nay," he whispered. "The women were hooded. We were in a forest near sunset, and I couldn't see their faces. No one spoke. The men—" His expression grew distant. He shook his head and looked at her levelly. "I don't know."

"You recognized my son, did you not? Was he alive?"

"Aye." Sighing, Angusel bowed his head. "He was."

"You failed to save him."

He drew a breath and puffed out his cheeks. "Aye."

Loholt might be nestled in her arms if not for Angusel's failure! Grief and anger began yanking her heart in opposite directions.

Anger won.

Fighting to retain control of her voice, she turned to address the High Priest. "For his inability to rescue Loholt mac Artyr, Exalted Heir of Clan Argyll, I propose that Angusel mac Alayna's trial be declared invalid."

"Gyanhumara, you can't!" cried Alayna. The High Priest waved for silence. With an impatient "Hrumph!" she folded her arms.

"My lady, your loss is the clan's loss, and I, too, grieve for our exalted heir." The High Priest looked sympathetic as he shook his head. "But except for receiving aid that he did not seek, Angusel completed his trial of blood as prescribed by law. My ruling stands." His staff made a hollow thump as he struck the platform, echoing within Gyan's heart.

Tears glistened in Angusel's eyes. He stepped forward, hands outstretched. "Gyan, I am so sorry!"

She didn't need his apology or his pity. His skill and strength, yes, but evidently that hadn't been enough.

If the High Priest wouldn't cooperate, then so be it.

"Kneel, Angusel mac Alayna," she commanded. In his eyes flared surprise—and perhaps fear, if he'd guessed Gyan's intent. To his credit, he obeyed. "Reaffirm your Oath of Fealty to me. Since you are unarmed"—Braonshaffir whined as it emerged from its sheath—"I will use my sword." She ignored the murmurs, the loudest coming from Alayna.

Gyan gripped the hilt with both hands. She lowered the blade to Angusel's neck, recalling her battle with Niall the Scáth to gauge how much force to use. But Niall had menaced those she had sworn to defend and would have taken her life.

Angusel had saved her life.

Though passing the deuchainn na fala made him a man by Caledonach law, he was only fourteen years older than her son. She had created this entire pathetic situation by succumbing to the vanity birthed by his hero-worship of her. What the ifrinn fuileachdach had she been thinking? She never should have sworn a boy into her service.

Her sword had never felt so heavy. Neither had her heart.

At the sound of her sword returning to its scabbard, Angusel opened his eyes and looked up. "Gyan?"

She raised a splayed hand. "Chieftainess."

"What?" He scrambled to his feet as quickly as his injuries would permit.

"Henceforth, you may address me by title only." She pitched her voice to carry to the farthest corners of the hall. "In the presence of this assembly, I hereby declare the original Oath of Fealty made by Angusel mac Alayna, Exalted Heir of Clan Alban, to Gyanhumara nic Hymar, Chieftainess of Clan Argyll, to be nullified."

Gasps swept across the hall.

Alayna stalked up to the dais, cheeks flaming as though she were in the throes of battle frenzy. "Chieftainess Gyanhumara, this is outrageous! Recant at once!"

"Mother, please. I deserve this." At her sharp glance, Angusel fell silent and dropped his gaze.

"If you do not recant, Chieftainess Gyanhumara," Alayna stated coldly, "then Clan Argyll will never receive aid from Clan Alban while I—or my son—live."

Just the sort of manipulative trick Gyan expected from the woman. "As you wish, Chieftainess Alayna."

Alayna fixed Gyan with a furious glare before regarding her son. "Come, Angusel. Let us be gone from this inhospitable place." Any stronger insult would have been a declaration of war.

Angusel didn't move.

Alayna tapped him on the shoulder. "I said come, son."

"I heard you." Pushing against the staff, he drew himself to his full height and faced Alayna. "But I'm not going with you."

"What?" Alayna's surprise forced her back a pace.

"Today, I have disgraced not just one clan but two."

"Angusel, no!"

"Mother, a dishonored warrior is of no use to his clan." He looked away. "Or to anyone."

"Angusel, my son, that's not true. The Argyll High Priest—"

"Was very kind, aye." He cast an appreciative glance at the man, but as he surveyed the Alban warriors, none would make eye contact with him. "There's no place for me in Clan Alban now. They know it." Gesturing at his clansmen, he looked squarely at his mother. "So do you. I am Angusel mac Alayna no longer. I am . . . Aonar."

Alayna whirled to face Gyan, rage contorting her features. "You!"

Alayna's finger jabbed the air in front of Gyan's chest. If she'd been wielding a sword, Gyan would have died where she stood. Not that it would have mattered; Gyan felt as if a part of her had already died with her bairn. "For the evil you have wrought upon Clan Alban, may you never have another day's happiness."

Gyan doubted she'd ever be happy again, curse or no.

As Alayna, in a violent flurry of motion, gathered her men to leave, Gyan sensed her father looming behind her. He laid a hand on her shoulder. "Gyanhumara—"

"Angusel mac Alayna's oath was to me, Father, and I stand within my rights to nullify it. You cannot override me."

He withdrew his hand, paced to the front of her chair, and lowered his face to hers. "Think of the consequences. Including the stain it will leave on Angusel," he said quietly. "He's a good lad at heart, Gyan. This wasn't his fault. He doesn't deserve to call himself 'Alone' any more than he deserves to be alone. Are you sure you won't change your mind?"

She folded her arms. "Absolutely." If her father was so concerned about a rift with Clan Alban, then he could bloody well try to make amends with Alayna himself. She didn't want to see anyone from that corner of Caledon for the rest of her life.

Ogryvan's expression hosted an odd blend of anger and sympathy. Straightening, he signaled Per, Seumas, Torr, and several other warriors to accompany him, and the group strode after Alayna.

As both parties disappeared through the far doors, Arthur stepped forward. "You haven't heard Angusel's account of the fight, Gyan. I can't believe he didn't try his best." What he didn't say, although she could read it plainly enough in his eyes, was that he thought she was being too hard on Angusel. On Aonar. "If you don't want his report, I do."

A few "ayes" chorused his request.

"The exalted heir-begetter will remember his place," she said icily.

"But, Gyan—Chieftainess, I—I did fight hard, but I was—"

"I am not interested in your excuses, *Aonar*." He winced. She stood. "You are alive, and my son is not. I command you to leave Arbroch. If you set foot within these walls again, it shall be upon peril of your life." His face adopted a stricken look before he turned away. For the first time, she noticed the condition of his wounds. Shivering, he clung to his staff as though without it he would die. She relented a little. "You have until sundown tomorrow."

"As you will." Angusel bowed stiffly. "Chieftainess."

He lurched through the silent crowd toward the feast hall doors.

Pressing a hand to her eyes, she dropped into her chair, wave after wave of fresh grief crashing and breaking upon her soul. To keep herself from being dashed to pieces, she tried to revive her anger against Angusel, Tira, and Cynda, as well as against the man ultimately responsible, Urien map Dumarec.

This time, grief won.

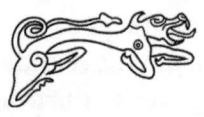

GYAN BURIED her face in her hands and wept, her chest heaving as though she battled for every breath.

Arthur knew exactly how she felt.

However, she didn't seem to recognize the political disaster she'd created. Urien undoubtedly would dance from one end of Dalriada to the other when he found out.

Conflicting desires warred within Arthur's heart. Angusel needed to hear that Arthur didn't blame him for what had happened to Loholt. Noting how quickly the lad slipped through the crowd, Arthur doubted he would stay at Arbroch any longer than necessary, but Gyan's distress vanquished all other concerns.

He gripped her convulsing shoulder. Without looking, she brushed his hand away. She might as well have beheaded him.

Arthur stooped to whisper, "Gyan..."

She sucked in a breath and blew it out. Her hands dropped to the armrests, her back stiffening. Face tilted upward, she clenched her jaw and shut her eyes. When she opened them, they burned with an intense inner fire. "I am going to kill him." Battle frenzy never had given her such a furious countenance.

"Angusel?" Arthur knew damned well what she'd intended when the lad had bared his neck to her blade.

Violently, she shook her head. "Urien." The name oozed from between her gritted teeth.

He clasped her hands and pulled her to her feet. Gazing at some point beyond his shoulder, she didn't resist him. "You can't mean it, Gyan. You have no proof."

She wrenched her hands free and slapped her chest. "Here is all the proof I need."

She drew her dagger and raised it level with her neck. Arthur caught her wrist. "Gyan, no!"

"The exalted heir-begetter shall stand aside," she growled. "Or be removed from this place."

Reluctantly, he complied. The crowd's buzzing escalated. Gyan grabbed her braid and hacked it off, stuck it onto the dagger's point, and thrust it overhead. Silence invaded the hall.

"I, Gyanhumara nic Hymar, vow to the exalted heir-begetter and Clan Argyll that everyone responsible for the death of Loholt mac Artyr shall feel the wrath of my blade. My head shall bear witness to the fulfillment of this oath."

By God, Arthur believed her.

She dashed the braid to the floor and sheathed her dagger. After scowling at him with a look that forbade intrusion, she stomped off the platform and through the shocked crowd. Near the doors, she paused long enough to give someone a reprimand. The oaken doors thundered shut behind her.

No one dared to pursue Gyan, not even the stalwart Cynda, who stood staring at the closed doors, wringing her hands and shifting from foot to foot.

With a leaden heart, Arthur retrieved Gyan's braid. He drew it slowly through his fingers, and it emitted a faint aroma of roses. Its softness mocked the many times he'd enjoyed its feel and scent. Saddened beyond measure, he coiled it about his fist.

He didn't understand what she had meant by having "proof." Intuition, perhaps. He'd seen grief strip reason from otherwise reasonable folk, himself included.

He couldn't blame her for the virulence of her response. Nor could he allow himself to succumb to similar temptations.

He could only hope that she would let him share this burden. At present, it didn't seem likely, and that grieved him more deeply than he'd have ever thought possible.

One person might benefit, though, if he acted quickly enough. Summoning his military bearing lest grief rob him of his sense, too, he signaled his decurion to form up the turma for departure, left the platform, and marched down the aisle.

NINIANE WATCHED the proceedings with growing horror. She didn't need to understand the words; the tones, gestures, and reactions revealed all. Her stomach clenched. This was her fault.

Most people glanced elsewhere as Angusel trudged by. Some turned their backs. If the look in Gawain's eyes had been a weapon, Angusel never would have left the hall alive. Angusel made no response except to appear even more devastated. Niniane yearned to fold him into a motherly embrace but feared that might violate another taboo. Instead, she reached out to catch his hand. The eyes that met hers—golden-brown eyes she'd Seen in more visions than she could count—brimmed with unshed tears. He pulled away and left the building.

The burden of prophecy and the necessity to keep it a secret from the world had never felt so heavy.

Gyanhumara's agitated countenance spoke volumes about her craving for solitude. Niniane respected that; grief could be a harsh master. Cynda tried to say something to the chieftainess and was scathingly rebuked. Tears sprang to the older woman's eyes.

Niniane closed her eyes, as much to erase the scene as to hold her tears at bay. All this misery because of her failure...

"I can guess why you're here, Prioress." Her eyes flew open to see Arthur standing before her, his face grim but resigned. "I'm afraid you're too late."

"I—I know. And I am so very sorry." More sorry than he could possibly imagine. She rubbed her shoulders, but the warmth failed to ward off the chill seeping into her soul.

"What happened? What did you See? Why in heaven's name didn't you come sooner?" Pain seared the edges of his tone.

Niniane had no desire to worsen that pain, but she couldn't withhold her confession from one of the few people she trusted with the knowledge of her gift. She drew a breath, let it out slowly, and in whispered tones revealed everything but the vision of Loholt in the peasants' hut, which must have occurred before his death, if at all. "Arthur," she said, "can—can you ever forgive me?"

He arched an eyebrow. "You didn't do anything wrong."

"My journey here—"

"Was delayed by misfortune, not by choice."

Small comfort. She averted her gaze, refusing to forgive herself.

"Niniane, I would ask a favor of you."

She looked up. "Anything, Arthur."

"It's Gyan." His fingers convulsed around the remains of Gyanhumara's glorious red hair, his sigh barely audible. "She needs your help."

"Me? She has family, servants, priests." She regarded him closely. "And her husband."

"I—" More pain flared in his eyes. "I can't get through her grief." Determination conquered the pain. "I was hoping you could."

"Angusel grieves, too, but he has no one."

"That's not true. He just doesn't realize it yet."

She hated to ask, "He's been banished, hasn't he?"

"From Arbroch, yes. And he faces rejection, public disgrace—I'm not sure I understand it all. Or agree with it. If Gyan comes to her senses, she may regret what she's done, but by then it may be too late. It may already be too late." Arthur grasped her hand. "I'll deal with Angusel. Help Gyan. For me."

"How can I, Arthur? Her religion—"

"Greet her in the name of the 'One God,'" he whispered, "and she should welcome you."

The One God? How strange, Niniane thought. But with failure binding her soul with guilt, she couldn't possibly refuse. "When you see Bishop Dubricius, please tell him I'll be delayed in returning to the priory. For how long, I'm not sure."

"Agreed." He squeezed her hand and released it. "Thank you, Niniane.

Cynda approached while they spoke, and she halted a respectful distance away. When Arthur turned to leave, she asked him a question in hesitant-sounding Caledonian. He glanced at the braid, nodded sharply, and gave it to her. Cynda's sobs erupted, and Arthur held her through the worst. With squared shoulders and set jaw, he strode from the hall. Cynda watched his departure, chin quivering, Gyanhumara's braid clutched over her heart.

WITHIN THE sanctity of her private chambers, Gyan at last felt free of meddlers prying into her grief.

Except there was nothing sanctified about this room. The cradle gaped from the shadows near the cold hearth like an open wound. Like the way her heart felt, empty and forlorn.

Her dear, sweet bairn was dead.

Gyan flung herself facedown on the bed, sobs wracking her body. Memories plunged her further into the abyss. She grabbed fistfuls of shorn hair and yanked, but it couldn't displace the pain lancing her chest. Worse than any fleshly wound, it wouldn't abate.

Why, she beseeched the One God, had Loholt been abducted? Why couldn't Angusel have saved him? Why had she let Cynda convince her nothing was amiss? Why did her bairn have to die so horribly? Why did he have to die at all? Why hadn't Urien gone after her instead, *why*?

Where was this all-seeing, all-knowing, all-powerful God when Loholt was murdered? Why didn't He act to prevent it? Didn't He care?

No answers came.

A tentative knock on the door wrenched her from her tirade. Cursing her stupidity for not bolting the door to the outer chamber, she called out to be left alone.

The knocking persisted. "Chieftainess Gyanhumara? I'd like to speak with you, if I may." Not Caledonaiche words but Breatanaiche. "Please?"

Gyan had no wish to see anyone, but her instincts objected. After swiping the back of a hand across her face, she rose and opened the door.

Prioress Niniane glided into the room, closing the door behind her and leaning against it. She held out a hand, palm up. "As a servant of the One God, I grieve with you, Chieftainess."

The One God. Gyan squeezed her eyes shut, wrapping an arm around the bedpost. Whatever Niniane had to say Gyan didn't want to hear.

Yet it stood to reason that Niniane's vocation put her into closer proximity with Him. Closer, surely, than Gyan felt. Perhaps the prioress could learn the answers Gyan had failed to obtain.

Regarding Niniane evenly, she fired her questions—except the one about Urien, which by its nature demanded silence. Several times, she paused to wipe her face or take a deep breath.

Sinking onto a nearby chair, Niniane murmured, "I'm sorry, my lady. Those matters are beyond my knowledge."

Hands on hips Gyan asked, "Why did the One God cause this misery?"

"He didn't. He loves us. He wants to see us happy, not miserable."

"Ha." Folding her arms, Gyan narrowed her eyes. "If the One God isn't responsible, then who is?"

"The prince of this world." Who did Niniane mean? Urien? The prioress continued, "The evil one. Lord of Lies. Ha'satan, the Adversary."

At her mention of the Adversary, Gyan shivered. Caledonaich called Lord Annàm "the Adversary" of his twin brother and Lord of Light, Annaomh. Their eternal battles across the groves and glens of the Otherworld bled into this one to spark conflict among mortal kind. Whether truth or fantasy, however, it made no difference. Gyan couldn't punish a bodiless manifestation.

On the verge of ordering the prioress to leave, she vented her frustration with a sigh. "Why mock me with your ignorance?"

Niniane shook her head. "Your husband sent me. 'Blessed are they that mourn, for they shall be comforted.'" Briefly, her eyes closed. "But I'm not much of a comforter, I fear."

In an odd way, though, Niniane was helping. "Talking... keeps my mind from—from..." Her chin started quivering, and she clamped her jaw shut. With her gaze fastened on Niniane to avoid looking at the empty cradle, Gyan sat on the bed. "Oh, Arthur..." she whispered. "I thought he'd hate me for what I've done."

For not dealing with Urien in a way that would have averted this tragedy, for failing to follow her instincts, for banishing Angusel and alienating his clan... for failing to be the wife Arthur needed or the mother Loholt needed. She loathed herself.

"My lady, please don't believe that." Niniane stood and crossed to the bed. She gathered Gyan's hands in her own as she sat beside her. "He knows this wasn't your fault."

"Wasn't it?" Gyan pulled free. "My inattention gave the abductors their opportunity." In more ways than one, she thought miserably. Gyan felt tears welling and blinked hard. Because of her selfishness and stupidity, she would never see her son again.

"That may be true," Niniane said gently, "but God forgives you. So does Arthur." Gyan couldn't believe any of it. Tears flowed anew. Niniane wrapped an arm around her shoulders. "You need to learn how to forgive yourself." A waver in Niniane's voice made Gyan look at her. To her surprise, she saw tears glistening on the other woman's cheeks. "Forgiveness of self is a lesson I must learn, as well."

The prioress didn't elaborate, and Gyan didn't ask. Gyan's own problems weighed too much. Her anguish had spawned political strife, the very thing she'd most feared that Urien would accomplish.

"I—I don't think I can ever forgive myself."

"It isn't easy, sometimes." Niniane gazed at Gyan hopefully. "Maybe we can learn together. That is, if you want me to stay."

Gyan considered the merits of Niniane's suggestion. She missed her chats with Dafydd about the One God and sensed she needed more.

Inadvertently, her gaze found the cradle. Fresh pain bolted through her body, and she gritted her teeth. Removing the bairn's things would avail nothing. She'd know where every toy, every swaddling cloth, every stick of furniture had been. She would still hear his cries, his laughter, his coos, and his sighs.

Gyan rose, crossed to a chest, and hunted around inside before finding the object she sought. After closing the chest, she strode to the door and turned to face Niniane. "Coming, Prioress?" Though wrapped in fabric, the metal imbued her with a sense of purpose.

The holy woman frowned. "My lady?"

"There's no need for you to stay here." Gyan gazed at Arthur's traveling cloak, debating whether she could live with the memories it evoked. Finally, she lifted it from its peg and folded it over her arm. "We shall both return to Maun."

OUTSIDE THE feast hall, Angusel braced himself against the timbers, eyes closed. His head wound throbbed unmercifully. Yet what was fleshly pain compared with the destruction of his world?

"Baby-killer!" someone rasped.

Angusel opened his eyes to see the men of First Turma, Sixth Ala, Horse Cohort marching past him toward the stables, many of whom he'd befriended during the weeks of cattle raiding for Chieftain Loth. Had one of them spoken with such vehemence?

Aye, the Pendragon's sister-son, Gawain map Loth. Though Gawain had moved on to keep in step, Angusel would have recognized that straight raven hair and stocky build anywhere.

He sighed. First Gyan—and he always would remember her by her familiar name. Then his own kin, now Arthur's. Only the gods knew who else despised him for his failure. His belly felt as though someone had thrust in a hot knife and twisted repeatedly.

Sundown tomorrow, she'd said. He wanted nothing more than to leave this gods-cursed place at once. And so he would, as soon as he could gather his belongings and horse and figure out where to go.

He couldn't hate Gyan. Not for the attempted execution, shattered oath, rage, or public humiliation. Or for taking from him the only things he'd ever wanted, the only things that had lent meaning to his life: being her sword-brother and friend.

For she'd been right. He had failed Loholt and, by extension, her. He knew it; she knew it. To his disgrace, everyone knew it.

Bandits might have him.

Yet even as the thought formed, he rejected it. He'd rather starve than resort to law-breaking. Better to live out the name he'd given himself.

"Angusel. I don't agree with what she did to you."

He turned and rubbed a hand across eyes that felt too wet for anyone else to see. "Lord Pendragon! I didn't hear you approach." He stared at the dusty ground. "Call me Aonar, sir. Please."

"I will not." The Pendragon's forceful tone made Angusel look up. "Call yourself whatever you like, but you are not alone. And you may use my given name. This isn't a battlefield or a legion post." He shook his head. "I'm not the one who insists on being unreasonable."

Angusel couldn't have disagreed more. "I failed her." He felt stinging in his eyes and looked away. "And you."

"So. You lied, then? Ran away before the first blow?"

"Nay, sir!" Words tumbled forth in a rush, describing every move, every grunt and thrust he could recall of the fight. "But when I woke up and found the blanket—" He averted his gaze.

A hand gripped Angusel's shoulder with a familiar, tingling warmth. "I grieve for Loholt, too." Arthur's features hardened into the mask Angusel knew well. "But grieving won't bring him back. You aren't to blame for this. Those people you saw are. Possibly others you didn't see."

"What do you mean, sir?" He had his guesses but craved Arthur's opinion.

The Pendragon gave a rueful smile. "Speculation can cause a lot of trouble." He set off toward the stables. After taking a few strides, he stopped and glanced over his shoulder. "Well, Angusel? Are you coming or not?"

"With you?" Angusel hurried to catch him. "Where?" He wanted to ask why but couldn't bring himself to voice it.

"The staging area," said the Pendragon, resuming his pace.

"Senaudon?" Angusel's astonishment stopped him. Had Arthur gone mad? "I'm sorry, my lord. I can't."

"Horse dung. You'll be in the legion. Officially." Arthur tapped his own fealty-mark. "You didn't break your oath. She is only refusing to accept your service. You still want to serve her, don't you?"

Do I?

An hour ago, he knew the answer.

"Your oath," Arthur said sternly, "binds you to serve Gyan by any possible means. If you join the legion, you will be serving me."

"And by serving you, I'll be serving her, is that it?"

"It's the only viable option you have." His eyes narrowed. "Unless you are an oath-breaker."

"Nay! But I—I'm not sure I'm ready to join the legion." Especially if he had to live at his birthplace, outcast.

Aonar.

"It won't be easy," said the Pendragon. "Think it over while you visit the physician and collect your gear. I leave within the hour." Arthur glanced at the stables, which were teeming with soldiers, servants, groomsmen, stable boys, and horses. "I need men who take their duties seriously. Not boys who choose to wallow in self-pity." He smiled slightly. "A wise man told me that having guilt is natural, but allowing it to consume you isn't. Today, you acted every inch the man I've expected you to become. I would be pleased to welcome you into the legion."

Duties, Angusel thought morosely. Mere days ago, Gyan had told him to join the legion at Senaudon. Yet he'd insisted on performing his *deuchainn na fala* first. If he'd obeyed Gyan, as duty demanded, she wouldn't have banished him today.

But there wouldn't have been anyone to try to save Loholt.

He sighed. The sword of duty cut both ways, but he deserved its every wound.

"I will join the Dragon Legion. The self-pity stays here." He stabbed a finger downward and regarded his new commander solemnly. "Arthur, I promise to serve you to the best of my ability."

The Pendragon grinned and extended his sword hand. As they clasped forearms, Angusel offered a tentative smile.

"Your best, Angusel, is all anyone can ask of you."

Perhaps, but that didn't free him from demanding more of himself. He vowed to become the best warrior ever. Not for his own sake or even Arthur's, but for Gyan. He prayed she would forgive him one day and allow him to serve her openly. That fragile hope sparked the volition to journey with Arthur to Senaudon and beyond.

Chapter 26

Gyan summoned Prioress Niniane's escort to the stables and was overseeing the preparations for their departure, amid the tumult created by Arthur's unit, when Arthur arrived. She stiffened at his approach, unsure of how he would react to her decision.

Hell would vanish before she'd let him stop her.

"Gyan, well met." He clasped her hands and drew her into an embrace. As his lips brushed her cheek, he whispered, "I didn't expect to have the chance to bid you farewell."

She laughed mirthlessly. She hadn't planned on taking her leave of him, either.

He nodded pointedly at Prioress Niniane's escort. "Isn't she staying?"

"They are my escort, too."

He released her hands and stepped back, his gaze radiating intense appraisal. "What do you mean?"

She removed her tricolor dragon badge, unwrapped the object

she'd brought from her chambers, and pinned it in the other brooch's place. "I have demoted myself." She gave him the gold brooch and fabric. "Keep it until you're ready to confer its true significance upon its bearer."

"What is this?" Glaring, he rapped a fingernail against Urien's discarded legion brooch. "Martyrdom?"

"I intend to resume my duties as a cohort commander." Fists on hips, she thrust out her chin. "If the Pendragon has no objections."

"What of Argyll and your duties here?"

"Ha." She rolled her eyes. "I am of no use to Argyll at present." Closing her fingers over her sword's sapphire, she said, "I intend to be of use to the legion."

Again, she bore his scrutiny. "You cannot escape the past."

"No," she conceded. "But I don't need its perpetual reminders."

Sighing, he nodded. "I understand." He stroked her arm, swathed in his traveling cloak, the only reminder she had intended to bring. "Where are you going?"

"Maun."

His hand stilled. "Out of the question. Unless you plan to deliver yourself into Urien's hands?"

He had a point, one she hadn't considered. It tempted her to change her mind, but her desire to get away outweighed all else. Only on Maun had she ever felt completely at peace.

She squared her shoulders. "Just let him try to take me! He has much to answer for." She folded her arms and shrugged. "With the Móran chieftainship so new on his shoulders, I presume he has more than enough to occupy him in Dùn At."

Arthur stared at her for what seemed like an eon. Once, their gazes had held naught but love. Not today, she realized miserably. But she resolved to remain firm.

Finally, he relented. "I will make the necessary arrangements on two conditions. First, that you take ship from Caerlaverock."

"Dùn Càrnhuilean? So Ygraine can counsel me?" Having her consort and blood-kin and the prioress prying into her grief, she could understand, but including a woman made kin by marriage pressed matters too far. "I think not."

"I suggest it for your health," he snapped. "A plague has decimated Caer Lugubalion. I cannot deploy the full legion against the Angli until spring. Providing they don't attack Dunpeldyr first."

The frustration soaking his voice made her overlook his use of those Breatanaiche names in their Caledonaiche conversation. "Attack Loth directly? I thought border-raiding was their game."

"It was. Until Loth summoned me, and what forces I could muster, based on a false report." His jaw tightened, and his eyes glittered icily. Whether his anger was directed at Loth, the Angalaranaich, or herself, she couldn't tell. "It may prove to be a costly mistake for us all." Quieter, he continued, "As to your traveling by way of Dùn Càrnhuilean, my mother does know the anguish of losing a child."

Gyan's cheeks flushed. She almost quipped that Ygraine had been reunited with her child but thought better of it. "And the second condition?"

"Gyan, lass—your hair! By the gods, what did you do?"

Arthur and Gyan turned to find Ogryvan striding toward them, with Per and the rest of his contingent in his wake. Gyan explained her vow and her decision to return to Maun. The fact that she hoped to escape her roiling emotions she kept to herself. Eyes downcast, she concluded, "Father, I am truly sorry for the hurt I have caused Argyll. And . . . you." Ignoring the sting in her eyes and nose, she looked up. Pain and compassion flooded her father's gaze, and her chin began to quiver.

"Ach, lass, I forgive you." Ogryvan folded her into a hug.

She buried her face against his chest, soaking his tunic with her tears. His arms tightened, and he swayed her gently like a bairn. Fresh grief shuddered through her body.

She stepped back, drying her face with her tunic sleeve. That her father had to do the same didn't surprise her. "I will miss you, Gyan. We all will." He glanced at the surrounding men, who answered with nods and words of affirmation. Arthur alone remained silent, which ripped open another wound, though Gyan fought to mask her hurt. "But I must admit your absence should make it easier for me to smooth Alayna's ruffled feathers."

"I don't think anything can help that," Gyan said, rage and regret facing off within her soul, "short of recanting what I did to her son." Rage won again; she couldn't deny the stark reality of Angus's—*Aonar's*—failure. "Which isn't going to happen."

"What Alayna wants from Argyll is the one thing she has always wanted," Ogryvan said. "She lost no time in reminding me of it."

Arthur arched an eyebrow. "And that would be?"

"She wants me as Alban's exalted heir-begetter," Ogryvan said. "That would rob Gyan of her rightful rank, son, and you of yours. I cannot do that to either of you."

Gyan raised her hands in supplication. "Father, I don't care about my rank"—*or my consort's*—"if it means more suffering for Argyll. If that's the only way to buy peace with Alban—"

"Nay, lass." He smiled briefly, brushing the graying Argyll Doves on his sword arm. "Your dear mother's grave bears witness to my vow that I shall never unite with the exalted heir-bearer of another clan." Ogryvan hugged her again. "You go and do what you need to do, Gyan. Don't worry about Argyll. Or me. I can handle Alban." After releasing her, he stared at Arthur, eyebrows furrowing. "I want my daughter back in one piece."

"I intend to post Argyll warriors to Maun with her, sir," he replied crisply.

"Your other condition?" Gyan asked Arthur as his announcement won exclamations of appreciation from the men.

"Yes."

Ogryvan shifted closer to Arthur. "See me privately before you leave, then. I have a—contribution for you." He held his son-by-law's gaze as if in challenge.

ARTHUR NODDED and watched thoughtfully as Ogryvan departed. In Brytonic and Caledonian, he called for volunteers. Enough stepped forward to fill two turmae, including Gawain and Per.

He cocked a questioning eyebrow at his nephew.

"I want to return to Tanroc's infantry unit," Gawain stated.

"Not one of its turmae?" Arthur asked. "They could use another fine horseman."

"Call it a respite from the saddle sores, sir."

Perhaps even a respite from Gawain's recent Dunpeldyr memories, though now bloody well wasn't the time to confirm that detail.

The Pendragon approved Gawain's request but denied Per's: "The Horse Cohort needs its prefect."

"Then appoint another one." Per stood beside Gyan. They exchanged a look; hers was one of irritation underpinned with the barest hint of affection. Per regarded Arthur frankly. "*She* needs me, whether she realizes it or not. Blood is thicker than"—he pulled off the red-ringed bronze dragon and held it up—"this."

Battling back a sigh, Arthur accepted the piece, wrapped it with Gyan's, and regarded his brother-by-marriage. "Guard her back well." His gaze shifted beyond Per, Gawain, Rhys, Conall, Mathan, and the other volunteers. "Gyan, you also have one new recruit."

The crowd parted. When the identity of this "new recruit" registered, dressed in black Caledonian armor, with freshly bandaged wounds and saddle packs looped over his arms, Gyan looked ready to refuse. Gawain and the Argyll warriors looked ready to lynch the lad.

Arthur leveled a glare at the men, and they eased their stances. Crossing his arms, he regarded his wife. "Angusel goes to Maun, or you, Gyanhumara nic Hymar, do not."

Angusel's countenance fell. "Lord Pendragon, I thought I—"

"In the Dragon Legion, soldier, you go where your commander orders." Arthur directed his gaze upon Gyan. "Understood, Commander?"

Gyan thinned her lips. "Understood, Lord Pendragon. *Aonar* goes to Maun." She removed Arthur's cloak and thrust it at him, keeping Urien's damned badge clenched in her fist.

As Arthur sadly took the garment from her, the fury smoldering in her eyes declared that she would not soon forget his intrusion upon her authority. Or forgive him for it.

SURROUNDED BY his escort, Urien urged Talarf into a trot, anxiety and resentment ravaging his heart. He ran a gloved finger beneath his gold-inlaid leather headband to release the sweat that had collected there. Not even a crown of inch-thick solid gold could make him forget the scar it concealed.

The main road to the God-forsaken Argyll border was the last place he wanted to be, but with Accolon overdue by a week, he needed to learn why.

He'd hoped to meet Accolon along the way. The border, however, stretched for miles. If Accolon were being pursued, he'd surely avoid the roads.

Talarf pricked his ears, tossing his head and wrestling with the bit. Urien tried to listen for other sounds, but the noise made by his company drowned everything else. He squinted down the road.

The traveler appearing from around the bend looked like hell, slumped over his horse's neck, with his face buried in the mane, one shoulder swathed in a dirty bandage, his clothes torn and dingy. The horse shuffled along, head drooping, barely lifting its hooves.

Urien halted his escort and ordered two men forward to investigate. The traveler raised his head.

"My lord!" shouted a soldier, looking back at Urien. "It's—"

Accolon, Urien mentally finished as his guard uttered the name aloud. He couldn't dismount fast enough.

Mindful of the wounded shoulder and possible injuries concealed by Accolon's clothes, the men eased Accolon from the saddle as Urien and the rest of the escort approached. While one soldier saw to the needs of Accolon's horse, Urien waved the others back so he could tend Accolon himself and, with luck, glean some information.

"Chieftain Urien." Accolon grinned wanly as Urien, supporting his good arm, helped him sit on a fallen log. "Well met."

"Well met, indeed." Urien made a show of examining the bandage. "Done?" he whispered.

Accolon nodded. He shifted on the log, grimacing.

"Trouble?" Urien pointed a nod at the wound.

"Nothing I couldn't handle."

With this being neither the time nor place to extract details, he deemed it best to concentrate on other matters. "Witnesses?"

"Dead."

Urien felt his eyebrows lift. "Anyone I might know?" The whore, perhaps, killed in the struggle over her baby? While it would deny him the pleasure of watching her beg for her life, he would not complain if good fortune landed upon his doorstep.

A fly tried to alight on Accolon's wound. He slapped at it, none too gently, Urien thought. The pest reeled, recovered its flight, and buzzed off. Accolon sucked in a breath, wincing, and slowly blew it out. "No one of consequence, my lord."

Elation surged through Urien's veins.

He indulged in the fantasy of seeing Gyanhumara, broken in body and spirit, cowering at his feet. He would take from her what he'd always craved, what had been rightfully his. And, oh, how he would savor the taking.

Pitching his voice for the others to hear, he said, "I can't do anything more for your wound, Accolon. We need to find a physician." He gave his friend a reassuring grin. "You'll be well and whole before you know it." For Accolon's ears alone he added, "Then you and I will celebrate your success."

UNLIKE THE first time Gyan journeyed on this road, she had nothing to celebrate. Then, the world had seemed fresh and exciting, bursting with promise and adventure. The road had led to her soul's mate.

Now, her soul's mate lived leagues away, immersed in his own concerns. Death allied with guilt and remorse to stalk her waking hours and haunt her sleep. "Adventure" lost its meaning, and the only promise she cared about was of being reunited with her wee bairn in the realm of the One God.

Her hand dropped to her hilt as she jolted along, caressing the grip's cool, familiar ribs, provoking the temptation to usher that promise into reality. "Life" was another meaningless word; she'd become a liability to her clan, consort, sword-brothers ... and her son. But Loholt had no reason to welcome an eternal reunion with her. Pain savaged her heart, and her grip tightened reflexively.

Too numb to live and yet too frightened to die, she surrendered to the journey's dictates.

The sixth night found the company at the gates of Port Dùn Ghlas. Gyan's spirits lifted a little at the prospect of speaking with Bedwyr. Unfortunately, he was out on patrol and not due back for several days. Nor were there enough warships at port to transport Gyan, Per, Niniane, Niniane's escort, and the Manx cavalry reinforcements, along with their mounts, remounts, and supplies, to Maun. Gyan greeted this news with stoic resignation. She had abandoned her remaining emotions at Arbroch like excess baggage.

She didn't confide in her brother or the prioress. Per wore a mask of forced cheer, and she couldn't risk breaching his barriers for fear of crumbling her own. Prioress Niniane displayed naught but kindness and caring, but by her request to stop at nigh unto every roadside shrine, Gyan surmised the holy woman was working through some inner turmoil, too. This left private prayer, but the One God seemed impossibly far beyond reach.

Concentrating on present needs, she insulated herself from the past as best she could. Each cold stroke of wind and rain upon the back of her neck galvanized her awareness that Urien would have to be dealt with, but not until after she'd collected incontrovertible proof, a daunting task regardless of the rewards. So she shut herself off from the future as well as the past and threw what energy she could summon into surviving each day.

Arthur hadn't exaggerated about the plague at Caer Lugubalion, she learned from the men of Niniane's original escort detail, all recently recovered from the illness. No one who'd survived the first infection caught it a second time, so their commander had selected them for this duty to reduce the risk of spreading the plague.

The company was walking their horses when they reached the fork where the road split to follow opposite banks of the Soluis Firth. Here the group splintered, with Niniane's escort and the nun Dorcas returning to regular duty at legion headquarters, and Gyan, the prioress, Per, and the rest of the warriors pressing on to Dùn Càrnhuilean. Gyan gave the order to mount and dismissed the Caer Lugubalion escort with her thanks, envying their shorter journey.

Torchlight atop the guard towers flanking the Dùn Càrnhuilean gates blazed like twin beacons. Night had long since fallen when Gyan's unit arrived. Chieftainess Ygraine led the unit that met them in the main yard, as if they had been expected.

"Of course you were, my dear," Ygraine responded to Gyan's query. "Arthur's courier arrived two days ago."

Gyan felt her face go ashen. "Th-then you know...?" She stopped, fearing her voice would betray her.

Arthur's mother fired off a rapid set of commands to her men. Reeling with emotional and physical fatigue, Gyan appreciated the way Ygraine took charge of the quartering and provisioning of Gyan's warriors and their horses. Ygraine delivered Niniane into the care of the house priest, who offered to conduct her to guest clergy quarters adjacent to the chapel. Gyan instructed Niniane to meet the company in the courtyard at dawn.

"So soon?" Ygraine sounded profoundly disappointed.

"My command awaits," Gyan said briskly, hoping she wouldn't prove to be a liability to them, too.

Ygraine gave her a slow nod. "Come, then. We must talk."

Must we?

Ygraine led her into a nearby building. Though built of stone, timber, and thatch in Breatanach style and heated with hearths and braziers, and though the ivory Càrnhuileanach Unicorn reared upon everything from wall hangings to the soldiers' badges, the elegant Ròmanach furnishings induced comparisons to Caer Lugubalion's praetorium.

"Why does Arthur favor this foreign heritage by choice?" Gyan wondered aloud, and in the next breath wished she hadn't. Ygraine paused to give her an odd look. "I thought his namesake and ancestor, Lucius Arturus Castus, was a Bryton who only earned his Roman citizenship by right of surviving twenty years in their army."

Ygraine smiled, and they resumed their course. "Castus was a namesake but not an ancestor. Uther liked 'Arturus'—mainly for that centurion's military record—and I invented the Brytoni form, 'Arthur.'"

"Which means...?"

"Uther's Bear. But our cub prefers to earn respect rather than relying upon family connections." Ygraine must have sensed Gyan's puzzlement, for she continued, "Arthur carries the blood of Roman emperors through the Aurelii."

Gyan felt her mouth drop open. "Marcus Aurelius? *That* Aurelia clan? The monks taught me he was one of Rome's wisest rulers."

"And his brother and coemperor, Lucius Aurelius Verus, and their father, Antoninus Pius, the emperor who ordered construction of a certain wall of your acquaintance."

Those names jarred Gyan's recollection of the monks' lectures about Marcus Aurelius's son and successor, Commodus, who was reputed to have been as cruel and dissolute as his father had been merciful and circumspect. Between the cruel man and the man responsible for erecting an earthen barrier between Gyan's people and Arthur's, it was no wonder Arthur had never mentioned his Ròmanach ancestry to her.

The thought vanished with the dawning realization that Ygraine had chosen to live amid myriad reminders of her dead husband. She shook her head in awe of the woman's strength of spirit.

They entered a guarded chamber—Ygraine's private workroom, to judge by the many tables stacked with parchment leaves, scrolls, and bound volumes. A scribe sat at a lamplit table, squinting over a page, the scratching of his quill making the room's only sound. Ygraine dismissed him with a word and a smile. He rose, bowed to both women, and closed the door behind him.

"How do you do it?" Gyan asked as she dropped into a chair.

"Do what, dear?" Ygraine retrieved a gold-embossed silver pitcher and a pair of matching goblets from a nearby table and poured two measures.

Gyan pointed at the goblet Ygraine gave her, the hanging oil lamps, the marble busts, the mosaic floor, and the backless, curved-legged chairs. "Everything you own must remind you of him. Your husband. How do you live with all those memories?"

Ygraine's smile adopted a sad cast. "It isn't always easy. They are a part of me, and I cannot escape them. Not even the bad memories, although, thankfully, those don't plague me as often as they once did." Her expression turned blunt. "What I cannot escape I have embraced." She twined a finger in the length of black cord supporting her gold dragon pendant. "Even celebrate."

"You and Uther had—what? A score of years together?" She suspected her words sounded more accusatory than she'd intended.

Caressing the undulating dragon, which flashed in the lamplight, her mother-by-law nodded. "Good years, too. For the most part."

Gyan whispered, "I didn't have two moons with my bairn." Cradling the goblet in her hands, she bowed her head and shut her eyes against the threat of tears. Her breasts ached abominably. She set the goblet aside and hugged herself tightly. In spite of the pressure, she could all but feel Loholt's tiny mouth working busily at her nipple, recalling her intense wonderment. Asleep, he'd looked so cherubic. A strangled gasp caught in her throat. She clenched her teeth.

Arms encircled her, and she leaned into the embrace. Memories assailed her of Cynda, the only mother she'd ever known, who headed the list of those she'd alienated by her grief.

The sobs would not be denied.

Ygraine said nothing, did nothing other than hold her close, stroking her bobbed hair until she'd cried herself out. Her tears soaked Ygraine's tunic. She straightened, scrubbed her face with impotent fingers while resolving to carry a cloth for these unexpected and altogether too frequent outbursts, and gave her mother-by-law a weak smile. "I am sorry about your tunic, Ygraine."

"Hush, it will dry." Ygraine casually brushed at the spot. "Feeling better, daughter?"

Daughter. A common title, but one Gyan had never heard from another woman, not even Cynda. It left her unprepared for the emotions coursing through her soul. With a single word, the woman whose name reminded her of the sun had woven into her void a thread of light.

She offered a thin smile. "Thank you ... Mother."

Ygraine's eyes brightened with sudden tears as she smiled and patted Gyan's knee. "I will pray the Lord will bless you and Arthur with more children."

Words fled. She couldn't tell her mother-by-law that Arthur was someone else whom she'd alienated, and that she had no idea how to repair that rift. Nor could she tell Ygraine that the One God had stopped listening to her pleas. Ygraine's daughter she might be, but the divine silence surely proved she no longer was God's.

With a parting hug and a murmur of thanks, she took leave of Ygraine and followed a servant down the corridor to the guest chamber. In the torchlight, she noticed a faint scar on the servant's neck, the legacy of years spent in a Caledonach slave-collar. It reminded her of someone else who had lost an infant son to death, not temporarily to politics.

And if he couldn't help her wrest answers from the One God, then no one could.

THE GROUNDS of St. Padraic's Monastery lay deserted, which seemed odd to her until she glanced at the sun and realized the brethren and students probably still crowded the refectory for their midday meal. She headed toward the Sanctuary of the Chalice.

The graves nestled between two wings of the cruciform church had settled since her last viewing of them, when they'd been freshly dug. Stone crosses had replaced the wooden ones and were carved with knots, Christian symbols, and names. Gyan visited each grave.

Some names she recognized, like her first tutor, Brother Lucan. With trembling fingertips, she traced the grooves of his Ròmanach name, Lucianus. It proved easy to remember Lucan in a more cheerful setting, not as a bloody, lifeless face.

With other names, she could summon only a single grisly image.

A few names stimulated no memories at all. To these fallen heroes, she gave an extra measure of thanks for their sacrifice.

Loholt had been sacrificed for her too: sacrificed to Urien's lust for revenge. Her heart clenched. Feeling the all-too-familiar sting of tears, she bolted around to the church's entrance, dragged open one of the doors, and slipped inside.

DAFYDD CHECKED himself to Brother Stefan's halting pace as they ambled from the refectory to the church. Stubborn pride would have forced Stefan to match Dafydd's pace, but Dafydd didn't wish to cause the crippled man further discomfort. Instead, he contented himself with the brisk, salty coolness of the afternoon breeze, listening to Stefan's reports about the students' progress.

At the base of the church's steps, Dafydd paused, frowning. Stefan cast him a puzzled glance. "Something wrong, Abbot Dafydd?"

"We have a visitor." Dafydd pointed at the right-hand door standing ajar. He recalled the letter and cage of pigeons he had received by way of a trader the day before, and guessed the visitor's identity and needs. "Brother Stefan, please resume your duties. I'll meet you in your workroom presently."

The master of students eyed him but made no comment. Dafydd waited until Stefan had begun hobbling toward the library before continuing up the steps and into the church.

He stopped inside the door and pulled it closed, searching the candle-lit chamber.

Silence dominated. No person interrupted the floor's expanse of gray slate. The Chalice sat undisturbed on its golden platform. The tapers' flames burned unwaveringly, and the incense-burners discharged straight wisps of spice-scented smoke as if the air hadn't stirred in a millennium. No shapes lurked behind the choir screen. Nor could he see anyone beside either of the sanctuary's main statues, those of Padraic and the Virgin. He widened his search.

If not for glimpsing a cloak's hem, he would have missed the hooded figure standing on the far side of a column near the altar. The person neither moved nor spoke.

Treading softly, he approached, praying with each step for wisdom, guidance, and comforting words.

With a head shake, the hood fell to reveal hair of Chieftainess Gyanhumara's hue but cropped unmercifully short. Had she taken holy vows? Her back was to him, and her plain-woven, dark blue cloak's hem dragged the floor, making it impossible to tell. Arthur had written of her devastation at their son's loss but said nothing of her entry into a religious order.

Perhaps the Pendragon didn't know.

A sick feeling churned in Dafydd's stomach.

She stood stone-still. What she gazed at or pondered, God alone knew. Experience had taught Dafydd that most people craved physical contact during periods of intense grief, even if only a handclasp. With the chieftainess, he opted for a more judicious course.

Clearing his throat, he began, "Chieftainess Gyanhumara?"

"Where is he, Dafydd?" She spoke in Caledonian and didn't look at him. Her tone sounded subdued yet plaintive.

He? Her son... or her God? A trickle of sweat made his slave-collar scar itch. He rubbed the spot beneath his robe's cowl, stepping closer to her.

His new position put him on a direct line toward the oaken statue of the crucified Christ. "Iesseu, my lady?" She gave a terse nod, and he prayed for guidance. "He dwells within those who believe."

She should remember this simple truth, but grief could be an insidious stealer of faith.

She grunted derisively. "That would explain why my prayers are not being heard."

Too late, taunted his inner demon.

"No!" Quieter, "No, my lady, you mustn't believe that. By your faith, God adopted you into His family. No one can nullify that, not even you. Chieftainess, God hears you no less than He hears me or Bishop Dubricius or any other believer."

She spun toward him.

He noted with relief that she wore her husband's badge, though a bronze dragon, not gold, with a jet eye rather than sapphire. He swallowed thickly. Dear Lord in heaven, Urien's legion brooch!

She is lost. Heart hammering, Dafydd tried to reject the lie.

Her face contorted into anguish, the gleam in her eyes bordering on madness.

Lost!

Earnestly, Dafydd prayed otherwise.

"Then why doesn't He answer me?" Her voice's quavering wrenched his heart. "Why didn't He give Angusel the strength to rescue Loholt? Or send an angel to do it? Or change the murderers' hearts?" Tears squeezed from her tightly shut eyes. He felt his own eyes moisten. "Dafydd, why didn't God save my son?"

Her words smote him like a challenge.

What makes me think I can help her?

He sent up an urgent petition for wisdom.

"He did save your son, my lady."

Liar. The child was unbaptized. Heathen. Lost.

Her raised eyebrows conveyed more skepticism than surprise. Dafydd forged on, "He saved Loholt from eternal destruction. The Lord God does not condemn innocent infants."

Liar! He did his best to ignore his demon-plagued doubts.

Folding her arms, the chieftainess looked down. "What a comforting thought." Her sarcasm made him wince. "I admire you, Dafydd. You lost a bairn and a grown daughter in less than a year. Yet here you are, serving the same God who took your children as though none of it happened." Shaking her head, she turned her back on the altar and the wooden Christ statue suspended above it. "I do not have that kind of faith."

Her tone didn't betray the depth of her sorrow, but the slope of her shoulders did. As she brushed past him, he caught her wrist. "My lady, please listen to me."

Yes, let's do feed her more lies.

She wrestled her arm free but stared at the church's doors like a caged beast yearning for release.

A pity I don't even possess the key to my own prison—

Behind his back, Dafydd clenched his fists. *In the Name of Christ, enough!*

Spreading his hands in a semblance of composure, he said, "Your feelings are not unusual. Please trust me; I have experienced similar struggles myself." He regarded her expectantly, but she made no comment. "God may seem distant to you, Chieftainess, perhaps even capricious and uncaring. Perhaps you feel you do not want to follow such a God. But that is not who He is. He is here, and He does care deeply for you, no matter what you have done—or will do. You are His precious child. He can do no less than love you with the fathomless breadth of His being." Dafydd sensed no demonic dissent and let out a soft sigh.

"I cannot feel His love." She shrugged. "I feel nothing."

Her simple declaration smote him with the pain he and Katra had endured for their children's deaths. They had challenged the existence of God's love, too—until they recalled its nature.

"God's love is not a feeling, my lady," he whispered. "It simply *is*. How we respond to it, and to God, is our choice."

Her continued silence made him unsure of how much she understood. "Faith works the same way. We may think we have lost faith, when all we have really lost is the volition to act in faith." Her upraised eyebrow invited him to continue. "Expressions of faith and love, my lady, whether to God or to other human beings, are never passive. They are conscious, deliberate acts of the will."

Hands on hips, she pursed her lips. "I did not will myself to fall in love with Arthur. It just . . . happened."

Why she'd turned the subject to her husband, Dafydd could only guess, but he sensed the need to tread carefully. "Strong passions can cloud judgment—"

"Ha. You're a monk now. Who are you to lecture me about passion?" She averted her gaze. "Forgive me, Dafydd. That was unworthy of me."

"That was your pain speaking." He clasped his hands. "It is my most earnest prayer, Chieftainess, that you will choose to act in faith. And in love."

She drew a deep breath, blew it out slowly, and drew another. "I will ponder what you have said." A determined light sprang to life within the windows of her soul. "I promise."

He watched her walk toward the doors. Had he said enough? Done enough? He glanced at the Chalice. The ancient alabaster vessel seemed to glow divinely.

"Chieftainess, please wait."

She obliged but didn't turn. A year ago, the Chalice had helped her through another grieving process. The urge to offer her the sacraments in this holiest of relics had been so strong that day, despite the prohibitions, that he had not dared to disobey.

Today, he felt no such urging. The Chalice was an object of veneration made sacred by He who had used it, he firmly reminded himself, not some mystical fount of healing and plenty, as in the pilgrims' fanciful tales.

His silence must have confused her, for she faced him, a question painted in the furrows of her brow.

"God be with you, my lady." Solemnly, he made the sign of the cross—yet another Christ-sanctified relic people seemed determined to worship for itself—in the air. She accepted his benediction with a brief nod and strode from the church.

He closed his eyes and tilted face and palms upward, praying fervently that Gyanhumara would allow God's love to restore her grief-ravaged soul.

A whir of wings in the rafters reminded him of another service he could perform for her, secular but no less vital. He concluded his prayer, left the sanctuary, and headed for the pigeon coop, working out the details of his message as he walked.

Chapter 27

THE BREEZES OF advancing autumn chilled the clear, moonless night. Prince Ælferd drew the edges of his cloak tighter about him as he stood at the prow of his flagship. A quick glance at his men revealed they were doing much the same. They exchanged brief nods and smiles. With a thumb thrust through his belt, Ælferd absently fingered the garnet-and-gold buckle his uncle had given him, inhaling deeply of the salty air.

On the heels of the thralls' doomed rebellion, the staging at Anderceaster of a third of the West Saxons' total muscle in ships and men had been fraught with more problems: illness, poor crops, fire, bad weather, ore shortages . . . the litany made Ælferd's head reel. He felt supremely thankful for his uncle's patience throughout this misbegotten affair.

Ælferd clamped off that dangerous thought. His men didn't deserve divine punishment for their prince's breach of faith.

With a grin, he stroked his golden mustaches as he envisioned his reward for the capture of Maun: marriage to Camilla. Her smile's memory warmed him better than a dozen cloaks; her kiss, like a hundred. Gods willing, he'd be basking in her embrace before the next full moon.

Maun's cliffs jutted into view. Ælferd signaled the dousing of his ship's running lights. The darkness deepened as the command transferred in turn to the remaining ships. Ælferd licked his lips. With surprise and fear as his allies, the Brædeas would be stinking in their graves before they knew what had killed them.

No Saxon saw the tiny fishing boat hugging the Manx coastline, hurrying home to port after a long day at sea. Its Brytoni captain watched the lights wink out aboard the approaching fleet. While Denu had no inkling of who they were or even how many, he knew trouble when he smelled it, and this stank as bad as a week-old catch. His bones ached for his bed, but sleep could bloody well wait until after he'd had a word with the siren-lovely but fathomlessly sad commander of Port Dhoo-Glass.

Gyan downed the dregs of her wine, grimaced, stood, and stretched. Little had changed since last she'd commanded the Manx Cohort. Reviewing and acting upon supply lists, requisitions, injury and discipline reports, and unit duty rosters still ranked a step lower than watching a tree grow.

Wiping her lips, she sighed. At least this duty improved upon living at Arbroch, watching Mardha's belly grow, or watching other women's children grow. Or being at Arthur's side, watching the gulf between them grow. She closed her eyes, again asking the One God when her heartache would abate.

Again, she received no answer.

As she bent to stow the tablets and parchment for the night, the door opened wide enough for Rhys to thrust his head into the workroom.

"Commander Gyan, I've a Breatanach fisherman named Denu in the antechamber. Wants to speak with you."

Glancing at the spluttering, stubby candles that shed more smoke than light, she creased her brow. "At this hour? Why?"

Rhys shrugged. "Wouldn't tell me, my lady. Insists on talking only to you. Claims it's urgent."

"Very well, Rhys." She dropped back into the chair, stifling a cough and fanning the smoke away. "I'll see him."

The fisherman shuffled in, holding a battered, salt-stained woolen cap in gnarled hands. He bobbed his balding head toward her.

"Your pardon, me lady, I don't mean to be a bother to ye. Got a bit of news, I do."

The odor of his trade conquered the candles' smoke. She leaned back in her chair, arms folded. No escape.

"Yes?"

"'Tis like this, me lady. I was heading to port, not an hour past, and I see these boats coming up from the southeast. Night trawlers, thinks I. Then all their lights go out."

"Night fishers don't do that, Denu?" Curiosity's arousal conquered her aversion to the smell, and she shifted forward.

"Nay, me lady. 'Tis aye dangerous in these waters, running without lights. Any sort of wind blows up, and ye can find y'self dancing with the devil on the rocks." Clucking his tongue, he slowly shook his head. "These were not fishermen."

An invasion fleet, then, she mused. Their approaching Maun from the southeast could only mean . . . "Sasunaich!" In response to Denu's confused look, she added, "Saxons."

His expectant appraisal of her was broken by a long blink.

So. Arthur's concerns hadn't been unfounded, just a year too early. Her warrior's blood began to tingle for the first time in far too long. She welcomed the feeling, allowing it to sweep through her body and purge her soul, exulting in the power it ignited within her.

She asked her fragrant visitor, "How many ships?"

Denu dropped his gaze to his hands, fingers and lips working silently. "Four hands. Maybe more." His shoulders, broad from ten thousand days of casting and hauling nets, scrunched into a lopsided shrug. "No moon. Tough to see."

Sasunach warships, she recalled from the intelligence reports, easily could hold sixty men. If Denu had counted aright, twenty ships meant twelve hundred warriors . . .

Her elation vanished. She tilted her head to meet the cold stone wall, a lump growing in the pit of her stomach. There weren't that many Caledonach and Breatanach troops on the entire island, and only three hundred seventy-five at Port Dhoo-Glass, most of them Breatanaich.

No moon. Tough to see.

How could she possibly defeat such a force when even the elements of nature conspired against her?

"Me lady?"

She'd been born for this moment and just might die for it. The idea, in fact, had merit.

Briskly, she said, "Thank you, good Denu. You shall be rewarded." She rose, preceded him to the door, and pulled it open. Rhys, seated at the table in the antechamber, rifling through a stack of reports, swiveled his head toward her. "Rhys, see that Denu gets—" She glanced over her shoulder at the fisherman. "What would you like?"

"A new net and sinkers." He displayed a hopeful, black-toothed grin. "If it please yer ladyship."

"See to it, Rhys. Who is on for courier duty?" The Manx Cohort had no need for a scout corps... until tonight.

Rhys studied the roster and regarded her levelly. "Aonar."

A noise rumbled in Gyan's chest, half growl and half groan. Her anger still smoldered at Arthur for foisting Angusel's presence upon her. Putting him on the courier roster had been the only way to follow the letter of Arthur's command and keep Angusel from her sight, leaving Rhys to give him his orders.

Tonight, however, Rhys would have more than enough to do. "Send him to me. Then have the centurions rouse their men quietly. Do not sound the general alarm. Order the lookouts to be extra sharp. If so much as a leaf trembles when it shouldn't, I want to know at once."

"Aye, Commander Gyan." The approval gleaming in Rhys's eyes salved her grief-weary spirit. They exchanged a nod. He saluted her and turned to leave.

Denu followed Rhys into the corridor, and the door swung to, making Gyan thankful he took most of the fishy smell with him.

She crossed to the window and stared into the night, hoping for some sign of the trouble marching her way. Like a cur with a bone, the inky vista held fast to its secrets.

No moon... she recalled a lesson Arthur had taught her, while repressing memories of more pleasurable activities they'd shared, resulting in the birth of—no. No. *No!*

Bracing against the window ledge with one palm, she pressed the other to her clammy forehead.

If that Hebrew general had defeated tens of thousands with a mere three hundred men, she might prevail against twelve hundred Sasunaich with the One God's help—if He would deign to grant it.

It seemed futile to ask.

Respond in faith, and in love.

She jerked her head, wondering where that thought had originated. Then she remembered. *Dear Dafydd, you care more about my well-being than I care about myself.*

Respond in faith.

For his sake, she had to try. She knelt.

And in love.

Love? For her clansmen, certainly, but for these Breatanach soldiers, who didn't spit at her only because they feared the Pendragon's wrath? Who didn't desert only because the sea penned them? Who would rather see her stiffening on a battlefield than follow her onto one? Did she wish the same fate for them?

Brutal memories surged forth: the mud and blood, the offal and vomit, the screams of dying men and horses, the flesh-greedy ravens, the stench of smoke and excrement, fear and death.

Tears streaming, she bowed her head and committed her men into the One God's hands.

At the sound of footsteps, she scrambled to her feet, sniffing and drying her cheeks. She knew that tread, although it sounded heavier. A knock rattled the door. Anger erupted.

Respond in love.

Violently shaking her head, she wiped her sweating palms on her leather-clad thighs and tightened her jaw. She would tolerate his presence if she must and trust him as far as she dared, but as for divine protection, Angusel was on his own. Alone. Aonar.

"Enter."

He marched in, eyes forward, body and head limned by the corridor's torchlight, uniform flawless. He had gained in stature as well as girth. An unadorned iron dragon shone dully from his shield-side shoulder, indicating the noncommand junior-officer rank of optio, held by all the legion's couriers. He halted and thumped his chest in the legion salute, which she acknowledged with a perfunctory nod.

"Optio, ride to South Cove to confirm the report of a Sasunach invasion force at least twelve hundred strong." His eyes widened slightly. She narrowed hers. "I trust you can manage with no light?"

An offended look briefly darkened his features. He drew a breath, held it, let it out slowly, and drew another. "Aye, Commander," he replied quietly.

"Good. The security of Maun rides upon your mission. Leave at once, and see that you do not fail." As he saluted and turned to go, she couldn't resist adding, "Again."

He flinched, but his stride didn't falter. In moments, he was gone. Regret pierced her heart.

Quelling it, she summoned the roster's next horseman, a Breatan, but easier to deal with than Angusel. She handed him a parchment leaf detailing orders for Per to march his detachment to Dhoo-Glass, which would add two hundred fifty. Far better to mobilize Tanroc based on an unconfirmed report than to wait on Angusel and risk sealing the island's doom.

As the courier started to leave, she considered giving him an additional order. But St. Padraic's monks had already suffered enough from the last war into which she'd dragged them. She couldn't do that to them again, no matter how much she craved their abbot's counsel.

She alerted another messenger to prepare for the ride to the Mount Snaefell signal beacon to send word to Arthur upon confirmation of the Shasunaich presence. Her consort had left the staging area to inspect recovering troops at headquarters, which she viewed as a mixed blessing. Her message would be delivered sooner, but the last thing she needed was Arthur's rebuke for assembling the legion needlessly should this fleet prove to be the phantom of an overtired imagination.

ANGUSEL LET Stonn pick his way through the hills south of Dhoo-Glass but balked at the pace, itching to put as much distance between himself and Gyan as possible.

She expected him to fail. *Again.* His face burned; sweat trickled down his neck.

He dashed moisture from his eyes, upbraiding himself for succumbing to her doubts. Succeed he must! Or die in the attempt.

Death seemed far better than suffering her scorn.

The brush rustled. Twigs snapped. Stonn's head jerked. Murmuring soothing words and stroking his stallion's neck, Angusel fixed his gaze to the path. A small creature ran squealing into the night. With the reins wrapped around one hand, Angusel dropped the other to his sword hilt.

He dared not push Stonn any faster and risk injury to either of them. Injury bred failure.

Near the top of the southernmost rise but far enough down the hill to hide their silhouettes, he halted Stonn, dismounted, and threw the reins over a limb. He squirmed on his belly over rocks, roots, grass, and sand to an outcropping.

The lowlands spread out before him like a great sable blanket, sprinkled with dozens of points of light that didn't belong. He puffed out his cheeks, releasing a breath. *Gods!*

His heart thudding, he squinted at the advancing army, yet several miles to the south. They appeared to be marching with just enough light to keep out of rodent burrows, snake dens, and cow dung, maybe one torch for ten men. He estimated the size of the force at close to fifteen hundred.

He chewed his lip, salty from sweat and sea spray. Four-to-one odds . . . five-to-two, if Tanroc's troops arrived in time. Ignoring the "if," it didn't sound too bad. The invaders might have the numbers, but the Manx Cohort knew the land, with or without light.

What a battle this would be!

Movement at the bottom of the ridge caught his eye. Instinct brayed a silent alarm. An enemy scout? He strained his senses, but the pounding breakers drowned all other sounds.

A sharp crack and a yelp of pain pierced the waves' thunder. Two voices exchanged a few guttural Sasunaiche words directly below him. Angusel grinned. Surprising them would be pathetically easy.

He freed his sword and crouched.

The memory of his time-devouring encounter with the one-eyed Dailriatanach traitor flooded back. Gyan needed time more desperately than numbers. He sheathed his sword and crept back to Stonn, thankful for the surf crashing against the cliffs to mask his departure. Surely, she would be pleased! He urged his stallion toward Dhoo-Glass.

OF THE duties around the fort assigned to those of his rank—one step above raw recruit, his choice and damned proud of it—Gawain map Loth rated nightwatch lower than stable mucking. Officers often congregated at the stables with news to share. Even if half of it proved false, it made for a far more exciting shift than tromping back and forth along the palisade beneath the mute stars.

Gazing northeastward, his thoughts turned toward Dunpeldyr. Worry gnawed at him for his mother, brothers, and baby sister. Even for his father.

At leave-taking this past summer, Loth didn't even grant him a farewell, which wounded far deeper than Gawain had expected. He couldn't help the fact that becoming Chieftain of Clan Lothian ranked lower in his mind than nightwatch duty.

His elbow tingled where it contacted the cold stone. Realizing he'd been standing too long in one place, he shouldered his spear and continued his rounds.

Gawain couldn't help the fact that his father chose to punish him for failing to live up to archaic notions of filial duty.

He had enjoyed the time spent with his younger siblings between the cattle raids, thankful that Loth's attitude toward him hadn't tainted theirs, and his mother had gone out of her way to smother him with love and kindness, as if her efforts could compensate for Loth's lack. For their sakes, Gawain regretted his decision to return to Maun with Aunt Gyan. If the Angli believed that Arthur and Loth could attack at any time, God alone knew what those foreign bastards might do as a preemptive measure . . . and Gawain wouldn't learn about it here until it was too late to attend the funerals.

But his aunt's anguish still wrenched his heart, causing fresh hatred for Angusel to gust through his soul.

He wondered where that vehemence came from. He loved Aunt Gyan—Commander Gyan—as kin, but there had to be something more. Like, maybe, by watching her devastation, it was like watching his own emotions regarding his father's choices being paraded for everyone.

But his father wasn't dead. He couldn't stop the thought before adding the damnable, inevitable *yet*.

Feeling a chill not entirely due to the night's breeze, he stepped into the guard tower to warm up and found Claudius adjusting his helmet. They exchanged grunts of greeting. The striped candle showed one ring, marking the last hour in their duty shift. Claudius retrieved his spear and left the tower.

As Gawain rubbed his hands over the brazier, he glanced through an eastern bow-slit. A distant flash caught his eye. He blinked hard and looked again. The apparition didn't vanish. He snatched his spear and stuck his head through the door.

"Claudius!" He restrained his voice to a loud whisper. "Someone's coming!"

Claudius whirled and ran back to the guard tower. "Where?"

Gawain pulled him onto the east wall and scanned the rolling hills. The bobbing light flickered through a clearing. He pointed.

The shadows resolved into a rapidly traveling horse and rider. Now, Gawain could hear the approaching hoofbeats and crackling twigs.

Claudius studied the horseman for several seconds. "I can't tell who it is. Better report this to Conall."

"Of course!" Gawain slapped the wall for not thinking of it himself.

Arms pumping, he pelted to the main gate tower. At his shout, Guard Captain Conall sat bolt upright on the cot, fully dressed save cloak and boots.

Gawain thumped fist to chest in salute, drawing a breath to steady his voice. "Sir, a horseman approaches from the east."

"A loner? How far?"

"At his pace, sir, he'll be at the hedge at any—"

"Hail, Tanroc!" called the Brytoni voice.

Conall strode to the window slit and shouted, "Suilean?" The signs and countersigns were Caledonian. This one meant "eyes."

"Suil a mhàin," the courier answered, confirming that he carried an "only one eye" dispatch—and that one eye belonged to the man in charge. Gawain's pulse quickened.

"Get Commander Peredur out here!" Conall ordered.

The troops were roused and ready before another candle-ring had vanished. Gawain, on the grounds that Commander Gyan was kin, talked his way out of guard duty to join them. His elation convinced him he could handle the entire enemy force by himself.

To say nothing of the chance to be on hand in case that whore-spawned Angusel failed her again.

Angusel kneed Stonn into a trot, hoping to stay ahead of the Sasunach scouts. He held his stallion to the valley's tree line to maximize speed yet minimize detection.

It didn't work.

At the foot of the ridge, he heard the unmistakable scrape of a sword being drawn. "Caraid!" he rasped, halting Stonn. *Friend.* The watchword applied to him, but only just. He subtly freed his sword hand from the reins in case he'd guessed wrong.

"Ainm," stated the soldier as he appeared from the brush, flanked by several companions. None carried torches, but Angusel needed no light to show him their readied weapons.

They wanted his name; standard protocol, conducting the exchange in Caledonaiche, since Gyan had deemed it unlikely their foes would know the language well enough to decrypt her signs and countersigns. He sucked in a breath, quelling the stab of remorse, and whispered the appropriate response: "Optio Aonar, Third Turma, Manx Cohort."

The lead soldier sheathed his sword, saluted, and motioned Angusel forward. As he complied, he noticed many men lugged bulging water skins. Stranger still, they began dousing the brush.

He knew better than to waste time asking but warned them about the enemy scouts. The men exchanged a glance, thanked him with their nods, and signaled the entire unit to slip back into cover.

That seemed like a fine idea. He pointed Stonn toward the trees, and they crossed the remaining ridge and valley to Port Dhoo-Glass.

The fortress, guarding the harbor from atop the promontory, looked dark and quiet. Too dark and quiet. His puzzlement mounted as he guided Stonn toward a portal near the closest harbor-defense tower. After identifying himself and gaining admittance, he posed his question. The porter relayed a message Rhys had left, directing him to report to the north infantry drilling fields. Angusel couldn't prevent the chorus of yaps as he spurred Stonn through the town toward the far wall, but he prayed the dogs' noise wouldn't destroy whatever surprise Gyan had devised for their unwelcome Sasunach guests.

He exited the opposite portal to find the infantry standing four abreast, paralleling the wall. Behind the signifer, who gripped the languidly fluttering cohort banner, the cavalry turmae headed the column, followed by units of archers and armed torchbearers.

Gyan, Rhys, and the other officers reined their mounts a few paces from the column to gaze pensively upward. As Angusel neared, a series of muffled hoots drifted over the wall. Gyan eyed him stonily.

"Optio, report," she demanded.

Rebuking himself for expecting a miracle, he delivered his estimate about the size and speed of the enemy force, as well as his sighting of the Sasunach scouts. The words marched out briskly to shield his hurt. She gave no reaction save a curt nod, which wasn't directed at him but at another courier mounted beside her. As that man galloped away and Gyan again cocked her head, more owl screeches split the night.

He couldn't hope to win her respect if he couldn't even claim her attention. "Commander, I—"

"Silence, soldier!" she snapped. "If Stonn is rested enough to fight, rejoin your turma. If not, stay to help guard the fort."

Some choice. He'd sooner die than relive the uselessness he'd felt atop Senaudon's walls while his clansmen's blood reddened the firth at Abar-Gleann. Stonn shook his head, snorting and wrestling with the bit as if in agreement. He calmed him with a pat, straightened in the saddle, and captured Gyan's gaze. "We fight, Commander."

She dismissed him to his assigned place, far too many paces behind the one he yearned to reclaim.

At a third set of hoots, she cantered Macsen to the column's head, the officers trailing behind her. Flanked by torchbearers, she wheeled her stallion to face the troops, her lips split in a grin made feral by the wild light. "The scouts are gone. We shall learn soon enough whether we have duped them. To arms, for Maun and honor!"

Her upraised fist set the column in motion.

Though midway through nightwatch, Ælferd felt no fatigue as he marched among his bodyguards near the head of the army, buoyed by excitement over his imminent victory. The scouts' report described a minimal force guarding the port's walls. Clearly, the Brædeas expected no danger.

So much the worse for them!

He wished Camilla could help him eradicate this nest of Brædan vermin, but her father had refused to let her join Ælferd's Manx expedition. Ælferd couldn't fault him. The King of the South Saxons didn't want his daughter to be so far from home with the man who loved her more than life itself.

He led his men to the first of three ridges separating them from their goal and signaled a slower pace. Only a fool would attack with warriors half-dead from the march.

The army topped the second ridge and poured into the valley. Ælferd had ordered silence, but he sensed the eagerness of his men, who surged like questing hounds against the leash. One more ridge separated them from their quarry.

As the first rank began to climb, an owl's haunting cry pierced the night. After several heartbeats, a second, fainter owl answered.

Arrows whined, drawing fiery arcs across the sky. The first flight fell into brush near the column's right flank. The twigs exploded into fireballs.

Oil-soaked brush!

As light flooded the valley, more deadly swarms followed. Too many good warriors fell under the steel-barbed onslaught.

Ælferd's standard-bearer took an arrow in the throat. His cry drowned in a bloody gurgle. Another soldier rushed forward to catch the Green Griffin, but a corner of the cloth dragged through a torch. As flames devoured it, Ælferd's men began to panic. Fear gripped his gut and loosened his bowels. Grimly, he ignored it and shouted more orders to the men. With his exhortations ringing in their ears, they regrouped and renewed the attack.

As ARROWS rained fire upon the valley floor, Angusel steadied Stonn, his blood beating its anxious tattoo in his ears.

Gyan had rejected him again.

He leaned over to stroke Stonn's neck, drawing comfort from its sleek warmth. The stallion answered with a toss of his head and a soft snort. Angusel sighed, wishing he hadn't been relegated to the turma fighting the farthest from Gyan's side.

Stonn's ears swiveled forward, and he impatiently chewed the bit. Angusel saw the turma's commander's signal and readied his first javelin. Tightening his grip with knees and hands, he cast a swift glance toward Gyan.

Looking like the warrior-goddess Nemetona in the flesh, the torchlit Braonshaffir a fiery beacon aloft in her fist, she sat proudly astride Macmuir, shouting encouragement.

Her words seemed to embrace everyone but him.

He couldn't hate her. Not while he despised himself.

As the turma decurion's arm dropped and Stonn surged forward, Angusel begged Nemetona for extra measures of courage, strength, and skill so he could do something—anything—to earn Gyan's favor.

Plummeting down the hillside, he banished his anxiety. Yelling helped. So did watching the Sasunach faces in the whipping torchlight twist into expressions of surprise and terror. The heat of answered prayer flooded his veins and braced his heart.

GAWAIN MARCHED as he'd been drilled again and yet again, with his gaze riveted to the helmet of the soldier in front of him. The bouncing torchlight challenged that directive but didn't prevent him from straining to catch the first sounds of the battle that surely must be taking place at Port Dhoo-Glass.

What he heard were the hoofbeats, snorts, and whinnies of the fifty horses at the head of the column, the crunching of two hundred pairs of booted feet upon dry grass and twigs, the creak of leather, the clink of metal, the rustling of branches, the sigh of the sea. Everything except what he sought.

What on earth had he been thinking when he'd asked Arthur for this assignment? He should have requested a turma posting. The view from horseback always furnished a definite improvement.

What if there was no battle? As disappointing as that would be, a night's reprieve from guard duty was worth the cost in blistered feet of the twenty-mile hike to Dhoo-Glass and back.

Perhaps Gyan's forces hadn't yet engaged the enemy. Ha! Against the entire Manx Cohort, they wouldn't have a prayer. Why, she could defeat them all by herself, according to the tales.

What if . . . what if they were too late?

Gawain spat out the fear on a rising tide of bile and continued stumping through the endless night.

Before Ælferd could press his advantage, javelin-casting horsemen came screaming down from the pine-shrouded ridge crest, followed by waves of foot soldiers.

He had no time to wonder how the Brædeas had been alerted. Shouting over the tumult, he commanded his men to fall back onto the valley floor, where the improved footing allowed the enemy horsemen to be more easily cut down. About the archers he could nothing except hope they ran out of arrows before he ran out of men.

He eyed a warrior astride a white stallion, the leader of the charge and his only chance to salvage success from this disaster. He readied his seax for the killing blow.

Chapter 28

Stonn's momentum carried Angusel deep into enemy ranks. The cavalry had been ordered to break off and circle to the Shasunaich left flank upon reaching the valley, to let the foot troops engage the front ranks. Angusel was in danger of being overwhelmed.

If the Sasunaich didn't kill him for failing to follow orders, Gyan would.

He wheeled Stonn around to fight his way out. Men rushed at him, screaming obscenities and brandishing war-knives, swords, spears, and torches. He cared naught. His sword reaped a bloody harvest, fires marking his trail as dropped torches ignited leaves and clothing. Sasunaich ran from him, and he quested for other targets. To his battle-frenzied delight, he discovered a plentiful supply.

During a lull, he searched for Gyan and the rest of the cavalry. Several dozen paces away, she bestrode Macmuir, towering over the writhing Sasunach sea, felling a foe with each stroke. Angusel's gut clenched. The charge had carried her too far too!

Heedless of how she might react, he urged Stonn toward her.

JUST WHEN Gawain thought the anticipation would drive him mad, a dull ringing arose, faint but clear. His body reflexively obeyed the command to double the pace, and the noise intensified into a din of heroic proportions.

He labored with the rest of his rank to the top of the ridge and its unobstructed view. His stomach lurched.

Scores of bodies littered the ground. Yet the enemy kept pressing forward, trampling the fallen to batter the Brytoni line, which was buckling in too many places. He spotted Gyan near the center of the conflict. Bitter dismay threatened to choke him as he watched Saxons close in. Orders be damned, he had to reach her side!

Logic ceased as he rushed into the fray.

AS THE Brædan leader plunged toward Ælferd, he realized he faced a woman screeching some weird battle cry as she hacked down Saxon after Saxon. Camilla's face flashed to mind, but he pushed the beloved vision aside. The woman bearing down upon him, face contorted with fury, bore no resemblance to the princess. And this warrior had already killed or maimed a score of his men.

Ælferd dodged from her path and leaped to thrust behind her shield as she flashed by. With a dull clank, his seax deflected off a wide metal belt, but the blow's force knocked her from the saddle. Her stallion bolted. Swinging his seax in a deadly arc as she tried to roll to her feet, Ælferd closed in for the kill.

ANGUSEL SAW Gyan disappear into a knot of Sasunaich and spurred his stallion with redoubled urgency. She could rebuke his disobedience later, and he'd gladly bear any punishment, if she survived.

If. The word powered his sword arm with fatal precision, fatigue and pain imprisoned in a remote corner of his mind.

Crossing the distance seemed to take a gods-cursed eternity.

He found her grappling with a richly armored Sasun, who had her pinned. Her helmet was gone. Gritting her teeth, she struggled to hold her attacker's war-knife from her throat. Her neck oozed blood where the Sasun had grazed it.

Angusel shed his shock and fear, kicked Stonn closer, scrambled to a crouch in the saddle, and jumped.

GAWAIN LOST his spear in the charge, buried in a Saxon belly. His enemy, shrieking, gripped the shaft, and it snapped when Gawain tried to yank it free. Another Saxon lost an eye to the broken spear's iron-capped butt. Gawain flung the shaft aside and drew his sword. Catching the torchlight, the blade seemed to writhe with an inner fire. For an instant, he stared agape at its uncanny beauty.

The blond onslaught began anew. Three screaming Saxons tried to overwhelm him by a concerted attack.

He hewed through them in time to see a Dhoo-Glass horseman leap from his mount to knock a Saxon off a companion.

Gyan! And that ill-begotten Angusel, both just moments from slaughter.

Not if he, Gawain map Loth, had any say!

The former heir of Clan Lothian called members of his unit to his side and grimly applied himself to his work.

ANGUSEL HIT the Sasun with bone-rattling force, and they rolled away from Gyan. Before the stunned warrior could recover, he tore off the man's helmet, grabbed two fistfuls of flaxen hair, and slammed his head repeatedly into the ground. The Sasun went limp.

As he reached for his sword, fingers dug into his shoulder and dragged him back. Angrily, he whipped his head around to find emerald eyes that blazed like a monster from his worst Otherworldly nightmares. Sweat cut through the blood and grime on her fury-contorted face. Her blood-streaked sword was leveled at Angusel.

Choking back despair, he deferred, head bowed, to the Hag of Death incarnate.

As time seemed to freeze, Gyan glared at Angusel. Rather, at the scar on his neck she couldn't see but knew all too well, the scar that signified his defunct Oath of Fealty. The scar that mocked her, reminding her of the son she never would see again because of the ineptitude of the scar's bearer. The scar she ached to obliterate.

Love or hatred: choose.

At her feet, the Sasunach commander moaned. Angusel stood beside him, bleeding from a dozen minor wounds, chest heaving, sword lowered, head bowed. The battle eddied around them as a knot of Manx Cohort warriors prevented Sasunaich from rescuing their fallen leader. Gawain led them, she realized dimly, which meant that Per's troops had arrived, freeing her to concentrate on her immediate threat.

She gazed at Angusel's scar.

Me or the Adversary. Choose.

Her neck burned as if branded with a fealty-mark. She removed her glove to touch the spot, not surprised to find it hot and sticky. A hair's breadth deeper and the wound might have been her last. Should have been her last! Rage welled at the thought that Angusel had thwarted her escape into eternity.

She smeared her blood between her fingers, replaced the glove, and gripped her sword in both fists.

Mine is vengeance, daughter. Mankind's is revenge. Choose!

This Sasun had invaded Maun without provocation, giving Gyan a wound that would bind her to Angusel and torture her to the grave with the very thing she'd hoped to avoid. Angusel's intervention violated honor. He'd had no right to affect the duel's outcome.

Angusel hadn't saved Loholt's life... but he had saved hers. Again.

A swift glance at the mangled corpses convinced her she wasn't ready to accept that fate.

But Loholt's loss and Angusel's role in it shrouded her heart. Grief demanded retribution. Honor demanded reward. Death for death; life for life. The misery emanating from Angusel's stance suggested a more prolonged retribution: life for death.

My Way is death for life; choose.

"Leave me alone! Your Way is impossible to understand!" she

shouted in Caledonaiche at the murky heavens. "Where were You when Loholt needed You? When I needed You?" She pummeled her thigh, heedless of the pain. "Why didn't You answer me?"

Were you listening?

A flush heated her face. Sweat chilled her spine. Her fist stilled. She licked her lips.

Were you?

Ignoring Angusel's confused stare, she whispered, "I am now."

Then choose.

She raised her sword, clenched her teeth, and chose.

THE SASUNACH commander's head rolled across the blood-slick ground.

Up jerked Angusel's head. He half feared he'd be next and half wished he would be. Oblivion never had seemed more appealing.

He met Gyan's gaze, praying for a sign of forgiveness. She bent to grab the Shasunach head and shouldered past him.

Her newest trophy tied by the hair to her sword belt, spattering blood as it bounced against her thigh, she lunged into the fray without a backward glance, a soul-freezing battle cry on her lips and steel death in her fist.

Through tear-blurred eyes, he watched her disappear, guarded closely by Gawain and other Tanroc soldiers, wishing she'd taken his own head. It would have hurt far less.

Grief collided with anger in his soul, igniting his battle frenzy with lightning-bolt force and searing away the tears. Screaming and brandishing his sword, he charged the Sasunach line.

He had nothing left to lose.

"BEDWYR!"

The son of Bann swatted at the offending hand. Like a hungry horsefly, it refused to go away.

"Bedwyr, wake up," buzzed the persistent voice. "I need the fleet. Now!" A shove rocked his shoulder.

Groaning, he rolled onto his back. His sleep-crusted eyes gradually focused upon the apparition looming over him. Arthur? At Caerglas? With no advance word? Surely not. He must be dreaming.

No, he wasn't. Nor was this Caerglas, he recalled. His patrol had docked at Caer Lugubalion the day before to enjoy a brief shore leave.

All too brief, apparently.

He glanced at the window. "Gods, Arthur, it's nowhere near daybreak." He pulled the woolen blanket to his ears and turned away from the annoyance he usually was happy to call friend. "Can't a man get any sleep?"

"Not with an invasion in progress."

"Invasion?" He sat up. Hair cascaded into his face. From the bedside table, he snatched a leather thong. "Here?"

"Maun." Bedwyr didn't miss the concern hiding beneath the hard edge of Arthur's voice.

"Again?" As his sleep-numbed hands fumbled behind his head, surprise stopped him midknot. "Cuchullain can't possibly be strong enough yet."

"Not Cuchullain. Saxons."

"Saxons? On Maun?" The knot secure at last, he flexed his fingers and stared at Arthur. "Are you certain?"

The oil lamp wavered as Arthur set it upon the table. Light glinted off the bronze rivets of his battle-kilt and baldric.

"At least fifteen hundred in twenty-five ships, according to the signal-beacon report. That's all I know." Arthur dug his knuckles into his palm.

"A journey like that would be . . ." Bedwyr squinted, wrestling with the calculation. "Six hundred miles. A lot more if they follow the coastline to avoid my patrols. That's a fortnight of sailing at the very least. Weeks to plan the affair, months more to gather men and weapons and provisions and—"

"I know."

"Why go to such trouble for that tiny spit of land?"

"It seems, my friend, that the Saxons have discovered its strategic value, like Cuchullain before them." Arthur's gaze intensified. "They must be trying a night attack on Dhoo-Glass."

Swinging his legs over the side of the bed, Bedwyr swore.

"Dress quickly." Arthur started for the door. "There's much to be done yet before we sail."

"I can handle the fleet, Arthur, and the men." He reached for his undertunic. "You don't need to suspend the Angli campaign."

"Yes. I do." Stark lines of worry creased his friend's brow.

"Oh, no," Bedwyr whispered. "Gyan..."

"Exactly." Arthur resumed his course. "Meet me at the docks."

"Lucky thing my patrol was in port tonight." The undertunic slid over his chest, a welcome shield against the chill. "And that you were here inspecting the troops." He stood and paced to his armor chest.

Arthur paused with a hand on the door handle. "You know I don't believe in luck." The worry yielded to grim determination. "Or coincidence."

"Come on, Arthur. You have to believe in luck." Arthur shot him a look that, for all its impatience, invited him to explain. Bedwyr grinned. "How else can you explain the success of your enemies?"

The Pendragon snorted and left.

BELLOWED ORDERS and pounding feet splintered Cynda's dreams. She sat up, gasping, and peered about the darkened chamber. Seumas, who had escorted her from Arbroch in response to Dafydd's urgent message, had also awakened and was struggling with the thongs of his battle-tunic. She rose and hurried over to help him.

Bitterly, she had protested Ogryvan's decision to send her to Maun. Gyan's accusatory words had branded her heart with guilt and shame. Cynda feared her reception would be nothing like the one she'd received from Lord Artyr the day before.

Seumas girded on his sword, lit a lamp, and inched forward as stealthily as leather and metal would allow. Voices sounded in the corridor, and he cocked his ear toward the door.

Cynda shrugged into her overdress, laced on her shoes, and joined him, gripping his arm. "Is this place under attack?" She hoped the whisper hid the tremor in her voice.

Ogryvan's best warrior lifted a shoulder noncommittally. "I cannot make out what is being said." The voices moved on. Seumas straightened and gazed at the ceiling, creaking under the passage of many feet. "They're aye preparing for something."

She fetched her cloak, flung it about her shoulders, and strode back to the door. Seumas, arms folded and countenance stern, barred her way. "What are you doing, Seumas? Please step aside."

"Carrying out my orders," he replied gruffly. "If we're under attack, you should not be in the midst of it."

Hands on hips, Cynda rolled her eyes. "But we might not be. I must know. Lord Artyr promised to secure my passage to Maun. I—" She heaved a breath, suppressing her doubts and fears. "I would rather be at Gyan's side." *If she'll have me.* "Not stranded here, waiting for her consort's return while he runs off on some mission."

"Nay."

"Seumas," she said, fighting to keep the exasperation to a reasonable level. "I birthed you and taught your mother how to change your swaddling. I also taught her to swat your arse when you misbehaved. If you don't want me to demonstrate that lesson—"

A sharp pounding cut her off. Seumas drew his sword, lifted the bolt, and eased the door open a crack. Cynda stood on tiptoe but couldn't see past the warrior's bulk. He sheathed his sword and opened the door wider, stepping aside.

Lord Artyr stood in the corridor, arrayed in Ròmanach battle-gear, his red-crested bronze helmet tucked under one arm and his short scarlet cloak replaced by the long, hooded black one that Gyan liked to wear. He greeted her with a terse nod. "Gather your gear and meet me at the docks. You're coming to Maun with me."

She glanced out the window, consternation and confusion furrowing her brow. "Now, my lord?" Then the greater implication hit. Her heart twisted. "Gyan—is she all right?"

"I don't know." Frustration bled through his tone. He said to Seumas, "Your duty to Cynda is discharged. I assume responsibility for her safety. Return to Ogryvan with the report that Maun is under attack, status of residents unknown. I will send word when I can." He began to turn away, stopped himself, and faced them, smiling faintly. "And thank him for the use of his pigeons. I plan to develop a flock for myself."

CONFRONTED WITH the death of their leader, the Shasunaich resolve began to waver. The arrival of Per's troops shattered it. By tens and scores and hundreds, the enemy fled into the predawn gloom.

Gyan stared at her reddened sword. Braonshaffir had served her much better, she thought with a wry smile, than Arthur's other gift.

The One God alone knew where that bedeviled horse had bolted. She stooped to wipe Braonshaffir on the tunic of the nearest corpse. The search for Macmuir would have to wait. With a solemn nod to Braonshaffir's dead benefactor—whether Caledonach, Breatanach or Sasunach, it remained too dark to tell—she sheathed the sword and shouted to her men to break off pursuit and regroup.

Let the michaoduin run tuck-tailed to their ships, she decided. If they left the island, so be it. If not, she'd deal with them later. Now was the time for assessment and desperately needed rest.

She found the nearest tree and braced a hand against its rough steadiness. Pain flared in every muscle. Her ebbing battle frenzy gave her a fair idea of how an empty nutshell must feel.

Even her grief had retreated. Though she seemed no closer to possessing answers about what had happened to Loholt or why, the questions had stopped tormenting her, for which she felt profound gratitude. Too much of the future lay ahead to expend too much emotional energy on the past.

Closing her eyes, she bowed her head in silent thanksgiving.

A hand gripped her shoulder. "You all right, Commander Gyan?"

She straightened to meet Rhys's gaze. Blood splotched his battle-gear, face, and hair. He clutched the cohort's banner. Though its edges were tattered, its emblem of three bent legs arrayed like spokes of a wheel remained intact, and no damage had befallen the staff's solid bronze Dragon Legion crest.

The signifer's fate, the One God alone knew.

"I—I think so, Rhys." She swallowed to banish the hoarseness, but it did little to help. "You?"

"Not a scratch, my lady." He grinned, released her shoulder, and planted the standard.

She could manage no more than a single nod. Rhys stepped closer and wrapped both arms around her, a gesture Arthur might have offered. Her heart ached. God, how she missed him! His smile, his laugh, his gaze, his touch—the intensity of her longing astounded her but gladdened her, too. Her emotions finally had escaped their grief-walled prison. She pressed her face against the cool bronze of Rhys's cheek guard, willing herself not to cry—and not succeeding—as the battle's clamor died around them.

Composure returning, she backed away to survey the field as the last Sasunaich stumbled over the ridge. Her soldiers approached, stepping around the scores of tiny fires spluttering across the valley, scattered among countless shadowy mounds. Some mounds moved feebly in the fickle light. Most did not.

"So many of our own..." She couldn't bring herself to finish.

"But you held the Sasunaich off," Rhys said with undisguised pride.

Only with the One God's help, though she couldn't admit that to Rhys. "Too many got away."

"With such short warning, in the dark, against those odds—my dear sister, what did you expect?"

She whirled toward Per's voice. He stood between a pair of horses, a white and a bay, his cheek smeared with blood but looking otherwise unharmed. Mentally thanking the One God and forgetting her fatigue, she ran to greet him. She didn't bother to fight these tears as she laid her cheek against his breastplate, reassured by his heart's steady rhythm. Per dropped Rukh's and Macmuir's reins to hold her tightly, as though loath to release her. She squeezed him even harder.

As they parted, Per pointed to her battle trophy with its circlet of bronze. "Their war-leader?"

She nodded, unwilling to risk unleashing her grief. "I'll tell you about it later." He cocked a skeptical eyebrow. "I promise."

Murmuring to Macmuir, she untied the trophy from her belt and fastened it to his chest-harness. Nostrils flared and muscles quivering, the stallion whinnied and snorted lustily. As she stroked his nose, his eyes lost their wild look, and he quieted again. A quick examination proved Macmuir had taken no injury. She took the reins from Per, and he mounted Rukh.

With Rhys's help, she climbed into the saddle. Too tired to ask where Macmuir had been found, she simply thanked Per for her stallion's safe return and extended a hand to Rhys. "Come. We can look for your mare."

"No need, Commander."

Rhys cupped hands to mouth and blew a long, wavering whistle. A tall black shape resolved out of the purple twilight. The mare trotted toward them, stepping neatly over the bodies. Rhys patted her flank and mounted.

Gyan's bone-deep fatigue couldn't suppress her laugh. "Nice trick, Rhys. You must teach me sometime." She rubbed Macmuir's sweat-streaked neck. "In case this demon-spawn decides to desert me again."

After the last men returned, Rhys called the roll from memory. One in five didn't answer. Gyan regarded the ragged ranks. Many leaned on whatever was available: swords, spears, shields, each other—Breatanaich and Caledonaich alike. Few seemed able to hold themselves upright. Far too few for what lay ahead, if her attempt to contact Arthur failed.

Through pain and exhaustion, each pair of eyes glowed at her with hopeful expectation.

Gyan cleared her dust-dry throat, knowing what her men wanted and needed most, but she had no idea how to begin. She glanced at Per. He nodded encouragingly: not much help from her beathach of a brother.

In the strengthening light, she recognized more of her clansmen's faces. Few had remounted. Most stood among men whom, a mere two years earlier, they would have gladly embraced with steel. Now, some helped their Breatanach sword-brothers to stand; others were the grateful recipients of such aid.

This shared crisis had done more to forge unity than a hundred treaties or marriages ever could.

"Well done, mo ghaisgich!" *My heroes.* The full significance might have been lost on the Breatanach warriors but didn't go unnoticed by the Caledonaich, who responded with fatigue-muffled claps and cheers. "Well done, my heroes, indeed. Together"—she paused to let the implication sink in for herself, as well as for her men—"*Together*, we have defeated the invaders. Their survivors flee, taking as their only plunder the tale of our awesome prowess." She signaled Rhys to raise the standard. A breeze ruffled the sigil, making the legs appear to kick. "The Saxons will think long and hard before crossing swords with the mighty Manx Cohort again!"

Husky cheers ripped the morning. Smiling, she beheld the filthy, bloodied faces and noticed one warrior who had remained silent.

Recognition inverted her smile.

He stood apart from the others, feet squarely planted and sword drawn. His helmet was gone, his curly hair formed a dark nimbus about his head, and his armor looked more red than black. He was swaying; apparently, not all that blood was Sasunach.

Their gazes met. He glared at her as though still gripped by battle frenzy. It was all too apparent that he despised her.

Angusel. Her lips shaped his name but birthed no sound.

Her grief strained at its shackles, but now that she finally felt alive again, she refused to let that emotion control her.

Lips pursed, she looked away and gave the order to return to the fort. As the men obeyed, she slid a glance toward Angusel, but he had disappeared. His absence wrought more sadness than relief.

She reined Macmuir around to lead her troops home, earnestly hoping the enemy had left the island. Not for her sake, but for the sake of her weary sword-brothers.

All of them, even Angusel.

Chapter 29

THE LAST SHIPS scraped onto the beach beyond Rushen Priory's walls as Arthur strode toward Niniane across the sand. "Did you bring enough men?" she asked him.

While most jumped fully armed from the vessels, one plump, robed figure descended shakily down a rope ladder, assisted by two soldiers.

"This"—his gesture encompassed the score of vessels and hundreds of soldiers—"is only half the force. Bedwyr's men are sailing straight to the Saxon beachhead, where we'll meet them." Determination creased his brow.

"The sounds we heard last night..." She closed her eyes and shivered, though it wasn't cold under the midday autumn sun.

"They didn't try to come here, did they? To the priory?"

"No, thank the Lord. But they passed close." Directing efforts to douse lights and hide valuables, struggling to remain calm lest the other sisters lose courage, ceaselessly praying the Lord would shield the priory... she shivered again. "Too close. Twice."

"Twice?"

"At compline, it sounded as if they were heading toward Dhoo-Glass. I made sure the priory was dark to prevent them from getting the notion to visit us." She shook off a fear-induced vision, the shreds of her prophetic power. "Just before matins, we heard them going the other way. Shouting, running, cursing, screaming..." She drew a sharp breath. "We feared we were next."

"Did you See anything?" he whispered. "Gyan?"

She winced. Why the Sight had abandoned her remained a mystery. Perhaps because she hadn't used it properly, God had withdrawn His gift? Whatever the reason, the pain wrought by its absence hurt as keenly as any vision she'd ever experienced.

"No, I—oh, Arthur, I'm so sorry!" Legs weakening, she stumbled into in his arms. "I—I Saw none of this!" Sobs wracked her body.

He cradled her head against his armored breast. The cool bronze doused the heat in her cheeks. When her tears had run their course, and she straightened, she found him looking not at her but at the cliffs hiding Port Dhoo-Glass from view, as if commanding them to divulge their secrets. His left hand dropped from her shoulder to close over Caleberyllus's ruby. Upon his face, anxiety reigned.

A centurion marched up behind him. "Lord Pendragon?" When Arthur rounded on the officer, his expression of supreme confidence made Niniane wonder whether she'd imagined the anxiety. "Sir, the scouts have returned from South Cove. The Saxons are boarding their ships. Our men are formed up and ready."

"Good, Marcus. Start leading them up that defile." He pointed at the draw slicing into the cliffs. "Reform them at the top. I'll be along shortly." The centurion saluted and left.

"What will you do?" Niniane asked.

"What I came to do, first." He sounded as bleak as the wind-ravaged cliffs at his back. "What she would have expected."

The confidence he'd displayed for his officer withered into resignation, and it disturbed her more profoundly than her failure to See what he'd needed most for her to See.

"Please don't speak as though your wife is dead," she whispered. "You don't know that."

"I don't know that she isn't."

She stared at the sand through moistening eyes, wishing she

could burrow into a hole and stay there.

He lifted her chin, compassion flowing from his gaze like a healing balm. "I'm sorry, Niniane. I know you can't help what you See—or don't See." He let go and balled his fingers. "It's just so bloody maddening! I could take not having her with me when I thought she was safe." He ground knuckles to palm. "God's bleeding wounds!"

She laid a hand on his arm. "I will pray for you, Arthur."

"I don't need it." She found his claim difficult to believe. "Pray for Gyan." She nodded as Cynda approached, muttering and dusting sand from her hands. Arthur exchanged a few Caledonian words with her before he said to Niniane, "Please look after Cynda until I determine it's safe at port."

Niniane voiced her agreement. Arms folded, Cynda stood beside her as Arthur quickly moved to join the unit marching past. Discipline forbade the men from audibly acknowledging his presence, but Niniane thought their pace seemed brisker, their shoulders more squared, their chins higher. Watching until Arthur disappeared into the draw, she prayed for him and Gyanhumara both.

Hesitation creased Cynda's face. Then she spat. "That, for *safe*."

Niniane felt her eyebrows knit. "What?"

"Gyan there, maybe hurt." The older woman pointed toward the port. "Maybe others hurt. You and me, we go and heal, aye?"

She fingered her chin. Losing the Sight hadn't left her utterly useless. Slowly, she nodded. "We will go and heal."

BEDWYR STOOD at the ornately carved prow of his flagship as it bucked the swells beyond the enemy beachhead. Around him clustered the other warships under his command, awaiting his lookout's report.

He stroked the snarling wolf's smooth oaken neck with renewed admiration for the Scotti shipwrights' art. Between patrolling runs, he'd spent the summer determining what made these vessels swifter and more maneuverable than the Brytoni design and found the answer in their knifelike keels.

Caerglas shipwrights still labored to refit the fleet with the new keel style, obligating Bedwyr and his men to sail the Scotti warships captured during last year's battle. Though the new additions had taken some getting used to by the crews, the commander of the Brytoni fleet was supremely thankful for this option. And today, gods willing, they'd have another ship design to learn.

"Commander! The Pendragon's forces are beginning to engage."

Shielding his eyes, he regarded his lookout swaying in the rigging atop the mast.

"Are the Saxons fighting or retreating?"

"Fighting, sir. Wait—" The lookout craned forward. "The Pendragon is pushing through, and the enemy is breaking off."

"Report when the first ship touches water."

"Aye, sir." The crewman returned his gaze to the land battle.

The cohort breaking through already—that was fast, even for Arthur. The Saxons didn't expect this, Bedwyr mused. It supported Arthur's theory of a night attack on Dhoo-Glass, one that apparently had failed.

Yet at what cost?

Bedwyr ached with his friend. Gyan had captured his heart, though in a different way. True, her bright beauty dazzled him. What lover of women could remain immune to it? And he admired her courage and respected her intelligence. Most of all, he loved her for the positive influence she'd exerted upon Arthur before tragedy befell their son. He'd have sacrificed his right hand to save the child, but by the time he found out, only grieving with Arthur remained.

He winced at the memory of the worst ale-head he'd ever suffered.

Good thing Arthur's work at South Cove was proceeding quickly.

Staring across his watery domain at the cliffs, he tried to imagine fighting on a surface that didn't constantly throw everyone off balance. Land troops had no need for the extra measures of strength and agility that made a good shipboard warrior. Nor did they need ironclad stomachs, he thought with an irreverent grin, no matter how loudly they complained about camp rations.

Bedwyr's men, all specially selected and trained for naval warfare, would acquit themselves with honor anywhere.

"My lord, the Saxons are shoving off," called the lookout.

"How many ships?"

"Twelve, sir. The remaining soldiers are trying to buy time." The crewman's teeth flashed a grin. "They don't have long."

Bedwyr moistened his salt-dried lips. "Raise the signal."

The lookout drew a length of cloth from under his tunic and tied it to the rigging beneath the Scarlet Dragon. As the saffron semaphore unfurled in the stiff breeze, he started down from his perch.

The warships set oars to water and lunged forward to cut off the Saxons' escape.

The enemy loosed swarms of arrows at the Brytoni fleet, but panic forced the archers to let fly too soon. Most of the arrows fell harmlessly into the sea. With a practiced eye for the distance, Bedwyr brought the fleet closer and answered with fire. Saxon volleys dwindled as more men devoted their energies to beating out the flames. The ships began wallowing like cows trapped in a bog.

A few set course toward the Brytoni line and the freedom lying beyond. One bore down upon Bedwyr's flagship at ramming speed.

Like a dancer, the Scotti-built vessel pivoted and glided out of the way. Bedwyr ordered out the grappling hooks. A tremor rocked the decks as the vessels scraped together. A few unwary crewmen from both ships fell overboard, their screams drowned by a horrific screeching and cracking of hulls.

The Saxons fought with desperate fervor to board the flagship. Bedwyr and his men battered them back to carry the fight aboard the enemy ship.

Hand-to-hand combat upon a wildly pitching deck sluiced with seawater and urine and blood, compounded by the danger of burning rigging, presented quite a challenge. Bedwyr harbored no doubt that Arthur had the easier task of this operation.

Fighting near the mast, he heard a shouted warning. He dived and rolled as the crosspiece crashed onto the deck. Its glowing end clouted his shoulder, and agony exploded in his brain.

His opponent lay pinned, screaming, beneath the burning beam, clothing alight. The stench of roasting flesh flooded his nostrils. Lifting his sword and gritting his teeth, Bedwyr performed the only merciful act.

Before the fire began to bite into the deck, he ordered the return to their ship, for the fighting on this one had ceased.

CALEBERYLLUS WAS a cruel taskmaster.

Arthur stared at the weapon dripping Saxon blood. What else could imprison him on this corpse-littered beach while he ached to discover the fate of his beloved Gyan?

Ridiculous. It wasn't his sword's fault.

These Saxons couldn't be blamed, either. They'd only gotten in the way, paying for their blunder in crimson currency.

What constrained the Pendragon to see the event to its inevitable conclusion was a precept embedded in him from the moment his fingers had curled around the hilt of his first wooden practice sword. Duty governed him so naturally that he seldom wasted a second thought upon his decisions.

Today, he felt the chafing weight as surely as if an iron band wrapped his throat. He swallowed thickly.

No predicting how she might react to him. If she was alive. Had time eased her grief or intensified it? Did she love him anymore? Or had she found—*God, please, no*—someone else to comfort her?

Would he have the chance to tell her any of this?

Clenching his jaw, he exiled his doubts about the future to concentrate on the present. Instead, perversely, his mind reviewed the raw memory of the afternoon's work. He grimaced. The exhausted enemy force had stood no chance against rested men lusting to avenge their companions' deaths.

"Wholesale slaughter" came closest to describing the grisly mess his men now labored to clean up. Untapped energy escaped in the form of boisterous joking as some soldiers stripped the dead of arms and armor and others stacked bodies and pieces of bodies for disposal.

Though battlefield humor might seem callous and out of place, with the corpses still limp and the wounded screaming for help, well did Arthur know its purpose. No soldier could look death in the eye without blinking. Those who failed to relieve the nervous tension went mad. Most chose to laugh about their daring exploits and narrow escapes, casting aspersions on the parentage and sexual preferences of the vanquished foe.

Today, their laughter stung him like brine on a gaping wound.

Upon Cai's suggestion after the Dun Eidyn debacle, he'd learned to find his release in a woman's arms. Besides the physical pleasure, it reassured him that life marched on, no matter how men tried to butcher each other. Those women hadn't meant anything to him.

Gyan had to be alive! If not, he'd never forgive himself... and he'd save some choice words for God. And if she lived, and still loved him, he never would let her leave his side again.

Squealing gulls drew his attention, squabbling over a fish. The gulls' raucous fighting reminded him of himself and his wife, with one marked difference. The birds shrieked and dived and pecked at one another with reckless abandon, free to follow their own choices. But no gull tried to hold any of the others back.

Pondering this revelation, he wiped Caleberyllus with a handful of grass pulled from the sandy bank. As the blade disappeared into its scabbard, he noticed the long cut on his right forearm. He couldn't recall any Saxon getting that close, though that was hardly unusual. The cut didn't hurt much, and the blood had already dried.

Recognition jolted him. The wound bore an uncanny resemblance to the one he'd accidentally inflicted upon Gyan's arm last year.

His left hand briefly touched the linen wrap covering the fealty-mark on his neck. That scar, symbolic of an oath far more profound than a bond between warriors, would forever bind his heart to hers regardless of how she acted toward him. His regret intensified.

Reluctantly, he returned to the task at hand.

Bedwyr appeared to be dealing with the Saxon warships with his usual efficiency. Golden flashes and black plumes erupted from the condemned vessels. Widening red circles marred the bay's greenish hue.

In combat, the Saxon warships were outclassed by their swifter Brytoni and Scotti counterparts, yet as troop transports they knew no equal. Arthur regretted that only half would be salvageable.

This seemed destined to be a day of regrets.

Mercifully, the fitful breeze coaxed the smoke out to sea, taking with it the stink of blazing destruction, though death smells clung stubbornly to the beach.

He watched Saxons jump ship and paddle for shore, only to be dragged under by the pounding surf. Many surfaced, choking and flailing. Some didn't. He sent Marcus with a unit to round up the survivors.

While the Brytoni fleet bobbed serenely offshore, the flagship split away and rode the waves onto the beach. Arthur strode forward as men disembarked to drag the vessel from reach of the covetous waters. Bedwyr stood at the prow, looking as if he'd stumbled through the caverns of hell.

"What in God's name happened to you?" Arthur asked.

Wincing, Bedwyr touched the blackened leather on his shoulder.

"I argued with a burning crossbeam." He smiled wanly. "Care to wager which of us won?"

Yet another damned regret: not having one iota of humor to banter with his best friend. "You should get that treated soon."

"I plan to. We're going to port," Bedwyr said. "Have you any wounded?"

"No. We suffered only minor casualties." As Arthur regarded his arm, sorrow provoked his sigh. "Nothing that can't wait." Duty's burden grew heavier. Small wonder he wasn't sinking into the sand. "Go. I'll meet you there later."

"Dolphin dung, Arthur! You're coming with me." Bedwyr raised his uninjured arm, palm open. Arthur checked his retort. "Marcus can finish here for you."

"You're right." Thank God for friends who possessed more sense than he did. "I'll tell him."

EMPTY BUCKET in hand, Niniane threaded between the drab tents toward the central clearing where the rock-lined firepits had been dug. She didn't need to glance inside the tents. The moans and screams and curses, and the stench of blood and offal and vomit, reaffirmed what she already knew.

Truly staggering, the many ways warriors could maim each other.

Being outside made it easier to steel herself against the suffering. The tent walls veiled the sights and muffled the sounds, and zephyrs purged the smells from the field-hospital compound erected on the Dhoo-Glass practice grounds.

Some part of her had rejoiced when she'd applied the last of the salve. Refusing her assistant's offer to fetch more, she'd latched onto this excuse to escape the gashes and burns and dislocated joints and broken bones and ruined eyes and missing limbs, if only briefly.

Niniane proffered the bucket to the woman minding the nearest cauldron. Her linen apron smeared with hog tallow and ragged black braids framing her sweat-streaked face, the woman looked as exhausted as Niniane felt. Grunting, she gave the thick, infection-fighting elder-leaf ointment a few stirs with her paddle before filling the bucket. Niniane murmured her thanks and managed a smile. Drawing the back of a callused hand across her forehead, the woman nodded.

After stopping by the supply tent to collect an armload of bandage rolls, Niniane returned to her patients.

The first young man to receive her attention had taken a spear above the heart, though not deep. Someone had removed the spearhead. She cleaned out the dirt and blood, applied a generous dollop of warm ointment, and covered it with a bandage. With a clean cloth dipped in cool water, she gently wiped sweat from the soldier's forehead. He stirred but, luckily, didn't wake.

As she collected her implements to move to the next cot, the ground began to waver and spin. She felt a pair of hands grasp her shoulders. Sister Willa, who'd accompanied her to assist with the wounded, said something Niniane couldn't make out. Pressing fingers to temple, she braced herself for a visitation of the Sight.

No visions came. Simply fatigue, she presumed, unsure whether to be relieved or not. Evening was nipping at afternoon's heels, yet so many soldiers remained in need of help.

The dizziness passed. Niniane turned with a sigh—and saw Arthur.

"Is she here?"

She noticed the cut on his forearm. "Chieftainess Gyanhumara is at the fort." It was the first question she'd asked upon arrival, and Cynda had left the field hospital shortly thereafter. "Cynda should be with her. But first, let me dress your"—she blinked and found herself talking to the air—"arm."

Bedwyr chuckled softly. This surprised her, for a melon-size burn branded his right shoulder. She reached for her knife and the bucket of ointment. Willa handed her a bandage roll.

"That's his way, Prioress." He groaned as she sliced away charred leather to expose his damaged flesh. She smoothed on the salve and watched his face's tension ease. He gazed at her through steady, moss-green eyes. "Especially with those he loves."

Niniane wrapped his shoulder. "I know, Bedwyr." She couldn't bear to tell him that Arthur's concern for others, which outweighed all thought of his own safety, would one day be his death. "I know."

Chapter 30

ARTHUR STRODE THE corridor toward the cohort commander's workroom. By all reports, she had suffered just minor wounds, but he needed the kind of proof only his eyes could provide.

What would happen after that, God alone knew.

He burst into the antechamber to find Rhys seated behind the table. From a ledge glared the embalmed head of the auburn-haired Niall, beside what had to be Gyan's latest trophy, its golden hair and mustaches drooping, mouth rounded in a shocked *O*, and its blue eyes reflecting eternity above the bloody, torn remains of the rest of the poor bastard.

Rhys scrambled to his feet, tipping his chair and scattering parchment, quills, and nibs across the tabletop. He saluted.

Arthur wrenched his gaze from the trophies to regard Gyan's aide, rendering a short nod. "Where is she, Centurion?"

"Resting in her quarters, Lord Pendragon. Left orders not to be disturbed by anyone." He pawed through the parchment to unearth a wax tablet and offered it to Arthur. "Preliminary report, sir."

Arthur's top priority lay in the adjacent building, probably asleep. He read the report anyway—and felt his eyebrows lift. Gyan's order of battle and its execution was nothing short of brilliant. A surge of love and respect deepened the wound her departure had wrought.

I was a fool to have let her go!

Hell, no. I was a fool for trying to hold her too tightly.

Rhys's hopeful expression reined in Arthur's thoughts far enough for him to make some encouraging remarks and offer a few suggestions. After returning the report to its author, he left the room.

Left orders not to be disturbed—by anyone.

He'd have flown to her on the wings of the wind; surely, she knew that. Had she meant to include him in her directive too? Even if she no longer loved him, seeing her again would be sufficient. He hoped.

Lengthening his stride, he battled the temptation to run.

He found her antechamber door bolted. Cynda's doing, no doubt. Would he interrupt their reunion? Would it matter?

Left orders not to be disturbed.

Bloody hell, I have more right to be here than any servant! Arthur's pounding rattled the timbers. The pain steadied him. He shook his hand, reformed the fist, and pounded again.

The door opened. To his surprise, an irate Peredur appeared, but the ire melted into a relieved grin. "Gods, Artyr, how did you get here so quickly? Nemetona's chariot?"

Caledonians believed their war-goddess drove a crimson chariot drawn by four winged, fire-snorting, ebony horses. Arthur grunted. "Something like that."

He stepped into the room, and Per closed the door behind them, his grin broadening. "You must have left the cavalry behind again."

Arthur chuckled at the old jest. "You're fortunate. I don't tolerate insubordination from just anyone." Gazing at the door to the inner chamber, he sobered. "How is she?"

Per crossed to the door, slowly worked the handle, and eased the door open a crack. "Why don't you see for yourself?"

Arthur's grief, doubts, and fears rooted him. Entire enemy armies didn't faze him a tenth as much as the prospect of losing her love.

"Well?" Per studied him intently.

He shrugged. "I don't want to disturb her."

Per crossed his arms, disgust puckering his face. "Artyr mac Ygrayna, I never figured you for a coward."

The accusation ignited his anger. Not because it was wrong, but because it came too damned close to being right. "This matter is between me and my wife. You have no right to interfere."

"Like hell I don't. I have her best interests and her happiness at heart." Eyes glittering, Per stalked up to Arthur. "Do you?"

They faced off, unmoving and silent. Did he, Arthur map Uther, have Gyan's best interests at heart? Did he even know what they were? Or what would make her happy again? The birth of another child seemed to help most women move past their loss. His own mother, for one. He ached to be intimate with Gyan and, God willing, to give her more children. Did she want a family?

Does she want me?

Only one way to find out. No battle could be fought without first scouting the land. By God, he'd win her back from wherever grief had imprisoned her, even if it took his very last breath.

"You're right, Per. I need answers." The rhythmic sound of her sleep-deepened breathing filtered through the crack. "Is Cynda with her?"

"Cynda? She's still at Arbroch."

Arthur swore under his breath.

"Isn't she?" Per asked, brow furrowed.

"I brought her with me but entrusted her to Prioress Niniane's care. In the field hospital, the prioress told me Cynda would be here."

Per's frown deepened. "Odd that she isn't. I'll find her." He aimed a nod at the bedchamber's door. "But not too quickly." Chuckling, he left the room.

Arthur stepped past his fears and into Gyan's bedchamber.

Left orders not to be disturbed.

He could understand why.

She sprawled on her back atop the furs. Of her armor, only the boots, helmet, and sword belt had come off. They lay in a neat pile at the foot of the bed. Her hair splayed about her head in a fiery halo. The reason for its shortness lanced his heart. Bowing his head, he briefly knuckled the ache.

The scratch at the base of her neck brought to mind her trophies, and profound thankfulness dispelled his grief. However, he knew that kind of fatigue. After Abar-Gleann, he didn't want even a sparrow to come within five leagues until he'd slept himself out.

Mesmerized by the gentle rise and fall of her chest, he drank in the glorious sight of her as a man gulps water after crossing the wilderness. In retrospect, that was exactly what his life had become: an arid wilderness of daily routine that maintained the outward semblance of normalcy while inwardly he struggled simply to survive, with little time to think and no time to feel.

Long-disused feelings pummeled him with redoubled force, beginning with the familiar twinge in his chest he'd felt each time their gazes met and held.

Left orders. Not to be disturbed. By anyone.

He had no desire to damage whatever relationship might remain by deliberately ignoring her wishes.

For this, he realized, was precisely what he'd done by trying to interfere with the calling of her warrior's blood, which had powered her heart long before she'd become his wife or the mother of their child. Her midnight rout of the Saxon invasion, against daunting odds, proved she could plan battles and lead men as well as anyone. Including him.

Casting about for a way to demonstrate the depth of his love and respect for her abilities as a warrior and leader, his gaze fell upon her cloak and rank badge.

Urien's damned badge.

It inspired the easiest military decision he'd ever made, and he prayed for sufficient time to implement it.

He kissed her sweet, sleep-parted lips and slipped from the room.

GYAN'S EYELIDS fluttered open. Pain wracked her muscles, and she groaned. Hearing the tattoo of receding footsteps, she glanced over in time to see the gold-trimmed cloak disappear through the door.

"Artyr?" Her whisper sounded hoarse. Desperate for assurance that he didn't blame her for Loholt's death, she said, "Please don't go."

The latch clicked with lonesome finality.

Tears burned her eyes as she rolled onto her stomach, buried her face in the pillow, and wept.

CYNDA SAT at an empty table along a wall of Dhoo-Glass's feast hall, trencher of cold pork, carrots, and bread lying untouched before her and her fourth mug of ale at hand. Almost empty, she observed, as she gazed sadly into its pitch-sealed leather depths.

Mayhap she should return to the field hospital, where she might be of some use. Her hands' tremors convinced her otherwise, and she tightened her grip on the mug.

She observed the comings and goings in the hall with bleary disinterest. Soldiers, mostly, swaggering this way and that with pints in their palms and lies on their lips, regaling anyone fool enough to stop and listen. At least, that's what she assumed they were doing, since she couldn't make out more than one Breatanaiche word in five.

The merchants, craftsmen, and farmers in the hall, many with families, kept to themselves. No one paid heed to an old Caledonach servant woman. Exactly as it should be.

When a group of Argyll horsemen tromped in, gazing about as if scouting a battlefield, she hunkered into her cloak and stared at her ale. Recognition meant questions she had no wish to face. Questions meant answers she wasn't prepared to render. Answers meant examining feelings she dared not resurrect. Feelings of guilt for failing the one person on earth she'd gladly have died for, and her son. Of burning shame for traveling all this way only to hide behind a rampart of fear. And of fathomless despair that Gyan would never forgive her.

Eyes stinging, she took her last pull of the bitter brew.

"There you are!" Decades of habit moved Cynda's head. Per stood before her, fists on hips, typical cocky grin painted across his face and a fresh cut adorning one cheek. Habit also forced her to note that the wound appeared clean and not too inflamed. "I was beginning to think my brother-by-law had lied to me." He beckoned. "Come, Cynda."

She didn't need to ask his destination. Hands braced on the tabletop, she rose. The drink fuzzed her senses and heightened her qualms. Head bowed, she shuffled from the hall in Per's wake.

"What ails you?" He glanced her way as they neared the officers' wing. "You look as if you're walking to a funeral."

She snorted softly. "Aye," she muttered. *My own.*

"If you're worried about Gyan, don't be. She's exhausted and has a few cuts and bruises, but nothing worse, thanks be to the gods."

Cynda mumbled her thanks; his remarks confirmed what she'd already heard. They entered the building between a pair of smartly saluting guards and trod the familiar route to the commander's quarters. Per pushed open the door and held it for her, but he didn't enter the chamber. She lifted an eyebrow.

"With you here, I can see to the needs of my men." The door banged shut behind him as he left.

"Artyr?" called a muffled voice from beyond the bedchamber's closed door.

Epona, please give me strength!

Cynda sucked in a breath and opened the door to her fate.

Gyan stood at the window, her arms crossed and her back to the door, looking out over the harbor, where Lord Artyr's war-fleet bobbed at anchor. When she turned, astonishment cascaded over her face, followed quickly by—joy?

Cynda shook her head in disbelief as Gyan rushed to her, arms wide, to fold her in a crushing embrace. Her second shock in as many moments came when she realized Gyan was weeping. Tears pooled in Cynda's eyes and spilled down her cheeks. Sweat, leather, and the pungent salve slathered on Gyan's cuts evoked a flood of memories, the most recent and painful of them riding the crest. Failure and guilt forced Cynda's sobs to erupt. She wanted desperately to run, to hide in her unworthiness and misery, but she could only cling to Gyan tighter and cry harder.

"I am so sorry, Cynda," Gyan whispered raggedly. "I've wronged you. Please forgive me."

"Gyan, my dove—"

My dove.

She had not believed she would ever use the old endearment again. Pain savaged her heart. "I should be begging your forgiveness." Pulling back, she clapped a hand over her mouth, choking on another sob. "If—if you can."

Gyan gripped Cynda's shoulders gently but firmly. "Of course, I forgive you." When Cynda refused to look up, Gyan gave her a little shake. "Grief made me blame you in part for Loholt's death." Sighing, she bowed her head. "That was wrong, and I'm sorry."

Nearly two decades ago, Cynda had lost her bairn and her husband to the killing fever; well did she know how grief could maul the soul. "Fret not about me, my dove, but set your heart at rest." She grasped Gyan's hand. "What of Lord Angusel? Have you forgiven him?"

Anguish dominated Gyan's face. "It may be too late for that." Their gazes held for a long moment. Finally, Gyan said, "The pain—it does go away, doesn't it?" The raw yearning in her eyes wrenched Cynda's heart.

She squeezed Gyan's hand. "In time, aye." Recalling how she'd learned to overcome her losses, she added, "Keeping busy helps."

"I don't think the men would appreciate my way of keeping busy." A sardonic smile bent Gyan's lips. "Yet they did seem to relish last night's activities, so perhaps—" Smile fading, she pulled her hand from Cynda's grip. "I must check on them." She moved toward her belt and boots. "And find Angusel."

While Cynda cinched Gyan's sword belt, she pondered the idea of encouraging her to rest. The darkness around her eyes proclaimed the need, even if she remained too stubborn to admit it. The strength of purpose in Gyan's movements as she donned her boots and straightened her battle-tunic, however, bespoke a different need, one no less vital to her soul's healing.

Gyan flung her cloak in place and, Cynda was dismayed to notice, casually pinned it with Lord Urien's old jet-eyed bronze dragon. What had become of Lord Artyr's bonding-day gift, Cynda hadn't a clue. Unsure whether to inquire about it, she asked instead, "What shall I tell Lord Artyr if he comes here looking for you?"

A confusing mix of emotions—fear, sorrow, uncertainty, regret, dread, annoyance—flashed across Gyan's features. "I am going to the field hospital and then the battlefield." She lowered her eyebrows. "If the Pendragon desires speech with me, he can seek me there."

Coldness gripped her gut as the breeze created by Gyan's departure enveloped her. Whatever was amiss between Gyan and her consort, Cynda vowed to help them resolve it. To atone for her part in Loholt's death and truly feel worthy of Gyan's forgiveness, it was the least she could do for either of them.

ASTRIDE MACMUIR, Gyan surveyed the Dhoo-Glass battlefield from the pine-crowned ridge where the charge had begun, searching for the one warrior who had made it possible for her to be there.

Soldiers in the valley were collecting adornments, usable weapons and armor, and separating friend from foe for burial. Arthur's men comprised the majority, though she recognized Gawain and other Manx Cohort troops among them while their companions recuperated in the field hospital or the barracks, depending on their skill and luck. Mounted patrols discouraged thieves and the morbidly curious.

Everywhere with impunity hopped raucously greedy, impartial, midnight-feathered scavengers.

Stonn had been safely stabled, but Gyan could find no sign of his rider in any of the places she'd searched.

At the western end of the battlefield, a huge pit had been dug for dead Breatanaich and Caledonaich. Though it wouldn't see nearly the same numbers as the Sasunach pyres, the grave was filling rapidly.

Most of these soldiers had sacrificed themselves to protect the lives and lands of strangers. She refused to believe Angusel had too.

A few women, some with squalling bairns riding their hips, lingered in wretched anguish near the pit. Hooded monks consoled the living and performed rites to send the valiant to eternal rest. If Dafydd worked among them, Gyan couldn't tell. The monks' chants lent a somber chorus to the mourners' wails and the violent percussion of the soldiers' labors.

The requiem coaxed a familiar tingling to course through her. Eyes closed, she silently recited the Caledonach warrior's lament.

A warrior is slain today, ne'er to fight another day...

The pyres, the common grave, taking items from the dead of both armies... *all his foes around him lay, the price in crimson blood to pay.*

It seemed so hideously impersonal.

None was comelier of face, wielding sword with braver grace; no bolder lover did embrace his lass, and none can ever take his place.

She understood the reasons well: custom, expediency, space limitations, and economics. She hoped she had masked overt signs of being affected. The moisture in her eyes dictated otherwise.

Leaders, she realized with abrupt clarity, were never meant to become hardened to war's tragic aftermath lest they forget its primary purpose as a method of enforcing peace.

Now fights he in the Otherworld, helmet golden, sword of pearl, bright banner proudly unfurl'd, dark minions into hell forever hurl!

The lament never would be sung for her son.

And because of her rash actions, it never would be sung for the warrior who had failed to save him.

Her heart felt as wrung out as damp linen.

Angusel she might never see again, but the monks reminded her of one final service she could perform for Loholt. She spurred Macmuir into a breakneck plunge down the hillside, an echo of the previous night's battle frenzy thrumming in her veins. She might have enjoyed it if grief weren't throttling her soul.

"God's wounds!" shouted a familiar voice behind her.

As the ground leveled, she halted Macmuir and twisted in the saddle to watch Arthur careen to the valley floor and rein his borrowed horse to a sliding stop beside her. With his cloak fretting in the breeze, sunlight exploded off his bronzed shoulders in a blazing aura.

"How many went lame in the charge?" His expression's fiery intensity made him seem less like her consort than Nemetona's.

She studied the steep, rock-strewn terrain and shrugged. "I haven't seen the reports yet." His disapproval smote her with palpable force. "It was a calculated risk. Something Gideon the Hebrew might have planned." Mentally, she girded herself for his inevitable rebuke.

He surprised her with a chuckle. "The Lord indeed granted you a miracle."

Obtaining Angusel's forgiveness and other such miracles seemed far beyond reach. Achieving peace with herself topped the list. Eyes watering, she looked away.

"Your victory didn't leave me a lot to do. The Saxons at the beachhead were exhausted. We took few prisoners." Sorrow lurked within his quiet words and not, she suspected, because of an easy win.

Nearby, a soldier swiped at a raven. The bird flapped lazily out of reach and fluttered down to peck at another corpse, gulping gobbets of flesh. Gyan grimaced.

"My victory? You don't intend to claim the credit?"

"The bards may insist on giving it to me, but I know you did a brilliant job. That hell-bent charge must have been divinely inspired." He groped inside a pouch dangling from his belt and withdrew a shining object. Her eyes widened with surprise spawned by recognition. "You have earned this, Comitissa Britanniam."

"'Lady-Companion of Brydein'?" she asked. Arthur, as the legion's war-chieftain, was called Dux Britanniarum, "Duke of Brydein." She'd never heard of this other Ròmanach title.

"That is one interpretation. Another is 'Countess of Brydein.'"

"An army designation?"

"More than a hundred years ago, the men filling the post were titled Comes Britanniarum." He offered her the cloak-pin. "I am officially reinstating the office."

"Ha. As what? The war-duke's bedchamber accessory? Heir-bearer? Chief shield-polisher?"

He rolled his eyes. "As my second-in-command, effective at once. We will conduct a formal ceremony in a few days, in conjunction with the presentation of unit and individual awards."

Her irritation rose. She craved love and forgiveness from him—and intimacy, if she hadn't driven him into someone else's bed. Not military accolades.

A wailing bairn reminded her of her destination. Leaving Arthur holding the cloak-pin, she jabbed Macmuir's flanks and raced off.

She didn't get far.

"Commander Gyan, come see what I found!"

Suppressing a sigh, she reined Macmuir toward the shout. Gawain cradled something in his upturned palm, which he surrendered to her.

"What is that?" Arthur asked as he joined them.

Hefting the garnet-studded treasure, she asked Gawain for the body's whereabouts, and he pointed to a headless corpse. "Prince Ælferd Wlencingsson, the Saxon commander. We extracted the name from one of the wounded prisoners," she explained to her consort. She dropped the buckle into Gawain's hands. "Put it back exactly as you found it, Gawain, and remove the body to Port Dhoo-Glass. It's not to be stripped and burned with the others."

"Now, Gyan—" Arthur began.

She knotted her eyebrows. "For what I have in mind, that body must not be looted."

"What, exactly, do you have in mind?"

"A way to inform the Saxons of their invasion's outcome by receiving a gift from me: Ælferd's body. His headless body, of course. I will not surrender my prize." Her glare defied Arthur to disagree. "And I will personally compensate you for the value of the prince's gear and adornments, if that is your concern."

He regarded her for a long moment but didn't countermand her order. She wheeled Macmuir about and kicked him into a canter to put the battlefield—and her consort—behind her as fast as possible.

Chapter 31

ARTHUR WATCHED GYAN'S diminishing form, his hopes for a joyful reunion dwindling just as rapidly. The brooch's weight dragged at his palm. He tightened his fist and cocked his arm.

"Lord Artyr!"

He lowered his hand and glanced toward the shout. At the valley's edge, Cynda stood struggling in a soldier's grasp. He stashed Gyan's brooch in his pouch, rode over to them, and dismissed the soldier. Cynda glowered at the man's receding back before returning her attention to Arthur.

"My men have orders to keep the battlefield clear until burial detail is finished," he said in Caledonian. "What are you doing here?"

"Gyan needs to rest. I came to tell her." She glanced westward, in the direction Gyan had disappeared. "Where did she go?"

He couldn't share his guess about her physical destination with Cynda. Of her emotional whereabouts, he felt far less certain. Gyan could have succumbed to anger, pride, grief, despair... "I don't know."

"You will follow her." Not a question but a command.

"She needs to be alone."

Cynda snatched the bridle and held it firmly. "Dog spittle! She has been alone, my lord, separated from clan and consort and most of her kin these past two turnings of the moon. It has helped her"—she spat, causing the horse to fidget—"that much."

Good point. And his vow to rescue Gyan from her grief wouldn't be worth a lake of dog spittle if he let her moodiness best him.

"You win, Cynda."

She released the bridle, and he tightened his grip on the reins. "Nay, my lord." She flashed a grin. "You and Gyan win."

As he set spurs to the gelding's flanks and the animal cantered forward, he earnestly hoped she would prove to be right.

GYAN KNEW what she had to do, but not in the Caledonach way.

At Arbroch, the hillside above the clan's burial site featured a vast granite slab gouged with dozens of cuplike depressions, many surrounded by rings or spiral patterns. Its carvers had lived and worked and died in mist-shrouded antiquity. Of their stone legacy's original purpose, not even the seannachaidhean could recall.

Clan Argyll used the slab to memorialize the dead. On a windless evening, candles set into the cups could be seen from the gate tower for all to share in the mourner's loss.

Regret and sorrow shredded Gyan's soul. Because Loholt's body hadn't been found—and likely never would be—she could not conduct the traditional outdoor memorial service for him.

Standing inside the Sanctuary of the Chalice, she gazed plaintively at the bank of candles on a table before her. Two tapers, flanking a basket of twigs, shed thin beams upon the rows of stubby votive candles, only a few of which had been lit.

The rest stood as dark monuments to dead unremembered.

She reached for a twig but stopped, unable to wrest her mind off her consort to focus upon her son.

That Arthur blamed her for Loholt's death was the only reasonable explanation for his actions in her quarters. He owed her the courtesy of telling her. By everything holy, Gyan had a right to know!

However painful the revelation might prove to be.

Her eyes stung. She rubbed them, trying to fault the pervasive incense, and despised the lie.

The bell's tolling and the choir's soft hymn signaled vespers. The chapel's doors opened, and threescore pairs of sandal-shod feet pattered past her. She had planned to conclude her memorial sooner, to prevent her presence from intruding upon the brethren's worship.

No. That was a lie, too. She felt utterly unworthy to join them.

Overwhelming remorse and guilt forced her to her knees. Tears spilled from her closed eyes, and she bowed her head lower and lower as the music swelled, until only her hands separated her forehead from the stone floor.

Loholt, my son, please forgive me!

The light touch of a hand on her head startled her. Expecting Dafydd, she straightened to find Arthur kneeling beside her, concern and questions engraved upon his face.

Embarrassment caused her to rasp, "Why are you here?"

Pain flared in his eyes, making her wish she could call the words back. "To grieve for my son." The pain transformed into frankness. "And for my marriage."

She arched an eyebrow. As she stood, so did he, and she beckoned him to follow her. They slipped outside, and she set a brisk pace across the monastery's grounds, ignoring the twilit serenity of their surroundings. Grief had expunged "serenity" from her vocabulary.

As they neared her intended destination, she groaned inwardly.

A year ago in this same apple grove, she and Arthur had reveled in the bliss of their private Eden. This night, they might find themselves banished from it forever.

She faced her consort, her feet planted and arms crossed. "You mourn our marriage? Because you have found someone else to warm your bed?" Sighing, she studied the broken, dead leaves underfoot, feeling just as broken and dead inside. "Not that I would blame you."

"God's wounds, Gyan!" She glanced up. "God's holy, bleeding wounds—another woman, is that what you think?"

"I know not what to think." She averted her gaze to hide her quivering chin. "Except that . . . you don't need a wife who insists on pursuing her own selfish causes. You don't need"—she twisted away, losing her emotional battle—"me."

"Yes. I do." His arms encircled her. "You, Gyanhumara nic Hymar, are the most precious person on earth to me."

Desperately, she yearned to believe him, but his eyes seemed hooded in the fading light, unfathomable. "Even after Loholt?"

Sorrow invaded his gaze, and he released her. "I grieve for our son, but I don't hold you responsible. I never did."

Self-loathing goaded her to say, "Then perhaps you don't know the whole story." Heaping fresh reproach upon herself, she confessed point after bitter point.

He gripped her shoulders. "Gyan, you cannot blame yourself. Any other woman would have acted exactly as you did."

I am not just "any other woman!"

Another lie. A leader she might be, but only by happenstance. She had proven no less selfish and petty than the most vulgar, mean-spirited varlet... and probably even more so.

Tears threatened, and she drew a shuddering breath.

He stroked her shorn hair. "I grieve even more for us."

"After what I did... can there be an 'us' anymore?" Not only for what she'd done to Loholt but to everyone else through her grief-induced rage, everyone except the one man truly deserving of retribution, who lay safely beyond her reach. She chewed a knuckle and looked down.

His fingertips beneath her chin brought her gaze back to his, where she found compassion and love in far greater measure than she deserved. "Gyan, I wouldn't—couldn't have it any other way."

Her throat tightened. She threw her arms about his neck, and he held her close, clasping her head to his chest while her tears washed away her remorse and guilt. The anguish remained, but at last she felt forgiven. And ready to forgive herself.

SHE DRIED her face on her undertunic's sleeve and offered him a wan smile. He lowered his lips to hers, tentatively, as if exploring unmapped territory. She increased the pressure, and he gladly answered in kind. Their arms and bodies twined like mistletoe to oak. Their lips worked ravenously together until he was unsure who would devour the other first. Her lips tasted sweeter to him than the finest wine.

"God in heaven, Gyan," he murmured. "I was so worried about

you."

"Because of the Saxons?"

"And our son." He motioned for her to sit on a nearby bench. She obeyed him as he marshaled his words. He dropped to one knee at her feet. "I need no oaths to remind me how much I love you." He tapped his neck. "But this scar does remind me that my obligation to serve you doesn't always mean protection." He clasped her hand. "You know I would die for you. What I vow to you this day, Gyanhumara nic Hymar of Clan Argyll of Caledonia, is to temper my instincts with judgment and to be more trusting of yours."

"My—what? Instincts or judgment?"

"Both." He branded the back of her hand with a lingering kiss.

"I must admit, your instincts about the Saxons were right all along. Arthur map Uther of Clan Cwrnwyll of Brydein, I vow to heed your warnings." She grinned. "No matter how mad they sound." As their chuckles faded, her expression turned pensive. "But what about when 'serving me' means permitting me the freedom to follow my conscience when my purposes differ from yours?"

"Even then." He rose and sat beside her. "But I trust you're not planning anything—risky."

"Against Urien?" Sighing, she drew up her legs, clasped her arms about them, and wedged her knees under her chin. "What can I do? Cultivate spies? His clansmen are as loyal to him as mine are to me. All the wealth of Argyll couldn't buy their treason." Her gaze seemed distant, unfocused. "And even if it could, the satisfaction of revenge isn't worth impoverishing my clan. I have but one choice to force his hand."

Arthur hugged her to him. Her too-short hair smelled of rose petals, and it amazed him how much he'd missed that simple sensation. Stretching out her legs, she leaned against his chest.

"That choice would be?" He had a guess but wanted her to name it. Otherwise, the truth would be much easier to dodge.

"We both know it's me Urien wants." She uttered a mirthless laugh. "But I doubt you would agree to my challenging him to single combat."

"Damned right." Though he respected Gyan's martial prowess, he knew she couldn't survive Urien's lust for revenge—and other things.

She expelled a heavy sigh. "Single combat would solve nothing, anyway. The loser's clan would declare a blood feud on the winner, and Caledonia and Brydein would plunge back to where we'd started. Before Abar-Gleann." Her hand felt as smooth and cool as a blade against his cheek, and she regarded him longingly. "Before you."

He captured her hand and brought it to his lips. "My love, I am so glad you've thought this through." As he gazed into the sea-green depths of her eyes, he lowered his voice to a throaty whisper. "Now that I have you back, I will not give you up again."

"Another vow, Lord Pendragon?"

"No, Chieftainess. Fact."

Wrapping both arms around her, he fastened his mouth to hers. Their armor blunted the pleasure of bodily contact, but he was enjoying the intimacy far too much to care.

"I love you, Artyr, and I want you—*need* you more than ever." A flash of fear eclipsed her desire. "But I can't bear to think that any more children we might have are fated to become Urien's targets."

Arthur glared at the bronze cloak-pin, gleaming dully in the waning light. He understood her fear but was heartily tired of their adversary coming between them. Caressing her cheek, he wished he could do more yet knew they had to proceed at her pace. "We can bring pleasure to each other in many ways, Gyan."

"I know." Her lips brushed his, lightly at first, then harder, harder still, and finally with a passion as hot and wild as kissing elemental fire. After they parted, she said, "But it isn't the same."

"Surely, there are ways to prevent conception."

"I wish the solution could be that simple." She shook her head resolutely. "It is my sacred duty to ensure the future leadership of the clan." The desire in her eyes raged hotter than before. "*We* must, Àrd-Ceoigin."

He stood, wanting nothing more than to act upon their passions, but propriety restrained him to helping her rise. Hand in hand, they left the orchard. When he would have angled toward the monastery's guesthouse, however, she continued toward the church. He stopped her on the threshold and voiced his query, submerging his disappointment.

"I cannot begin working toward the future," she whispered, "until I make peace with the past."

That he could well understand.

She tugged open the door and stepped inside. Although most monks had departed, some still clustered near the altar for private prayer and meditation. She strode to the tiered bank of votive candles and pulled a twig from the basket.

So did Arthur.

Her raised eyebrow invited him to explain. "When you and Loholt needed me most, I was too obsessed with my plans to retaliate against Colgrim." The confession didn't come easily, for those plans might yet effect a wider impact than anticipated, and not necessarily for the better. "Can you forgive me?"

She frowned. "I blamed many people for Loholt's death—rightly or wrongly—but it never occurred to me to blame you. The Angli war was your responsibility." She slowly rolled the unlit twig between her fingers and sighed. "As Loholt was mine."

"It occurred to me. Often." He swept an errant lock from her forehead and cupped her cheek. Her eyes shimmered with compassion. "I swear to you, Gyanhumara nic Hymar, Àrd-Banoigin of Clan Argyll, that I will protect our sons until my final heartbeat."

"Or daughters?"

Rejoicing to see the teasing twinkle return to her eyes, he nodded, praying that the Lord God Almighty would deliver the world from a daughter even half as feisty, strong-minded, and glorious as her mother.

Abbot Dafydd slowly approached them. Gyan motioned him closer. "For Caledonians, the act of honoring the dead is not complete until it is shared outside the immediate family."

"Bear ye one another's burdens." Dafydd inclined his head. "I am indeed honored to participate, Chieftainess."

She unpinned Urien's badge. "I shall make arrangements for an endowment to the monastery." Clutching her slipping cloak with one hand, she used the other to thrust the brooch toward an astonished Dafydd. "Please consider this my promise of payment."

"Payment?" asked the abbot.

"For your help, your wisdom, your prayers—but mostly because you continued to believe in me and *for* me until I could regain the volition to act in faith." She smiled faintly. "And in love."

As she dropped the brooch onto Dafydd's palm, she glanced slyly at Arthur. "Is that promotion is still available, Lord Pendragon?"

"Absolutely, Commander." With immeasurable pride, he retrieved the sapphire-eyed gold dragon from his pouch and pinned it in its rightful place. "Abbot Dafydd, you stand as witness to the elevation of

Commander Gyanhumara nic Hymar to the post of Comitissa Britanniam." As Arthur regarded her, everything else seemed to melt away. "Though you have always ruled my heart, Gyan, and always shall."

"And you mine," she murmured, her eyes misting.

Together, they lit a candle for Loholt. By tacit consent, they lit another candle for every pledge they repeated to each other. The combined brilliance bathed Gyan's face in a rosy glow. The radiance of her smile warmed Arthur's soul.

"You won't protect our children, Artyr." Her smile deepened as his eyebrows shot up. "But *we* will."

"Indeed, Gyan, we will."

He anticipated their reborn partnership with more joy than any treasure or accolade the world could possibly offer.

Explicit Liber Secundus

KDH, MMXIII
PSALM 30:5 (NIV), Soli Deo Gloria

Author's Notes

For my original thoughts regarding my historical approach, names, and whatnot, please refer to *Dawnflight*, either edition.

Morning's Journey is the first novel to have benefited from my work in expanding the idiomatic language employed throughout this series. I then went back and revised *Dawnflight* accordingly, prior to releasing the second edition. If I seem to have gone a bit overboard, ha, well, that's why the glossary is included here, with terms and place-names that apply to this text. Likewise, the appendix of people lists characters and, in many cases, updates to their descriptions, as applicable.

The sequel, *Raging Sea*, concentrates on Angusel's story as he hones his skills in the crucible of more of Arthur's battles and other events. According to some traditions, there were three Elaines in Lancelot's life. Thus far, I have introduced readers to two: Angusel's mother, Alayna, and one of his early mentors, Centurion Elian. Both characters return in the sequel, which also features the introduction of the third and most emotionally meaningful, Eileann, the "island" destined to become the serene center of Angusel's "raging sea."

People

ENTRY FORMAT:

Full Name (Pronunciation). Brief description, which may include rank, occupation, clan, country, nickname(s), name's origin and meaning, banner, and legendary name. Place-names and other affiliations are given in the person's native language.

Approximate pronunciation guidelines are supplied for the less obvious names, especially those of Scottish Gaelic and Brythonic origin. When in doubt, pronounce it however it makes sense to you.

Astute fans of the series may notice differences in pronunciations of some of the names from those given in *Dawnflight*. These differences represent updates in my research, based on working with the voice artist for *Dawnflight's* audiobook edition.

Accolon. Centurion in First Ala, Horse Cohort, Dragon Legion of Brydein; Urien's second-in-command and friend. Clan: Moray, Dalriada, Brydein. Legendary name: Sir Accolon.

Ælferd Wlencingsson. West Saxon prince. Son of Wlencing; nephew of Cissa; betrothed to Camilla. Banner: green griffin on gold.

Ælle (ALE-leh). King of the South Saxons. Father of Camilla. Banner: gold Woden's hammer and fist on black. Historically, he reigned in Sussex (the "South Saxons") from 477 until perhaps as late as 514, though no document officially recording his death exists.

Airc. Centurio Equo, Fifth Ala, Horse Cohort, Dragon Legion of Brydein. Clan: Argyll, Caledon. Name origin: Scottish Gaelic *àrc* ("cork").

Alain. Heir to the chieftainship of Clan Cwrnwyll of Rheged, Brydein. Husband of Yglais; Arthur's brother-in-law. Legendary name: King Alain Le Gros.

Alayna (ah-lah-EE-nah). Chieftainess and Àrd-Banoigin of Clan Alban, Caledon. Widow of Guilbach (Gwalchafed); Angusel's mother. Name origin: Scottish Gaelic *àlainn* ("beautiful, elegant, splendid").

Ambrosius Aurelius Constantinus. Late Dux Britanniarum. Elder brother of Uther; father of Merlin. Nickname: Emrys (EM-rees). Legendary name: Ambrosius.

Aneirin (ah-NAY-rin). Brytoni bard in the service of the chieftains of Clan Moray, based on the historical Aneirin, who probably lived about a hundred years later than the setting of this story and did compose a ballad about the historical Urien.

Angusel mac Alayna. Àrd-Oighre of Clan Alban, Caledon. Son of Alayna and Gwalchafed. Nickname: Angus. Name origin: inspired by Scottish Gaelic *an càs* ("the trying situation"), *sàl* ("sea"). Legendary name: Sir Lancelot du Lac.

Annamar ferch Gorlas. Daughter of Gorlas and Ygraine; Arthur's half-sister; wife of Loth of Clan Lothian; mother of Gawain, Gareth, Medraut, and Cundre. Clan: Cwrnwyll, Rheged, Brydein. Legendary name: Queen Margause.

Antoninus Pius. Second-century A.D. Roman emperor, of the Aurelii family, who ordered the construction of the Antonine Wall in Britain.

Aonar. A name Angusel gives himself, based on events in this story. Name origin: Scottish Gaelic *aonar* ("alone").

Arthur map Uther, a.k.a. Arturus Aurelius Vetarus, a.k.a. Artyr mac Ygrayna. The Pendragon, Dux Britanniarum (succeeded Uther). Àrd-Ceoigin of Clan Argyll, Caledon. Son of Uther and Ygraine; husband of Gyanhumara; father of Loholt. Clan: Cwrnwyll, Brydein. Nickname: Artyr. Banner: scarlet dragon rampant on gold. Legendary name: King Arthur Pendragon.

Arturus Aurelius Vetarus. See Arthur. Latin name loosely based on the ancient Roman format and in this story means "Arthur of the

Aurelii, son of Uther." After Abar-Gleann, some of his officers suggested that he add "Caledonius" ("Conqueror of Caledonia") to his string, in grand old Roman tradition, but he declined.

Artyr mac Ygrayna (ar-TEER). See Arthur. Caledonaiche matronymic name format meaning "Arthur, son of Ygraine." Name origin: Scottish Gaelic *ar tir* ("our country").

Badulf Colgrimsson. Angli prince. Son of King Colgrim.

Bann. Chieftain of Clan Lammor of Gododdin, Brydein. Father of Bedwyr.

Bedwyr (BAYD-veer) map Bann. Highest-ranking officer of the Brytoni fleet. Son of Chieftain Bann. Clan: Lammor, Gododdin, Brydein. Legendary name: Sir Bedivere.

Boudicca. First-century A.D. queen of the Iceni tribe in southern Britain famous for leading the rebellion against the Roman occupying forces that fell one battle short of Emperor Nero withdrawing all Roman troops from Britain.

Bryalla. Maidservant at Arbroch. Clan: Argyll, Caledon.

Byrn mac Lorana. Late Chieftain and Àrd-Ceoigin of Clan Argyll. Hymar's first consort; Peredur's father.

Caius Marcellus Ectorius. General (legate) in the Brytoni army, Camboglanna garrison commander. Son of Ectorius; Arthur's foster brother. Nickname: Cai. Legendary name: Sir Kay the Seneschal.

Calpurnia. Wife of Ectorius; mother of Cai, foster mother of Arthur. Distantly descended from the ancient patrician Roman Calpurnii family.

Camilla Ællesdottr. South Saxon princess. Daughter of King Ælle; betrothed to Ælferd.

Cato. Decurion in First Ala, Horse Cohort, Dragon Legion of Brydein. Clan: Moray, Dalriada, Brydein.

Cissa (KEE-sah). King of the West Saxons. Ælferd's uncle. Banner: white horse crowned on purple. Historically, Cissa probably was King of the South Saxons, ruling jointly with Ælle until Ælle's death, though no reliable Saxon monarch genealogy exists, and titles and territories may have been more than a little bit fluid.

Claudius. Soldier in the Brytoni army stationed at Tanroc.

Cleopatra. Cleopatra VII Philopator, of Greek ancestry and the last pharaoh of Egypt; she ruled during the mid-1st century B.C.

Colgrim. King of the Angles. Banner: crimson eagle on white.

Commodus. Roman emperor who succeeded his father, Marcus Aurelius, in the late 2nd century A.D.—and didn't inherit his father's wisdom or pragmatism.

Conall. Centurion, second-in-command at Tanroc garrison, Manx Cohort, Dragon Legion of Brydein. Clan: Argyll, Caledon.

Cuchullain (ku-CUL-len) og Conchobar. Laird of the Scáthaichean of Eireann (succeeded Conchobar). Son of Conchobar; husband of Dierda. Nickname: Cucu. Banner: silver wolf running, on pine-green. Legendary name: Cú Chulainn.

Cundre ferch Loth. Daughter of Annamar and Loth; Arthur's niece. Clan: Lothian, Gododdin, Brydein. Legendary name: Kundry.

Cynda (KEEN-dah). Gyanhumara's maidservant, confidante. Clan: Argyll, Caledon.

Dafydd (DAH-veeth) the Elder. Monk at St. Padraic's Monastery. Katra's husband; father of Dafydd the Younger. Name origin: Brythonic variant of the name David.

Dafydd (DAH-veeth) the Younger. Son of Dafydd the Elder. Name origin: Brythonic variant of the name David.

Denu. Brytoni fisherman. Clan: Moray, Dalriada, Brydein. Name origin: Welsh *denu* ("attract").

Dileas (DIE-lay-ahs). Caledonach courier (rank: optio) in the Brytoni army. Name origin: Scottish Gaelic *dìleas* ("faithful").

Dorcas. Nun and healer living at Caer Lugubalion.

Dumarec. Chieftain of Clan Moray of Dalriada, Brydein. Urien's father. Banner: black boar's head on gold.

Dwras map Gwyn, a.k.a. Dwras Gwyn Peldyr (Brytonic, "Dwras White Spear"). Brytoni farmer. Son of Gwyn; husband of Talya; father of Gwydion. Clan: Lothian, Gododdin, Brydein.

Ectorius. Late general (legate) in the Brytoni army. Father of Cai;

foster father of Arthur. Legendary name: Sir Ector.

Galen of Pergamum. Roman physician of Greek origin who practiced in the court of Emperor Marcus Aurelius in the 2nd century A.D. His research and methodologies greatly advanced knowledge in the fields of anatomy, physiology, pathology, pharmacology, and neurology, and it's estimated that as much as 80% of his writings remain valid by modern standards.

Ganora. See Gyanhumara. This is one of many variants of "Guinevere" found in ancient literature; others include Vanora and Wander. In this story, "Ganora" is a mistaken pronunciation of "Gyanhumara."

Gareth map Loth. Heir to the chieftainship of Clan Lothian. Second son of Loth and Annamar; Arthur's nephew. Clan: Lothian, Gododdin, Brydein. Legendary name: Sir Gareth.

Gawain map Loth. Foot soldier in the Brytoni army. Firstborn son of Loth and Annamar; Arthur's nephew. Clan: Lothian, Gododdin, Brydein. Legendary name: Sir Gawain.

Gereint map Erbin. Prefect of the Badger Cohort (Praefectus Cohortis Meles), Dragon Legion of Brydein; commander of the occupation force at Senaudon. Son of Erbin. Legendary name: Sir Geraint.

Gideon. Hebrew general who destroyed a Midianite encampment of thousands of men using only 300 warriors hand-selected for the way they drank water at a stream. Biblical reference: Judges 7.

Gorlas. Late Chieftain of Clan Cwrnwyll of Rheged, Brydein. Ygraine's first husband; father of Annamar and Yglais. Legendary name: Duke Gorlois of Cornwall.

Guenevara. See Gyanhumara. Name origin: Angli/Saxon variant of Gwenhwyfar.

Guilbach (GOOL-bahk). Late Chieftain and Àrd-Ceoigin of Clan Alban, Caledon. Alayna's consort; Angusel's father. Clan: Tarsuinn, Caledon. Nickname: Gwalchafed. Name origin: Scottish Gaelic *guilbneach* ("curlew").

Gwalchafed (GWAHL-kah-vehd). See Guilbach. Nickname bestowed on Guilbach by Uther the Pendragon honoring his battle prowess. Name origin: Brythonic *gwalchafed* ("summer falcon").

Gwydion. Son of Dwras. Clan: Lothian, Gododdin, Brydein.

Gyanhumara (ghee-ahn-huh-MAR-ah) nic Hymar, a.k.a. Gwenhwyfar ferch Gogfran, a.k.a. Guenevara. Chieftainess and Àrd-Banoigin of Clan Argyll of Caledon. Daughter of Hymar and Ogryvan; wife of Arthur; mother of Loholt. Nickname: Gyan (GHEE-ahn). Banner: two silver doves flying, on dark blue. Name origin: Scottish Gaelic *gainne amhran* ("rarest song"). Legendary names: Queen Guinevere, Guenevere, Guenever.

Hippocrates of Cos. Greek physician who lived in the 5th-4th centuries B.C., widely considered the father of Western medicine.

Horace. Quintus Horatius Flaccus, a 1st-century, B.C. Roman poet.

Hymar (HEE-mar). Late Chieftainess and Àrd-Banoigin of Clan Argyll, Caledon. Ogryvan's wife; mother of Peredur and Gyanhumara. Name origin: Scottish Gaelic *amhran* ("song").

Iesseu (ee-ay-SAY-oo). Caledonaiche variant of Jesus.

Iesu (YAY-soo). Brytonic variant of Jesus.

Iomar mac Morra. Àrd-Oighre of Clan Rioghail, Caledon. Son of Morra; Ogryvan's cousin. Name origin: Scottish Gaelic *iomair* ("to row").

Iulius Caesar. Roman Emperor Gaius Julius Caesar, best known to Caledonians as having ordered a failed invasion of Caledonia in the 1st century B.C., though he managed to subjugate the rest of Brydein into the Roman Empire (Britannia Province).

Katra. Brytoni freedwoman. Wife of Dafydd the Elder; mother of Mari, Dafydd the Younger, and Samsen.

Liam. Brytoni farmer. Clan: Cwrnwyll, Rheged, Brydein.

Lir. Abbot of St. Padraic's Monastery; Keeper of the Chalice.

Livy. Titus Livius Patavinus, a turn-of-the-millennium Roman historian most famous for his books about the several-hundred-year history of the Roman pre-republic, republic, and empire, collectively titled *Ab urbe condita libri* ("Books since the city's founding" or, less literally but more descriptively, "A History of Rome").

Loholt mac Artyr. Àrd-Oighre of Clan Argyll, Caledon. Firstborn son of Arthur and Gyanhumara. Name origin: Scottish Gaelic *lo h-oillt* ("for terror").

Loth. Chieftain of Clan Lothian of Gododdin, Brydein. Arthur's brother-in-law; Annamar's husband; father of Gawain, Gareth, Medraut, and Cundre. Banner: amber bear on forest green. Legendary name: King Lot.

Lucan. Monk and teacher at St. Padraic's Monastery. Latin name: Lucianus.

Lucius. Decurion in First Ala, Horse Cohort, Dragon Legion of Brydein. Clan: Moray, Dalriada, Brydein.

Lucius Arturus Castus. Roman centurion stationed in northern Brydein in the mid-fifth century whose military record was impressive enough that Uther appropriated the man's middle name for his son even though he was not a blood relation.

Lucius Aurelius Verus. Brother of Emperor Marcus Aurelius who ruled as coemperor in the late 2nd century A.D.; a.k.a. Lucius Vero.

Lughann (LOO-ahn, Scotti, "Lugh's Man"). Scáthaichean slave at Caer Lugubalion, a warrior captured during the First Battle of Port Dhoo-Glass.

Marcus. Centurion in the Brytoni army; Arthur's aide-de-camp. Legendary name: King Mark.

Marcus Aurelius. Roman emperor who ruled in the latter half of the second century A.D.—and one of the few of that club who wasn't a raving megalomaniac.

Mardha (MAHR-ah). Maidservant at Arbroch. Clan: Argyll, Caledon.

Mari. Late daughter of Dafydd the Elder and Katra.

Mathan. Horseman assigned to Fifth Ala, Horse Cohort, Dragon Legion of Brydein. Clan: Argyll, Caledon. Name origin: Scottish Gaelic *mathan* ("a bear").

Medraut map Loth. Third son of Loth and Annamar; Arthur's nephew. Clan: Lothian, Gododdin, Brydein. Legendary names: Sir Mordred, Modred.

Merlinus Aurelius Ambrosius Dubricius. Bishop; general (legate) in the Brytoni army, garrison commander of Caer Lugubalion. Son of Ambrosius; Arthur's cousin. Nickname: Merlin. Latin name is loosely based on Roman format and means "Merlin of the Aurelii, son of Ambrose, called Dubric." Known in Welsh ecclesiastical history as St. Dubric (or St. Dyfrig, depending upon the source). Legendary name: Merlin.

Morghe (MOR-ghee) ferch Uther. Daughter of Uther and Ygraine; Arthur's younger sister; betrothed to Urien. Latin name: Morganna Aurelia Vetara. Legendary name: Queen Morgan Le Fay.

Morra. Chieftainess and Àrd-Banoigin of Clan Rioghail, Caledon. Ogryvan's second cousin; mother of Iomar. Name origin: derived from Scottish Gaelic *móire* ("bag" of *pioba-móire* ("bagpipe")).

Niall. Late Scáthaichean general, killed by Gyanhumara in the First Battle of Port Dhoo-Glass.

Niniane. Prioress of Rushen Priory. Legendary names: Niniane, Nimue, Lady of the Lake.

Ogryvan (OH-gree-van) mac Glynnis. Chieftain of Clan Argyll, Caledon. Hymar's consort; Peredur's stepfather; Gyanhumara's father. Nickname: "the Ogre." Legendary name: King Leodegrance.

Owen. Brytoni farmer. Clan: Cwrnwyll, Rheged, Brydein.

Padraic, Saint. Founder of the monastery on Saint Padraic's Isle; patron saint of Ireland (a.k.a. St. Patrick, St. Paddy).

Paul, Apostle. Paul (formerly Saul) of Tarsus, Christian missionary in the 1st century A.D.

Peredur mac Hymar. Centurio Equo, Seventh Ala, Horse Cohort, Dragon Legion of Brydein. Hymar's son; Ogryvan's stepson; Gyanhumara's half-brother. Clan: Argyll, Caledon. Nickname: Per. Name origin: Scottish Gaelic *pòr dùr* ("stubborn seed"). Legendary name: Sir Percival.

Quintus. Late monk at Saint Padraic's Monastery. Name origin: Latin *quintus* ("fifth"), a common naming convention among Roman families indicating, in this case, the fifth male child born to the same parents.

Reuel. Seannachaidh of Clan Argyll, Caledon; preserver of law and lore. Name origin: Second "R" of J.R.R. Tolkien.

Rhys (HREES). Centurion, second-in-command at Port Dhoo-Glass garrison, Manx Cohort, Dragon Legion of Brydein. Clan: Argyll, Caledon.

Riothamus. Late Franco-Brytoni warlord who governed Armorica and possibly a portion of southern Britain in the mid-fifth century. Some scholars identify him with Ambrosius or even Arthur, citing the fact that his name in Brythonic means "high king" (*rigotamos*). By that logic, every man named Richard (an inversion of Scottish Gaelic *àrd rìgh*, "high king") also would be in contention for a crown.

Rudd (ROOTH). Former Brytoni slave at Arbroch.

Samsen. Late infant son of Dafydd the Elder.

Seumas (SHAYoo-mahs). Caledonach warrior; Ogryvan's most trusted bodyguard. Clan: Argyll, Caledon. Name origin: Scottish Gaelic *Seumas* ("James").

Sichuan. Brytoni warrior, one of Morghe's escort whom she'd brought to Arbroch from Caerlaverock. Clan: Cwrnwyll, Rheged, Brydein.

Stefan. Brytoni monk and master of students and the library at St. Padriac's Monastery. Latin name: Stephanus.

Suetonius. Gaius Suetonius Tranquillus, a late-1st- to early-2nd-century A.D. Roman historian best known for his collection of works titled *De Vita Caesarum*, "Of the lives of the Caesars," biographies of the twelve consecutive Roman rulers beginning with Julius Caesar.

Talya. Wife of Dwras; mother of Gwydion. Clan: Lothian, Gododdin, Brydein. Name origin: Brythonic *tal* ("bright").

Tira. Brytoni slave who chose to remain at Arbroch after being granted her freedom; Loholt's wet nurse.

Torr. Caledonach warrior. Clan: Argyll, Caledon. Name origin: Scottish Gaelic *tòrr* ("conical hill"). Legendary names: Sir Tor, Sir Torre.

Ulfyn. Centurion, First Century, Badger Cohort, Dragon Legion of Brydein; Gereint's second-in-command. Legendary name: Sir Ulfin.

Urien map Dumarec. Prefect of the Horse Cohort, Dragon Legion of Brydein. Son of Dumarec; betrothed to Morghe. Clan: Moray, Dalriada, Brydein. Legendary names: King Urien, Uriens.

Uther map Custennin. Late Dux Britanniarum (succeeded Ambrosius). Ambrosius's younger brother; Ygraine's second husband; father of Arthur and Morghe. Latin name: Vetarus Aurelius Constantinus. Legendary name: King Uther Pendragon.

Vennolandua. Ancient and possibly mythical Queen of Cornwall, wife of King Locrin—whom she killed in battle after he divorced her in favor of a mistress. Vennolandua proceeded to rule Cornwall as queen until her son came of age.

Vergul. Priest of Clan Argyll, Caledon.

Vortigern. Late Brytoni warlord who employed Saxon mercenaries against the Caledonians and Scots.

Willa (WEE-thlah). Nun at Rushen Priory.

Wlencing. Late West Saxon prince. Younger brother of Cissa; father of Ælferd. Historically, Cissa, Wlencing, and Cymen appear to have been sons of Ælle, though the latter two men rarely appear in Arthurian tradition.

Ygraine (ee-GRAY-neh). Chieftainess of Clan Cwrnwyll of Rheged, Brydein. Widow of Gorlas; widow of Uther; mother of Annamar, Yglais, Arthur, and Morghe. Nickname: Ygrayna. Banner: ivory unicorn on crimson. Legendary name: Queen Igraine.

Ygrayna (ee-grayEE-nah). Caledonaiche variant of Ygraine. Name origin: Scottish Gaelic *a'ghrian* ("the sun").

Glossary

THIS APPENDIX INCLUDES place-names and foreign terms. Pronunciation guidelines are supplied for the less obvious terms, especially those of Brythonic or Scottish Gaelic origin. In the case of a term having multiple translations used in the text, the most commonly referenced term is listed first. Word and phrase origins and English translations are given wherever possible.

My choices of word selection, translation, spelling, suggested pronunciation, and the use of accent marks reflect an attempt to imply a "proto-language" to today's version, especially with regard to the Scottish-Gaelic-based words, compounds, and phrases. Terms identified as having a Pictish source are based on studies of Scottish place-names, since there are no known documents that were written in ancient Pictish. Brythonic-sourced words are derived from ancient Welsh literature, such as the *Mabinogion*.

Astute fans of the series may notice differences in spellings or pronunciations of some of the terms from those given in *Dawnflight*. These differences represent updates in my research.

Abar-Bhàis (Caledonaiche, "Mouth of the River of Death"). Site of the Angli attack on Arthur and Gyanhumara's traveling camp while she was pregnant with Loholt. The name is selected to evoke the "River Bassas," site of the sixth of twelve battles traditionally ascribed to Arthur in the 9th-century *Historia Brittonum*, which I moved up to 4th for the purposes of *Morning's Journey*. Origin: proto-Celtic/Pictish *abar* ("river mouth"), Scottish Gaelic *a'bhàis* ("of death").

Abar-Gleann (Caledonaiche, "Mouth of the River Valley"). Site of Arthur's first battle as Dux Britanniarum, where he defeated the Caledonians, located at the eastern end of the Antonine Wall on the south bank of the Firth of Forth near the present-day town of Bo'ness, Falkirk, Scotland. This equates to the first of Arthur's twelve battles, the "mouth of the River Glein," recorded in Chapter 56 of the *Historia Brittonum* (written in the early 9th century). Origin: proto-Celtic/Pictish *abar* ("river mouth"), Scottish Gaelic *gleann* ("valley").

Aconitum. A poisonous plant. Origin: Greek *akonitos* ("without dust; without struggle").

Add (ATH) Valley. Lands surrounding the River Add near Dunadd.

Adversary, the. Euphemism for Caledonach demon overlord, Annàm, and Satan; see also Ha'satan.

Ærish (AIR-ish; Eingel/Saxon, "Brazen Ones"). Origin: inspired by Old Anglo-Saxon *æren* ("brazen").

1. Of or pertaining to the inhabitants of the western portion of the island Latin-speakers call Hibernia; i.e., the Scots (Irish).

2. Name applied to the body of water between Æren (Hibernia) and Brædæn (Brydein); i.e., the Irish Sea.

Ainm (ah-EEM; Caledonaiche, "name"). Used as part of the sign-countersign codes in the Manx Cohort. This challenge is usually given to determine friend-or-foe status; the correct response is rank, name, and unit designation as listed on the duty roster. Origin: Scottish Gaelic.

Ala (pl. alae; Latin, "wing(s)"). Cavalry unit usually consisting of five turmae, commanded by a centurio equo.

Alban ("The Wild People"), Clan. Caledonaiche: *Albainaich Chaledon* (poss. *h'Albainaich*; "of Clan Alban"). Member of the Caledonach Confederacy. The clan's name tracks to the ancient name for Scotland and is deliberately evocative of an alternate legendary name for Arthur's realm, "Albion." Banner: rampant white lion on cerulean blue. Cloak pattern: sky blue crossed with crimson and green. Gemstone: aquamarine. Name origin: inspired by Scottish Gaelic *am bàn* ("untilled") and *Albainn* ("Alba," "Scotland").

Àmbholc (AY-mulk; Caledonaiche, "Time of Spring"). Brytonic: *Imbolc*. Winter ritual celebrated by non-Christian Caledonians and Brytons on February 1. Joinings taking place on Àmbholc night can be nullified the following Àmbholc with no shame clinging to either person. Caledonaiche name origin: Scottish Gaelic *àm* ("time"), *bòlc* ("to spring").

A'mi (Caledonaiche, "to me"). Exclamation used in battle to regroup forces. Origin: Scottish Gaelic.

Anderida (Latin). Saxon: *Anderceaster*. Brytoni-controlled port on the Narrow Sea near the present-day town of Pevensey, East Sussex, England.

Angalaranach (poss. Anghalaranach, pl. Angalaranaich, poss. pl. Anghalarannaich; Caledonaiche, "(of the) Diseased People"). Unflattering terms the Caledonaich apply to the Angli people. Origin: Scottish Gaelic *an galar* ("the disease"), *a'ghalar* ("of the disease").

Angle(s) (Brytonic). Name applied to one or more inhabitants of the eastern coast of Brydein.

Angli (Latin). Of or pertaining to the inhabitants of the eastern coast of Brydein.

Annàm (ahn-NAIM), Lord. Caledonach demon overlord; a.k.a. "the Adversary." Annaomh's twin brother; leader of the evil Samhraidhean of the Otherworld, symbolized by a pair of crossed bloody cudgels. Name origin: Scottish Gaelic *an nàmh* ("the enemy").

Annaomh (AHN-nuh), Lord. Caledonach supreme deity; ruler of the Otherworld and leader of the Army of the Blest, symbolized by the sun. In Caledonach mythology, his evil twin brother is Annàm. Name origin: Scottish Gaelic *an naomh* ("the saint").

Antonine Wall, the. Latin: *Antoninorum murum*. Caledonaiche: *Am Balla Tuat* ("The North Wall"). Frontier fortification built in southern Scotland by Roman Emperor Antoninus Pius in the mid-second century A.D. Extends from the Firth of Forth to the Firth of Clyde.

Aonar (EYE-nar, Caledonaiche). "Alone." Origin: Scottish Gaelic.

Arbroch (Caledonaiche, "Exalted Town"). Brytonic: *Ardoca*. Latin: *Alauna Veniconum*. Seat of Clan Argyll and home fortress of Gyanhumara and Ogryvan; Roman fort captured in 1st century A.D.

by the Caledonaich, located near the present-day village of Braco in Perthshire, Scotland. Caledonaiche origin: Scottish Gaelic *àrd* ("exalted"), *broch* ("burgh").

Àrd-banoigin (aird-ban-UH-ghin; pl. àrd-banoigainn; Caledonaiche, "exalted heir-bearer(s)"). The female member of the ruling family through whom the clan's line of succession is determined. Typically, the clan's chieftainess serves as àrd-banoigin while she is of childbearing age and passes this status to a daughter or niece when the younger woman reaches physical maturity. Origin: Scottish Gaelic *àrd* ("exalted"), *ban* ("woman"), *oighre* ("heir"), *gin* ("beget").

Àrd-Ceann Teine-Beathach Mór (aird-KAY-ahn TEE-neh BAYah-tahk more; Caledonaiche, "High-Chief Great Fire-Beast"). Since Caledonaiche has no word for "dragon," this is the closest that the Caledonaich can come to rendering "Pendragon" in their language. Usually, they don't bother. Origin: Scottish Gaelic *ceannard* ("leader;" I switched the suffix to a prefix for consistency with other invented terms), *teine* ("fire"), *beathach* ("beast"), *mór* ("great"). There is no word for "dragon" in Scottish Gaelic, either.

Àrd-ceoigin (aird-kayUH-ghin; pl. àrd-ceoiginich; Caledonaiche, "exalted heir-begetter(s)"). The consort of the clan's àrd-banoigin. Marrying the àrd-banoigin gives the man access to her wealth but does not automatically grant him the chieftainship of her clan. Modern analogy: Queen Elizabeth II's husband, Prince Phillip. Origin: Scottish Gaelic *àrd* ("exalted"), *céile* ("husband"), *oighre* ("heir"), *gin* ("beget").

Àrd-oighre (aird-OOreh; pl. àrd-oighreachan; Caledonaiche, "exalted heir(s)"). The male heir of the àrd-banoigin and àrd-ceoigin. The àrd-oighre may serve as clan chieftain in the event that the àrd-ceoigin is dead or incapacitated, upon ratification of a vote by the clan's elders and the chieftainess. Origin: Scottish Gaelic *àrd* ("exalted"), *oighre* ("heir").

Argyll (AR-gayeel; "The Tempestuous People"), Clan. Caledonaiche: *Argaillanaich Chaledon* (poss. *h'Argaillanaich*; "of Clan Argyll"). Member of the Caledonach Confederacy. The clan's name tracks to the former County of Argyll, Scotland, though at this point in the story, the clan hasn't yet expanded in that direction. Banner: two silver mourning doves in flight, on dark blue. Cloak pattern: dark blue crossed with saffron and scarlet. Gemstone: sapphire. Name origin: Scottish Gaelic *ar gailleann* ("our tempest").

Armorica (Latin). Brytoni-settled region of Brittany, France.

Astarte. Morghe's black mare, named for the Eastern Mediterranean fertility goddess from which Easter derives its name. Origin: Greek *aster* ("star").

Attacot(s) (Latin). Scáthaichean: *Aítachait.* Name applied to one or more inhabitants of the western portion of Eireann.

Attacotti (Latin). Scáthaichean: *Aítachasan.* Of or pertaining to the inhabitants of the western portion of Eireann.

Aurelia (pl. Aurelii; Latin). One of the original Roman patrician families; its progeny includes 2nd-century A.D. Roman emperors Antoninus Pius and Marcus Aurelius, and in this story, Ambrosius Aurelius Constantinus, Merlinus Aurelius Ambrosius Dubricius, Vetarus Aurelius Constantinus, Arturus Aurelius Vetarus, and Morganna Aurelia Vetara.

Ave (Latin, "hail"). Commonly used as a greeting, or as an invitation for someone to enter a room.

Badge. Rank insignia worn by members of the Brytoni army: a cloak-pin fashioned in the shape of the legion's symbol (e.g., dragon). Enlistees' badges are bone or hardwood. Officers' badges are wrought of different metals depending on rank and are ringed by green (infantry), red (cavalry), or blue (navy) enamel, or a combination thereof, to indicate breadth of command. If the officer is of the nobility, the badge includes a gemstone representing the clan's dominant color.

Badger Cohort. Latin: *Cohortis Meles.* Unit in the Brytoni army occupying Senaudon.

Banasròn (BANas-rone; Caledonaiche, "woman's head"). Euphemism for female genitalia. Origin: Scottish Gaelic *ban* ("woman"), *sròn* ("headland").

Bannock. Small, hard cake made from barley or oat meal and cooked on an open griddle.

Bear of Lothian, the. Symbol of Clan Lothian of Gododdin, a rampant amber bear on forest green. Also called the Lothian Bear and the Amber Bear.

Beathach (BAYah-tach; Caledonaiche, "beast"). Origin: Scottish Gaelic.

1. An element of the Caledonaiche term for "Pendragon," *Àrd-Ceann Teine-<u>Beathach</u> Mór.*

2. An epithet often used affectionately.

Belteine (bel-TEE-neh; pl. Beltean; Caledonaiche, "Passion Fire"). Brytonic: *Beltain*. Fertility ritual celebrated by non-Christian Caledonaich and Breatanaich culminating on May 1 with firelight activities that would make a Ròmanach orgy participant blush. Caledonaiche name origin: Scottish Gaelic *boil* ("passion"), *teine* ("fire").

Bernicia (Latin). Brytonic: *Brynaich*. Coastal Angli-controlled territory east of Gododdin.

Berwych (Old English, "Barley Farmstead"). Caledonaiche: *Bearruig* ("Pursuit to the Precipice"). Angli-controlled fortress on the border of Gododdin, corresponding to present-day North Berwick Law conical hill in East Lothian, Scotland. Caledonaiche name implies something along the lines of "last-ditch defense" and is inspired by Scottish Gaelic *Bearruig* ("Berwick"), *bearradh* ("precipice"), *ruaig* ("a pursuit", "defeat").

Betony. Medicinal herb.

Betrothal-band, -mark. Caledonaiche: *lorg a'bhanais-geall* (fem., "mark of the betrothal;" m., *aileadh a'bhanais-geall*). A tattoo roughly one inch wide, depicting two ropes braided together, usually painted with dye extracted from the woad plant. By Caledonach custom, this mark is inscribed around the left wrist of the àrd-banoigin and her future consort as a visible display of their promises. Origin: Scottish Gaelic *lorg* ("mark," fem.), *aileadh* ("mark" or "scar," m.).

Bian-sporan (Caledonaiche, "pelt-purse"). The accessory crafted from an animal's pelt collected during the deuchainn na fala rite, symbolizing a young warrior's passage into adulthood. Origin: Scottish Gaelic *bian* ("animal skin"), *sporan* ("purse").

Boar of Moray, the.

1. Symbol of Clan Moray of Dalriada, a black boar on a field of gold; also referred to as "the Black Boar."

2. Nickname of Urien map Dumarec.

Bonding ritual. Caledonaiche: *dean am bann naomh* ("make the holy bond"). The Caledonach ceremony wherein the àrd-banoigin is tattooed with her consort's clan-mark and he with hers. Origin: Scottish Gaelic *dean* ("to make"), *am bann* ("the bond"), *naomh* ("holy").

Brædæn (BRAY-dane; Eingel/Saxon). Brydein. Origin: inspired by Old Anglo-Saxon *brædan* ("to extend"), with the modified second syllable to distinguish it from "Brædan."

Brædan (BRAY-dan; Eingel/Saxon). Of or pertaining to the Brytoni inhabitants of Brydein. Origin: Old Anglo-Saxon *brædan* ("to extend").

Bræde (BRAYD-eh; pl. Brædeas, Eingel/Saxon, "roasted meat(s)"). Slang terms the Angli and Saxons apply to one or more Brytons. Origin: Old Anglo-Saxon.

Braonshaffir (Caledonaiche, "A Drop of Sapphire"). Gyanhumara's sword, named for its distinguishing feature. Name origin: Scottish Gaelic *braon* ("a drop"), *shaffir* ("of sapphire," transliterated from Latin *sapphirus* and rendered with possessive form (*sh-*)).

Breatan (BRAYah-tan; poss. Bhreatan; Caledonaiche, "(of the) Bryton"). Terms used by the Caledonaich to refer to a single Brytoni individual; also may be translated as "(of the) Deceiver." Origin: Scottish Gaelic *Breatunn* ("Britain" and "British"), *bràth* ("to deceive").

Breatanach (brayah-TAHN-ach; poss. Bhreatanach, pl. Breatanaich, poss. pl. Bhreatanaich; Caledonaiche, "(of the) Bryton(s)"). Terms used by the Caledonaich to refer to one or more inhabitants of western and mid-Brydein; also may be translated as "(of the) Deceiver(s)." Origin: Scottish Gaelic *Breatunnach* ("a Briton"), *bràth* ("to deceive").

Breatanaiche (brayah-tahn-EESH; Caledonaiche, "tongue of the Brytons"). Term used by the Caledonaich to refer to the Brytonic language.

Brigid. A deerhound bitch belonging to Loth and Annamar, named in honor of the Brytoni hearth-goddess.

Brydein (Brytonic). Latin: *Britannia*. Caledonaiche: *Breatein* (poss. *Bhreatein*, "(of) Brydein"). Britain, a.k.a. the Island of the Mighty.

Bryton(s). Name applied to one or more inhabitants of western and mid-Brydein.

Brytoni. Of or pertaining to the inhabitants of western and mid-Brydein.

Brytonic. The native language of the Brytons, also known as "Brythonic" or *P-Celtic* in present-day anthropological usage.

Buill-coise (bool KWEES-eh, Caledonaiche, "ball-feet"). Football; i.e., soccer. In this era, the ball is an inflated goat or sheep stomach. The only time the game is played with a human head is in the case of a warrior failing to have his Oath of Fealty accepted by the one to whom he attempted to swear the oath. Origin: Scottish Gaelic *buill* ("ball"), *coise* ("feet").

Caer Lugubalion (Brytonic, "Fort of Lugh's Strength"). Latin: *Luguvalium* ("Lugh's Valley"). Caledonaiche: *Dùn Lùth Lhugh* (doon LOOT hloo, "Fort of Lugh's Power"). Brytoni-controlled fortress near the western end of Hadrian's Wall, headquarters of the Dragon Legion of Brydein, located in what is now Carlisle, Cumbria, England. Caledonaiche name origin: Scottish Gaelic *dùn* ("fortress"), *lùths* ("power"), and my invented possessive form of the name Lugh, *Lhugh*.

Caer Rushen (Brytonic, "Rush's Fort"). Brytoni-controlled fortress near the southernmost tip of the Isle of Maun, located in present-day Castletown, Isle of Man.

Caerglas (Brytonic, "Green Fort"). Caledonaiche: *Dùn Ghlas* ("Locked Fort"). Brytoni-controlled fortress on the western end of the Antonine Wall that doubles as a garrison and headquarters of the Brytoni fleet, located in present-day Glasgow, Scotland. Caledonaiche name origin: Scottish Gaelic *dùn* ("fortress"), *ghlas* ("locked").

Caerlaverock (Brytonic). Caledonaiche: *Dùn Càrnhuilean* ("Fort of the Rock-Elbows"). Roman-fortified and Brytoni-controlled hill-fort and seat of Clan Cwrnwyll, located on the northern bank of the Solway Firth in southwestern Scotland, due south of present-day Dumfries. Site of Arthur's birth; Ygraine's home fortress. Triangular Caerlaverock Castle was built atop its ruins in the 13th century; hence my inspiration for the "rock-elbows" Caledonaiche designation. Caledonaiche name origin: Scottish Gaelic *dùn* ("fortress"), *càrn* ("rock pile"), *na h'uilean* ("of the elbows").

Caleberyllus (Latin, "Burning Jewel"). Arthur's sword, known through various sources as Caliburnus, Caliburn, Caledfwlch, and Excalibur. This name is my invention, derived from the Latin words *calere* (heat, origin of "calorie") and *beryllus* (beryl, a classification of gem) as a poetic description of the sword's distinguishing feature. Technically, a ruby is a cabochon, not a beryl, but I suspect that nobody was making that fine a distinction in the 5th century A.D.

Caledon (poss. Chaledon; Caledonaiche, "(of the) Place of the Hard People"). The name the Caledonaich apply to their territory, encompassing what is now the Scottish Highlands and northern Lowlands. Origin: Pictish/proto-Celtic *caled* ("hard").

Caledonach ("Caledonian"), Caledonaich ("Caledonians" and "The Hard People"), Caledonaiche ("Caledonian language"), Chaledonach ("Caledonian's" or "of the Caledonian"), Chaledonaich ("Caledonians'" or "of the Caledonians"). Idiomatic terms of my own invention, based on Scottish Gaelic linguistic rules for indicating group membership (*-ach* (sing.) and *-aich* (pl.) suffixes), and the possessive form (*Ch-* prefix). Language designation (*-aiche* suffix) is my own invention.

Caledonach Confederacy, Caledonian Confederacy. Caledonaiche: *Na Cairdean Caledonach* ("The Caledonian Friends"). Caledonach political entity. Member-clans mainly consist of those living closest to Breatanach-controlled territories. Historically, the region of Caledonia may have been divided into seven major kingdoms, each with many client-kingdoms, and it most likely wasn't a united nation. Caledonaiche name origin: Scottish Gaelic *na cairdean* ("the friends"), plus my invented term, *Caledonach* ("Caledonian").

Caledonach law, Caledonian law. Caledonaiche: *Sgianan na Chaledonaich* ("Laws of the Caledonians"). Unwritten code memorized and recited by seannachaidhean, and administered by priests. Caledonaiche phrase origin: Scottish Gaelic *sgianan* ("knives"), plus my invented term, *Chaledonaich* ("of the Caledonians"). Although there is a word in Scottish Gaelic meaning "law" (*dlighe*), I opted for a more poetic approach.

Caledonia (Latin). The name that Latin- and Brytonic-speakers apply to the home of the Caledonaich, the region encompassing what is now the Scottish Highlands and northern Lowlands.

Caledonian(s). Of or pertaining to the inhabitants of the nation of Caledonia, terms used by Latin- and Brytonic-speakers.

Calends. The first day of any month on the Roman calendar—and the origin of the word "calendar." Origin: Latin *kalendae* ("the called").

Camboglanna (Brytonic, "Crooked Bank"). Fortress near the western end of Hadrian's wall, built on a high bluff overlooking the Cambog (Cambeck) Valley, located in present-day Castlesteads, Cumbria, England.

Caraid (Caledonaiche, "friend"). Used as part of the sign-countersign codes in the Manx Cohort. This response is usually given to indicate friend-status to the other party. Origin: Scottish Gaelic.

Càrnhuilean (cairn-WHEEDL-ayan; Caledonaiche, "The Rock-Elbows People"), Clan. Caledonaiche term for Clan Cwrnwyll of Rheged, Brydein. Full Caledonaiche designation: *Càrnhuileanaich Rhiogachd Bhreatein*. Name origin: Scottish Gaelic *càrn* ("rock pile"), *na h'uilean* ("of the elbows").

Càrnhuileanach (cairn-WHEEDL-ayan-ach; pl. Càrnhuileanaich; Caledonaiche). Of or pertaining to Clan Cwrnwyll of Rheged, Brydein, a term of my invention referring to Arthur's Brytoni heritage that uses the *-ach* suffix convention for indicating membership in a given group. Also translates to "Man of the Rock-Elbows Clan," a reference to the physical layout of the clan's seat, Caerlaverock, as a triangular fortress of "elbows." Name origin: Scottish Gaelic *càrn* ("rock pile"), *na h'uilean* ("of the elbows").

Centurio equo (Latin, "commander of horse"). A cavalry centurion, usually an ala commander. Badge: copper brooch with a red enamel ring around the legion's symbol.

Centurion. Latin: *centurio* ("century commander"). Mid-grade military officer; in Arthur's army, this is usually a century or ala commander, or commander of a garrison staffed with fewer than four centuries or alae. Badge: copper brooch with appropriately colored enamel ring around the legion's symbol.

Century. Latin: *centuria*. Infantry unit consisting of 80–100 soldiers, commanded by a centurion.

Chalice, the. Cup once used by Iesu the Christ, enshrined at the Sanctuary of the Chalice.

Chamomile. Medicinal herb; also can be used as a rinse to lighten hair color.

Chieftain's Rock, the. A tall, large, flat rock standing inside Dunadd's innermost defensive perimeter, inscribed with a series of notches, a boar, and the indentations of a basin and a footprint. In this story, the rock figures prominently in a pre-Christian Brytoni ritual to confirm the new Chieftain of Clan Moray.

Clan-mark. Caledonaiche: *fin-cìragh* ("clan-crest"). A tattoo representing the Caledonach clan's symbol, usually painted with woad dye. A woman receives the clan-mark on her right forearm when she achieves the status of àrd-banoigin. During the bonding-ritual, the àrd-banoigin receives her consort's clan-mark on her left forearm. Likewise the àrd-ceoigin is tattooed with her clan-mark, also on the left forearm. Infant heirs of the àrd-banoigin receive a simple version of the clan-mark during the naming-ceremony. The clan-mark is a special classification of warding-mark. Origin: inspired by Scottish Gaelic *fine* ("tribe," fem.), *cìr* ("cock's crest," m.), *carragh* ("monument," fem.).

Clota's River. Caledonaiche: *Ab Chlota*. Caledonach term for the River Clyde, which forms the northeastern-most end of the Firth of Clyde. Caledonaiche name origin: inspired by Scottish Gaelic *abhainn* ("river") and proto-Celtic/Pictish *abar* ("river mouth"), plus my invented possessive form of the name Clota, *Chlota*.

Cohort. Latin: *cohors* ("company"). Military unit usually consisting of ten centuries or alae or combination thereof, commanded by a prefect (non-nobleman) or tribune (nobleman).

Comes Britanniarum (Latin, "Count of Brydein"). Female version: Comitissa Britanniam. The historic Roman army title was applied to the soldier who commanded all field action against enemy threats between the Antonine and Hadrianic walls. In Arthur's army, it applies to his second-in-command. Also can be translated as "Companion of Brydein."

Common(s), The. Caledonaiche: *An Coitas* (pl. *A'Choitais*). The beehive-shaped buildings scattered throughout Caledonach settlements. Caledonaiche name origin: inspired by Scottish Gaelic *coitcheann* ("common," adj.).

Compline. The last of eight Christian canonical hours of the day, occurring at approximately two hours past sundown. Origin: Latin *complere* ("to fill up").

Council of Chieftains, the. Conclave of Brytoni chieftains that convenes to pass judgment on matters involving more than one Brytoni clan.

Cù-puc (KOO-puck; pl. cù-puic; Caledonaiche, "dog-pig(s)"). An epithet. Origin: based on Scottish Gaelic compound *cù-muc* ("dog-sow"), with a change in consonants to make it sound more satisfying when spoken aloud.

Curule (Latin, "consul"). A curved, backless, cushioned, gilt chair of state.

Cwrnwyll (KEERN-weedl), Clan. Caledonaiche: *Càrnhuileanaich* ("The Rock-Elbows People"). Brytoni clan occupying the region of Rheged. I invented this clan name to be evocative of Cornwall, the region ascribed by tradition for Arthur's birth. The fact that it renders very nicely into Caledonaiche is something I didn't discover for almost 25 years. Banner: rampant ivory unicorn on crimson. Cloak pattern: dark red crossed with sky-blue and saffron. Gemstone: ruby.

Dalriada (Latin). Caledonaiche: *Dailriata* (poss. *Dhailriata*; "(of the) Necessary Meadow"). Political region in the northwest sector of Brydein consisting chiefly of the Kintyre Peninsula and western islands of Scotland plus the Isle of Man. At the time of this story, the Scotti incursions into this region were just getting underway, and historically the Isle of Man was never considered part of the later Scotti kingdom of Dál Riata. Caledonaiche name origin: Scottish Gaelic *dail* ("meadow"), *riatanach* ("necessary").

Dalriadan(s). Caledonaiche: *Dailriatanach* (poss. *Dhailriatanach*, pl. *Dailriatanaich*, poss. pl. *Dhailriatanaich*). Of or pertaining to the inhabitants of the Brytoni region of Dalriada.

Dance of the Sun, the. Caledonaiche: *Ruidhle a'Ghrian*. One of the Caledonach activities performed on Àmbholc day to encourage the sun to provide days with increasing amounts of daylight. Caledonaiche name origin: Scottish Gaelic: *ruidhle* ("dance"), *a'ghrian* ("of the sun").

Dance of the Virgins, the. Caledonaiche: *Ruidhle na Righinnean*. One of the Caledonach activities performed on Belteine night to invoke fertility blessings. Caledonaiche name origin: Scottish Gaelic: *ruidhle* ("dance"), *na rìghinnean* ("of the young ladies").

Death-loyal. Caledonaiche: *bàs-dìleas*. Compound adjective applied to someone who has sworn the Oath of Fealty to another person. Origin: Scottish Gaelic *bàs* ("death"), *dìleas* ("faithful").

Decurion. Latin: *decurio* ("commander of tens"). Junior-grade military officer, usually a turma commander. Badge: iron brooch with appropriately colored enamel ring around the legion's symbol.

Deira (Latin). Brytonic: *Deifr*. Coastal Angli-controlled territory south of Bernicia and east of the Brytoni-controlled fortress, Eboracum.

Deuchainn na fala (Caledonaiche, "trial of blood"). The rite of passage for Caledonach warriors. Clad in a loincloth and armed with a dagger, the candidate is taken into the forest and charged to return in at least three days. Being early is taken as a sign of cheating and cowardice. Origin: Scottish Gaelic *deuchainn* ("trial"), *na fala* ("of blood").

Diana (Latin, "divine" or "heavenly"). Roman virgin goddess of the hunt, the moon, and of childbirth and women. In this text, it refers to the statue adorning the fountain outside Caer Lugubalion's praetorium.

Doves of Argyll, the. Caledonaiche: *Na Calamaig h'Argaillanaich*. Symbol of Clan Argyll of Caledon, a pair of silver doves in flight on a dark blue background; also referred to as "the Argyll Doves." Origin: Inspired by Scottish Gaelic *na calamain* ("the doves" and rendered in the plural feminine form with the *-aig* suffix), and my invented term, *h'Argaillanaich* ("of Clan Argyll").

Dragon Legion, the. Latin: *Legio Draconis*. Northern Brytoni army unit, whence the term "Pendragon" originates. When Arthur took command after Uther's death, this was the only legion in existence—what was left of it.

Dragon King. Eingel-Saxon translation of "Pendragon."

Dumnonia (Latin). Brytonic: *Dyfneint*. Brytoni kingdom, established during the waning years of the Roman occupation, located in the southwestern peninsula of Brydein, occupying during the period of this story what is now Cornwall, as well as the western portions of Devon and Somerset. The Latin name originates from the name of the indigenous Celtic tribe, the Dumnonii.

Dunadd (doon-ATH, Brytonic, "Fort on the River Add"). Caledonaiche: *Dùn At* ("Swelled Fort"). Hill-fort near the town of Kilmartin on the Kintyre Peninsula in Argyll and Bute, Scotland, that is believed to have been the capital of the ancient Scotti kingdom of Dál Riata. In this story, it is the Seat of Moray, home fortress of Urien and Dumarec. Caledonaiche name origin, which is the oldest written form of the fort's name: Scottish Gaelic *dùn* ("fortress"), *at* ("to swell").

Dunpeldyr (Brytonic, "Fort of the Spear"). Caledonaiche: *Dùn Pildìrach* (doon peel-DEER-ack, "Fort of the Turning Ascent"). Traprain Law hill-fort near Haddington in East Lothian, Scotland, which serves as the Seat of Clan Lothian and the home fortress for Annamar and Loth. Caledonaiche name origin: Scottish Gaelic *dùn* ("fortress"), *pill* ("to turn"), *dìr* ("to ascend").

Dun Eidyn (Brytonic, "Fort of Eidyn"). Caledonaiche: *Dùn Éideann* (doon EE-day-ahn, "Well-Armed Fort"). Hill-fort on the summit of what is known today as Arthur's Seat, Edinburgh, Scotland, located on the south bank of the Firth of Forth. Site of the battle where, prior to the opening of *Dawnflight*, Uther was killed by King Colgrim and his invading Angli army, forcing Arthur to take command of the retreating Brytoni troops to prevent a rout. Caledonaiche name origin: Scottish Gaelic *dùn* ("fortress"), *éideadh* ("armor").

Dux Britanniarum (Latin, "Duke of Brydein"). Caledonaiche: *Flath Bhreatein*. Roman military title applied to the commander of the legions stationed between the Antonine and Hadrianic Walls. Prior to the Roman military exodus from Britain in the early part of the 5th century, this force consisted of two legions. When Arthur took this job, approximately 80 years later, there weren't enough trained soldiers available to form a single legion. Badge: gold dragon, with a red, green, and blue braided enamel outer ring. Historically, this title was applied only to the commander of northern stationary defenses (i.e., troops guarding the Hadrianic and Antonine walls), and it was not a field command. My Arthur doesn't have that luxury. Caledonaiche name origin: Scottish Gaelic *flath* ("prince"), plus my invented term, *Bhreatein* ("of Brydein").

Dyfed (Brytonic). Post-Roman Brytoni kingdom occupying the promontory of what is now southwestern Wales.

Eala (ay-AH-lah, Caledonaiche, "swan"). One of Alayna's cats (female, solid black). Name origin: Scottish Gaelic.

Eingel(s). Terms the Eingel people apply to themselves that are more Germanic pronunciations than the Latinized form, "Angli."

Einglaland (Eingel, "Angle-land"). Eingel name for their collective kingdoms; England.

Eireann (Scáthaichean, "Ériu's Head"). Ireland. Latin: *Hibernia*. Caledonaiche: *Airein* ("Men of the Plow"). Eingel/Saxon: *Æren* ("Brazen"). Caledonaiche name origin: Scottish Gaelic *airein* ("plowmen"). Eingel/Saxon name origin: Old Anglo-Saxon *æren* ("brazen").

Elder. A medicinal plant.

Epona. Caledonach/Brytoni deity: Horse-goddess symbolized by a prancing mare.

Falcon of Tarsuinn, the. Symbol of Clan Tarsuinn of Caledonia, an attacking falcon.

Fates, the. Greek goddesses presiding over the destinies of mortals' lives.

Fealty-mark. Caledonaiche: *dìleas-tì*. A scar on a Caledonach warrior's neck made by his or her sword wielded by the person to whom the warrior has sworn the Oath of Fealty. Origin: Scottish Gaelic *dìleas* ("faithful"), *tì* ("intent").

Feast of Christ's Passion, the. Easter.

Ferch (VERK, Brytonic). "Daughter of," followed by the father's name; e.g., Morghe ferch Uther.

Fiorth (Brytonic), the. Caledonaiche: *Ab Fhorchu* ("River of the Flowing Hound"). Firth of Forth, southeastern Scotland. Caledonaiche name origin: inspired by Scottish Gaelic *Abhainn Fhorchu* ("River Forth"), *forasach* ("forward," adj.), *cù* ("hound").

Fleet Commander, the. Latin: *Navarchus Classis Britannia*. Admiral in charge of the Brytoni war-fleet. Since the word "admiral" originates from Arabic, I considered it appropriate to employ a different title; technically, in Arthur's Roman-based military force, the fleet commander is equivalent in rank to a legate. Badge: silver dragon brooch with a blue enamel outer ring.

Frisians. Coastal Germanic tribe culturally similar to the Eingels and Saxons. Historically, they began migrating to Britain in the early 5th century A.D.

Games helm. Ornate helmet specially designed for Roman cavalry games rather than combat in order to attract the attention of potential wealthy patrons.

Geall Dhìleas (Caledonaiche, "Oath of Fealty"). See Oath of Fealty. Origin: Scottish Gaelic *geall* ("promise"), *dhìleas* ("of faithfulness").

Glaschu Monastery. Christian men's religious community located near the Brytoni fort Caerglas in present-day Glasgow, Scotland. The monks are famed for their uisge beverage.

Gododdin (go-DOTH-in). Brytonic: *Guotodin*. Caledonaiche: *Gò Do-dìon* ("Deceptively Difficult Defense"). Brytoni-controlled territory corresponding to modern southeastern Scotland and northeastern England. The Brytonic name is derived from the Latin name of the Celtic tribe inhabiting the area at the time of the Roman occupation, the Votadini. The Caledonaiche version implies that the region is deceptively well-defended. Caledonaiche name origin: Scottish Gaelic *gò* ("deceitful"), *do-dìon* ("difficult defense").

Green Griffin, the. Symbol of Prince Ælferd of the West Saxons, a green griffin on gold.

Gwyddbwyll (Brytonic, "wood sense"). A strategy board-game that figures in many ancient Arthurian tales, such as *The Dream of Rhonabwy* in the *Mabinogion*. Although *gwyddbwyll* translates to "chess" in modern Welsh, the game apparently predates chess's introduction to Europe and so most likely was played very differently than chess.

Gwynedd (GWIN-eth). Mountainous and sparsely populated region corresponding to present-day northwest Wales. Name origin:

Brythonic variant of the Latin designation of tribal residents during the Roman occupation collectively known as Venedotia.

Hag, the (also the Crone). Caledonaiche: *An Cronag h'Eugais*. Late-life manifestation of the Life-Goddess. Caledonaich who see the Hag believe they soon will die; hence, she is also referred to as "the Hag of Death." Origin: inspired by Scottish Gaelic *cron* ("evil," "harmful"), *eug* ("death"), both of which are masculine nouns.

Ha'satan (Hebrew, "The Accuser"). Satan.

Hauberk. Saxon chain mail shirt that reaches to mid-calf.

Heliodor. Caledonaiche: *clach-gréin* ("sunstone"). Ancient Greco-Roman name for the greenish-yellow form of golden beryl, a semi-precious gemstone, from Greek *helios* ("sun"). Caledonaiche name origin: Scottish Gaelic *clach* ("stone"), *gréin* ("of the sun").

Horse Cohort. Latin: *Cohortis Equitum*. Unit in the Brytoni army consisting of eight cavalry alae and no foot soldiers, formed as a result of the Brytoni-Caledonian treaty forged after the battle of Abar-Gleann. First Ala is comprised of Brytoni horsemen; the remaining alae are comprised of Caledonians.

Ifrinn (EEF-reen, Caledonaiche, "hell"). In Caledonach mythology, this is the realm of Lord Annàm and the Samhraidhean, as well as other malevolent spirits and demonic beings. Origin: Scottish Gaelic *ifrinn* ("hell").

Ifrinn fuileachdach (EEF-reen FWEE-layach-dach; Caledonaiche, "bloody hell"). An expression of frustration. Origin: Scottish Gaelic *ifrinn* ("hell"), *fuileachdach* ("bloody").

Ifrinnach (EEF-reen-ach; pl. ifrinnaich, Caledonaiche, "hellion(s)"). Evil spirits other than Samhraidhean. Origin: based on Scottish Gaelic *ifrinn* ("hell").

Illegitimus (Latin, pl. illegitimi, "illegitimate (ones)"). An epithet carrying obvious parental connotations but extremely tame compared with the Caledonaiche equivalent, *machaoduin*.

Ivory Unicorn, the. Symbol of Clan Cwrnwyll of Rheged, Brydein, a rampant ivory unicorn on crimson, deliberately evocative of the unicorn supporter on the present-day coat of arms of the United Kingdom.

Joining, joining ceremony. Caledonaiche: *a'phòg naomhair* ("the holy kiss"). The Caledonach marriage ritual, optional. Origin: inspired by Scottish Gaelic *a'phòg* ("the kiss," fem.), *naomh* ("holy").

Jutes. Powerful Germanic tribe that originated on the Jutland peninsula in modern Denmark and began migrating to Britain in the late 4th century A.D.

Keeper of the Chalice, the. Christian holy man selected to guard the Chalice and maintain its shrine; usually also serves as Abbot of Saint Padraic's Monastery.

Lady's mantle. Medicinal herb.

Lammor, Clan (Brytonic). Caledonaiche: *Làmanmhor* ("People of Great Hands"). Full Caledonaiche designation: *Làmanmhoranaich Srath-Chlotaidh Bhreatein*. Brytoni clan of the region of Strathclyd, Brydein. Banner: emerald-green stag's head on silver. Cloak pattern: grass-green crossed with silver and black. Gemstone: heliodor. Brytonic name origin: inspired by the Lammermuir Hills of southern Scotland, where this clan is located. Caledonaiche name origin: Scottish Gaelic *làmhan mhor* ("of great hands"), i.e., craftsmen and -women; *Srath-Chluaidh* ("Strathclyde"), *srath* ("low-lying land near river"), and my invented term, *Chlotaidh* ("bank of Clota's River").

Lann-seolta (Caledonaiche, "blade-cunning"). The term applied to Caledonach warriors who are particularly adept at predicting their opponents' moves in battle, especially in regard to swordsmanship. Origin: Scottish Gaelic *lann* ("blade"), *seòlta* ("cunning", "skillful").

Lauds. The second Christian canonical hour, occurring at dawn. In some religious communities, this office is combined with matins. Origin: Latin *laus* ("praise").

Lavender. Medicinal and aromatic strewing herb.

Legate. Latin: *legatus*. Senior Roman military officer, usually a legion commander, equivalent to a brigadier general. Badge: silver with appropriately colored enamel ring around the legion's symbol.

Legion. Latin: *legio*. The largest unit in the Roman military infrastructure, usually consisting of six infantry cohorts and at least one cavalry ala, commanded by a legate. Technically, Arthur is *Legatus*

Legio Draconis ("Legate of the Dragon Legion"), but his status as Dux Britanniarum is more descriptive and therefore supersedes the "legate" title, so I don't use the term "legate" in this text.

Lion of Alban, the. Caledonaiche: *An Leóghann h'Albainaich*. Symbol of Clan Alban of Caledon, a white lion rampant on a field of cerulean blue. Also referred to as the Alban Lion. Origin: Scottish Gaelic *an leóghann* ("the lion"), plus my invented term, *h'Albainaich* ("of Clan Alban").

Lothian, Clan (Brytonic). Caledonaiche: Clan *Lùthean* (LOOT-hay-ahn, "People of Power"); full designation is *Lùtheanaich Ghò Dodìon Bhreatein*. Brytoni clan of the region of Gododdin, Brydein. Banner: rearing amber bear on dark green. Cloak pattern: forest-green crossed with dark blue and gold. Gemstone: amber. Caledonaiche name origin: Scottish Gaelic *lùths* ("power").

Lugh. Caledonach/Brytoni Lord of Light, symbolized by a bull.

Lugh Longarm. Scotti deity—possibly the same as the aforementioned Caledonach/Brytoni god Lugh, although the Scots would never admit this.

Lugnasadh (loo-NAH-sah). Summer festival celebrated by non-Christian Caledonaich and Brytons on August 1, characterized by horse racing and livestock sales; named for the god Lugh.

Mac (Caledonaiche). "Son of," followed by the mother's name; e.g., Angusel mac Alayna. Origin: Scottish Gaelic.

Machaoduin (mahk-EYE-dween; pl. michaoduin; Caledonaiche, "son(s) of the unmanned"). An epithet with obvious parentage connotations; can apply to jerks, cowards, the condemned, the exiled, and traitors. Female form is *nichaoduin* (pl. *naichaoduin*). Origin: Scottish Gaelic *mac* ("son"), plus my invented compound, *aoduin* ("un-man"), inspired by *ao-* (negation prefix), *duine* ("a man").

Macmuir (Caledonaiche, "Son of the Sea"). Gyanhumara's horse (white stallion), sired by Macsen.

Macsen (Brytonic, "Great One"). Arthur's horse (white stallion), named in honor of a predecessor of Ambrosius, Macsen Wledig ("Great Prince").

Mansio (Latin, "abode"). The inn reserved for use by high-ranking military officers and civilian dignitaries; most Roman fortresses quartering a half-cohort or more had one.

Manx Cohort. Latin: *Cohortis Mavnium*. Unit of the Brytoni army stationed on the Isle of Maun consisting of one infantry century posted to Ayr Point (with the men from that century being rotated to guard the Mount Snaefell signal beacon, as well), two centuries at Caer Rushen, two centuries plus two cavalry turmae at Tanroc, and three centuries and three turmae at Port Dhoo-Glass.

Map (Northern Brytonic). "Son of," followed by the father's name; e.g., Urien map Dumarec. Brytons of southern clans use the variant *ap*, also in conjunction with the father's name.

Mark of Argyll, the. Caledonaiche: *Fin-cìragh h'Argaillanaich*. Designation of Argyll's clan-mark, a pair of doves in flight. See clan-mark and Argyll, Clan.

Matins. First of eight Christian canonical hours of the day. Properly occurring at midnight, the prayer service is sometimes combined with lauds, which is held at dawn. Origin: Latin *matutinus* ("of the morning").

Maun. Latin: *Mavnum*. Isle of Man in the Irish Sea.

Mo ghaisgich (mo HEYE-sitch, Caledonaiche, "my heroes"). A term of respect and endearment. Origin: Scottish Gaelic.

Mo laochan (Caledonaiche, "my little champion"). A term of encouragement usually applied to boys; female version: *mo laochag*. Origin: Scottish Gaelic, a diminutive of *laoch* ("hero, champion, warrior").

Mona (Latin). Brytonic: *Ynys Mon*. Anglesey Island, just off the coast of Wales. The island was a noted center for Druid worship and training until the Romans got nervous in the 1st century A.D. and destroyed their shrines and groves.

Móran (Caledonaiche, "The Many People"), Clan. Chaledonaich moniker for the Brytoni Clan Moray of Dalriada, Brydein, coined simply because there are so many of them. Full Caledonaiche designation: *Móranaich Dhailriata Bhreatein*. Origin: Scottish Gaelic *móran* ("many").

Móranach (pl. Móranaich; Caledonaiche). Of or pertaining to the Brytoni Clan Moray of Dalriada, Brydein. Origin: Scottish Gaelic *móran* ("many").

Moray, Clan. Brytoni clan occupying the region of Dalriada, Brydein. Banner: black boar on gold. Cloak pattern: black crossed with gold. Gemstone: jet.

Most Sacred Ground, the. Caledonaiche: *A'Bhruach Mò*. Area in the Nemeton within the innermost circle of stones where the altar resides. Origin: Scottish Gaelic *a'bhruach* ("the small area of high ground"), *mò* ("greatest", "greater").

Mount Snaefell. Highest point of the Isle of Maun; location of the main Brytoni signal beacon and Wyllan's forge.

Naming ceremony. Caledonach ritual wherein the week-old infant of the àrd-banoigin and àrd-ceoigin is presented to the clan to be confirmed as an heir and tattooed on the heel with the clan's symbol.

Narrow Sea. Latin: *Angusta Mare*. English Channel.

Navarchus Classis Britannia (Latin, "Commander of the Brytoni Fleet"). The Brytoni fleet commander's official title, though Bedwyr seldom uses it.

Nemeton, the. Caledonaiche: *Nèamhaitan*. A Caledonach holy place, a clearing surrounded by two sets of standing stones or live trees; each clan seat has its own. Caledonaiche name origin: inspired by Scottish Gaelic *nèamh* ("heaven", "sky"), *àite* ("a place").

Nemetona. Caledonach/Brytoni Goddess of War, symbolized by a lioness, said to drive a crimson chariot drawn by four winged, fire-snorting black mares.

Nic (Caledonaiche). "Daughter of," followed by the mother's name; e.g., Gyanhumara nic Hymar. Origin: Scottish Gaelic, contraction of *nighean mhic* ("young woman offspring").

Oath of Fealty, the. Caledonaiche: *Geall Dhìleas*. The rite wherein a warrior pledges loyalty to a warrior of another clan; precursor of the knighthood ceremony. If trust is an issue for the person accepting fealty, the rite can be used for execution. Origin: Scottish Gaelic. The person holding the sword asks, *"An dean thu, [Name and Title(s)], an Geall Dhìleas chugam, [Name and Title(s)], gus a'bàsachadh?"* (Literally, "Make thou, [Name and Title(s)], the Oath of the Faithful to me, [Name and Title(s)], until the dying?") The person swearing the oath responds, *"A chaoidh gus a'bàsachadh."* ("Ever until the dying.")

Old Ones, the. Caledonaiche: *Na Déathan Sean*. Collective name applied to the Caledonach deities. Origin: Scottish Gaelic *na déathan* ("the gods"), *sean* ("old").

One God, the. Caledonaiche: *An Díaonar*. Caledonach term for the Christians' deity. Origin: inspired by Scottish Gaelic *an dia* ("the god"), *aonar* ("alone").

Optio (Latin, "assistant"). Lowest-ranking military officer, usually a centurion's clerical assistant, courier or scout; this officer typically does not command other soldiers. Badge: iron legion symbol, no enamel on the ring.

Otherworld, the. Caledonaiche: *An Domhaneil*. In Caledonach mythology, this is the realm of the Old Ones, roughly analogous to Heaven but with more traffic of mortals and spirits back and forth between both worlds. Origin: based on Scottish Gaelic *an domhan* ("the world"), *eile* ("another").

Pendragon, the. Brytonic: *Y Ddraig Pen* ("The Chief Dragon"). Latin: *Draconis Rex* ("Dragon King"). Caledonaiche: *Àrd-Ceann Teine-Beathach Mór* ("High-Chief Great Fire-Beast"). Honorific applied to the Dux Britanniarum, commander of the Dragon Legion.

Phalanx. A closely spaced, heavily armed, wedge-shaped military formation employed in charges for the purpose of opening a gap in the enemy's line. Tactical origin: ancient Greece.

Pict(s) (Latin, "Painted Folk"). Epithet applied by Latin-speakers to one or more inhabitants of Caledonia.

Picti (Latin, "of the Painted Folk"), Pictish. Of or pertaining to the inhabitants of Caledonia.

Port Dhoo-Glass (Manx). Brytoni-controlled port named for its location at the confluence of the rivers Dhoo ("Black") and Glass ("Green"), present-day Douglas, Isle of Man. "Above the river called Dubglas" is the site of battles 2, 3, 4, and 5 of Arthur's twelve battles on the list cited in chapter 56 of the 9th-century *Historia Brittonum*. On my list, Port Dhoo-Glass is the site of battles 2 (in *Dawnflight*) and

5 (in *Morning's Journey*). Technically, Gyanhumara led #5, and Arthur was present only in its aftermath.

Powys (Brytonic). Post-Roman Brytoni kingdom occupying territory in what is now northeastern Wales.

Praefectus Cohortis Equitum (Latin, "Prefect of the Horse Cohort"). Senior military officer commanding Arthur's only all-cavalry cohort. Badge: bronze brooch with a red enamel ring around the legion symbol.

Praetorium (Latin, "governor's residence"). The living quarters of the garrison commander; also may be translated as "palace."

Prefect. Latin: *praefectus*. Senior military officer; in Arthur's army, this is usually a cohort or garrison commander. Badge: bronze brooch with either a red or green enamel ring around the legion symbol, or both colors if the garrison also has a cavalry unit.

Rheged (Brytonic). Caledonaiche: *Rioghachd* (poss. *Rhioghachd*; "(of the) Royal Land"). Political region of Brydein encompassing what is now northern England and southern Scotland. Caledonaiche name origin: Scottish Gaelic *rioghachd* ("kingdom"—though it's interesting to note that this is a female noun).

Rioghail ("The Royal People"), Clan. Caledonaiche: *Rioghailanaich Chaledon*. Member of the Caledonach Confederacy. Banner: purple eagle standing, on gold. Cloak pattern: black crossed with pale purple and red. Gemstone: amethyst. Name origin: Scottish Gaelic *rioghail* ("royal").

River Fiorth (Brytonic). Caledonaiche: *Ab Fhorchu*. Firth of Forth. See Fiorth, The.

Ròmanach (poss. Rhòmanach, pl. Ròmanaich, poss. pl. Rhòmanaich; Caledonaiche, "(of the) Roman(s)"). Usually uttered in derision—though not always. These terms are also used by the Scáthaichean.

Ròmanaiche (roh-mah-NEESH; Caledonaiche, "tongue of the Romans"). The Latin language.

Rukh. Peredur's horse (bay gelding).

Rushen Priory. Christian women's religious community located on the eastern coast of the Isle of Maun, presided over by a prioress.

Sacred Flame, the (also the Flame). Caledonaiche: *An Lasair Naomh*. Caledonach symbol of religious purity, analogous to Christian holy water. Origin: Scottish Gaelic *an lasair* ("the flame"), *naomh* ("holy").

Sacred Ground, the. Caledonaiche: *An Làr Naomh*. The portion of the Nemeton between the inner and outer rings. Origin: Scottish Gaelic *an làr* ("the ground"), *naomh* ("holy").

Saffron. An herb that yields a yellow dye.

Saint Padraic's Isle. Islet off the western coast of Maun, opposite Tanroc; site of Saint Padraic's Monastery. Present-day St. Patrick's Isle.

Saint Padraic's Monastery. Christian men's religious community founded by St. Padraic (Patrick) in the mid-5th century, located on Saint Padraic's Isle and presided over by an abbot. Site corresponds to Peel Castle, St. Patrick's Isle, which existed as a Celtic monastery for several centuries, until the Vikings turned it into a fortification.

Samhainn (SOH-wen; Caledonaiche, "Summer's End"). Brytonic: *Samhain*. Harvest festival celebrated by non-Christian Caledonaich and Brytons on November 1. Name origin: Scottish Gaelic *samhainn* ("Hallowtide").

Samhradh (SOW-hrah; pl. Samhraidhean; Caledonaiche, "Summer Wraith(s)"). Evil resident(s) of the Otherworld; demon(s). In the Caledonach worldview, a warrior who dies dishonorably becomes a Samhradh, doomed to fight against the Army of the Blest for all eternity. Name origin: Inspired by Scottish Gaelic words *samhradh* ("summer") and *samhladh* ("ghost" or "replica").

Sanctuary of the Chalice, the. Shrine established for the Chalice at Saint Padraic's Monastery.

Sasun (SAH-soon; Caledonaiche). Term referring to a single Saxon individual.

Sasunach (sah-SOON-nach; pl. Sasunaich, poss. Shasunach, poss. pl. Shasunaich; Caledonaiche, "(of the) Saxon(s)"). Terms applied by the Caledonaich to the Germanic inhabitants of southern Brydein. Origin: Scottish Gaelic *Sasunnach* ("English", "Englishman").

Sasunaiche (sah-soon-EESH). Caledonaiche term for the Saxon language.

Saxon(s) (Brytonic). Of or pertaining to the inhabitants of the southern portion of Brydein; name possibly derived from their weapon of choice, the *seax*.

Scarlet Dragon, the. Standard of the Brytoni army, a scarlet dragon passant on a field of gold, very similar to the present flag of Wales; also referred to as "the Dragon."

Scot(s) (Brytonic). Caledonaiche: *Scáth* (poss. *Scháth*, pl. *Scáthinaich*, poss. pl. *Scháthinaich*). Terms applied to the inhabitants of the eastern portion of Eireann.

Scotti (Latin). Caledonaiche: *Scáthinach*. Of or pertaining to the inhabitants of the eastern portion of Eireann.

Sea holly. A plant that can be used as an aphrodisiac.

Seannachaidh (SHAWN-a-kay; pl. seannachaidhean (shawn-ah-KAY-jhayan); Caledonaiche, "storyteller"). The clan's keeper of law and lore, roughly equivalent to a Brytoni bard. Seannachaidhean only recite the law; priests administer it. This is the Scottish Gaelic word for "male storyteller," but it appears to be a compound of *sean* ("old") and *an achaidh* ("of the field"), perhaps an echo of the ancient practice of reciting battle tales.

Seat of Alban, the. Caledonaiche: *Cathair h'Albainaich*. Clan Alban's administrative headquarters at Senaudon, Caledon. Origin: Scottish Gaelic *cathair* ("chair" and "city"), plus my invented term, *h'Albainaich* ("of Clan Alban").

Seat of Argyll, the. Caledonaiche: *Cathair h'Argaillanaich*. Clan Argyll's administrative headquarters at Arbroch, Caledon. Origin: Scottish Gaelic *cathair* ("chair" and "city"), plus my invented term, *h'Argaillanaich* ("of Clan Argyll").

Seax (Saxon). War-knife, usually measuring 15-18 inches from point to end of hilt.

Senaudon (Caledonaiche, "Place of Charmed Protection"). Angusel's birthplace and Alayna's home fortress located in present-day Stirling, Scotland. Origin: inspired by Scottish Gaelic *seun* ("a charm for protection" and "to defend by charms").

Sennight. Measure of time: one week (contraction of "seven nights," analogous to "fortnight" being a contraction of "fourteen nights").

Sight, the. Otherwise known as Extrasensory Perception. This version manifests in prophetic visions and dreams.

Signifer (Latin, "standard-bearer"). The soldier charged with carrying the unit's banner—and guarding it in battle.

Soluis Firth, the. Solway Firth, the body of water that divides southwestern Scotland from northwestern England.

South Cove. Site of Saxon beachhead on the Isle of Maun, near Caer Rushen but not near enough to be detected by that fortress's lookouts. On my list of Arthur's twelve battles, this is the site of number 6, though it's more of a cleanup operation.

Stonn. Angusel's horse (gray stallion).

Suilean (SHOO-layan; Caledonaiche, "eyes"). Used as part of the sign-countersign codes in the Manx Cohort. This response is usually given as a challenge to an approaching visitor. Origin: Scottish Gaelic *sùilean* ("eyes").

Suil a mhàin (shool ah wane; Caledonaiche, "only one eye"). Used as part of the sign-countersign codes in the Manx Cohort. This response indicates the courier carries an encoded message only to be read by the unit's commander, implying great urgency. Origin: Scottish Gaelic.

Talarf (Brytonic, "Silver Hair"). Urien's horse (chestnut stallion).

Tanroc. Brytoni-controlled fortress on the western coast of the Isle of Maun and site of the 3rd of Arthur's twelve battles on my list (technically, Cai leads this one in Arthur's stead). No present-day equivalent.

Tarsuinn ("The Crossing People"), Clan. Caledonaiche: *Tarsuinnaich Chaledon*. Member of the Caledonach Confederacy, so-named because they run a large ferry business from several points across the Firth of Forth. Banner: gold falcon in flight, on azure. Cloak pattern: saffron crossed with blue and red. Gemstone: golden beryl. Name origin: Scottish Gaelic *tarsainn* ("across").

Trews. Loose-fitting trousers made of leather, wool or linen, worn by Brytoni men and by Caledonaich of both sexes.

Tribune. Latin: *tribunus*. In Arthur's army, this is a high-ranking military officer (usually a prefect) of noble birth. Badge: bronze brooch, with appropriately colored enamel ring and the clan's gemstone.

Turma (pl. turmae; Latin, "squad(s)"). Roman cavalry unit consisting of 10-30 horsemen, commanded by a decurion. In Arthur's army, the typical size averages 20.

Uisge (OOS-ghee; Northern Brytonic, "water"). A strong alcoholic beverage distilled from barley. I chose to employ a dialectic shortening of Scottish Gaelic *uisge-beatha* ("water of life;" i.e., whiskey) because humans during that era rarely drank unboiled water lest they run the risk of getting sick.

Valerian. Medicinal herb.

Vectis (Latin). Isle of Wight, English Channel.

Vespers. Seventh Christian canonical hour, occurring at sunset. Origin: Latin *vespera* ("evening").

Warding-mark. Caledonaiche: *seunail*. A tattoo believed by Caledonaich to be a physical manifestation of divine protection. Origin: Scottish Gaelic *seun* ("a charm for protection"), *aileadh* ("mark").

Way, the. A Biblical term for Christianity.

Wintaceaster (Saxon, "Market Castle"). Winchester, Hampshire, Wessex, England.

Wintaceaster Palace. Residence of King Cissa of the West Saxons.

Woad. An herb that yields a blue dye.

Woden. Eingel/Saxon deity; ruler and father of the gods. In their worldview, Woden's Hall houses the souls of dead warriors. "Woden's Day" survives in modern usage as "Wednesday." Also known as Wodan, Wotan, Odin.

Acknowledgments

As always, I must first thank my family for putting up with this lifelong obsession of mine. My husband, Chris, is supportive of me and my work in his eternally pragmatic way. Jonathan, our firstborn, has been very helpful recently with his insights regarding photography and lighting, saving me from looking as if I were telling ghost stories around a campfire during my first Skype interview for promoting *Dawnflight*. And special thanks go to our daughter, Jessica, who got me back into the literary saddle by telling me to "just shut up and write." Of course she was absolutely right. I wish I could do more to express my gratitude, but, "unfortunately, sainthood is not in my power." (Richard Harris as King Arthur in *Camelot*, Warner Brothers, released 25 October 1967).

To this list I add fellow writer Robin Allen, who also helped shepherd me through the process of looking good for video interviews and is one of the best friends—online or off—that anyone could ever wish for; my editor, Deb Taber, a wellspring of advice and encouragement; and my cover designer, Natasha Brown, with whom I hope to work for many more projects to come.

kih, Lynchburg, Virginia
September 28, 2014

Interior Art

Gyanhumara

Argyll Dove, lead: original artwork ©1998-2014 by Kim Headlee.

Gyanhumara

Argyll Dove, 2nd: original artwork ©1998-2014 by Kim Headlee.

All other character totems are line-art adaptations ©2012-2014 by Kim Headlee, based on photographs of the following Pictish stones found throughout Scotland:

Ælferd

Griffin: detail on the end of Meigle 26 in the Meigle Sculptured Stones Museum, Angus, Perthshire and Kinross.

Angusel

Lion, standing: inspired by a detail on the side of Meigle 26 in the Meigle Sculptured Stones Museum, Angus, Perthshire and Kinross.

Angusel

Lion's Head: inspired by a detail on the Daniel Stone, Rosemarkie, Black Isle, Easter Ross, depicting a lioness with a man's head in her mouth.

Annamar — Flower: detail on the front of the Dunnichen Stone at the Meffan Institute, Forfar, Angus, Perthshire and Kinross.

Arthur — Dragon, horizontal: the Dragon Stone, Portmahomack, Tarbat, Ross and Cromarty.

Arthur — Dragon, vertical: detail on the front of stone Meigle 4, Meigle Sculptured Stones Museum, Angus, Perthshire and Kinross.

Badulf — Leopard's Head: detail on a silver plaque found in the hoard at Norrie's Law, Fife. The glyph's orientation on the plaque is vertical.

Bedwyr — Stag, walking: detail on the front of the Eassie Stone, Eassie, Angus.

Cynda — Mirror Case: detail on the Brough of Birsay Stone, Orkney.

Dafydd — Scholar: detail on the front of stone Kirriemuir 1, Forfar, Angus.

Denu — Kelpie/Dolphin/Seahorse: detail on the back of the Ulbster Stone, Thurso Museum, Highland Caithness. The glyph's orientation on the stone is vertical.

MORNING'S JOURNEY

Dwras — Z-Rod, canted: detail on a silver plaque found in the hoard at Norrie's Law, Fife. The glyph's orientation on the plaque is vertical.

Gawain — Bear, walking: the Bear Stone, Scatness, Shetland Isles.

Gereint — Notched Rectangle: detail on the rear of Aberlemno 2, Aberlemno Kirkyard, Angus, Perthshire and Kinross.

Lughann — Double-crescent: detail on the back of the Ulbster Stone, Thurso Museum, Highland Caithness.

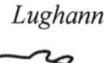

Merlin — Salmon: detail on the Golspie Stone, Craigton 2, Highland Sutherland.

Morghe — V-Crescent: detail on the Brough of Birsay Stone, Orkney.

Niniane — Disc-cross: the Dyce 6 stone, City of Aberdeen.

Urien — Boar: the Boar Stone of Clune Farm, Dores, Highland Inverness.

About the Author

Photo Copyright by Chris Headlee

KIM HEADLEE LIVES on a farm in the mountains of southwestern Virginia with her family, cats, fish, goats, Great Pyrenees goat guards, someone else's cattle, half a million honey bees, and assorted wildlife. People and creatures come and go, but the cave and the 250-year-old house ruins—the latter having been occupied as recently as the midtwentieth century—seem to be sticking around for a while yet. She has been an award-winning novelist since 1999 and a student of Arthurian literature for nigh on half a century.

http://www.kimheadlee.com
http://kimiversonheadlee.blogspot.com/
https://twitter.com/KimHeadlee
http://www.facebook.com/kimiversonheadlee

Other published works by Kim Headlee

Twins, e-book and paperback, the novella genesis of *Sundown of a Dream*, The Dragon's Dove Chronicles, volume 6, Pendragon Cove Press, 2017.

The Business of Writing, nonfiction e-book and paperback, Pendragon Cove Press, 2016.

King Arthur's Sister in Washington's Court by Mark Twain as channeled by Kim Iverson Headlee, illustrated by Jennifer Doneske and Tom Doneske, e-book, audiobook, hardcover, and paperback, Lucky Bat Books, 2016.

"The Challenge," e-book, paperback, and audiobook, Pendragon Cove Press, 2015.

Liberty, 2nd Edition, with character-totem art by Jessica Headlee, e-book and paperback, Pendragon Cove Press, 2014.

Snow in July, with character-totem art by Jessica Headlee, e-book and paperback, Pendragon Cove Press, 2014.

"The Color of Vengeance," e-book, paperback, and audiobook, short story excerpted from *Morning's Journey*, Lucky Bat Books, 2013.

Dawnflight, The Dragon's Dove Chronicles, volume 1, e-book, audiobook, and paperback, Lucky Bat Books, 2013; cover and interior updated 2014.

Liberty, writing as Kimberly Iverson, paperback, HQN Books, Harlequin, 2006.

Dawnflight, first edition, paperback, Sonnet Books, Simon & Schuster, 1999.

Forthcoming:

Raging Sea, The Dragon's Dove Chronicles, volume 3, Pendragon Cove Press.

Prophecy, the sequel to *Liberty*, Pendragon Cove Press.

CPSIA information can be obtained
at www.ICGtesting.com
Printed in the USA
FFHW011217191118
49371098-53711FF